CW01456711

Q

Vaseem Khan is the author of two award-winning crime series set in India, the Baby Ganesh Agency series set in modern Mumbai and the Malabar House historical crime novels set in 1950s Bombay. He is also the author of *The Girl in Cell A*, a psychological thriller set in small town America. His first book, *The Unexpected Inheritance of Inspector Chopra*, was selected by the *Sunday Times* as one of the 40 best crime novels published 2015–2020 and is translated into 17 languages. In 2021, *Midnight at Malabar House* won the Crime Writers' Association Historical Dagger. Vaseem was born in England, but spent a decade working in India. In 2006, he returned to the UK and joined University College London's Department of Security and Crime Science, where he has helped manage the Dawes Centre for Future Crime. In 2023, Vaseem was elected Chair of the UK Crime Writers' Association.

vaseemkhan.com

@VaseemKhanUK

/VaseemKhanOfficial

IAN FLEMING PUBLICATIONS

QUANTUM OF MENACE

VASEEM KHAN

ZAFFRE

First published in the UK in 2025 by
ZAFFRE
An imprint of Bonnier Books UK
5th Floor, HYLO, 105 Bunhill Row,
London, EC1Y 8LZ

Copyright © Ian Fleming Publications Limited, 2025

James Bond and 007 are registered trademarks of Danjaq LLC,
used under licence by Ian Fleming Publications Ltd

The Ian Fleming signature and the Ian Fleming logo are both trademarks owned by
The Ian Fleming Estate, used under licence by Ian Fleming Publications Ltd

All rights reserved.
No part of this publication may be reproduced,
stored or transmitted in any form or by any means, electronic,
mechanical, photocopying or otherwise, without the
prior written permission of the publisher.

The right of Vaseem Khan to be identified as Author of this
work has been asserted by him in accordance with the
Copyright, Designs and Patents Act, 1988.

This is a work of fiction. Names, places, events and
incidents are either the products of the author's
imagination or used fictitiously. Any resemblance to
actual persons, living or dead, or actual
events is purely coincidental.

A CIP catalogue record for this book is
available from the British Library.

Hardback ISBN: 978-1-80418-865-1
Trade paperback ISBN: 978-1-80418-867-5

Also available as an ebook and an audiobook

1 3 5 7 9 10 8 6 4 2

Typeset by IDSUK (Data Connection) Ltd
Printed and bound in Great Britain by Clays Ltd, Elcograf S.p.A.

MIX
Paper | Supporting
responsible forestry
FSC
www.fsc.org   FSC® C018072

The authorised representative in the EEA is Bonnier Books
UK (Ireland) Limited.
Registered office address: Floor 3, Block 3, Miesian Plaza,
Dublin 2, D02 Y754, Ireland
compliance@bonnierbooks.ie
www.bonnierbooks.co.uk
www.ianfleming.com
www.vaseemkhan.com

DEDICATION

*To Bond fans everywhere who, as much as they have loved 007,
have retained a soft spot for his friend and armourer, Q*

Q loves a good puzzle. So this book is also dedicated to
puzzle solvers everywhere. If you can solve the riddle below,
your name will go into a draw to receive a 'Bond and Q
goodie bag'. Three winners will be picked from all those
submitting the correct answer. To enter, and for full
terms and conditions, please go to www.vaseemkhan.com
or www.ianfleming.com ... Here is the riddle:
Who am I referring to below?

Nemesis of our favourite spy
A man of cunning, none can deny
He lost his hands to his own greed
Golden dollars, did his empire seed
On an island fortress he now awaits
Heart reversed, fomenting Cold War hate

Prologue

INSIDE A LARGE, FORMLESS GREY building, as forbidding as any ogre's keep in a fairy tale, a man in a dark suit hurried through night-time corridors.

Arriving at a room on the building's uppermost floor, he nervously adjusted his tie, then knocked on the door.

Moments later, he was speaking with the room's sole occupant, a small, blunt-headed man in a white shirt and grey tie, seated at a shiny desk, a collage of papers spread before him. And a half-eaten pizza, set beside a glass of what might be whisky. 'Sir. I have the recording you requested.'

The man slipped a USB stick from his pocket and inserted it into the hard drive of a desktop computer. 'This is from a speech made by Dr Peter Napier two years ago at the Symposium on Quantum Computing held at MIT – that is, the Massachusetts Institute of Technology in the USA.'

The seated man raised an eyebrow. 'I *have* heard of MIT.'

An image flickered to life on the monitor. A dark-haired white man speaking at a podium. The accent: English. '*How can a man be both dead and alive? This question was recently posed to me . . . by a priest. Quantum science is one of those rare phenomena where faith, science and fiction coincide. Religion tells us that man never truly dies.*

1

The body fails, but our essence – call it the soul, if you like – lingers on, eventually finding its way to heaven, hell, nirvana, or off to haunt some old country pile back in England.' [Laughter, from an unseen audience, off-screen.] *'Fiction goes one step further. The body – and brain – die, but, with a little ingenuity, might be reanimated. And so we have vampires, zombies . . . and undergrad students in morning lectures.*

'Science – now, this is where it begins to get tricky—'

An interruption as a bearded man clambers onto the stage and throws several eggs at Napier, whilst shouting anti-tech slogans. Security personnel appear, and the protestor is led away. Moments later, Napier continues. *'The quantum computing revolution will change the world. Some, as we have just seen, are terrified by this prospect. The truth is that any new and powerful technology is open to misuse. But it's not the tech that's evil. After all, we don't blame the dinosaurs in* Jurassic Park *for chomping on a few humans. Blame the humans for building bad cages!*

'People say quantum science defies logic. In the quantum realm, the classical rules that govern physics break down . . . and so cats – and humans! – can be both dead and alive. But the truth is that even uncertainty has its rules. Soon we will master those rules. And then we will truly change the world.'

Grey static.

The seated man lit a cigarette. 'Our . . . partners in England believe this man can deliver what they have promised?'

'Yes, sir.'

'Very well. You may proceed.'

After the underling had left, the seated man continued to look at the image of Peter Napier on the screen. *The man is either a liar or a magician.* If the latter, the world would face the consequences soon enough.

He picked up a slice of pizza, bit off a large mouthful. Anchovy and sauerkraut. *Delicious.* His gaze fell to a photograph in a golden frame, a dour-faced woman looking at him disapprovingly. Setting the photo down flat, he doused the cigarette in his whisky glass and resumed his work.

So much to do. So little time.

1

Two Years Later

ZAK HADN'T ANTICIPATED THE RAIN.
Rain was something he would never get used to. Back in Syria, rain, when it bothered to turn up, tended to be quick, violent and messy, like a bad case of the runs.

The runs. There wasn't much he liked about this country, but the English certainly had a way with words.

He walked along the deserted street until he came to the house he was looking for.

He knew that the pebble-dashed McMansion was empty. Police tape still cordoned off the property.

A glance over his shoulder; and then he clambered, catlike, over the low iron gate, landing on the far side with the deftness of a gymnast. Staying in the crouch, he looked up at the house.

Why had they sent him to steal a car from a dead man?

A late night fox paused its investigation of a battery of bins, aimed a possessive eye at him. *Bugger off. This trash is spoken for.*

But Zak had bigger things on his mind than rummaging through Peter Napier's rubbish.

Napier. The man's name brought up uncomfortable memories. Napier had visited Zak's school, soon after he had set up his lab

4

on the edge of town. To deliver a lecture. Quantum computing. Zak had been fascinated. There had been a lot of maths. Maths had been about the only subject Zak had ever cared for. Maths had rules. Rules that didn't suddenly change, pulling the rug out from under you.

Napier had noticed Zak. Had told him he had *potential*. Quantum computing was the future. And Zak could be a part of it.

The cars were parked in the garage. A Range Rover Sport, a Jaguar and a Bentley 100 XT.

Just your basic runarounds in an age of austerity.

Zak slipped his kitbag off his shoulder, twisted his baseball cap back to front and got to work. He had made the box himself. You could order the chip online. Plenty of places on the Dark Web.

The box bleeped, and the Bentley's locks sprang open.

Bingo.

Minutes later, he was roaring down the road. Nought to sixty in four-point-four.

This was when he felt alive again, when the past loosened its grip and the future seemed almost bearable. The thought brought with it a prick of guilt. He imagined his mother, her never-ending angst.

But why should he feel guilty? He hadn't asked to be here. Hadn't asked for the war back home. At seventeen, he was a man, and a man made his own decisions.

Besides, it wasn't stealing when you took from the rich. Especially the dead ones.

The 100 XT had a self-drive function. He jabbed a button; the steering wheel took on a life of its own.

His thoughts returned to the dead man. Peter Napier.

Napier had talked about changing the world. But Zak came from a world that had already changed beyond all recognition. Most days, Syria was a half-remembered dream. Vivid pops of colour set beside charcoal drawings of a nation under siege.

Soldiers at check-posts in Damascus's Old Quarter. A man trembling against a wall, rifles pointed at his chest.

Why couldn't he remember his father's face?

For an instant, Zak imagined Peter Napier's face superimposed on the shadows that made up his father's head. And then the image of the conjoined man wavered, dissolved and was replaced by a darker one, from the night Napier had died.

Zak thought about what he had seen. What he knew. What he had *done*.

Perhaps he should have gone to the police.

But real gangsters didn't talk to cops.

It began to rain, a violent squall like a bucket of water thrown at the windscreen. The wipers erupted to life . . . to reveal a small, dark shape huddled in the middle of the road.

Instinctively, Zak grabbed the wheel, swerved the car to the right, fighting the self-drive function. His foot jabbed downwards. The car bucked under his hands, then seemed to speed up of its own accord. In the split-second before he lost control, it occurred to him that he had stabbed down on the accelerator instead of the brake pedal.

The last thing that flashed through his mind, an instant before the car hurtled through the gates of the chapel: *quantum entanglement. Two bodies acting on each other from an impossible distance* . . . It seemed that Peter Napier had found a way to get to him, after all, even from beyond the grave.

2

B ASTARD WAS ASLEEP.
Well, that made one of them.
He wondered what had awoken him. A sound. A muffled boom, like a thunderclap, rolling in through the open window.

For a moment, he stayed motionless on the bed, a knight atop his tomb.

Around him the house settled on its foundations, soft-sighing creaks and the squeaks of what might have been mice. The sounds were the first thing he had noticed on his return to Wickstone. Both the symphony of country noises and the nightly *absence* of noise, as clanging – to a city-dweller – as the racket of church bells.

Q blinked, once, twice, and sat up. A moment while the past whispered into his ear. He saw M – the old M – frowning at him. *There are no more true believers, Q . . .* Now what had that been about? . . . M. MI6's hoary old dragon. Not so much passive-aggressive, as aggressive-aggressive . . . Good old M . . . Now, nothing but a memory. Like MI6. Like his old life.

He switched on the lamp, gaze falling to the newspaper cutting on the bedside drawer. The headline, above an image of a deserted riverside jetty, read:

CORONER RULES LOCAL SCIENTIST DROWNING
DEATH 'MISADVENTURE'

A photograph of the dead man was inset. Peter Napier.

A tremble in reality. The past speared in once more. Two boys, aged fifteen, at a science fair. Pete and Q, in their school uniforms, Pete's tie loose and limp, Q's perfectly Windsor knotted. Pete grinning, dark haired and obliquely handsome; Q, a cardboard cut-out set beside his charismatic friend.

His eyes picked out strings of words. *Speculation around coroner's verdict: misadventure or suicide? . . . Full report withheld . . . Napier Labs established in Wickstone-on-Water to great fanfare . . . Secretive research on next-generation quantum computing . . . Tragedy for the local community.*

He slipped out of bed, headed to the bathroom.

Turn on tap. Splash water onto face.

Nice sink. Armitage Shanks. A punk rock band from the nineties had adopted the name. And the company's original founder had been named Bond.

Hah! Had he ever told 007 that? Must have done.

The thought reminded him that Bond had been in touch: *Call me.*

The face that looked back at him from the mirror – fifty, sandy-haired, clean-shaven, handsome – in the right light and if you asked the right person – looked pensive.

Major Boothroyd. The artist formerly known as Q. Erstwhile head of Q Branch, the research and development arm of the British Secret Service aka the Secret Intelligence Service aka SIS aka MI6.

And now . . . Well, who was he, exactly?

The world had changed while he had been down in his bunker.

For a quarter of a century he had served as a cog in a very important machine. A machine that, for all its faults, sought to make sense of the world, to divide the world into good and bad, and then side with the good, make the good *happen*. And Q had had a small but integral role to play in that.

Q Branch. A government-funded warren of facilities in which inventions, big and small, were built, tested, rebuilt and then – perhaps more often than the taxpayer might approve of – blown up. The climate-controlled office that was too cold in summer and too warm in winter. The plastic in-tray that sat on his desk, welcoming him each morning with its papery recriminations. The dog-legged corridor leading to the cramped little kitchen area, with its tiny fridge, Styrofoam cups and a coffee maker that, on a good day, dispensed something slightly less drinkable than river pollutant. A little further along was the conference room, dominated by a photograph of a monocled Sir Mansfield Cumming, the first Chief of the Secret Service, progenitor to them all. Cumming had lost a leg in a road accident; his habit of wrongfooting visitors by jabbing a compass into its wooden replacement had always seemed to Q one of the better urban myths hanging around the Service.

Above all, there was the work. Project meetings and steering committees. Confabs with engineers, computer geeks and idiot savants with fluff in their navels. Mission planning with M and the Double Os. Mission post-mortems. Occasional excursions outside of Q Branch. Scientific symposiums in exotic locales, the sort to drive a travel agent to drink: Reykjavik in winter; Gaborone in high summer. Field testing new kit at the Porton Down military campus in Wiltshire, clods of earth flying in all directions. And, in recent years, the increasingly regular battles with bean-counters and bureaucrats; a merry-go-round of operational and budget reviews, run by gangs of lobotomised hobbits who wouldn't know an armour-piercing round if it hit them in the behind.

What he wouldn't give to warm his hands at such a gathering now.

How long had it been? Time had all but become a blur. Three months? Three months since the new M – in post less than a year – had called him into her office to deliver the coup de grâce. No surprise retirement party, no teary speeches, no glass of Lithuanian shiraz pressed into his hands by the office temp, together with a humorous leaving card featuring an old man with trousers at half-mast.

Hands are tied, Q. Restructuring in the wake of the spending review. You'll land on your feet, no doubt. And there's a generous redundancy package, of course.

The words 'walk the plank' had hovered over the conversation. Conversation? Conversation would imply a batting of balls back and forth. But the only balls being batted had been his ow—He remembered the savage satisfaction in M's eyes. They had never got on. Not since Q had testified at a Joint Intelligence Committee hearing on the dangers of AI deployment within Britain's defence infrastructure, exposing the fact that the then-prospective M knew as much about artificial intelligence as she did the actual thing: as in, neither had ever had occasion to burden her grey matter. The woman was a political animal, a mouthpiece for the brick-faced PM who had appointed her; a self-serving, lickspittle careerist that would have made a political spin doctor seem a model of integrity by comparison.

Back in the bedroom, he sat down at his desk, reached into a drawer and pulled out a plastic foolscap folder in neon orange.

From the folder he extracted a single item. A letter. Handwritten.

Not actually a letter. Barely a handful of lines. The note was from Pete.

If you're reading this, I'm dead.
I can't tell you everything – I don't have all the answers.
That will be your job. Should you choose to come back.
Mort won't be pleased. But that's neither here nor there, is it?

Q picked up a glass of last night's camomile tea from the desk, stood and walked to the open window.

Behind him, Bastard shifted around at the bottom of the bed, tail wagging in a dream. Above: a sprinkling of stars, diamonds thrown against velvet.

The house – a rental property grandiosely named Sanctus Villa – was the last on the road, standing at the apex of a minor hill known locally as 'Holy Hill'. The double-storeyed cottage was said to mark the end point of an easterly ley line that connected a Neolithic long barrow and – as locals were wont to joke – the new Waitrose in the centre of town.

Locals. Strange to think that, once upon a time, he had been a local too.

His memory tentacled into the past, caught hold of the old nuclear bunker out on the edge of town, now the site of Pete Napier's lab. As a boy, he remembered hopping the fence with Pete, groping their way through the catacombs, torches in hand. Losing their way.

History, repeating itself.

Q had lost his way. Or the way had lost him.

In medieval Japan, a samurai who had lost his position had two options.

Become *ronin*, an outcast, wandering the barren wastes like a dispossessed ghost.

Or commit *seppuku*.

He imagined walking into the centre of Wickstone-on-Water and disembowelling himself in front of the town hall. Probably some sort of local ordinance forbidding it.

A glance at the bottom of the letter, eyes lingering on the mystery inscribed there; then he walked back to the desk and fired up his laptop, before navigating to the encrypted site he used to communicate with the few acquaintances from his former life he still had left.

Bond's number hovered below an avatar of Paddington Bear.

It occurred to Q that he had never asked Bond: *Why Paddington?* Possibly because he was afraid of the answer.

11

Probably involved murdering several people and then sleeping with someone glamorous.

If there was one thing Q would never admit to, it was that he had quite enjoyed Bond's salty stories. The man was an insufferable egomaniac, with a penchant for shooting people in the face rather than bringing them in so that justice might be served or, heaven forbid, sitting them down for a cup of tea and a chat. But at least he lived life at a hundred miles an hour.

And beneath the smooth spy exterior there lurked a man that Q had, against all odds, found himself warming to. There was something noble about Bond, an unyielding, old-fashioned adherence to values that were fast vanishing from the world. An acknowledgement that, in an age of venality and vice, there were still those who believed in something greater than themselves. In goodness. In decency. In doing the right thing, even if it wasn't always obvious where the lines were drawn.

Values that bound them together. Even Bond had recognised that, in time.

It would explain why the man had remained in touch after Q's eviction from the Service, when all his other colleagues had deserted him as if he had admitted to watching *Bake Off Russia*.

Q dialled Bond's number. After a while, the dial tone clicked off. Nobody home.

Q shut the laptop and returned to Napier's letter. Once again, his gaze was drawn to the enigma at the very bottom:

UUSCVILCTRAKYMJCKNMKHEA
WIUGXUJYHAKRVA
GANCETWKTTGP
LIUQYNLJIOFCS

And below that, a single word: *Easy!*

Q had been around enough ciphers to know one when he saw it. Despite Pete Napier's assertion, there was nothing 'easy' here, or he would have cracked it already.

The real question was: why?

Why would Pete send Q a letter like this – dated the day of his death? Why the cipher?

It made no sense. Except that it did.

Pete had known something bad was going to happen. And he had reached out to Q. Presumably because of that tenuous bond that connected them.

The letter had found Q at precisely the right moment. Still reeling from the shock of his dismissal from MI6. *Don't fight it, Q. You won't win.* It was the brutality of the end that had taken him by surprise. They might as well have taken him into a field and put a bullet in the back of his head.

In the months since, he had tried to take stock of his life . . . Transferable skills: isn't that what they called them, these days? Was the ability to fashion weaponry out of almost anything a transferable skill valued in the modern workplace? His role at MI6 had been highly specialised. His dismissal – and M's vindictiveness – had queered the pitch when it came to other intelligence agencies. Which meant a role in the civilian sector. Somehow, Q couldn't imagine himself designing airport hand dryers for the remainder of his days.

And then, just a fortnight earlier, Pete's letter had finally reached him. The letter appeared to have been posted several weeks *after* Pete's death. Clearly, he had left instructions – with a lawyer, perhaps, or a friendly face at the post office. Until the letter, Q hadn't even heard of Pete's demise, so utterly had he cut himself off from the news cycle.

The letter had ignited something in him. A sense of mission. At a time when he badly needed a purpose. The letter implied that Pete expected him to return to Wickstone to dig up answers. But answers to what? Could a handful of lines in a note really indicate the possibility that there was more to Pete's death than misadventure?

Only one way to find out.

And so here he was.

They said you could never go home.

Whoever said that had never received a letter from a dead man.

3

DEATH.

A subject much on DCI Kathy Burnham's mind of late. Occupational hazard, to some extent. Bodies found under collapsed cardboard roofs. Corpses in filthy terraced houses, arms purpled with needle marks. Stabbings. A shooting – once. An incident with a bull terrier and a lollipop lady. Gruesome, that one.

Death was never an easy proposition. Even the natural ones.

A year earlier, she had sat by her father's side as he had breathed his last. That was the way to go. Surrounded by family, with the hope that some of them, at least, weren't counting down the seconds.

She turned the BMW into the hospital's forecourt, parking just ahead of a space reserved for ambulances.

Getting out, she headed briskly for the main doors.

Behind her, DS Lazarus wheezed along in the spring sunshine, already out of breath. No surprise there. The last time Bob Lazarus had passed a physical, dinosaurs roamed the Earth.

They plunged into the tiny general hospital, a relatively recent addition to the town, made their way up to a second-floor ward.

A constable lounged on a chair reading a sports magazine, sandwich in hand. The young man scrambled hastily to his feet. 'Ma'am. Sir.'

'At ease, Dobbs.' Bob Lazarus flashed a smile, warmly returned.

Lazarus had that easy quality with the troops, Kathy had often noted, not without a little envy.

Sometimes she wished she could be a bit more Bob.

But wrestling colleagues into headlocks and ramming their faces into the vending machine rarely won you popularity contests.

To be fair, that had only been the one time, and the condescending arse had *totally* had it coming. But the stink had followed her around ever since. Followed her all the way back to Wickstone.

And so now she had a certain *reputation*.

Fair enough. She was a big girl.

Better to be disliked for who you were, rather than liked for being a doormat.

The boy was sitting upright in bed, an iPad on his lap, right ankle encased in a cast.

A woman – his mother – sat next to the bed, in jeans, a flower-printed blouse and a peach headscarf.

Kathy knew that her name was Sameera Youssef. That was about all she knew.

'Sam!' Bob grinned. 'Nice to see you.'

'And you, Detective Sergeant Bob.'

'How many times have I told you? Call me Bob.' He patted his ample belly. 'That speciality baklava box almost killed me. My better half has banned me from setting foot in your shop. On pain of pain.'

'Mrs Youssef, my name is Detective Chief Inspector Kathy Burnham. We would like to talk with your son.'

The woman looked pensive. 'Please excuse me, but should not a lawyer be present?'

16

'Sam,' cut in Bob, 'we're trying to keep this unofficial for now. An informal chat.'

'Your son has committed a serious crime,' Kathy said.

'Got two boys myself,' said Bob. 'Right pair of tearaways when they were Zak's age.' He put on his most avuncular expression, the one he thought of as Father Christmas-meets-David Attenborough. Melt the heart of a Nazi. 'We know you're a good kid, Zak. Got yourself into some bad company. It's not you we want ... Who asked you to steal the Bentley, son?'

Kathy leaned in. 'Was it the Albanians?'

Zak glanced at his mother.

Kathy: 'Zak, if you know anything, anything *at all*, you must tell us.'

Sameera stood up. 'I am sorry, detectives, but my son is not well enough to answer your questions.'

'Looks fine to me,' said Bob. 'In fact, I'd say it's a miracle he's come out of that crash with nothing more than a fractured ankle. Which is more than I can say for the Bentley. Courts don't take kindly to young hooligans helping themselves to other people's motors. Especially those belonging to the recently deceased.'

Zak twitched at the mention of the dead man.

'If Zak cooperates, we can put in a good word,' said Kathy. 'He might avoid a custodial sentence.'

'No need to be afraid, son,' said Bob. 'We can protect you.'

A cynical laugh erupted from the boy. 'That's what they said to us back in Syria.'

Kathy stared at him. 'OK. I guess we'll just have to come back and arrest you when your doctors give us the go ahead. Think I'll go have a chat with them now.'

'What if I know something about Peter Napier? His death?'

Kathy frowned. 'Napier's death was an accident.'

'What if it wasn't?'

Bob spoke. 'Zak, is there something you want to tell us?'

'I'll tell you once I have a signed deal.'

'Someone's been watching too much TV,' muttered Kathy. 'I suggest you tell us what you know. *Now*.'

They stared at each other.

Sameera took a deep breath. 'I do apologise ... But I cannot allow this to continue.'

'Sam—' Bob began, but the Syrian woman cut him off. 'I am sorry, but I know my son's rights. He cannot be questioned until he is medically fit. And not without a lawyer present.'

'This isn't going to go away,' said Kathy. 'The next time we talk to Zak, we won't be so friendly.'

4

YOU HAD TO HAND IT to the Russians.

If you didn't, they'd probably take it anyway.

He had awoken with Nikolai in his head. A meeting, fifteen years in the past. Back in that narrow window of time when Russia was, if not quite an ally, then at least not the big bad wolf once again huffing and puffing at Europe's door. When an Englishman and a Russian might still share a bottle of vodka in a dimly lit bar in Moscow without attracting the attention of the *politsiya*.

Nikolai Sakharov: Q's mirror, the head of Directorate X – the Russian Q Branch at the Foreign Intelligence Service – the Russian MI6. A Cold War veteran with the stomach ulcers to prove it. A decade older than Q, he had befriended his British counterpart at a time when such friendships were frowned upon, if not actively discouraged.

Nikolai had been in a sour mood that day. He had just been drafted to the Historical Truth Commission, a bald-faced attempt to revise recent Russian history, to glorify the Soviet Union and sweep some of its more irreducible crimes under the rug. 'Those slack-sphinctered old walruses ask me to dance, Q. Like a bear with a gun to its head.'

'I sympathise, old friend. I've seen you dance.'

'Hah.' He lifted his vodka, shot it back, flagged down another. 'Mark my words. War is coming. Not today, maybe not tomorrow, but soon. My masters eye Kyiv like men in the gulag eye a juicy steak.' He looked sideways at Q, dark brow furrowing, handsome Neanderthal that he was. Nikolai with his two ex-wives, three estranged children and four cats. 'If they knew I spoke to you this way, they would put me against a wall.'

Q had said nothing. There was no need. Trust was a rare commodity in the circles of hell in which they moved. When you gave it, you gave it freely, expecting nothing in return. Expecting, more often than not, to be repaid with betrayal.

But they were not field agents. They were scientists. Who would want to eliminate scientists during peacetime?

And so it was a shock, when a month later, sitting in his office back at MI6, Q had opened a report fresh in from the Moscow desk to discover that Nikolai was dead, his body discovered in an alley less than a mile from the Lubyanka, knifed twice through the heart. The Russians' official conclusion: a mugging, no leads. The unofficial assessment: MI6 had been behind the killing. And, trembling in Q's hands, confirmation that 007 had wielded the blade.

He had never asked Bond for details. The one question that was taboo in MI6's Double O section: why? The report had been redacted. He had never known why his friend/not friend had had to die.

Q sat up in bed. Why was he suddenly thinking of Nikolai?

A strange burning flamed his lungs. A sensation he had felt too often of late. There were moments when the whole thing – his summary ejection from MI6, the hallucinatory quality of the three months since – seemed a cruel dream, a jest of fate, soon to be undone by M – the old M – bursting out of a cupboard, vuvuzela in hand, to tell him that, sorry, old chap, they had simply been having a massive wheeze at his expense, and he was to report back at his desk the next morning, ready and raring to go.

It was a terrible thing, he thought, to be valued for so very long, and then to no longer be needed.

His thoughts returned to Nikolai.

Nikolai's death had haunted Q for years. The not knowing.

And now here was another old friend, once his very best friend, calling to him from beyond the grave.

Peter Napier.

This time Q's hands weren't tied.

This time the truth was out there, waiting.

If he had the courage to find it.

He showered, then dressed. Stood a moment before the full-length mirror.

His tailored woollen suit in charcoal grey looked impeccable. The shirt: classic white with a herringbone weave. Spit-shined shoes you could use to check the underside of diplomatic vehicles for explosives. A tweak of the tie and he was set. He had bought the navy and polka-dotted tie at Ferragamo in Rome.

He picked up a broad silver tie-pin, balanced it in the palm of his hand, then slipped it on. A Montblanc pen – a combination of gold-coated hammered metal and deep blue lacquer – was pushed into a pen loop sewn into the lining of the jacket.

Now he was ready.

Downstairs, Miss Honeypenny was waiting for him, humming quietly to herself in the corner.

Honeypenny. The choice of name hadn't been accidental.

*Money*penny had been M's secretary back at MI6, a woman Q had greatly admired, not least because she had managed to resist Bond's advances.

Bond had laughed grimly when Q had told him about the latest addition to his household.

Q had authorised a batch of the robots months before his ousting from MI6. Social robots were going to be the next big thing. 'A robot in every home by 2035,' one American tech baron had recently trilled on CNN. It was only a small leap from 'every home', to 'every government facility'. Q Branch had begun several projects looking at how social robots might be compromised by 'bad actors'. In the best traditions of science, Q had started by experimenting on himself, taking one home and setting it to work in the environment in which it was designed to operate. Now that he was out of the Service, he had held on to the robot. It was either that or take a hammer to it.

Q had known that Bond's thoughts would flash instantly to the robot's namesake.

Miss Moneypenny.

The one that got away.

Q had decided not to tell Bond that he and Moneypenny had had a bit of a thing. For a while. Bond's head might have exploded. Besides, a gentleman never told . . . The affair had run its course and ended amicably.

And so now he had Honeypenny – technically, Yamagoshi Labs Model 550-X. A humanoid torso, set on a wheeled base. Artificial brain powered by an NPU – a neural processing unit, the latest in computer chip technology. The 550-Xs had been designed as companions for the elderly. Or the lonely.

Q wasn't exactly elderly and he wasn't exactly lonely.

'Good morning, Q.'

'Good morning, Honeypenny. Did you hunt down the information I asked for?' He turned to the coffee machine, a Sage Oracle Jet, jabbed at various buttons. Settled on a double espresso.

'Yes, Q. The initial investigation into the death of Peter Napier was conducted by a local detective team, led by a DCI Kathy Burnham.'

Q froze. He turned back to Honeypenny. 'Did you say *Kathy* Burnham?'

'Yes, Q.'

Q felt his stomach twist. His trousers tightened until the blood was being squeezed back up into his brain.

Kathy Burnham.

It wasn't possible. But it was.

Honeypenny cut into his thoughts. 'You also have three new messages from PerfectPartner. Would you like me to read them out?'

'No. Delete them.' Shock continued to reverberate through him. *Kathy.*

'Are you sure, Q? I calculate a 75.8 per cent probability that you will find Rebecca Morris highly compatible. She is forty-seven years old, divorced and a chartered accountant at Grant Thornton.'

Modern dating was a minefield. Once you made it past the manic depressives and the weekend Satanists, there was precious little left for a normal human being. Q longed for the days when a man could meet a woman in the old-fashioned way. Clashing umbrellas in the rain. A chance meeting in a bookshop. Anything was better than the hell of online matchmaking.

'Very sure, Honeypenny. Delete them all.'

As Q commenced Operation Breakfast – oats with kefir, fruit, flaxseeds, brazil nuts and a spoon of ginkgo biloba extract – he considered the day ahead. There was little doubt that it was going to be unpleasant. Just how unpleasant remained to be seen. They said time healed all wounds. Whoever had said that clearly hadn't been punched in the face by the past.

Q hoped to make progress on the 'case'. Strange, calling it that. As if he were a gumshoe in a hardboiled noir film. A sort of British Philip Marlowe, but without the hat and the effortless Bogart cool. And the chain-smoking.

Which had killed Bogart. So probably not that cool.

Oesophageal cancer. At fifty-eight. Q knew that because it had come up in a pub quiz. And also, because his late mother had been a chain-smoker.

Back to Pete Napier.

His first task was to get a lay of the land, at least as far as the police investigation into Pete's death went. Easier said than done.

Kathy Burnham.

Christ. You couldn't make it up.

Why was he here? Why was he doing this?

Questions with no easy answers. Pete's letter had set something in motion. Q had returned to Wickstone with a vague notion of reinvestigating his old friend's death. But he hadn't seen Pete in years. Why had the man's death hit him so hard?

Because Pete had once been his *best* friend. And because the truth mattered. Because, in the world Q had come from, men – and women – died for the truth. Pete's letter hinted at fore-knowledge of his end. Had he killed himself? Q couldn't believe that. That wasn't the Pete he had known. Neither could he imagine Pete dying of 'misadventure'. Not by drowning, at any rate. If you knew anything about Pete, you would know *that*.

Instincts were a terrible thing. You could never be sure that they weren't leading you up the garden path.

But Q had spent too long relying on them to ignore them now.

And if he didn't know the first thing about investigating a death, now was as good a time as any to learn. The basic principles were straightforward enough. Motive, means, opportunity. How hard could it be? 'Honeypenny, can you get me the address for the police station where DCI Kathy Burnham is based?'

Moments later, Q was typing the information into his phone.

Bastard padded into the kitchen, flopped into his basket, doing his impression of the World's Most Depressed Dog. Again.

Q set a water bowl below the animal's nose, then picked up his own bowl and headed for the garden.

5

THE DAY HAD BEGUN BADLY.

Mortimer – Mort – had arrived at the Wickstone Library to find Dave Potts taking a chainsaw to the box hedge.

'What are you doing?'

Dave pushed the safety goggles onto his head, wiped a sleeve over his brow, plastered with bits of chopped leaf. 'What do you reckon?'

Mort looked at the topiary, mystified.

'It's Churchill,' Dave elucidated. 'God bless him.'

Mort turned his back on the man, wandered inside, up a flight of steps and into the sanctuary of his office.

Shrugging off his jacket, he hung it on the coat-rack. As he turned, he caught sight of his reflection in the Victorian mirror hung beside the bust of Marcus Terentius Varro.

No one could fault him on looking the part.

Bow tie. Tweed waistcoat. Crisp white shirt. A man had to keep up standards, after all. Seventy-eight was the new forty-eight.

Couldn't do much about the hair. Or rather the absence of it. A neatly trimmed beard – still peppery – and piercing blue eyes completed the picture. Well, *he* thought they were piercing.

The thought of Pete Napier, the state of his body after it had been in the river, turned Mort away from the mirror.

You shouldn't have lied to the police.

He put a foot on the thought, pushed it back down into the cellar of his subconscious.

Mort sat down at his desk and turned on his computer.

As usual, there were few emails in his inbox. After retiring from Oxford University's Faculty of History he had settled into a new sort of life. A quiet life.

That had been twelve years ago. Twelve years of renegotiating his place in the world, his place in Wickstone.

Strange, the way the past drifted and flapped around you.

Like stories.

His story. Bella's story.

Not every story had a happy ending.

And now Mort's thoughts came, eventually, inevitably, to *him*.

Mort had heard he was back in town. But no contact had been initiated. Just as well.

Mort was spoiling for a fight.

Yes, indeed. If Major Boothroyd was stupid enough to turn up on Mort's doorstep ... God help him.

6

'Loved the good cop, bad cop vibe we had going there.'

Bob Lazarus pulled a packet of mints from his pocket. 'Lot easier in the old days, of course, before the world turned into a steaming pile of wokery. I remember when you could just whack Mr Big over the head with a telephone directory. Bish. Bosh. Ten minutes later, he'd be singing like Beyoncé . . . That's a joke. Obviously . . . So, what do we do now?'

Kathy, head over phone, checked her messages as she stalked ahead of him. 'We do what we said we would. Arrest him. Shake him upside-down by the boots till his teeth rattle.'

'I suppose you're right. It's just—' A grimace. 'The boy's been through a lot.'

'And that gives him a free pass, does it?'

'I didn't say that. It's his mum I'm thinking about—'

Bob saw Kathy stutter to a halt. A man was standing beside their black BMW, seemingly waiting for them. Bob didn't recognise him. Tall-ish, late forties, early fifties. Sandy haired, with a little grey at the temples. OK-looking, if you liked them a little on the constipated side. Beautifully tailored suit. Tie – with tie-pin. Fancy! He looked like an advert out of a clothing catalogue for the sort of posh gent whose head Bob Lazarus would have greatly enjoyed introducing to the bowl of the station loo.

27

Q tucked his hands into his pockets. Mainly because he didn't know what else to do with them. He had tracked DCI Kathy Burnham down to the hospital by calling in at the town's only police station, another recent addition to the local landscape. When Q had been young, the nearest police station had been a twenty-minute drive away in a neighbouring town.

Q had driven over, found her car and waited, bracing himself for the encounter to come.

But it was still a shock seeing her in the flesh.

Kathy stood there as if struck by lightning.

'You,' she breathed.

7

MEDIUM TONY HAD PROBLEMS.

And they didn't stem from his nickname.

Yes, the moniker had caused him a certain degree of aggro. All rebranding did. But it wasn't as if he had had a choice. The Boss had decided that this was what Tony was going to be called and that was that. You didn't argue with the Boss.

When the new outfit had come to town it was like one of those Wild West films. Not as much shooting in the high street, admittedly, but if you knew what was good for you, you kept your head down, drew the curtains and saved your complaints for the whisky glass.

When Tony – then known as Big Tony – had introduced himself to the Boss, the man's brow had crunched into confusion. 'But you are not big.'

'Well. No.'

'You should be called Short Tony. Or Small Tony.'

They had settled on Medium Tony.

Small Tony. Christ.

The call had come through earlier that morning. The Boss's chief henchman. The one they called 'Papa John', with the look in his eye that suggested he had just finished smothering his grandmother with a pillow and was considering what to do for an encore.

Tony knew the type. Didn't matter where they came from, they were all the same.

Callous. Soulless. Ruthless.

The man had spoken to Tony about the kid, Zakaria. The boy had made a pig's ear of the Bentley job. Rammed the car into a church. Pete Napier's car.

Zak was in hospital, talking to the cops. God only knew what he was saying. And about who. Or whom? Tony never knew which and didn't much care.

Tony had warned Papa John about taking on someone that young.

But the kid had skills, and this lot had no compunction about recruiting the young. Younger the better. Get them out on the streets as soon as they could walk, slinging dope, running errands, ferrying guns around. And if they got caught – well, what could the law really do to a minor? As long as you kept them at arm's length, they couldn't tell the cops anything useful anyway.

But Zak was different. Zak was smart. Smarter than anyone Tony knew. A lot bloody smarter than him, for a start. The kid had revolutionised Tony's chop shop operation. Absolute whizz with the tech stuff. Well, you had to be these days. Back in Tony's day, you could steal a car with a twisted coat hanger. Now you needed a PhD to get into a bloody Škoda.

But Zak's smarts also made him a liability. The kid knew way more than was good for him.

And now it was somehow Tony's problem.

Tony was no fool. His education may have begun and ended in the garage, but he could smell what was in the wind. The new outfit were into some heavy shit. And Pete Napier had been up to his neck in it.

Tony remembered the man. Napier had come in a couple of times, to get his cars serviced. Always seemed distracted.

Somewhere more important to be. No time to spare for a friendly word with the hired help.

Tony had a word for people like that. Arsehole.

But the man had been important to whatever Tony's bosses had cooking in Wickstone.

Wheels within wheels.

Tony had a motto: Keep your head clean and your nose down.

But that was assuming you had a choice.

Papa John had been very clear.

Something had to be done about Zak.

So, no. Being called Medium Tony didn't bother him.

That was the least of his worries.

8

'SO, THE PRODIGAL ARSE RETURNS.'
The pub was quiet. A background hum came from
a handful of bleary-eyed barflies and a TV tuned to a
soothing daytime soap that no one was watching.

The Knight Shift Inn. Q hadn't been in the place for thirty
years. The surroundings, as much as Kathy's words, had momentarily thrown him. He remembered coming in here as a young
man, a misguided attempt to find a home away from home. All
he had found was another space where no one needed him.

The pub sat on the town square, the old wooden-framed
guildhall to one side, and a row of charming civic buildings clad
in grey ragstone on the other. In the centre of the square, a
bronze knight wielded a long sword, the destrier beneath his
bottom charging into the fray, hooves raised. Legend had it that
The Unknown Knight had founded the village following his
return from the Crusades.

Q noted that an attempt had been made to steer the pub
upmarket. Esoteric libations in novelty glasses. A gastro vibe to
the chalkboarded menu. Charcoal-infused pizza. Deconstructed
ham sandwich, served on a shovel.

Q focused on DCI Kathy Burnham.

He had known this would be a mistake. But it wasn't as if he had a choice. 'Kathy, I—'

'Don't bother.'

Q's mouth flapped. His insides churned. He met Kathy's eyes, saw nothing but pitch-black hatred. He had never been good at this. Fathoming emotion. This was where science failed you. He knew that his colleagues at Q Branch had often thought of him as 'dispassionate', lacking in 'people skills'. Which were what exactly? Q Branch hadn't employed him to be a therapist. Or a babysitter.

He began again. 'I didn't come here to rake over the past. I came here for Pete.' He dug into his pocket, took out the letter Pete Napier had sent him, folded it out onto the table.

Kathy's eyes continued to flamethrower him. Q was sure his face was beginning to melt.

Eventually, she looked down, picked up the sheet. 'What the hell is this?'

'Pete sent it to me. It arrived a few weeks after his death. I think he knew he was in danger.'

'Pete Napier died in an accident. Or, quite possibly, killed himself.'

'What if it was neither?'

Kathy set down the letter. Her hand was shaking. Q suspected it wasn't early onset Parkinson's. 'Are you telling me you tracked me down because of an investigation I headed up?'

'Yes.'

Kathy was silent a long time. Her body language seemed calm, but her eyes were reading aloud from a different script. Her eyes were saying she wished she had a chainsaw.

'I know this isn't ideal,' said Q. *And the Oscar for Understatement of the Year goes to . . .*

Kathy steepled her hands together. At that instant, she reminded him of one of Bond's nemeses: Blofeld or Goldfinger. Or at least how Bond had described them. 'What do you want?'

'I want the case files. I want you to talk to me about the investigation.'

Her face went very still. A very nice face, he had to admit. A few lines of silver in otherwise still lustrous dark hair, swept back and kept tidy by a hair clip. Crow's feet at the corners of her green eyes lent a quality of worldliness to her features. A shade to her skin that spoke of a wild Mediterranean gene somewhere in her ancestry.

Something unnameable tugged at his heart.

Kathy was still beautiful, both objectively and in a way only a first love could be.

'Why, in the name of all that is holy, would I help *you*?'

Q took a deep breath. 'Because a man is dead. Because that man was once my friend. *Our* friend.'

'Let me get this straight. You rock up after thirty years and the only reason you're here is because you want to pump me for information? Information that I legally cannot share with you?'

'Yes. Though the second part doesn't matter. I signed the Official Secrets Act when I joined ... Well, you know.'

Kathy did know. Had heard it through the town grapevine. Small-town boy made good. You couldn't keep it a secret, no matter the cloud he had left under. No matter that he had ripped out her heart, torn it to shreds then set fire to the pieces.

'Q,' she breathed, as if testing out the moniker.

'Yes.' He wanted to say more, but the words halted at his lips like reluctant parachutists sensing a distinct possibility of aerial bombardment down below.

Kathy continued to stare at him, then abruptly stood up. 'I could use a drink. Guess who's buying?'

9

Zak's father had once told him that mirrors didn't lie.

You could fool other people, but you couldn't fool a mirror.

Zak hated lying. When his father had been around, he had lectured him endlessly about a man's worth being weighed by his integrity, his virtue and so forth. Zak's grandfather – his father's father – had been a judge in the old Syria, a man known for his vigorous application of these principles. OK, so perhaps he'd handed out a few more death sentences than might be considered cool in today's climate, and he was a devil for a good stoning, but nobody was perfect.

Zak remembered him as a tall man, with enormous hands and a mane of white hair. Grandfather had believed in the old adage that children should be seen and not heard. And, preferably, beaten when not seen. Nothing instilled moral fibre more effectively than a big stick.

Zak's father had wept bitterly when the old man had passed. It was the first time Zak had seen his father cry. It had shocked him. Men didn't cry. That was the work of women and professional mourners. Like his Aunt Lilia, who had made a good living turning up at funerals and wailing the roof down. Proper top-notch ululating.

Aunt Lilia, another casualty of the war. Cut down in a half-bombed street in Raqqa by a sniper's bullet. Zak's father had warned his sister not to go there. But that was Aunt Lilia for you. Enterprising. A lot of work for a professional mourner in Raqqa, she had told Zaq. She wasn't wrong about that. But you couldn't wail at your own funeral.

His thoughts swung back to the visit from Bob Lazarus and Kathy Burnham.

The pigs were right about one thing— Actually, he couldn't call them pigs as pigs were *haram*. His mother had told him it wasn't very nice to call anyone pigs, even the cops.

They had him 'bang to rights'. Another English phrase Zak had heard a lot recently. For instance, from Medium Tony, who ran the local chop shop. Zak had had no idea what a chop shop was until it had been explained to him. A garage engaged in dismembering or otherwise processing stolen cars. Tony had made it sound like a friendly butcher's store back in Damascus.

Medium Tony worked for Zak's ... benefactor.

Zak wondered what his benefactor would think when they found out Zak had screwed up the Bentley gig.

The thought of letting down the benefactor filled him with dismay. And fear.

Zak owed the benefactor everything. The benefactor was the one who had recognised Zak's capabilities and offered him a vision of a different future. One where Zak's 'very particular set of skills' would be put to good use. Like Liam Neeson in *Taken*. Zak liked Liam Neeson. He particularly liked how Liam Neeson could punch people in the face whenever he felt like it.

In truth, it hadn't taken much for the benefactor to convince Zak. The benefactor had told him that if Zak wanted respect in this country he needed money. If you had money, all your problems went away.

Pete Napier's face bubbled to the front of his thoughts.

They said secrets died with you. Had Napier taken his secrets with him, down to the bottom of the river? Zak hoped so.

Could he lie to the police and get away with it? Was it wrong to use a dead man?

Probably. But Zak didn't owe Napier anything. Yes, Napier had taken an interest in him. But that interest had been mercenary. As subsequent events had shown.

Napier had treated him as a project. The little immigrant boy from Syria with the dead dad and the mum struggling to stay afloat.

Thoughts of his mother stabbed at his conscience.

She didn't get it. She still thought they could live like they'd lived in Syria. But they were *nothing* here. The bakery she had opened, with borrowed cash ... How long would that last?

Zak felt in his pocket for the stone that he kept there. A stone from the deepest part of the Badiyah, the Syrian desert. A reminder of everything that had been lost. Everything to be regained.

Zak had to be the man of the house now.

He had to do whatever was needed to get them back home. Back to Syria.

10

'OK. SAY I HUMOUR YOU. What do you think you're going to achieve, raking over Pete's death?' Kathy picked up her beer. As a rule, she didn't drink when on duty. But rules were meant to be broken and she couldn't think of more fitting circumstances.

The blunt force trauma of seeing Q again (hah! What a stupid title! But she couldn't bear to call him by his real name) was wearing off. To be replaced by a sense of enraged wonder ... The fact that he wanted *anything* from her, after everything he had put her through. Textbook narcissism.

But still. He did have that letter. Did it mean anything?

Something about Pete's death *had* struck Kathy as odd. But there had been no evidence, nothing she could point to, to counter the coroner's verdict of death by misadventure. And there were so many other cases, and not enough hours in the day. Nor staff in her outfit. She had already lost a detective inspector. The bosses kept promising her a full strength team, but so far those promises had proved hollow.

On the surface Wickstone was a sleepy market town. Scratch that surface and you had a crime rate going through the roof like one of those graphs you saw of the price of tomatoes. It was the reason the county brass had finally decided to establish a police outpost here, the reason they had sent her back after building a career in a nearby town. A *proper* town. A place Wickstone's size rarely boasted – or needed – a DCI. But with criminality gradually chipping away at the town's halcyon way of life, the authorities had had to act.

'I don't know,' said Q. 'Frankly, I hope I'm wrong and it turns out that Pete *did* die of . . . misadventure.'

'But you don't believe that.'

A hesitation. 'No.'

'Why?'

'Because Pete would never have entered that river willingly.'

Kathy made a decision. 'What do you want to know?'

'Lead me through the case. The basics.'

'Fine . . . Victim's name was Peter Napier. Fifty years old. Caucasian. Five eleven. Brown hair. Brown eyes. Quantum computing scientist. Discovered drowned in the River Wickstone. No signs of assault. No defensive wounds. His car was found parked beside the wooden jetty at Bishop's Point. We think that's where he went into the water.'

'Was there a suicide note in the car?'

'No.'

'In his house?'

'No.'

'On his computer?'

'No.'

'Did he write or mention to anyone that he was going to kill himself?'

'Not that we know of.'

'Then I think we can rule out suicide, don't you?'

'The coroner didn't conclude suicide. She concluded death by accidental drowning.'

'Pete would never have gone into the river.'

'You keep saying that. Why?'

'Because Pete couldn't swim. He was terrified of open water.'

Kathy's eyes widened, just briefly. 'We never came across that anywhere in our investigations.'

'He lied about it. Even when we were kids. Don't you remember?'

A beat. 'Doesn't that just make it more likely that he committed suicide? Why else would he be out there? The time of death is estimated at around two a.m. There's no earthly reason for him to be out on that jetty, especially if he was scared of open water.'

'What reason would he have to kill himself?'

'His colleagues told us he'd been unhappy for some time.'

'Unhappy? About what?'

'His life. His company. Work. He was under enormous stress. There was also the fact that he took off his clothes and laid them neatly on the passenger seat of his car. Together with his phone and watch. Why would he do that if he wasn't planning to go into the water?'

'Was there any sign that anyone had been out there with him?'

'No. It's a pretty isolated spot. There's only one access road going out to Bishop's Point with a road camera covering it. The footage shows Pete headed up there – alone – a few hours before his death. No one else passed the camera that night.'

'No forensic artefacts of any kind?'

'None that we could find.'

'Did he contact anyone, make any calls, just before going out there?'

'No.'

Q shifted in his seat. 'Who found the body?'

'Local cyclist. Or rather, the cyclist found the car. Thought it looked suspicious. Called us. We sent the divers in. They found the body pretty quickly. Hadn't drifted far.' Kathy picked up the letter again. 'What makes you think *this* indicates foul play?'

'The tone of it. "If you're reading this, I'm dead." Pete clearly foresaw his own death. He was frightened by something. Or someone.'

'Don't you think you're reading too much into it? Besides, it's dated the day he died. To me, *this* reads like a suicide note.'

Q changed direction. 'The coroner's report wasn't made available publicly. Why?'

'National security reasons. At least, that's what we were told.'

Q blinked. National security? An alarm began ringing somewhere in the basement of his mind. 'I presume *you've* read it?'

'I've seen it.'

'And?'

'And what?'

Q sighed. 'Kathy. Please.'

'Those records are sealed. Or at least only available to involved parties.'

'I *am* an involved party.'

'Really? When was the last time you saw Pete? For Christ's sake, you haven't set foot in Wickstone for three decades.'

A man at a nearby table, slumped over a beer, frowned at them from under a Rastafarian hat. Odd headgear for a grown white man, but who was Q to pass judgement? 'There's also the cipher,' he said. 'At the bottom of Pete's letter.'

'He was a scientist. Probably wrote ciphers in his sleep ... Have you worked out what it says?'

'Not yet.'

'Wow. Stop the presses. Call the PM. Q doesn't have all the answers.'

Q frowned. 'I never claimed to have all the answers. That's why I'm talking to you.' He looked down, rotated his pint glass through a quarter-turn, looked back up. 'I want access to your case files.'

'Not a chance.'

'Please, Kathy. Don't turn this into a turf war.'

'What turf war? There is no turf. You have no turf! This is a police investigation and you're a civilian.'

'I headed up Q Branch for over two decades. A division of the British Secret Service charged with developing top-secret field technologies. I believe that gives me just a smidgeon of turf.'

She stared at him.

'Look. I can get hold of those files myself, if I have to. Through other channels.'

'Over my dead body.'

'I'm just trying to help.'

Kathy stood up. 'No. You're not doing this for anyone but yourself. You came back because of guilt. Well, you can take your guilt and shove it.'

Q's mouth gaped. But no sound emerged. Finally, he said, 'Why are you calling me Q? It sounds strange when you say it.'

'Because that's all you are to me now. A grown man identified by a stupid letter.'

11

MIRKO DEMAÇI HAD NEVER WATCHED *The Godfather*. Too close to home. Besides, he had never liked the Italians. He had tried to do business with them once and they had laughed him out of the door. They weren't laughing now.

And that business with the horse's head. Why would you want to cut off a perfectly good horse's head? What had the horse ever done? You want to frighten someone, go frighten them. Don't bring horses into it.

Mirko loved horses. His stables out in Essex cost a small fortune to maintain. An investment in his sanity. Horses didn't give him blood pressure. Horses didn't invite him to weddings and then get upset when he didn't show up. Horses didn't accidentally kill the wrong person.

Mirko had never wanted this life. He had grown up in the Albanian mountains. As a boy he had wanted to play the flute. His father had caught him at it one day and broken the flute over his knee. Told him it was a woman's instrument. Threatened to break the girl who had given it to him.

Where was that girl now?

Gone. Lost to him when his father had moved them all to the city.

Gangster. Mirko had never really liked the word, or at least, the way some people used it. Reducing an entire way of life to a caricature. What did he do that was so bad? He provided a service. Drugs. Sex. Assault rifles. Basic human needs.

Granted, he had built a business that flouted the law. But whose law was it, anyway? Not God's law.

Mirko abhorred violence. Yes, the side-effect of his line of work was that occasionally people got hurt. Sometimes you had to stuff men into barrels and set them on fire. Came with the territory.

Now, at this advanced age, all Mirko wanted was a peaceful life. He wanted to retire. Tend to his horses. Listen to his grand-children's recitals.

What did the old have to cling to except the young, anyway? And lost dreams.

He still dreamed of that girl who had given him the flute. What was her name, now?

Gangsters rarely got to dance through fields of tulips, deliri-ously in love. Rarely got to end their lives in their own beds. Life was unfair. You built an organisation that provided gainful employment for hundreds. You gave men a purpose. And what did you get in return? Society's brickbats.

The door opened and Papa John came in.

Mirko could tell by his deputy's expression that this was going to be a serious discussion. Not that Papa John was known for being the life of the party. The only party that Papa John had ever been the life of was a wake.

Mirko had found him many years ago, a young man on the make. A boy who wanted to run before he could walk. There had been a moment when Mirko had thought he would have to have Papa John killed. But something had stayed his hand. He had never regretted that impulse. Papa John – he had been just *Gjon* in those days – had been the rock upon which Mirko had built his church.

In truth, it amazed Mirko that Papa John remained content to play second fiddle. For years he had expected the man to make a play for the throne. That was the life they led. Never turn your back on anyone, not even your friends. *Especially* your friends.

But Papa John had stayed loyal. More than loyal. The man had no family of his own. No woman. A lonely life. But some men were like that. Content within themselves.

Mirko had no sons. Four daughters before his wife had given up. *No more playing roulette with my womb!*

Formidable woman. And from a noble Albanian family. Couldn't even get rid of her. Didn't need a blood feud on his hands. Mirko knew of blood feuds that had lasted seven generations.

She had died five years ago. Peacefully. Surrounded by her daughters and granddaughters. No grandsons. Not yet, at any rate.

'We need to talk about Wickstone,' said Papa John.

'Pass me the remote.'

Papa John walked to the table, picked up the remote and handed it to Mirko.

Mirko flicked through the channels and landed on *The Great Pottery Throw Down*.

He settled into his armchair. Whirred up the footrests.

Mirko loved the show. Unknowns given the chance to shine. The big presenter who kept breaking into floods of tears. Magic.

'The boy, Zak,' said Papa John. 'He's talking to the police.'

Mirko picked up his mocktail and slurped at it through a straw.

'He hasn't said anything. Yet. But he's offered them something. About Napier.'

Mirko put down the glass. Raised the volume. Some woman named Dora had made a Sgraffito cockatoo. Mirko had no idea what Sgraffito meant, but the cockatoo was impressive. He wondered how it would look in his bedroom.

'The boy's under police guard. I'm monitoring the situation.' A pause. 'There's something else. An old friend of Napier's. Just arrived in Wickstone. He's asking questions.'

'And?'

'I had him checked out. Until recently he worked for the intelligence services.'

Mirko stiffened. He muted the television. 'Is this a problem?'

'I'll take care of it.'

'I don't want any more disruption in Wickstone. Our ... friends abroad are getting jumpy.'

'There won't be.'

Mirko gave Papa John a look. 'How is your hair transplant settling in?'

Papa John stiffened. 'It's fine.'

'Does it hurt?'

'Not anymore.'

Mirko eyed his lieutenant. Vanity, thy name is gangster.

'In the meantime, I've asked Medium Tony to deal with Zak,' said Papa John.

Mirko picked up his glass again. 'And Adem? The car was one of his, wasn't it?'

'Yes.'

Mirko shook his head. He loved his nephew, the closest thing to a son he had. But the boy made mistakes. Headstrong. That was the next generation for you. Never content. The old ways, the old staples, weren't good enough. Now it was all online fraud and cyberterrorism and ransomware.

The future.

All Chinese to Mirko.

County lines. *That* was something he could understand. If the junkies won't come to the mountain, take the mountain to the junkies. Wickstone was one of a dozen small towns ripe with

46

potential. The gang had established early inroads, in part thanks to Peter Napier.

But Napier was no longer in the picture.

Matters were becoming complicated. A delicate balance was being upset.

Life in the mountains. That had been simple. Locals called them the Accursed Mountains. It was said the Devil had created them in a single day, when he had escaped from hell.

Mirko had loved the mountains. Boar-filled forests. Lakes as blue as the eye of God.

Sometimes, in the dead of night, Mirko would weep for those lost mountains.

12

T
HE SILVER BIRCHES WERE SHADING towards green.
Following the meeting with Kathy, Q had needed to
clear his head.

He drove out from the town centre, parked outside the
Wickstone Woods, an arboreal mishmash of oak and ash and
elm and lime and alder and Scots pine. And birch. Dapples of
golden sunlight lit up the undergrowth: tufts of wild grass and
bracken; red campion, purple thistle, and foxgloves; a flourish of
bluebells. The colours of the ancient world.

As a boy, he had loved these woods. The solitude. The pagan
necromancy deep among the trees. His leather-bound set of
Encyclopaedia Britannicas had informed him that the forest was
a remnant of the great wildwood that had once smothered Britain.
Somewhere in here, perhaps, the last aurochs had been hunted
to extinction. Druids had made blood sacrifices in Neolithic
groves.

He followed an old walking trail, not minding, for once, that
his shoes were getting mucky. He hated mucky shoes. Pete had
laughed at him, back in school. Q's habit of polishing his black
brogues each day.

He broke through the woods and out into a dazzle of sunlight.

The church had been around since before the Black Death. Deconsecrated – for a reason lost to time – then reconsecrated, and partially burned down in the 1500s, it had been lovingly restored, a faithful reconstruction in grey stone with a red roof and three tiers of blind arcading rising to a castellated upper storey. Carved scroll-work depicted a combination of winged angels and fabulous beasts.

From a distance it appeared as if the two were engaged in outstanding feats of sexual congress.

Q walked along a bramble-lined path, clusters of wild black-berries shooting from the thickets, and to a round-arched doorway. A momentary hesitation – never quite seen eye-to-eye with God – and then he entered, walking past a heavy octagonal font, and then along the nave, flanked on both sides by dark wood pews.

A rear door let out to the graveyard.

Pete's grave was over by the site's eastern edge, out past the war dead.

Q crunched his way along a pebbled path. No one else around.

The grave was distinguished by its simplicity: a bed of black stone chippings, and a small rectangular headstone inscribed with a few pithy words.

Here lies Peter Robert Napier. Blah blah blah.

A low maintenance arrangement. Made sense. No one to maintain it.

What was life but a series of humiliations, anyway? Ostracization at school, the daily grind of career and mortgage payments, then, once you had outlived your usefulness, booted out the door to a chorus of platitudes. Grim rounds of golf. If you were lucky. Then death. More platitudes. *He was a lovely man. A good friend. A great husband and father.*

Lies and half-truths and exaggerations.

And then, the final indignity. Stuffed in a box and folded into the earth like a heap of old turnips. A cathedral of bleached bones for the damp creatures of the earth to use in the way children crawled in and out of an abandoned playground castle.

The thought would have appealed to Pete. One of nature's cynics.

A sudden vision of his old friend elbowed its way in: Pete, in the river, thrashing around, face contorted by terror. *Help me.*

Q walked across the graveyard, stopped halfway towards the southern edge, looked down at another grave.

To his surprise, the grave was well maintained, the kneeling angel tinged with green, but otherwise intact.

No great epitaph on the stonework.

Dates. A name.

Annabelle Boothroyd.

Three decades. Three decades in the dirt and the memory of his mother's passing was still as sharp as a knife drawn across the palm.

Q pulled out his phone, logged on, sent a message to Bond. The reply was instant.

>Tied up.

Tied up. With Bond that could mean anything. From hang-gliding off a cliff with a bomb strapped to his back to ramming a motorboat into an oil tanker. Or perhaps he meant literally tied up. Wouldn't put it past him. Q's fingers moved over the phone.

>Need help.

Several seconds, then Bond's reply:

>???

>Access to police and coroner files. Peter Napier. British. Quantum scientist. Recently deceased.

>Other channels?

>I'm persona non grata.

Q checked that the apostrophe was in place, then pressed send. Just because he was using an encrypted messenger service, it didn't mean standards had to slip. What if he died and they had to go through his messages at a closed-doors inquiry?

Seconds ticked by.

>Leave it with me.

Q had often wondered what it must be like. Being out in the field. With the ability to call upon almost limitless resources. Until recently, Q had been one of those ensuring that agents such as Bond were given such resources. Now the shoe was on the other foot.

In truth, he hadn't expected Bond to help.

But, if there was one thing Q had learned during all their years together, it was that 007 was nothing if not surprising.

13

MEDIUM TONY HAD NEVER SEEN the inside of a prison cell.

A fact he was proud of, even if no one believed him. It wasn't something he bandied about, certainly not around his new employers. He had the impression they didn't trust anyone who hadn't done a stretch.

Tony had grown up in Wickstone. The furthest he had ever been was Malaga. Hadn't really liked it. Not really his speed. More drunken British yobs in knock-off football shirts than you could shake a stick at. If he wanted that sort of experience, he would take the train to Newcastle.

Tony's dad had run the local garage. The Wickstone Autoshop. By the time Tony was six he could strip the engine on an Austin Metro in under an hour. By rights he should have been on one of those TV shows about kids who played the violin at a ridiculously young age. Tony would like to see a violinist replace a leaky transmission on a ten-year-old Ford Focus. Hah.

But the world wasn't fair. Tony had learned that early on when one of the garage's customers had reversed over Tony's dad in a minivan. Massive chest trauma. Tony had held his dying dad's hand while he spewed blood and muttered something about Mrs Patterson's carburettor.

Tony got out of his car and walked into the hospital.

The lad outside Zak's room looked barely out of his teens.

Tony recognised him. Dobbs. He knew the kid's father. Navy blue Renault Megane.

Tony shifted the paper bag in his arms to one side and stuck out a hand. 'Steve, right?'

Dobbs nodded uncertainly, had a go at shaking Tony's hand. Then seemed to realise he probably shouldn't be doing that sort of thing. Not in uniform, anyway.

'I'm sorry, sir, but you can't go in.'

'Zak's my employee. I've come to see how he's getting on.'

'Technically, he's under arrest. Restricted visitation.'

'Technically? He's not *actually* banged up, is he?'

'Well, no. But he soon will be.'

'In that case there's no reason for me not to pop in and give him this bag of peaches.'

Tony waited. The peaches smelled lovely. He'd got them for nothing at the market. Old girl behind the stall owed him for a clutch repair. Owner wouldn't miss them.

'No. I suppose not.'

Inside, Tony was relieved to find the lad's mother was AWOL. Sameera. Formidable woman. When Zak had started working for him she had been so relieved that her young tearaway of a son had found gainful employment, she hadn't bothered to look at the small print. He wondered if she had been purposefully oblivious. The pair had been through hard times. And that bakery of hers wasn't exactly thriving.

The boy was slumped on the bed, watching TV.

'You've not been picking up your phone,' said Tony.

'The police have taken it.'

'Of course.' He set the bag down, then lowered himself into an armchair. His knees creaked like accordions.

'We have a problem.'

'I'm fine. Thanks for asking.'

Tony poured himself a glass of water from a jug on the bedside unit. 'How are you?'

'I'll live.'

'Good. I hear the cops were in to talk to you.'

'I didn't say anything.'

Tony wanted to tell Zak about the day one of his new employers had brought a car round for him to stick in the compactor. Tony had had the crusher installed a few years ago, one of those American models that compressed vehicles into dense metallic cubes.

Tony had noticed the thumping on the inside of the car's boot. Perhaps he should have said something?

Then again, best not to see things like that.

'You've made a right pig's ear of this.'

'I don't eat pig.'

'Our mutual acquaintances are not best pleased.'

Zak said nothing.

'The first rule of this business: don't get noticed. You got noticed.' Tony leaned in. 'Now listen to me carefully. If you tell the cops anything about Pete Napier, it won't just be you in the meat grinder. Do you understand?'

Zak blinked back his anger. He knew that Tony's words came from elsewhere. From men who wouldn't hesitate to – to—He looked away, not wanting Tony to see the tears in his eyes. Seconds passed. 'Do you think about him? Napier? About what happened to him?'

'Napier isn't your problem. Nor mine. This is the wrong business to grow a conscience, son.'

The door opened and a doctor came in. Brown chinos. Checked shirt. Stethoscope. He looked even younger than the cop at the door.

Tony stood up.

He had no love for doctors. Or hospitals. When he was seven, he had had to go in for a rash on his nether regions. He couldn't swear to it, all a bit hazy now, but the doctor who had examined him had been a little too hands on.

'Hi, Zak. How are we today?'

'*You* look fine,' said Zak. 'I'm still in this cast.'

The doctor grinned as if Zak had just said the funniest thing he had ever heard.

'I'll leave you gents to it,' said Tony, getting to his feet. 'Don't forget what we talked about, will you, Zak?'

14

THE ROAD OUT TO NAPIER Labs speared through a patchwork of muddy fields.

Once upon a time Wickstone had constituted a handful of farms and a chapel, a little blister of civilisation surrounded by deep forest. A royal charter had established an open-air market in the centre of town sometime back in the 1200s. A few hundred souls – and as many pigs – soon grew into the sort of market town enterprise England did so well, cosseted in a bubble of gentility, sheltered from the ravages of change by a timeless inertia.

All gone now.

Q had noted the signs. Change wrought across the faces of buildings he had once recognised. In the people scurrying through the streets, heads down.

This wasn't the Wickstone he had grown up in. Once upon a time you could have scratched the topsoil and uncovered Bronze Age relics. Now everything was tarmac and glass and concrete, and the only relics seemed to be of the human variety, those who had survived the Blitzkrieg of modernisation and now shambled about in bewilderment, dazed and confused. And angry.

When he had returned he hadn't known what to expect. Would word of his ousting from the corridors – or, at least, the hidden basements – of power have arrived here before him? Would the ruddy-faced locals greet him with the sort of reception usually reserved for incoming paedophiles, the kind required to go around knocking on everyone's door to inform them that they were on the Sex Offenders Database, and, by the way, how are your lovely children?

The smear of a horn jerked him back to the road.

A Deliveroo rider on a motorcycle was aggressively weaving behind him.

Q glanced at his speedometer. He had one of those insurances where they installed a black box in your car. A mile over the speed limit and dire consequences would ensue. Q wasn't sure exactly what those consequences might be. The engine might judder to a halt. Keanu Reeves might pop up to commandeer the vehicle.

The helmeted Deliveroo rider took advantage of a sudden widening in the road to scrape by, taking the time to flash Q a middle finger as he roared past.

Napier Labs was housed in the architectural folly once known as Bunker 11, a mad scheme dreamed up by Whitehall back in the 1960s.

The existence of a secret British war bunker located on the outskirts of Wickstone-on-Water and to be used in the event of World War Three had been leaked in the early nineties, though the site itself had remained closed off to public view. Not that that had stopped a teenaged Q – and others – from making it past the abandoned security perimeter.

There hadn't been much to find. Miles of empty underground caverns once designated for offices, dormitories and comfy berths for the PM and his Cabinet, a safe haven to plan retaliation while Soviet H-bombs rained down on London.

Later, when a cash-strapped Tory government had begun looking around for family silverware to pawn, no one had thought that Bunker 11, with its bare limestone and breezeblock walls and fluorescent lighting, would qualify as anyone's idea of prime office space.

They would have been wrong.

Q was forced to a halt by a steel gate, looked down upon by spherical, 360-degree surveillance cameras mounted on stanchions. A grey panel fence, some fifteen feet in height, marched off to either side. Curls of razor wire glinted in the sun.

A uniformed guard had emerged from a guard booth to meet the Deliveroo rider.

The rider had shed the helmet, revealing that *he* was in fact a *she*.

The dark-haired young woman gave Q a hard glare as he dismounted from the Caterham. He wondered if it was the car that had attracted her attention. A vehicle for the 'distinguished gentleman with one eye on the past and one on the future'. Q had no idea what that meant, but, on a visit to the Caterham factory in Dartford a couple of years earlier, he had instantly fallen in love with the vehicle's elegant design. The acid green Caterham Seven had come in kit form – it had taken Q two weeks to build with almost every component custom-ordered from the factory's build book – from the burgundy leather dashboard to the retro magnolia instrument gauges to the anthracite gearknob with 'R' insignia denoting the Caterham's race car pedigree. He hadn't had this much fun with a car since his university days when, for a prank, he had rewired a friend's Ford Fiesta so that every time he pressed the brake pedal it honked the horn.

The woman, clad in biker leather, looked intimidating. As if she had honed obscure martial arts skills in a hilltop monastery for just this moment. He waited until she had left, then walked to the gate where the guard was examining the label on the takeaway.

Q introduced himself. 'I'm here to see Jed Ellis.'

The guard, an elderly man with a forehead like a brick slab, took out a tablet, checked something. 'You're not on my list.'

'I don't have an appointment. I'm a friend of Peter Napier's. I need to speak to Ellis.'

The man looked uncertain, but went back to his booth to call it in.

Poking his head back out, he said: 'Someone will meet you inside. Here, you can take this in.' He thrust out the takeaway bag.

Q was met in a small but efficient-looking reception by a young woman in a white lab coat. Tall, dark-haired and wearing glasses with fire-engine-red frames. 'My name is Astrid Simmons. May I see some ID, please?' The accent was European, possibly Scandinavian, with a mangling of varsity-American.

Q took out his wallet and handed her his driving licence. 'Please wait here.'

She vanished, leaving Q alone with a male receptionist who looked a bit like Joseph Stalin. Stalin watched Q warily as he took a seat. He guessed Napier Labs didn't get many unscheduled visitors.

There wasn't much to see in the reception area. A giant corporate logo – an interlocking N and L – blazed from one wall. Another held a blow-up photograph of Peter Napier standing behind a whiteboard covered in equations, grinning from ear to ear.

Genius.

Q had always known that he possessed above average intelligence. But Pete's IQ had been an order of magnitude higher. And Pete had known it. Even in school, he hadn't bothered to hide it. It hadn't made him many friends. Perhaps that was why he and Pete had bonded. Outsiders. Or, as Pete had put it, giants in a land of pygmies.

That sort of comment explained why the other boys had once stripped them down to their underwear and shoved them into the playground.

They had kept in touch, for a while, after Q left Wickstone.

Pete had charted his own course. A PhD at Oxford, followed by a research fellowship. Academic appointments in France, the USA and Canada. A decade ago he had returned to the UK to take charge of his own research team at University College London, a lab funded by IBM. Seven years later, he had left UCL to found Napier Labs, returning to his hometown of Wickstone-on-Water to set up a facility shrouded in secrecy.

Q had found minimal information online about Napier Labs. Beyond the odd press release, little had come out of the lab or those that ran it. That Peter Napier, one of the world's leading pioneers in the field of quantum computing, was working on next-generation technology was a given. But how far the company had progressed along that path and what exactly they had been doing remained a mystery.

Astrid returned and handed Q's driving licence back to him. 'You'll have to leave your phone at reception. No recording devices allowed inside. Mr Ellis has agreed to see you. Please follow me.'

They walked along windowless whitewashed corridors. At regular intervals, intimidating steel doors blocked forward progress, negotiable only via biometric identification: iris scans and fingerprints.

'We're all still in shock.' Astrid walked past an open doorway. A pair of heads bobbed up from a table strewn with papers to watch them go by. 'It's hard to believe he's gone.'

'I've been told that Peter's colleagues felt he was unhappy. That some think his death was a—'

'Suicide? Yes. I've heard the theory. I don't know about Peter being unhappy. Then again he wasn't the type to bare his emotions.'

She said no more. They arrived at a door. A plaque on the wall declared it to be the office of Jed Ellis, Chief Operating Officer.

The COO turned out to be a short man with curly red hair, streaked with grey. He wore square-framed glasses and a white lab coat. A feeble moustache hung out on his upper lip, feigning nonchalance.

Q looked around. The office was spacious and looked as if a storm had blown through it. He hated the sight of slovenliness. An untidy desk was the sign of an untidy mind.

'Sorry about the mess.' Jed's accent was American. Californian, to Q's ears.

Q handed him the takeaway bag.

Jed took the bag and cleared a space on his desk. A handful of papers fell to the floor. Jed ignored them. Q resisted the urge to pick them up.

'So, you knew Pete ... Sorry, what was your name again?'

'Boothroyd. Major Boothroyd.'

'Major?'

'Yes.'

Jed looked mildly impressed. Q had long ago discovered that there was a certain type of person who found military rank intoxicating. He rarely referred to his stay in the army but wasn't averse to using it when the occasion demanded.

'And you're here because ... ?'

'Pete and I grew up together. I have questions about his death.'

'Don't we all. Terrible thing, drowning. Wouldn't wish it on anyone.'

Jed took out a burger, opened up the bun, squirted three packets of ketchup onto the patty, then put the top half of the bun back on.

Q's stomach did a loop-the-loop. Hell was too good for grown-ups who drowned defenceless food items in ketchup. It wasn't even organic.

Jed took an enormous bite, wiped his mouth with a sleeve, put the burger down. 'Sorry. Haven't had time to eat today. Pete mentioned you. You work at MI6, don't you? Are you here in an official capacity?'

Q was surprised. He hadn't heard from Pete in years.

'No. I've left MI6.'

'Pity. Always wondered what you guys do over there. Are you thinking about the quantum revolution yet? Game-changer. Major security threats coming down the pike. Big. Huge.'

Q had a rudimentary grasp of quantum mechanics, but the intricacies and practical applications of the science were beyond his area of expertise. He imagined trying to explain quantum mechanics to Bond. Bond would want to know if he could use it to blow someone's head off at fifty paces. Or undo a bra.

Jed picked up a bottle of Coke and guzzled at it. 'Important to stay hydrated.'

'How long did you work with Pete?'

'You're looking for closure. I get that. Very important, closure. When my dad died it was months before I cried.' Jed seemed to be making up his mind as to whether he would cooperate. Or not ... 'OK. I'll play ball. Least I can do for an old friend of Pete's ... To answer your question, Pete brought me in three years ago when he decided to build this lab. Poached me from IBM. I'm a hardware guy.'

Q looked blank.

'How much do you know about quantum computing?'

Q hesitated. He didn't like the idea of appearing ignorant in front of an American. 'A little. But let's pretend I'm a novice.'

'I'll take that to mean you know diddly squat.' Jed grinned. Bits of burger wriggled between his teeth. 'Quantum computers aren't just going to be faster than the most powerful supercomputer we have, they're going to be orders of magnitude faster. Light speed. Warp speed.'

As explanations went it left everything to be desired.

Jed slurped his Coke. 'OK. I can see you're a little lost here. Let's go back to basics . . . Classical computers work on the binary model. Two states to represent all data. Zeroes and ones. We call them bits. You probably know that. Maybe. Quantum computers use quantum bits – qubits, the smallest possible units of quantum information. Essentially, qubits are subatomic particles and thus use properties of the quantum mechanical world. Superposition. Entanglement. Stop me if I'm going too fast.

'What this means is that each qubit can take on a great many states – not just two. And that means that quantum computers can simultaneously perform far more logic operations per second than classical machines. To give you an idea, back in 2015, a Google–NASA D-wave quantum computer solved an optim-isation problem a hundred million times faster than a classical computer could have. It would have taken the average laptop ten thousand years to solve the same problem.'

'And that's what Napier Labs does? Builds next-gen quantum computers?'

'That was 2015. The Stone Age. Napier Labs is building the world's *fastest* quantum computer. A machine so powerful it makes everything else look like a Casio calculator.'

Q had owned a Casio calculator. His mother had bought it for him. It had been his pride and joy. Other boys took racy magazines to bed. Q had his calculator.

'And you're building it *here?*'

'Don't look so surprised. Setting up here was a brainwave. Pete's brainwave. He grew up in Wickstone, knew about this site. Negotiated a deal with the government. We have a thou-sand-year lease. In ten years, we'll be the world's biggest quantum tech outfit. We'll need the space.'

'You sound very sure of yourself.'

'I'm sure of the tech. Pete Napier wasn't just any quantum guy. He was *the* guy. First guy to break the hundred-qubit barrier. At IBM, he set up the first cloud-based quantum processor. Changed the field. After that anyone – with the right clearance – could experiment with the tech. If they can understand it, of course. Even you could have a go. Maybe.'

The burger lost another bite-sized jigsaw piece.

'If everything was going so well, why was Pete so unhappy?'

Jed put his burger down, dug a tissue from his lab coat, wiped his mouth. 'Look around you. This is an incredibly high-pressured environment. We have millions – tens of millions – invested in the success of this project. VC money. Pete's own life savings. Pete was a worrier. A perfectionist. Working for himself was a whole different ballgame. He felt responsible for everything. The stress got to him.'

'It doesn't make sense.'

'Look, this isn't official, and I'll deny it if you breathe a word anywhere else ... But I think Pete cracked up. I think he killed himself.' A beat. 'He'd set himself a crazy timeline. Impossible. He wanted BETSY up and running by the end of this year. He had us lined up for a stock market flotation. The company will be worth a boatload when it goes public.'

'Who's BETSY?'

'Sorry. That's what we call our quantum computer.'

'What does it stand for?'

'It stands for Betsy.'

'Oh.' Acronyms were de rigueur in government circles. Q had attended meetings where virtually every word spoken had been an acronym.

'It's the name of his daughter?' Jed raised an eyebrow.

Q knew that. Pete had mentioned it years ago, before they lost touch. He tried to remember the name of Pete's wife. Ex-wife. 'He was divorced.'

'Yep. Celestine McAvoy. Canadian. They split years ago. Celestine took the kid and got out of Dodge. Last I heard she was shacked up with some Irishman in LA. Pete took it hard. Frankly, I think it was still playing on his mind.'

Q changed tack. 'Were you and Pete close?'

'Sure. Yes. I'd say so. Though Pete never really let anyone in. You know?'

'What sort of person was he?'

'Pete? I thought you said you grew up with him?'

'That was a long time ago.'

'He didn't suffer fools, I can tell you that.'

'How did he get on with the staff here?'

'He was the boss and he made sure everyone knew it. Pete set high standards. Expected others to follow.'

'And made it clear when he felt those standards weren't being met?'

'Sure. If asses needed kicking, he kicked them. I'm not sure what you're getting at?'

'Did Pete upset people? Did he make enemies?'

'The police asked me this. He was a scientist, not Scarface.'

'He didn't have enemies?'

'None that would have wanted to kill the guy. That's what you mean, right?' Jed was shaking his head. 'Pete pulled the pin. It's that simple. It happens. Do you know that the highest rate of suicide in the UK is among men aged fifty to fifty-four?'

Q fell silent a moment. There was something evasive in the man's manner. Something about his responses. For most of his life, Q had rarely had to rely on his instincts. In a lab, things either worked or they didn't. Algorithms, logic, technology. Hard science. No room for sentiment or fuzziness. No room for guess-work or attempting to intuit what others might be holding back. That sort of thing was best left to politicians and bureaucrats. People like M.

'Did you see Pete on the day he died?'

Jed nodded. 'He was in the lab that day.'

'How did he seem?'

'Agitated. Tense. We were carrying out a big test.'

'What was the test?'

'I'm afraid that's classified intellectual property. I'm sure *you* understand.'

'But you think the failure of this test could have driven Pete over the edge?'

'I didn't say the test failed.' Jed's mouth became a bloodless line. 'Look. Pete was strung out. Drinking too much. Spent every second of the day catastrophising. We were making progress, but it wasn't fast enough for him. I tried to calm him down. But the guy was on an express elevator to his own private hell.'

Q thought about the letter Pete had sent him. How did that fit into what Jed Ellis was telling him? Pete's letter indicated that he had thought *something* was wrong. But the tone of the letter didn't match the image that Jed was painting of a stressed-out Pete, a man who just might have talked himself into the river. Pete's letter suggested an *exterior* threat. At least to Q. And then there was the cipher ... Q considered showing the letter to Jed but decided against it. There was something about the man's cavalier attitude that bothered him.

Jed checked his watch. 'I'm sorry, but I've got to get back to work. Astrid will see you out. I hope you got what you came for.'

15

'**J**ED ELLIS SAID YOU WOULD show me BETSY.'

Astrid halted, looked unsure. 'I should probably check with him.'

'He was going to show me himself, but he's tied up. Said you would take care of it.'

The lie had popped out before Q could consciously form the thought. He felt his pulse racing. He was sure beads of sweat had appeared on his forehead. How in the world did men like Bond do this sort of thing? Lie as easily as they breathed? At this rate, Q would soon have the silver-tongued dexterity of a Number 10 aspirant.

Astrid seemed to make up her mind. 'Of course. This way.'

They walked along identikit corridors, through more security doors, eventually arriving in a large chamber lit by diffused light flowing down from rectangular ceiling plates. They were on a gantry overlooking the space. Several technicians in lab coats floated around a large machine comprised of what looked like a giant chandelier made of gold. Wires criss-crossed the space, entering and leaving the guts of the machine. Around the edges of the chamber, enormous terminals stood sentinel, lights winking across their surfaces like fireflies.

Q followed Astrid down a set of steel steps. Curious glances swept his way. Q felt almost at home. A lab was his natural habitat . . . The past jerked at him like a blunt saw: leading Double Os through Q Branch, demonstrating the latest piece of field kit; warning Bond to return the kit in one piece, if at all possible.

Q stood in front of the quantum computer.

The machine seemed to pulse with unimaginable power. A sense of awe moved through him. It seemed perverse that he, a creature of flesh and blood, should now feel the insignificance of his own mortality in the presence of this machine. What did it say about a species, he wondered, that it had reached a point in its own evolution when it could create something greater than itself?

'Isn't it beautiful?'

Q saw that Astrid's eyes were glistening behind her red spectacles. He realised that this was the reason she had agreed so readily to bring him here. She wanted to show off this supreme demonstration of humankind's ingenuity. She wanted Q to know that this was something *she* had played a small part in.

'It's the world's first ten-thousand-qubit machine. Light years ahead of anything else.'

Q could see rows of strange hoops, like golden bracelets, and sparkling rods, hanging by the hundreds, inside the machine. The whole thing shimmered in a way that seemed to deceive the eye. His mouth felt dry. He touched his tie-pin. 'What does it do?'

'It's too early to say,' breathed Astrid. 'But a sufficiently powerful quantum computer will change everything. Imagine millions of brains working on millions of problems simultaneously. That's the potential of quantum computing. We'll be able to map the molecular world, the behaviour of subatomic particles, revolutionising chemistry and medicine. We'll model climate systems and accurately forecast the weather while predicting longer-term climate change. Financial modelling will allow us to streamline global economic structures, preventing recessions, perhaps even eradicating poverty. And artificial intelligence will leap forward several generations.'

'Is that a good thing?'

She glanced at him. 'I thought you were a techie?'

'I am. But I've worked with plenty of tech that has the power to harm. A note of caution is no bad thing. We're racing into the future and we're not even sure what that future will look like.'

'You sound like Helen.'

'Helen?'

'Helen Banner. She was the chief scientist here. Until recently.'

'She left?'

'Yes. That's the official line, anyway.' Astrid realised she had probably said too much. 'We should get back.'

'Was Pete close to anyone here in Wickstone? Someone he may have confided in.'

'Pete wasn't the confiding sort.' The chamber's flat white light swam in her irises. 'There *was* someone. A mentor. A man he'd known from when he'd grown up here. Pete would see him, now and again. Funny sort of name . . .'

'Mort?' said Q.

'Yes. That's it. Means "dead" in French.'

Jed Ellis looked thoughtfully at the photograph of a strontium atom on the wall.

When is a photo not a photo?

You couldn't actually photograph an atom. Because you couldn't bounce light off an atom to capture its image – atoms were too small. But you *could* make an atom glow by firing lasers at it.

People were a little like that. You rarely saw the reality, but you could see the glow.

Pete Napier had glowed. But beneath the glow: darkness.

Jed loved big words. Words such as *game-changing*. Or was that two words?

The world was full of good people who had achieved absolutely nothing. Who lived, breathed for a while, then died, having made as much impact as a fart in a high wind. And there were plenty of bad people out there who did the same.

But, somewhere in between, there were men like Jed. Neither good, nor bad, but who saw an opportunity and weren't afraid to take it.

Jed had put too much of himself into this lab to see it fail.

Besides, if Pete's example was anything to go by, it wasn't as if he would be given a choice. Sometimes, failure *really* wasn't an option.

He opened a drawer, took out a locked box. Unlocking it, he extracted a phone, switched it on. He rarely used *this* phone. This phone was only for emergencies.

He dialled a number. A voice came on the other end. 'Yes?'

'I've just had a very interesting visit,' said Jed.

Back outside Napier Labs, Q googled Helen Banner.

He discovered a brief press announcement to the effect that Banner was leaving Napier Labs for 'personal reasons'. Exactly two weeks before Pete's death.

Banner's background made for intriguing reading.

A Brit by birth, she had worked in the field for years, rising to become the *directeur de recherche* at the Quantum Sciences Institute of the Université de Paris.

And then Pete had somehow lured her to Wickstone to serve as his chief scientist.

Why had Banner left the lab? Astrid had hinted that there was more to Banner's departure than the official explanation.

Had Pete booted her out?

A woman who knew the most intimate secrets of his lab.

A woman bearing a grudge.

16

MORT HUNG AT THE BACK of the room watching Delight Ambrose, the library manager, chat with the members of the Historical Society as they hoovered up the last of the Syrian desserts and discussed the session.

She was good at this, he had to admit. Patience of a saint. Kind word for everyone.

Which, given the nature of the congregation, took an extraordinary feat of mental dexterity.

Mort had heard a lot of guff over the years about community spirit. A sort of good-natured bloody-mindedness that convinced ordinary people that they could achieve anything *if only they could learn to work together.*

The trouble with communal endeavours was that they were invariably beholden to the loudest voice in the group. History had taught Mort that. Nazi Germany was a communal effort. The slaughter by Hutus of the minority Tutsis in Rwanda over-flowed with community spirit – as long as you were a Hutu.

Unlike Delight, Mort had never been good with people. Academia favoured monomaniacs, the type of person who will send an email to the colleague sitting next to them rather than face the horror of an actual conversation.

And yet.

It was the local council under the previous head, Geraldine Bennett – eminently sensible woman – who had approached him. A historical society? Who better than a retired historian to take on the job?

Mort had known some of these people for years. Fellow Wickstonians. Neighbours. Friends? Only in the theoretical sense. But that was the thing about groups like this. If they persisted long enough, barriers came down. Prejudices dissolved.

At least, that was the theory.

'You all right, Mort? You look like someone's just told you you've got a dodgy prostate.'

Dave was fiddling with the giant thermos on the foldaway table.

Dave Potts, the library's deputy manager, had intrigued Mort since they had first met. Dave had been around the library system for decades and looked like a Viking who had been on the wrong end of the looting and pillaging. He was dressed in jeans and a shirt with a cartoon camel on the front. His blond hair was tied into a plaited braid, as was his beard. His bottle-bottomed glasses made his eyes look enormous.

'I'm fine.'

'Talk went well.'

'Yes.'

'Good crowd. Sam's cakes went down a treat. Shame she couldn't make it. That son of hers is in trouble again. Stole a car and crashed it into the side of a church. As if God hasn't got enough on his plate without yobs crashing Bentleys into his gaffe.'

'Dave!'

They turned to find Delight approaching: a middle-aged black woman in dark trousers and an embroidered velvet jacket. 'The boy is seventeen. He came from a war-torn country. He lost his father. Have you any idea how that impacts a child?'

'Yeah, well, growing up in East London was no cakewalk either. Don't see me making a big deal out of it. Everything's mental trauma this, mental trauma that these days.'

Mort's thoughts drifted to Pete Napier. Pete had been going through his own struggles. Could Mort have helped him? Why hadn't he seen the signs?

It had been different with Bella. Bella had slalomed her way downslope for years. The end, when it came, hadn't been entirely unexpected. Not that that had stopped others from blaming Mort. Blame was like a mud pie in a Hollywood film. Anyone could fling it at anyone else and it seemed like a lot of fun. For the one doing the flinging, at any rate.

What Mort could have done about Bella, he did not know.

But people weren't rational. Not when it came to this sort of thing.

Mort didn't do guilt. But there were times when guilt's cousin, regret, came to visit. Slithered into Mort's bed and slipped its fish-clammy hands around him, spooning till the cold hours just before dawn.

Mort remembered Pete as a boy. Precociously intelligent. Ambitious. Not too hot on the social niceties. The boy had reminded Mort of himself.

Pete had lost his father while still in his teens. His mother had faded into herself, a walking, talking ghost. There, but not there. Pete had adopted Mort as a mentor. Or perhaps it had been the other way around?

Mort had done the best he could.

But Pete had been a force of nature.

A thundering express train, no one in the driver's cab.

And then the tracks had run out.

Q slid the Caterham to a halt outside the Wickstone Library.

The visit to Napier Labs had thrown up more questions than it had answered. For one: Jed Ellis's presumption that Pete had ended his own life. Yes, the pair had worked closely together for years, but Q couldn't imagine Pete killing himself just because things weren't going to plan. That wasn't the Pete he remembered. The Pete he remembered would have bulldozed his way to a solution. If Pete had been a soldier he would have been the kind to charge machine-gun nests. Not because he was brave, but because he thought the rules didn't apply to him. Getting turned into Swiss cheese by machine-gun fire was for lesser mortals.

Q looked up at the library. Its outer aspect hadn't changed. The buttery brickwork. The gargoyles lining the roof. The air of learning that wrapped around the place like a forcefield, repelling some, drawing in others.

Memories elbowed their way in.

Being dragged here by his mother twice a week so he could spend an hour in a corner with his nose in a book while she went to the pub. Teenage Saturdays spent volunteering, helping grumpy pensioners find the toilet, while his peers were out playing footie or chewing each other's faces off at the cinema. Ordering in esoteric science books with Pete for projects they had assigned themselves.

Happy memories. Bittersweet memories.

A ball of dread rotated slowly in Q's stomach. His legs felt leaden. He had about as much desire to get up and go inside as a Yorkshireman had to enter a nail salon.

He knew what awaited him. The idea of bracing Mortimer about Pete ... The thought alone made him shiver. Ice followed by heat.

He could feel the anger rising.

This moment had been a long time coming.

Q got out of the car and walked across the road.

Mort ran his hands under the tap, palpated his face.

Death. He could feel it, just at the edges of vision. Whispering. Snickering. Waiting to be allowed in. Couldn't be long now. He could feel it in his bones. The dying of the light.

But he wouldn't go gentle into that good night. He would fight it with everything he had. Rage, and burn and rave at close of day, just as Dylan Thomas had commanded.

But what if he couldn't?

There it was again. That insidious voice. In the dead of night, when he would reach out, seeking the warmth and reassurance of another human body, encountering only the cold vacuum of Bella's absence.

Thirty years and still she haunted him.

The ancient Greeks had built an execution device known as the Bull of Phalaris. A bronze bull into which sentenced convicts were locked. A fire was lit and the prisoner inside slowly broiled to death as the metal rose in temperature. A clever mechanism converted the sounds of the doomed into the roars of an enraged bull.

You had to love the ancients. Greeks. Romans. Persians. All distinguished by their innovative approaches to cruelty.

But the bronze bull had always seemed to Mort particularly barbaric.

Because this was how it felt. The long-term absence of a loved one. Day by day the pain built, from uncomfortable to unbearable to a sort of living death.

Mort picked up a towel and wiped his face.

Stepping back into the library, he saw that the crowd had thinned, though a small huddle remained, gathered around a tallish male figure with his back turned. Mort didn't recognise the man, though there was something familiar in his frame.

He patted his bow tie, fiddled with the top button on his waistcoat and approached the group.

The newcomer seemed to register his presence as those around him fell silent.

He turned to face Mort.

Mort felt his legs give away. His knees were suddenly made of rubber. He stumbled to a halt.

Q looked at Mort.

75

Light falling from the tubelight above washed out the older man's features but couldn't disguise the expression of shock.

Seconds ticked away, stretching and twisting into a noose that draped itself around Q's neck. He opened his mouth, but the machinery of his throat had rusted.

Finally, he spoke. 'Hello ... Dad.'

17

KATHY WAS ON A DATE.

The date had been set up by a well-meaning friend. Worst timing ever. But Kathy didn't want to let Lizzie down. She would never hear the end of it, for one.

Her mind was fizzing. With Q. His sudden irruption back into her life. After all this time.

Strange how memories long blunted suddenly became razor sharp again.

Old hurts, freshly awakened.

What did she really feel for him? She barely knew the man. Not this version of him.

They barely knew each other.

Her date had said something.

What was his name again? Roderick. Roddy. Rod. Odd name for a grown man.

At least he seemed normal. The last guy Lizzie had set Kathy up with had taken her paintballing with his son's friends, all at least twenty years younger than her. Her date had shot her in the face. Twice. For two weeks she had had to go to work with a pair of massive bruises on her forehead, like horns.

Roderick was telling Kathy how exciting her job must be. All that chasing after criminals. CSI forensics. Rod was some sort of glorified council administrator. Spent his days steering a desk, filling out forms. What he wouldn't give to be out on the mean streets of Wickstone, roughing up suspects, laying down the law.

'I'm just going to the bathroom. I may be some time.'

Kathy walked to the toilet, then to the restaurant's rear entrance. She had picked the place precisely because it had an escape route.

Sorry, Liz. Bad timing.

Outside, she stood by the bins a moment. A graveyard of waiters' cigarette butts made a heap by her foot. Was that a used condom? It looked recently vacated.

She resolved never to eat here again.

Her head felt fuzzy. Probably shouldn't have had three vodka martinis before the starters had even been ordered.

Kathy took out her phone. Q had given her his number ... What would she say to him anyway? Had he really come back here to investigate Pete's death?

Pete and Q. Too smart for their own good. And as thick as thieves. Though Kathy always got the impression that the friendship was lopsided. Pete had been the pied piper, Q the one dancing to Pete's tune.

When Kathy and Q had started dating there had been an awkward moment. She had never told Q that Pete had tried it on. Only the once, and she had instantly set him straight. Even then, Kathy wasn't one to mince her words.

When Q had told her he wanted to ask Pete to be his best man at the wedding, Kathy had phoned Pete up and told him to make an excuse. Pete had duly obliged.

The wedding-that-never-was. They had both been twenty, Q at university, Kathy going through basic training at the police academy. Too young to be engaged, let alone married. Crazy kids.

And then Q's mother had ... died, and the whole thing had fallen apart anyway.

After all these years, he was back. A lifetime lived in the interregnum. For them both. The world had changed. Whole galaxies had imploded. Probably. Cosmology had never been Kathy's strong suit. Was it three vodkas or four?

Her thoughts gravitated towards Pete's death. *Had* they missed something? It wasn't beyond the bounds of possibility. Police investigations were rarely an exact science. Even when a scientist was involved. Hah!

If nothing else, Pete's death had dragged Q back to Wickstone.

Kathy remembered the day Q had first caught her eye. A knock-kneed sixteen year old haunting the local library. She had only come in for a book about the police service.

A rainy day. Afterwards, Q had shrugged off his sweatshirt and stuck it over a puddle for her. Where had he got that idea? It was the most ridiculous thing she had ever seen. She could have just walked around the puddle.

But something about that strange boy had stuck.

Kathy had come back the next weekend looking for another book. Or so she'd told herself. The rest, as they said, was history.

Ancient history, now.

Her phone rang.

Kathy cursed.

It was Jeremy.

Her husband.

18

WHEN CAESAR HAD FALLEN OUT with Pompey, he had chased him across the known world, to the shores of Egypt. Pompey had once been Caesar's son-in-law. But Caesar's daughter had died, her death dissolving the last tie binding the two men.

By the time Caesar arrived in Alexandria, Pompey had been murdered by eager-to-please locals.

Mort wondered what Caesar would have done had he caught up with his former son-in-law. Would he have forgiven him? Would he have allowed bygones to be bygones?

Fat chance. Caesar was a vindictive bastard. You didn't become dictator for life by being an easy-going, kiss-and-make-up sort.

Mort sat at his desk looking at his son. The anger had vanished. How could he be angry? He barely knew the man sitting before him.

The boy had changed. Well, you would, wouldn't you? *Thirty years.* Thirty years since the lad had shown his face in Wickstone. Mort had seen the odd picture of him over the years. A photo in some obscure article on the Internet.

Q. Head of Q Branch. MI6. The Secret Service. His son!

Mort's eyes continued to examine Q's features. The changes that time had wrought. Was there anything of himself in there? Not really. The boy had always favoured his mother, Annabelle. Bella.

It was Bella's death that had caused the rift. Or the manner of it. The boy had blamed Mort. Unfairly. But you couldn't explain the workings of a marriage to a twenty year old who had only ever had one girlfriend.

Mort still remembered the rage the boy had directed his way. Wild. Unreasoning. Implacable. Things said that couldn't be unsaid.

To be fair, Mort *had* tried, over the years. Overtures via intermediaries. Only to be rebuffed. And then, one day, he had just stopped. Either the boy would come around or he wouldn't.

He hadn't.

What right did the boy have to blame him for Bella's death?

If anyone had a right to be angry it was Mort. Whose seed had given the boy life? Who had catered to his every whim until he could stand on his own two feet? Ask a crack den baby whether they would prefer Mort as a father or the drug-addled street thug destiny had saddled them with?

Not that Mort knew many crack den babies. He wasn't entirely certain what went on in a crack den, but he doubted they were nurturing environments for the young.

'Why are you here?' Mort's voice emerged as a croak. He had known the boy was back in town, had imagined confronting him a thousand times. But seeing him here, now, in the library, was a shock.

'Pete wrote to me just before he died. He mentioned your name. I'm looking into his death.'

'Why?'

'Because he was my friend.'

'My understanding was that you hadn't spoken in years.'

'Pete told you that?'

Mort said nothing. A fishbone had stuck in his throat. He didn't want to answer questions about Pete. He focused on his son. At least the boy was properly dressed. *Something* of Mort had rubbed off on him. Nowadays, offices were populated by dress-down-Friday yobs.

Mort picked up a jug of water and poured himself a glass. 'The police have already investigated Pete's death. It was an accident. A terrible accident.' A twinge of guilt. He wondered if it was visible on his face.

'I don't believe that. Pete was too careful to let something like that happen.'

Mort hesitated. 'He was under a lot of strain. That company of his, out in Bunker 11 ... Things weren't going the way he wanted. There were personal issues. The situation with his ex-wife—'

Q cut in. 'Are you saying you think Pete committed suicide? You knew Pete. Probably better than anyone in Wickstone. He wasn't the kind to give in. He wouldn't have killed himself.'

Mort picked up his glass. 'For someone who lost touch with Pete a long time ago, you seem to have no problem knowing his mind. But then, you always did think you knew us better than we knew ourselves. All of us.'

Q stiffened. His father's words were a shot across the bows. But he had no wish to talk about his mother. That wasn't why he had returned to Wickstone. He took out the letter Pete had sent him, handed it to his father, watched as Mort scanned it. 'Pete was in trouble. And now he's dead. And I'm here.'

Mort's face betrayed nothing.

'What do you think he meant by "Mort won't be pleased"?'

'I don't know. Perhaps he simply meant I wouldn't be pleased by you coming back here.' Mort hoped that his voice hadn't trembled. He hated lying. Lying was a sign of weakness. But there were occasions when the truth would be impossible to explain. When the truth could cause more damage than a lie.

Another silence. The conversation lay there, unmoving, waiting to be buried.

There was so much Q wanted to say to this old man. Thirty years of accumulated words. He wanted to pour them over Mort, boiling oil thrown from the battlements. But what good would it do? He remembered how his father had taken an interest in Pete after Pete's own father had vanished, never to be seen again. Mort had become another acolyte of Pete's genius. Later, he had steered Pete towards Oxford, where Mort held a professorial post. Q remembered Mort helping Pete fill out his application forms. He had never done that for Q. Or rather, when Q had said he had no wish to go to Oxford, Mort had accepted without protest.

'What do the strings of letters mean?' Mort said.

'It's a cipher. I haven't worked it out yet.'

'Why would Pete send you a cipher? Why didn't he just tell you what he wanted to tell you?'

'I don't know.' What Q didn't say: that as teenagers he and Pete had regularly sent each other encoded messages. Both trying to outdo the other. A girl they fancied. A humorous anecdote about a teacher. Some tidbit they had come across in *National Geographic* or *New Scientist*.

Q felt a great ballooning of emotion under his ribs. He couldn't sit here anymore. The sight of his father, after all these years. The reawakening of the past, lurching at him. He had thought he would handle it better than this . . . He stood up. 'I have to go.'

Mort seemed to compress into his seat. 'Fine.'

'Fine,' said Q. Why wouldn't his legs move?

'Fine,' Mort repeated.

Q turned and left the room.

19

ON THE WALL OF HIS office at Q Branch: an acrylic panel, embossed with the MI6 logo.

The logo, derived from the British coat of arms, included the words: HONI SOIT QUI MAL Y PENSE. Old Norman French meaning 'shamed be whoever thinks ill of it', the motto of the Order of the Garter. The Order had been the brainchild of King Edward III, back in 1348, and the quote was deemed a riposte to those who denied his somewhat dubious claim to the French throne. According to Edward himself, the Order represented a revival of King Arthur's Knights of the Round Table.

Discovering that little piece of trivia, not long after joining MI6, had sent a frisson through Q. The Arthurian legend had been one of his and Pete's teenage obsessions.

Now, as he stood in front of Pete Napier's home, Q remembered something Pete had said: 'One day, I'll live in my own Camelot.'

This wasn't Camelot. This was The Gables, Winifred Road, in the town of Wickstone-on-Water. An impressive pile, but no Camelot.

The gate was locked, police tape strung between the railings.

Q looked up and down the street, then clambered over the gate. As he crested the top, he became tangled up and fell, crashing to earth on the far side, breath momentarily knocked out of him.

He got to his feet, slapped dust off his trousers, then jogged to the front door.

He had come prepared. A quick online recce had told him that the houses on this road had been built with smart locks, only accessible via smartphones. Or a piece of kit designed to circumvent the virtual keys needed to open such locks. Q Branch had been fashioning such 'break-in boxes' for years. No self-respecting field agent left home without one.

The door lock beeped, went from red to green, and the door swung back.

Q slipped the soap-dish-sized box back into his pocket, went inside and closed the door behind him.

It took him less than an hour to search the house.

He wasn't sure exactly what he was looking for. The truth was that he was feeling his way through this. As head of Q Branch his job had been strategic. There were no mysteries to be solved at that level. Area 51 didn't house alien remains and the CIA hadn't killed JFK. At least, that was what his counterpart at America's foreign intelligence agency – namely, the head of the Office of Technical Service – had assured him.

At Q Branch, he had dealt with known unknowns. Equipping field agents to operate behind enemy lines. The neutralisation of new technologies developed by bad actors.

When field agents died, it wasn't Q Branch that carried out investigations into their deaths.

Upstairs, he found two stripped-down bedrooms, and a wardrobe with a box of old toys: ping-pong balls, tennis balls, wrapping paper, tin foil and a water pistol. Leftovers, he presumed, from whoever had lived here before Pete.

The master bedroom looked equally unlived-in, the bed perfectly made. The wardrobe contained a selection of expensive clothing. Q knew most of the brands. Science wasn't the only umbilical cord that connected him with his childhood friend.

In the bedside unit, he found an old scrapbook. Inside, among assorted papery flotsam from Pete's childhood, he found a swimming certificate. A fake, designed and printed by Pete to show to his parents. Why had Pete held on to this? It revealed a sentimentality at odds with the Pete Q remembered. And a reminder of the lengths his friend would often go to rather than allow others to believe less of himself.

At the back of the scrapbook he discovered a photograph of himself, Pete and Mort. The picture, taken in the garden of Q's home, arrested him.

Pete was grinning broadly. Q and Mort were unsmiling.

They had never seen eye-to-eye.

Mort had been a hard man. Hard to love. Ambitious. Demanding. Particular. *Don't go into my study. Don't touch the paintwork. Why an A minus?* ... Had Mort ever wanted children? Q wasn't sure. He had always felt himself an unwanted distraction, an obstacle to be negotiated along Mort's highway to success. In many ways, his father reminded him of Pete. Perhaps that was why the pair had bonded. More so after Pete's father had departed the scene, leaving Pete alone with just his mother – and with Mort as a replacement dad ... Perhaps this explained why Pete had resumed contact with Mort when he had returned to Wickstone. Or perhaps they had never lost touch.

He shook himself back to the present, set down the scrapbook and walked out of the bedroom and into a room Pete had clearly used as an office.

He was stopped short by a model of the Millennium Falcon on Pete's desk. The model was old, with bits missing. Q remembered helping Pete put the thing together. Another of their shared passions: *Star Wars*.

A lump formed in his throat.

It was a delusion to think he had a choice in this. Whatever the truth, be his death accident, suicide or foul play, the fact was that Pete had cried out for help.

And Q had answered the call.

He searched Pete's desk, but found nothing of interest, aside from a cigarette lighter. The Pete he had known hadn't smoked. He imagined his old friend sitting at his desk, chain-smoking the day's stresses away.

Q stepped back. Disappointment coursed through him. Had he really expected to find anything useful? The police had already been through the house. What could *he* possibly discov—

A noise, coming from downstairs.

Q walked out onto the landing, leaned over the railing, listened carefully.

Someone was in the house.

His heart began to thud. He began to move back, then changed his mind. He calmed himself, thought the situation through. There was no reason for anyone else to be here. Unless they had followed him here.

He slipped off his shoes, then padded down the stairs in his socks. Crouching down, he peered between the banisters.

A shadow moved across the doorway of the front drawing room.

Q's heart leaped. The shadow had been holding something in its hand. A gun.

He felt fear trickle into his bowels. A centipede crawled along his spine.

He walked back up the stairs and across to Pete's office. Leaned against the wall.

His knees felt like jelly.

Suddenly, Bond's voice was in his ears. *The difference between the agent who lives and the agent who dies is not freezing in that critical moment.*

Q forced himself to breathe out.

Work the problem.

He was facing an unknown foe, armed. Q's only weapon was his Swiss Army knife. Not inconsequential, but not much use against a gun. His adversary was probably a trained professional. The hand-to-hand combat training Q had undergone during his stint in the army was thirty years out of date. Going head-to-head with the man downstairs wasn't really an option.

What he needed was a distraction.

And then he had it.

He walked to Pete's desk, picked up several pencils from a penholder, together with Pete's cigarette lighter, then walked out and across to the spare bedroom with the box of abandoned toys. Rummaging through the box, he took out the ping-pong balls and the roll of tin foil. A quick look told him all he needed to know: the balls were made of nitrocellulose.

He stabbed a pencil into one of them, then covered it in tin foil, including an inch of the pencil. Then, carefully, he removed the pencil, leaving a foil spout protruding from the ball. His hands trembled, and he willed himself to calm.

He repeated the procedure with several more balls.

Walking back to the stairs, he crept down, slipped the lighter from his pocket and lit a flame below each of the ping pong balls. Smoke began to pour from the crudely fashioned spouts.

Q rolled the balls down onto the landing. Soon the space was thick with white smoke.

He heard a noise, footsteps moving onto the landing, a man coughing, lost in the smoke.

Q pulled a silk handkerchief from his pocket, held it to his mouth and nose, and walked briskly down the stairs, through the smoke, and out towards the front door.

He had just made it onto the front porch, when a shape lumbered up from behind, barrelling into him, and carrying them both to the gravelled forecourt.

Q's head bounced off the ground. He grunted in pain as his shoulder twisted.

His opponent, coughing madly, clung to Q's torso. Q twisted around, thumped at the man's skull. A whirling fist caught Q on the chin. A gasp escaped him. He struck out with his elbow, felt it connect with the man's nose. The man cried out, released his hold.

Q wriggled free, scrabbled to his feet. His opponent rose from the floor. The man wore a balaclava and appeared to have lost his weapon. He continued to cough, looked unsteady on his feet. The smoke had clearly incapacitated him. Perhaps he was an asthmatic? Stood to reason. Not every killer was a perfect physical specimen.

A fistfight isn't about the rules, Q. Bond's voice, again. *It's about winning.*

Q lashed out with a foot, caught the man squarely between the legs.

His opponent went down, a goat-like bleat escaping him.

Q didn't wait. He jogged to the gate, scrambled over, and was in his Caterham moments later, roaring down the road.

20

A HOT SHOWER CLEARED HIS HEAD but left his bruises throbbing.

His twisted shoulder cried out as he pulled on a T-shirt. Scrawled across the front of the shirt: GUNS & VASES. Moneypenny had bought him the customised garment following a visit to his London home, raising an elegant eyebrow at his choice of décor. 'A man in love with vases. How novel.'

His jaw ached. Q had sat through enough HR-mandated first aid training courses to convince him that no major damage had been done. No need for a trip to the hospital.

The damage to his psyche was a different matter.

After thirty years in a lab, he wasn't prepared for this sort of thing. He was a scientist, not a field agent. Scientists didn't go around firing rocket launchers at enemy tanks or leaping across moving train carriages whilst chasing foreign agents.

To be fair, Q *had* fired the occasional rocket launcher: Q Branch had developed several over the years, with very specific modifications. But fistfights?

Who in the world was following him? And why?

Because he was asking questions about Pete. That much was obvious.

Q recalled another of Bond's maxims. *If they're trying to kill me, it means I'm on to something.*

Should he inform the police? Call Kathy? ... No. It would only give Kathy ammunition to use against him. She would probably arrest him for breaking into Pete's house.

He headed down for dinner.

Normally, he would cook. Cooking relaxed him. Living alone, he had learned to fend for himself. But he was still getting used to a kitchen that wasn't his own. His arsenal of Santoku Japanese knives remained in London. He had no idea how long he would be in town.

Q settled in the living room and ordered dinner. The menu for Mr Singh's Curry Palace promised 'untold exotic delights'. Q frowned. What exactly was 'untold' about Mr Singh's delights? Each dish was literally explained on the menu. He couldn't abide hyperbole.

He ordered a lamb rogan josh and a garlic naan. Couldn't go wrong with a rogan josh.

He picked up the remote control, searching for something soothing on the TV. His favourite shows: *Frasier. Antiques Roadshow. Slow Horses.* Though the latter was a little too close to home, like watching an adult film starring people you knew.

Q opened his MacBook. He rummaged in his pocket and took out the tie-pin he had been wearing earlier. Turning it over, he removed the backing and extracted a customised micro SD card. He inserted the card into an adaptor, then slipped the adaptor into the laptop.

A few clicks later and he was looking at photographs of the quantum computer.

The tie-pin was a souvenir from MI6, with an inbuilt micro-camera. Similar models could now be purchased over the Internet.

Q's thoughts churned.

An investigation felt a lot like designing new kit for the Double Os. Problems in need of solutions. At the start you rarely had all the data. But you chipped away at it and soon you had a blueprint. A plan. And then you followed through, refining the design. Iteration after iteration.

That was the job and he had loved it. Or *had* been the job.

On his last day Moneypenny had taken Q aside. Had there been a glimmer in her eye? Moneypenny didn't cry. No use for sentiment.

You won't miss it. Go be all that you can be.

Go be all that you can be. Very Tom Cruise. Except that Q wasn't Tom Cruise. Tom Cruise was riding motorcycles over cliffs at age sixty. Tom Cruise was abseiling into Olympic stadiums, cheered on by millions. Q hadn't ridden so much as a bicycle in almost forty years. He could take one apart and probably fashion something else from it – a jetpack, a siege engine – but the idea of riding one to his death hadn't occurred to him.

In ancient Troy, Odysseus took the credit for entering the city and winning the war. But who remembered the guy who designed the Trojan horse? Epeius of Phocis. Soldier. Athlete. Carpenter ... Q had never asked for fame. Or riches. Just a decent-sized budget for his work, a final salary pension and a place to call home.

Yet now, here he was.

Q focused on the quantum computer.

He wasn't sure why he had felt the need to photograph it. But something about the machine had spooked him. He had seen pictures of one before, but nothing compared to the reality. It was far larger than he had expected, hanging suspended in the air like an alien spacecraft. Or a giant metallic jellyfish.

Otherworldly. And perhaps it was.

Peter Napier truly had been a genius.

More than ever Q was convinced that Pete's death was neither accident nor suicide. Pete simply wouldn't allow that. To work his whole life towards creating something like this, and then to throw it all away? That didn't sound like Pete.

Jed Ellis's explanation of stress-related suicide made no sense to Q. Granted, he had lost touch with Pete, but if life had taught Q anything it was that people didn't change. Not fundamentally. Not at a cellular level.

Pete was a massive narcissist. Ego the size of Saturn. Q couldn't imagine him ever believing that he would fail. He couldn't imagine Pete falling into despair.

A beep on his phone.

A notification alert.

He logged in to a secure forum.

Bond had come through. A set of scanned files awaited Q.

Whatever else you might say about James Bond, the man got things done. Need an Armenian warlord despatched? Call Bond. Nuclear scientist slipping into bed with the wrong crowd? Call Bond. Top secret files need rescuing from an uncrackable vault? No problemo.

Q went through the list of files. It was more than he could have hoped for. His excitement was tempered by the fact that he now owed Bond a favour. A dangerous proposition at the best of times. Like owing a hormonal lion a debt.

The files included investigative reports from the police team charged with looking into Pete's death – led by DCI Kathy Burnham – a scene of crime report, various forensic analysis reports, the autopsy, key interview transcripts and the coroner's report.

Q began with a cursory look at the documents, settling an overview of the material in his mind. Time passed.

The doorbell rang. His curry order.

A Deliveroo rider was waiting for him at the door, holding out his order. The same rider from earlier in the day. Biker lady with the alien helmet.

She lowered his order to the ground, then slid her visor up. Her expression was unsmiling. He had no idea what he had done to upset the woman. Sticking to speed limits was not a crime. On the other hand, road rage had led to a surge in traffic-based violence. Statistically, it was a no brainer.

'Hi,' said Q.

The woman folded her arms.

Q coughed, then began reaching down for his order.

'Passcode.'

Q looked at the woman. His mind had gone blank. 'I— Well, I can't seem to recall.'

'No passcode, no food.'

'But the order has my address on it.'

'No passcode, no food.'

Q looked around desperately. There was no one in the street to witness this injustice. This was worse than police brutality.

Bastard appeared, slinking around Q's legs to snuffle at the order. The dog had an addiction to restaurant food. Q had discovered this by chance when Bastard had torn through an order of Peking duck and seaweed-and-pork wontons while Q had been on the phone.

'Is that your dog?'

'Yes.'

The woman's expression softened.

Q leaned down and aggressively stroked Bastard. 'Good dog.'

Bastard ignored him and pawed at the parcel.

'Is the food for the dog?'

'Yes.'

She looked dubious. 'What's his name?'

'Bastard.'

She stared at him. 'You named your dog Bastard?'

'I inherited him. Together with the name.'

The dog had belonged to Q's neighbour, an anchorite by the name of Cruikshank, who, in the short period Q had known him, had redefined the boundaries of misanthropy. Cruikshank had turned up a day after Q's return to Wickstone, beady-eyed and malodorous, with a dire warning. *Park in front of my property again and I won't be responsible for the consequences.*

The dog – a piebald bulldog – had waggled along behind the old miser, bow-legged and rheumy-eyed. As its snout grazed the back of its master's calf, the geriatric tyrant had whirled on the animal to aim a kick at its head. *Get away, bastard!*

Cruikshank had died in his sleep two days later. Q had watched the ambulance ferry the body away, and then promptly forgotten about both man and dog.

The next day, he had noticed the beast hunkered down under the beech tree across the road, eyes trained steadily on Q's front door.

Two days of this and Q's nerve had broken.

He had opened the door, set a bowl of Pedigree's Finest on the front stoop and muttered: 'Well, come on, then.'

Q waited for the Deliveroo lady to make up her mind.

And then she simply snapped her visor shut, turned, got on her bike and rode off in a storm of exhaust fumes.

21

THE HOUSE WAS QUIET.

It always was. Had been for more years than Mort cared to remember.

He set the keys in a Faraday box on the sideboard, by the terracotta amphora given to him by a colleague at the University of Bologna. Dead now. Like so many of Mort's contemporaries.

Where had time gone?

The great wheel turned and, in the blink of an eye, you were lost. Fumbling in the weeds of old age, battling past and future.

He shrugged off his coat, walked through to the kitchen, grabbed a bottle of Montrachet from the fridge, poured a glass.

A false witness shall not go unpunished, and he that speaketh lies shall perish.

Mort remembered his mother's words, fired at him after he had spoken an untruth that had seen him sent home from school. She had added, with relish: 'All liars shall have their part in the lake which burns with fire and brimstone, which is the second death.'

His mother had been a fiend for the Good Book. Could quote chapter and verse. The benefit of growing up a vicar's daughter.

Mort had been too young to know much about brimstone, but 'second death' sounded ominous.

Lying to his son felt different to lying to the police.

But what could he have said? What could Mort have told his estranged son about Pete Napier, the boy who had taken Q's place?

Back at the library, Mort had felt Bella's presence in the room.

Many had asked him why he had never remarried. There had been abortive attempts, of course. No man was an island. And he had never claimed to be a monk. Never that. But he had been on the verge of fifty by the time Bella had died. Subsequent relationships had withered beneath the shadow of her passing.

How much the boy looked like his mother! The same grey eyes. The sandy hair, turned darker with age, now streaked with fine lines of grey.

Mort knew that his son had never married. A fact that had always eaten away at him. Had Bella's death, the tragedy of his parents' marriage, somehow soured the institution of marriage for the boy?

The walls of the kitchen closed in. His breathing became laboured.

Mort pulled at his tie, went into the living room, stumbled onto the sofa. His hands found the remote; the TV snapped on.

The news was full of death and destruction. War and earthquakes.

Positively cheerful compared to how Mort was feeling.

The boy would be back. If he continued to pursue his investigation, it was inevitable.

And what would Mort say then? What would he be *forced* to say?

About the night Pete died.

About what Mort had told him.

About what Mort had done.

22

THE FILES TOOK MOST OF the night to go through.
Having eaten, Q settled down at the dining room
table with his laptop and a notebook. And a good bottle
of Rioja Reserva, together with a hunk of Manchego. Essential
to the investigative process.

He began with the scene of crime report. Not much new there.

Kathy had laid out the bare facts, and here they were, confirmed
on paper.

Pete's car – a brand-new all-electric Lexus RZ – had been
found at the scene. Inside, Pete's shoes and clothes, neatly piled
on the front passenger seat, together with his phone, wallet and
keys. The car's GPS system showed that he had driven from his
home to Bishop's Point – the wooden jetty on the River Wickstone
from which it was surmised he had entered the water. There had
been no stops en route. A journey time of some twenty minutes.

Q recalled going out to Bishop's Point with Pete when they
had been boys. Ill-considered attempts at fishing, sitting there
with their legs dangling from the jetty, rods in hand, waiting
for something to happen. Fishing, it turned out, was the most
boring activity yet invented by humankind. It was like that old
saying. Give a man a fish and you feed him for a day. Teach

him to fish and you guarantee him a lifetime of mind-numbing drudgery.

Next: the reports of the searches at Pete's home and office. The police had turned up nothing untoward. Pete lived alone and spent very little time there. He arrived early at Napier Labs each morning, worked late, often ate at his desk. Sometimes he stayed the night, sleeping in a small room dedicated to the purpose.

Pete's office had been a no-go zone, at least until his death. If anything of interest had been there, his colleagues had cleared it out by the time the police arrived.

Pete's laptop, computer, phone and Internet history had been checked. Digital forensics had turned up empty-handed. Nothing pertinent to the investigation. No phone calls to unknown parties. No social media presence. A blizzard of emails, almost exclusively to work colleagues. The general tone was condescending. With a side order of demanding. A sociopathic belief in exclamation marks. But nothing to indicate any virulent enmities.

The autopsy report was equally straightforward. Death by drowning. No other wounds on the body. No signs of a tussle.

The only note of surprise was thrown up by the toxicology analysis. Recent and sustained drug use. Pete: burning along the cocaine highway at a hundred miles an hour. In the wrong direction ... Cocaine. Street names: Charlie. Snow. Nose Candy. White Lady. And Q's personal favourite: Percy ... Why Percy?

Q had known cocaine users during his time at MI6. Invariably Double Os. The ever-present likelihood of being maimed, tortured, disfigured or killed. And that was only in M's office. Alcohol and drugs became useful crutches. Not for long, of course. Regular testing, ever more stringent, as the years had passed.

Bond had never succumbed. Though he liked a martini and, in the past, had used amphetamines to give himself 'an edge'. Bond's habit of mixing the drugs in Dom Perignon was just so ... Bond.

Q imagined Pete's stresses at the lab had led him down that path. Did it make it more or less likely that he had killed himself?

Another question: where did Pete get the drugs? This was Wickstone, not central London, where you could practically pop down the local newsagent's and buy cocaine by the kilo while chatting about the football.

County lines. The catchy name the police had given to London-based gangs making inroads into places such as Wickstone-on-Water. Bored housewives. Repressed husbands. Anxiety-ridden teens. Middle-class angst in all its splendour. Clamouring for something to take the edge off.

The interviews the police had conducted with Pete's colleagues proved equally banal. No speaking ill of the dead, despite what they might privately have felt. They were all shocked. Stunned. The loss had hit them hard. Pete had been more than just their boss. He was the visionary behind the quantum computing revolution. A prophet of the technological age. And he was going to make them all rich and famous.

Q noted that Kathy had interviewed Helen Banner, the woman who had recently left Napier Labs. Banner had said little except to repeat that Pete was a genius. She claimed she harboured no ill will towards her former boss. Her departure from Napier Labs had been by mutual consent. Personal issues.

Q made a note of Banner's address.

His interest was piqued by a brief phone call between Kathy and Pete's ex-wife.

Celestine McAvoy was an American, of Scottish heritage. She lived in California, together with Pete's daughter, fifteen-year-old Betsy. Celestine claimed that they rarely heard from Pete. The man was too absorbed in his work. Had practically no relationship with his daughter. Not that they cared. Pete was not missed. He was dead? Maybe killed himself? Boo hoo.

Celestine McAvoy did not strike Q as a sympathetic woman.

But what did he know? Perhaps Pete had been awful to her. It wouldn't surprise Q. Pete had never struck him as particularly good with women. Or other human beings, in general. Too wrapped up in himself. Aggressively pursuing his destiny. It had come as a surprise to him that Pete had ever married, had a child.

Q had thought about it himself, over the years. Domesticity. Fatherhood. Never really come close, not since Kathy. It wouldn't have been hard to find someone. An eligible bachelor. Higher-than-average post-tax income. Own home. Non-snorer. Happy to empty the bins. No weird fetishes. Unless you counted collecting cricket statistics. But cricket wasn't merely a sport. It was a philosophy. Like Bushido.

The police had investigated Pete's personal finances. Lot of money flowing into and out of his accounts. Venture capitalist money. Pete had a robust sense of his own worth, paying himself a handsome salary as CEO of Napier Labs. He also had expensive tastes.

The rent on his Wickstone home was extortionate. And he liked cars. Among those he owned: the Lexus he had driven on the night of his death, a Range Rover Sport, a Jaguar and a Bentley 100 XT.

Aside from his penchant for lavishness, there was nothing untoward in Pete's finances ... How had he paid for his cocaine habit? As far as Q knew, drug dealers rarely accepted Mastercard. But there seemed no evidence of regular cash withdrawals from Pete's account. Cryptocurrency? Possibly. Perhaps that was why the police hadn't picked up on it. Anonymous crypto accounts were notoriously difficult to trace.

The coroner's report summed up the evidence, arriving at the conclusion that the most likely scenario was that Peter Napier had driven out to the River Wickstone on the night of his death and, for reasons unknown, entered the water at around 2 a.m., drowning shortly thereafter.

One mystery remained. The details of the coroner's report had been withheld from public scrutiny, under a 'national security' tag. What had Pete been doing that could have necessitated such an action? Q had enough acquaintance with the workings of national security to know that such determinations were not lightly made.

Peter Napier. Q's friend. Once upon a time: his *best* friend.

He was struck, once more, by his need to pursue this investigation. Yes, he had known Pete but that had been a long time ago. Did friendship remain, in any tangible sense, after such a lengthy absence?

Pete had obliged him. With his cryptic letter. And he had caught Q at the perfect moment. Still at sea following his ejection from MI6. A man struggling with his own demons.

MI6 retained a bank of therapists. The Double Os were regularly subjected to psychological assessments. It came as no surprise that most were borderline sociopaths. They spent their lives taking on fake personas, lying, cheating, stealing and murdering. And, in Bond's case, blowing things up. Yes, it was all in the service of the nation – and the wider cause of liberty – but it took its toll. Even Bond had had to take his turn on the couch. Though it was usually his therapists who ended up needing counselling.

Q had considered discreetly contacting one such individual. He had never seen a therapist before, but a couple of sessions might help clear his head.

He had always assumed he would carry on at MI6 until retirement. And then he would be retained in some sort of emeritus capacity. A consultant. A special advisor.

He hadn't expected to be cast adrift. Out on the choppy seas of middle-age, with sharks in the water.

Bastard shambled into the room, took up residence in the corner, head on paws. The very picture of misery. Did animals suffer from depression? Q had never had a pet. Perhaps he should contact a vet. Misery loves company. Perhaps Bastard had sensed it, that first day, and had come a-knocking because in Q he recognised a kindred spirit.

But Q wasn't depressed.

At least, he didn't think so.

23

DS Bob Lazarus had never made a bad cup of coffee.

At the station they called him the Gordon Ramsay of coffee. Other people banged on about quality of beans, the water-to-coffee ratio. But Bob knew it was more than that. He used an old-fashioned French press – la cafètiere, if you were feeling a bit la-di-da – and a coarse grind. Nothing fancy. Marks and Spencer's Fairtrade.

The French press was brilliant for whipping up coffee by the batch. Bob was always happy to do the honours. Made him popular with the lads – and laddesses – at the station.

Not so sure about the nickname, though. He would have preferred something less confrontational. The Coffee Whisperer. Not that he had anything against Gordon Ramsay. But Lorna didn't hold with all that shouting and swearing. Personally, Bob thought it was all an act. Gordon Ramsay was probably a big softie in real life. Probably went gooey at the sight of puppies and kids with cancer.

Talking of which. Bob took the coffee upstairs on a tray together with a plate of McVitie's Hobnobs – Lorna's favourite – and her various medications.

His wife was propped up in bed, listening to music. Mendelssohn. Before Bob had met Lorna he wouldn't have known Mendelssohn from armpit music.

Lorna had been a music teacher. A little more than that. In her younger days, she had played for a year with the London Philharmonic. Clarinet. Her biggest claim to fame was that she had played on the soundtrack of the first *Lord of the Rings* film.

Bob couldn't watch the film anymore without blubbing into his hanky.

'Hello, love.'

His wife smiled at him. Bob loved the way Lorna smiled. Properly. No making a pained face, as he had seen celebrity cancer sufferers do. As if to broadcast to the world: *Look at me. What a brave soul I am. Battling the big C.*

Sure. People with cancer were brave. But cancer was something that happened *to* you. It wasn't the same as a man running into a burning building to save a small dog. Or a kid standing up to a bully. Real bravery was in *choosing* to put something on the line.

Bob had been putting it on the line his whole life. Went with the territory.

He had joined the force as a rough-and-ready eighteen year old. Back in the days when you could still take a hoodlum by the scruff of the neck and give him a good seeing to. All different now, of course. Lay a hand on some young thug making merry hell and the brass couldn't wait to string you up.

Bob had worked all over. Itchy feet. Eventually washed up in London, where he had met Lorna quite by chance. A call out to the Royal Festival Hall, following a burglary.

He had no idea what the petite blonde with the clarinet had seen in him. Although, to be fair, he had cut quite the figure back then, in his pristine uniform, with his jet-black hair and winsome smile. But Lorna could have done a lot better. A woman like that.

Six months later, they had married. A small wedding. Neither of them had any family. A few of the lads came along. None of

Lorna's colleagues from the Philharmonic. Lorna had been cast out by then. A new artistic director ringing the changes. Never really recovered from it. Never tried to join another orchestra. She had always told Bob that she had had her fill. Gave her more time to work on Bob. It was Lorna who had urged Bob to take his detective exams. She had seen something in him that he hadn't seen in himself. Behind every great man: a woman who won't take no for an answer.

Bob hadn't regretted it. Took a while to find his feet, but his qualities had soon been recognised. A doggedness in pursuit. A willingness to put in the hard yards. He had hit his own glass ceiling at detective sergeant. That was fine. Bob had no wish to sit in the hot seat. Heavy hangs the head, and all that.

They had moved to Wickstone-on-Water fifteen years ago. Back then, Lorna worked at the local school and Bob drove out to a neighbouring town each morning. When the bigwigs had decided to establish a police HQ in Wickstone, Bob had been moved across. A no brainer.

Over the years, Bob had seen the town change. He had seen the growing unease, felt it in his water. Had predicted trouble. At first, they came in a trickle. A handful here, a handful there, some on their own steam, some sent over by those in charge in Whitehall. And then the floodgates opened.

Lorna, bless her heart, had welcomed them. *Everyone needs a safe harbour, Bob.*

But Bob had heard other sentiments expressed. Darker sentiments. He had seen the pressure build. Had to come out somewhere. But that was the point of democracy, wasn't it? Other nations lied to themselves, hid from uncomfortable truths. But in a grown-up country, you let the people decide.

Not everyone agreed, of course. Some wanted spectacle and scapegoats, not facts and reason. Political pageantry. Fair enough. That was human nature.

But Wickstone wasn't the Third Reich. The people here, by and large, were sensible. Judged the situation on its merits. Crime had gone up. The pressure on resources had increased. No sensible person could deny that. And so, yes, some of Bob's neighbours had voted Brexit. Others had taken in refugees. And some had done both.

They were all good people, and Bob would go a long way for them.

Lorna was watching some sort of talent show. An opera singer was singing the most beautiful aria. While juggling a pair of flaming bowling pins.

Lorna's face was lit up. That smile. How had he got so lucky?

He entwined his fingers with his wife's. Everyone's trauma was real. But perhaps some trauma was realer than others?

Bob thought about Kathy Burnham. He had worked with the DCI for just over a year now. Her heart was in the right place. And she was obviously as sharp as a tack. But Bob wasn't sure Kathy had that ruthless streak you needed to deal with the elements that had recently come into Wickstone. He had seen a lot of that in London. The gangs. The traffickers and the drug barons. The type that made Vlad the Impaler look like a Care Bear.

Bob thought about the man who had come to see Kathy. Q. Not his real name, obviously. Kathy had given Bob the basics. An old friend. Some sort of techie in the Secret Service. Childhood bunkmate of Peter Napier, come back to do some amateur sleuthing.

Napier's death had made a big splash. How could it not? Local boy made good returns to set up a hush-hush big-money science lab on the edge of town. And then dies in mysterious circumstances. The media had descended on Wickstone. And then, as the news cycle ticked over, had just as quickly vanished. In a heartbeat, Peter Napier was forgotten.

But his legacy was important. Napier Labs was important. To Wickstone. And to those who had a vested interest in its success.

Bob agreed with Kathy that something hadn't been right about Napier's death. It didn't *track,* as they said on Bob's favourite American cop show.

But what more could they have done? A lack of evidence. A coroner's report that concluded death by misadventure. No point butting your head against a brick wall.

Still. Bob was intrigued by this development. By Q. Why had Napier written to him?

Bob settled his glasses on his nose.

No point worrying about it. All would become clear in due course. Or not.

Now it was time for a cup of coffee, a nice biscuit and some quality time with his wife.

God only knew how much time they had left.

The aria singer launched one of the bowling pins miles into the air, then hit a high C and caught the pin as it came down. All without missing a beat.

Lorna applauded, a little laugh escaping her.

Bob felt his heart expand. Tears sprang to his eyes.

He reached, once again, for his wife's hand.

24

GOOD NIGHT'S SLEEP WORKED WONDERS. Or not. Q awoke in pain. His jaw was on fire. Bruises groaned the length of his body.

And yet, he felt strangely exhilarated. Last night's maudlin thoughts had vanished. Cobwebs brushed from his mind. The encounter at Pete's home confirmed that he was on to something. His instincts – in returning to Wickstone to investigate Pete's death – had proved correct. It occurred to him that part of his newfound sense of buoyancy came from the fact that he was back in the saddle of his own destiny. His emasculating exit from MI6 could be set to one side. He had a mission. And this time no one could force him to give it up.

He had ended the previous evening by searching the Internet, digging up background information. Peter had made several major breakthroughs in the quantum computing field whilst at UCL – University College London. Yet there was little inform- ation about why he had suddenly chosen to leave. A single article on a science blog seemed to indicate that Pete had fallen out with the university and with his industry sponsors. No further details. And then, less than a year after his departure, he had popped up in Wickstone at the helm of his very own lab.

Q noted down the name of the head of UCL's Quantum Science Institute, a Professor Mike Huang. Pete had been the previous director of the institute. Huang had been the institute's deputy director. It would be worth a visit to UCL to speak with the man.

But first things first. To begin with, he wanted to interview Helen Banner, the woman who had left Napier Labs just before Pete's death, under mysterious circumstances. And, in due course, another chat with Kathy, now that he had gone through the investigative reports. Assuming she would see him. He hoped so. Kathy had led the investigation into Pete's death. Q needed her cooperation. All strictly professional. Nothing to do with any personal desire he might have to see her again. At least, that's what he told himself.

As Q sat down to breakfast, he turned to Miss Honeypenny. 'Honeypenny, can you find me a vet in Wickstone-on-Water?'

'Yes, of course, Q.' A second later: 'The nearest vet is the Horse and Hound Veterinary Clinic on Tapworth Street.'

'Can you book me an appointment?'

'I will do so now, Q.'

Q spooned at his oats. Beside his bowl was the letter Pete had sent him.

Q had spent another hour hacking away at the cipher, with little success.

UUSCVILCTRAKYMJCKNMKHEA
WIUGXUJYHAKRVA
GANCETWKTTGP
LIUQYNLJIOFCS

And the single word: *Easy!* below the cipher. Pete, taunting him. From beyond the grave.

Q strongly suspected the cipher was a Caesar cipher. It had been Pete's favourite; the cipher purportedly used by Julius Caesar to communicate with his generals. A Caesar cipher simply shifted letters along the alphabet by a given number of places – the 'key'. So if the key was two, then each letter in the message would be shifted by two along the alphabet. Thus an A would become a C. B would become D. And so on. The word ANT would become CPV when encoded using the Caesar cipher.

But when Q applied a key of two to Pete's cipher he got only gibberish.

Perhaps the key wasn't two?

Q used an algorithm to apply various other keys. A shift of one, two, three, four, five and so on, all the way up to a shift of twenty-five letters where an A would become a Z.

Nothing.

Clearly, Pete had been cleverer than that.

Q thought about it. Pete had loved the Caesar cipher. If he wanted to write to Q in code then surely that would be the one he would use? ... There was another possibility. What if Pete had used a *double* Caesar cipher?

The double Caesar cipher was a variation on the Caesar cipher that was far harder to crack. It worked just like the original but each letter in the message was shifted by a *different* amount, based on a keyword. Each letter in the keyword told the decoder how many letters to shift. Thus with A set as zero, B is a shift of one letter, C is two, D is three, E is four ... and so on.

Thus if the original message was, say, HELLOWORLD, and the keyword was DOG, then this would mean that the first letter in HELLOWORLD would be shifted by three letters – because D represented a shift of three from the letter A. But the second letter in HELLOWORLD would be shifted by *fourteen* letters, because O represented a shift of fourteen from the letter A. The pattern would then be repeated. So the fourth letter in HELLOWORLD would again be shifted by three – because it would be aligned with D again.

The million-dollar question: *What was the keyword that Pete had used?*

Q looked at Bastard. The dog was somehow managing to graze from his dog bowl whilst the rest of his body lay recumbent. He looked like a puddle that had sprouted a canine head. 'Any ideas?'

Bastard kept eating. A trumpeting sound emerged from the windier end of his torso.

'Helpful,' said Q. He picked up his bowl of oats, walked out into the garden.

Sitting down at a garden table, he looked at the letter again.

Easy! Why would Pete say that? They hadn't been in touch for years. Somehow that single word seemed out of step with the rest of the short letter. Jocularity had never been Pete's strong suit.

Easy ... Q's spoon froze halfway to his mouth ... What if the word *easy* was part of the cipher?

Q put down his spoon. Excitement throbbed slowly against his ribcage.

Easy. *Easy* was the keyword.

Q got up and fetched his notebook and a pen. He wrote out the alphabet. Under this he wrote the numbers 0 to 25, representing the number of letters to be shifted if the Caesar cipher was being applied.

A B C D E F G H I J K L M N O P Q R S T U V W X Y Z
0 1 2 3 4 5 6 7 8 9 10 11 12 13 14 15 16 17 18 19 20 21 22 23 24 25

Q wrote the word EASY and compared it to the alphabet he had just written out. Thus E was the fourth letter along from the start point of A, i.e., a shift of four. The next letter in the keyword, A, *was* the start point. So a shift of zero. S was eighteen letters along, and Y was twenty-four letters along.

Q went back to the original cipher.

He wrote out the first line, then the keyword EASY, repeated below that line. Under this, he wrote out the number of letters each letter of Pete's message would have to be shifted *backwards* by in order to decipher the text.

U	U	S	C	V	I	L	C	T	R	A	K	Y	M	J	C	K	N	M	K	H	E	A
E	A	S	Y	E	A	S	Y	E	A	S	Y	E	A	S	Y	E	A	S	Y	E	A	S
4	0	18	24	4	0	18	24	4	0	18	24	4	0	18	24	4	0	18	24	4	0	18

Thus U would have to be shifted back by four letters and would be deciphered as Q. But the second letter, also a U, was aligned with the letter A in the keyword EASY – a shift of zero – and thus would not be shifted back at all and would remain U. Next, the S would be shifted back by eighteen letters in the alphabet and would thus become an A. C would be shifted back by twenty-four places and would become an E. And so on.

He continued in this fashion until he was able to decipher the line.

QUAERITEPRIMUMREGNUMDEI

Disappointment hammered at him. It looked like another line of nonsense. He had been almost certain—

Q stopped. Something about the string of letters stuck a familiar chord.

With growing excitement, he inserted spaces into the line.

QUAERITE PRIMUM REGNUM DEI

It was the Latin that Q had recognised. Or at least he was fairly certain that this was Latin. It made sense. Pete had studied Latin at A level. An extra course, one of many. Pete had always had brain capacity to burn. Q had never bothered with Latin but, thanks to his father's obsession with the ancient Romans, could recognise the odd word. Dei was God. Or something related to God. And regnum ... That meant country or kingdom, didn't it?

Only one way to find out.

He logged on to a Latin translator, typed in the words. The translator came up with:

SEEK YE FIRST THE KINGDOM OF GOD

Q sat back. He had intelligible words but was no further forward in understanding Pete's message. *Seek ye first the kingdom of God.* What could Pete have meant? The kingdom of God? Pete had never been religious. At least not when Q had known him. Had he found God later in life?

It seemed unlikely. Q recalled the many debates he and Pete had had over the true nature of God. Each day science uncovered more of the wonders of the cosmos. Infinity hinted at something beyond the ken of man, a greater power. There had been many times when Q had needed faith. Faith in himself, in something beyond the veil. A world without faith would be a pitiless place, human existence no more than a dismal comic operetta. Q would rather not believe in such a world.

Perhaps the rest of the message would provide context?

Q repeated the process with the remaining lines from the cipher until he had a complete decoded message.

He stared at the revealed lines of text, none the wiser. Whatever Pete had intended with his missive, Q didn't get it. What he had before him made no sense.

It occurred to him that the translator might not be completely accurate. There were nuances – particularly with an ancient language such as Latin – that no algorithm could completely capture.

What Q needed was someone who spoke Latin fluently.

It just so happened that he knew such a person.

Agitation drove him back into the kitchen where Bastard appeared to have fallen asleep with his face in his bowl. Q walked across and gently lifted him clear. Bastard snorted dog food from his nostrils, then settled back on his paws.

Q's feelings following the meeting with his father had been a raging torrent. Memories of his mother; the beast of the past.

But that had been a long time ago. He had held onto anger, nursed it even when logic and common sense had told him it was time to let go.

Before Wickstone, the previous occasion Q had seen Mort was ten years earlier. To be accurate, it had been an *image* of Mort, looking scholarly, on the back of a book in Waterstones Piccadilly. Mort had written several well-received Roman histories over the decades.

Mort had been due to visit the bookshop. Q had thought about attending. In the end, he had decided against it. A part of him had hoped that Mort might get in touch whilst in London. But Mort hadn't called.

And now here they were.

Q knew that he would have to see his father again.

The prospect was grim.

25

ZAK WAS WORRIED.

The visit by Medium Tony had thrown him. The Tony he had known until now had been a genial sort. Twinkle in his eye, friend to man and beast alike. A smile for everyone, even when he was busy changing the registration plate on a stolen BMW.

Yes, Tony was a criminal, but he was also a nice man.

Or so Zak had thought. But nice men didn't come into hospital and threaten you.

OK, so Tony was probably under orders. Probably from Zak's benefactor.

That didn't change the fact that Zak was now in the firing line.

Zak wasn't stupid. When he had agreed to join Tony's operation, he had quickly hacked into the garage's primitive online systems. In films, they always said 'follow the money'. So Zak had followed the money. And any other trail he could find. He knew exactly who was behind the chop shop. He knew the pies they had their fingers in. And he knew – or thought he knew – how Pete Napier had slotted into this crooked jigsaw.

Zak was under no illusions. The people he worked for were not the type to pat him on the back for an honest mistake.

Tousle his hair and send him on his way. He had cost them money. A lot of money. Not just for the bashed-up Bentley but for lost future business.

More importantly, they thought he was talking to the cops. About Pete Napier.

If they knew how much Zak knew, about what Napier had been doing in Wickstone, about Napier's death, Zak doubted they would wait. He was in danger. No matter which way he turned. Could the cops really protect him? Protect his mother?

Back in Syria, talking to the cops was not optional. If the cops wanted to talk to you, they came around in a truck and escorted you to the station. If you didn't feel like being escorted they cracked you around the knees with a truncheon and dragged you into the truck. If you ran, they shot you in the back. What better way to encourage cooperation between the police and the community they served?

How long could Zak hold out? How long could he lie?

To the cops.

To his mother, to himself.

To the people who could hurt them both.

26

HELEN BANNER LIVED IN A large house not far from Peter Napier's home.

Q supposed that the influx of tech staff that Napier Labs had brought to Wickstone preferred to congregate close to one another. Birds of a feather.

He parked his Caterham on the gravelled front courtyard of the triple-fronted Victorian. A silver Mercedes sparkled in the sun.

Q crunched up the drive and rang the doorbell.

When the door eventually swung back, it was to reveal a very tall and broad-shouldered youth in what looked like a rugby outfit. Airpods stuck out of his ears. Q pegged the boy at around seventeen or eighteen. He had the sort of chiselled cheeks and boy-band hair Q wished he had had at that age.

Q remembered playing rugger as a kid. He and Pete had been all but useless. Uncoordinated and uninterested. Couldn't catch a cold, let alone the ball. All that running around tackling each other, clumping together in a scrum. The punching. The gouging. The tweaking of testicles. And that had just been the sports master.

'Yes?'

Q introduced himself. 'Is Helen Banner at home? I wonder if I could speak with her?'

'What about?' The boy had an odd accent. French, though not quite.

'I'm an old friend of Peter Napier's. I was hoping I could talk to her about his death.'

The boy's cheeks flushed. 'Don't you think you lot have done enough? Mum had nothing to do with Pete's death. And she doesn't owe your lab a thing.'

'I don't work for Napier Labs.' Still the boy hesitated. 'Look, it won't take long. And I'd rather not try and track her down elsewhere.'

He hovered on the doorstep, then turned and walked off into a spacious hallway. An elephant's foot umbrella stand stood to one side. An abstract painting in primary colours hung on a wall. An expensive-looking bicycle leaned against the opposite wall.

Q was led through the house and out into a garden so vast it deserved its own game warden. A patio gave way to a mani-cured lawn. Beds of spring flowers merged into trees. Was there a hedge maze in the far distance? Probably.

A woman was sitting on a garden sofa, glass in hand, laptop open before her. Tawny-haired, she wore a sleeveless chiffon summer dress in pastel colours. Her arms were corded with muscle, an Apple watch prominent on one wrist. Her face was arresting, with a strong jawline and dark eyes. Grooves around her mouth. She had the look of a yachtswoman, one who had sailed around the world, surviving against all odds, and was now writing her memoir. Q pegged her age around the mid-forties.

'Mum, this is—' The boy paused, looked back over his shoulder.

Q introduced himself to Helen Banner. 'I'm sorry to interrupt your morning, but I was hoping you would answer a few ques-tions about Pete Napier's death for me. He was an old friend.'

The woman stared at him, then turned to her son. 'Aren't you getting late for your game?'

The boy dug out his phone, checked the time. 'I should make a move. Do you know where my boots are?'

'More mud than boots. They're in the back room. In the same bag you brought them home in.'

He glanced uncertainly at Q, as if he didn't trust this well-groomed stranger with his mother.

'Drive carefully,' said Helen.

'Yeah. Sure.' The boy walked away and vanished back into the house.

'He's only just passed his test,' Helen explained to Q. She gestured at an armchair.

Q sat.

'Something to drink?'

'No. Thank you.'

'He's seventeen. Grew up in Paris. And now he's here. In Wickstone. Safe to say, he hasn't quite forgiven me.'

'How long have you lived here?'

'About three years.'

'Is it just you and your son?'

'Ricky. And no. My husband moved here with us. Henri. He's French.'

'What does he do?'

'Complains about the bread, mainly.' A beat. 'He works for a logistics firm. Travels a lot. He's currently in France. He's been very supportive.' Said almost as an afterthought. Q imagined it couldn't be easy, uprooting your family, no matter how much you were paid.

The sun was battling hard to make itself known. It had been a schizophrenic spring, wet and warm in equal measure. Records had been broken.

Helen put down her glass and picked up a vape. She drew on it and puffed out a sweet-smelling vapour. 'How is it that you think I can help you?'

'I'm trying to understand the circumstances of Pete's death.'

'Pete's death was an accident. Tragic, but I don't see what I can tell you that the police can't.'

'You knew him well?'

'As well as anyone, I suppose. We'd worked together before, in France. When he set up Napier Labs, he offered me the position of chief scientist. Though that was a bit of a misnomer.'

'How so?'

'Well, Pete was the real chief scientist. But he preferred to go by the title of CEO. That isn't to belittle my own contribution. It's simply a fact.'

'What *was* your contribution?'

'How much do you know about quantum computing?'

'I'm learning as I go.'

'I'm a software scientist. Designing the hardware for quantum computing is just half the problem. Computing hardware is only as useful as the software that you can run on it. Quantum programming is the process of turning high-level algorithms into physical instructions that can be executed on quantum computer processors. That's what I do.'

'Sounds pretty integral to the project at Napier Labs.'

'Think about it this way. Without the ability to code algorithms, a quantum computer is just a shiny mass of circuitry.'

Q shifted in his seat. 'Some of your colleagues think Pete may have drowned himself. But the Pete I knew would never have done that.'

Her jaw rippled. 'Perhaps you didn't know him as well as you thought? Pete was under enormous pressure. I've seen people crack before. It's never pretty.'

Q pulled out Pete's letter, then found himself hesitating. He hadn't felt comfortable showing it to Jed Ellis, but Helen Banner had known Pete from a time before he established Napier Labs. And now she had left the organisation. He handed her the letter. 'He sent me this just before his death. I think it shows that he was worried. Not suicidal.'

120

'Worried about what?'

'His safety.'

She scanned the sheet, frowning. 'The coroner concluded death by misadventure.'

'I know. That's why I'm asking questions.'

'You don't believe the verdict?'

'I'm not sure. And I have to be sure.'

She tucked her feet up onto the sofa. Q saw that she was barefoot. Strong calves. Cyclist's calves. He recalled the bicycle he had seen in the hallway.

'He was an incredible man,' she said, eventually. 'Utterly driven. Oblivious to everything but the success of his project.'

'Ruthless?'

'When he had to be.'

'Is that why you were kicked off the project?'

She stiffened. Her eyes drilled into him. And then she looked away. 'Who have you been talking to? Jed Ellis?'

'I have.' Q didn't mention that Ellis had said nothing about Banner.

'I wasn't kicked off the project. I left by mutual agreement.'

'So did I,' murmured Q.

She looked at him strangely.

Q leaned forward. 'Look. I'm not the police. I just want to know what happened to Pete.'

'I'm bound by a non-disclosure agreement.'

Q looked around the garden. 'When we were seventeen Pete and I climbed Ben Nevis together. Three quarters of the way up, I slipped and twisted an ankle. I couldn't go on. I knew that Pete had set his heart on getting to the top. He was driven by milestones, even then. The weather was terrible. I told him to go on, I'd wait for him. He said OK, and then moved on. The weather worsened. Twenty minutes later, Pete came back. "If you get yourself washed off the mountain, I'll have to spend the rest of my life explaining why I left you behind." He was smiling when he said it. But I could see what it cost him to come back. It's about the only time I ever saw him do something completely unselfish.' Q paused. 'Pete wasn't perfect. But he was my friend.'

'I want to help you. But I can't. Breaking my NDA will disqualify my stock options. When Napier Labs goes public, they're going to be worth a lot of money. Last year, three quantum computing firms listed, all for several hundred million dollars each. Do you understand?'

'I understand.' Q was more than familiar with NDAs. In the clandestine world that he had inhabited, they were part of the fabric.

'Look, I get what you're doing. But sometimes it's better to let sleeping dogs lie.' She drew on her vape, then: 'Pete and I had a scientific disagreement. That's all I can tell you. We didn't see eye-to-eye on the direction of travel.'

'Is there any reason you can think of for someone to want to harm Pete? Someone at Napier Labs, perhaps? I'm asking off the record.'

'Nothing is off the record.'

Q changed tack. 'Who replaced you at Napier Labs? As chief scientist?'

Helen's cheek twitched. 'That would be Astrid Simmons.'

Astrid Simmons. The young woman who had met Q at Napier Labs. And who had told him about Banner's exit from the firm but hadn't mentioned the fact that *she* had replaced the woman. Something about the way Helen had spoken about Simmons struck Q as odd. Once again, he felt himself navigating unfamiliar seas. Human beings were difficult to fathom. He had always been more comfortable with machines. 'With you off the project, how will Napier Labs develop the software you were working on?'

'Most of my protocols are finished. I think Pete had the idea that my understudy will finish them off.'

'Your understudy?'

'Astrid. Pete had a lot of faith in her.'

Again, Q sensed the tension in Helen's voice. Understandable, perhaps. Being replaced by a younger model was never easy. Q knew that better than anyone.

A short, awkward silence, broken by Helen: 'Did you ever see the film *Oppenheimer?*'

'Yes.' Q had quite liked it. Though a bit more nudity in a science film than he had expected. And a lot of standing around looking glamorous. Which, in his experience, didn't really happen in science much.

'Pete was obsessed by Robert Oppenheimer. Pete knew that the machine he was creating would change the world. But it also brings with it the potential for immense harm. Pandora isn't just out of the box, she's busy flashing her knickers, kicking over bar stools.' A dry smile. 'I'm sorry that Pete's dead. If he had lived he would have won a Nobel prize. In time. When I think about the loss to humankind, the work he had yet to do.' A shake of the head. Q thought he saw the possibility of tears.

Yet Helen Banner didn't strike him as the sentimental sort.

Curious.

As he was getting into his car, Q's phone rang.

It wasn't a call. It was the security system at his home back in London.

Q didn't trust off-the-shelf video doorbells – often susceptible to wireless evil-twin attacks. A hacker could copy the network onto their own infrastructure and gain control. Q had installed a specially modified version. Modified by himself, at Q Branch.

He had been receiving videos while he had been away. His only visitors had been a pair of black-suited Jehovah's Witnesses, a courier delivery guy – who had nonchalantly lobbed a parcel over the side fence – and the postman.

But the person now prowling around the back door was different. Clearly, he had hopped the side gate and walked down the alley that ran alongside Q's house to his garden.

The man wore a baseball cap pulled low, wraparound sunglasses and a close-fitting dark beard.

Q pressed a button on his phone. 'The alarm system on my house is bespoke. Believe me, it won't be worth your while trying to break in.'

The man's head jerked up in shock. His eyes quartered the door, finally focusing on a camera built into the brickwork high above.

'Don't believe me?' Q pressed another button. A high-pressured jet of water shot out from the wall, hitting the intruder square in the face, dislodging his sunglasses. He cried out, staggered back, tripped, fell to earth. Another jet shot out, focusing on his crotch. The man scrabbled away, got to his feet, ran for the alley leading back to the front of the house.

Q sat in the Caterham, considering the development. Adrenalin coursed through him.

They had found his home. His *home*!

He had to assume it was the same people who had followed him to Pete's home in Wickstone. Who were they? What did they want? *How much danger was he in?*

Perhaps they were simply covering their bases. Checking him out. After all, he had breezed into Wickstone, started asking questions about Pete's death. Questions that someone clearly didn't want him to ask.

If nothing else, it proved that there was more to Pete's death than met the eye.

And if Q kept going, there was little doubt that the risks would escalate.

But backing off wasn't an option.

For better or worse, he was committed.

27

IRKO HATED DOCTORS EVEN MORE than he hated accountants.

At least accountants were definitive. They told you what was possible and how much it would cost. At Mirko's age, doctors promised nothing. And they rarely told the truth. Bad news was presented as an opportunity. Exercise more and live longer. Don't eat the things you like and live longer.

Mirko needed to pay a fortune for this?

Dr Kozumi was almost as old as Mirko. He came from the same region in Albania as Mirko, had set up shop in London decades ago. Kozumi had been a good doctor to the family. His private practice had flourished under Mirko. Mirko's men often needed urgent medical care, the sort that invited questions from NHS doctors, questions his men were not in a position to answer. Such as: How did you get that bullet in your shoulder?

The NHS truly was broken.

Now, as the Angel of Death pinched Mirko's cheeks and winked slyly at him each morning, the visits by Dr Kozumi had become more frequent.

Mirko watched the man roll down Mirko's sleeves, then pack away his blood pressure cuff. He listened with half an ear as Kozumi went through his routine.

When the doctor had left, Mirko ordered Papa John to get his nephew online.

Fifteen minutes later, Adem appeared onscreen. His dentally enhanced grin was blinding. As was his shirt. Mirko could hear loud music in the background. Rap music. 'Yo, PopPops. What's cooking?'

Mirko hated the nickname. Adem had picked it up in some film when he had been young. Mirko's sister had thought it the 'cutest thing'. Mirko had doted on his sister and so had allowed it. He hadn't expected the little boy to grow into a man and still be attached to childish things. That was the thing about Adem. Mirko knew, in his heart, the boy wasn't all there. But what could he do? Adem was his sister's only son. The one thing she had asked of Mirko on her deathbed was that he look after her son.

'Have you been in a fight?'

'What? No, PopPops. What makes you say that?'

'You're wearing sunglasses. Inside.'

Adem slipped off the sunglasses. Grinned again. 'Yo, PJ. My man. Nice hair.'

Mirko felt Papa John stiffen behind him. It was a good thing for Adem that he was Mirko's nephew.

'Did you speak with Tony?'

'I did.'

Mirko waited.

'He went to see the kid. Gave him our message.'

'Did the boy understand?'

'Chillax, PopPops. I've got this.'

'Is that why you sold Napier those cars? When I told you to stay away from him?'

Adem looked wounded. Mirko's sister had employed the same expression every time she had got herself into trouble. Usually

126

with another boy. Such as Adem's father. A man who, having soiled the Demaçi gene pool, had subsequently vanished. Or had been made to vanish. Mirko had never quite been sure. His late father had remained tight-lipped on the matter.

'The man had a thing for cars. I'm the only dealership in town. We have a contract with Napier Labs. A very lucrative contract, in more ways than one. You know all this.'

Mirko thought about his father again. In Albania, in the mountains, they had lived hand-to-mouth. In London, in the early years, his father had worked fifteen-hour shifts in a bread factory. And for what? He had quickly discovered that he was, and always would be, a second-class citizen. Mirko's father had wanted more. And so he had decided to do something about it.

Later, Mirko had taken his father's fledgling criminal enterprise and turned it into the organisation that had truly changed the family's fortunes. His father hadn't lived long enough to see that. Shot through the heart in an altercation with a rival. Mirko's father had been armed with a knife. Literally the man who brought a knife to a gunfight.

'Why did the boy try to steal the car?'

'I wanted it back. After Napier's death, the police cordoned off his property. I couldn't wait. I had an overseas customer lined up. Everyone wins, PopPops.'

'And now the police are talking to the boy.'

Adem hesitated. 'Yeah. That wasn't part of the plan. But he's a good kid. Smart. There are things we could be doing, online scams—'

'Don't go near him.'

'But—'

'Do I need to repeat myself?'

Adem looked sullen. Once again, he reminded Mirko of his sister. If only he didn't see her come alive in the boy! Mirko had hoped that, by giving Adem responsibility, by sending him to Wickstone, the boy might actually learn something.

But that was what came of not having a father.

Mirko had hated his own father. But he missed him too. And now he understood him. He understood the responsibilities of running a family. You did what you did. For them. And then you went to confession and begged forgiveness.

No one could say Mirko was a bad man. Well, technically, they *could* say that. Not in his presence, of course. But that was like blaming a shark for eating other fish. 'There's something else. An old friend of Napier's. Boothroyd. He's in Wickstone, asking questions. If he arrives on your doorstep, send him away. Do not engage.'

Adem looked as if he was about to protest, but then simply said, 'Sure. Whatever you say.' Mirko ended the call, then waved a hand at Papa John. Out. The big man hesitated, then left the room.

Mirko felt tired. Being a gangster was a young man's game. All Mirko wanted now was a firm mattress, a watertight bladder and to be left alone with his memories. He missed his wife. He missed his youth.

Mirko had read somewhere that elephants went to the same graveyard when they knew their time was up.

Where did old gangsters go to die?

28

THE DRIVE TO LONDON WAS uneventful.

There was a moment of tension around Junction 5 on the M25 when traffic ground to a halt and a helmeted biker came up to hover in Q's blind spot. He had thought for a second that it was the Deliveroo rider who had taken an inexplicable dislike to him. Absurd. But he slid up the windows anyway. You couldn't be too careful. Nutters everywhere.

London's gleaming outriders came into view just after lunch.

Even in the short time he had been away he had missed the city. He might have grown up in a small rural town but Q had long ago evolved into an urban creature. Designed to shuffle between concrete-and-glass pillars reaching for the sky. The background radiation of noise and light and colour. The constancy of people, from all over the world.

His heart gladdened at the thought of London's familiar staples: the traffic-and-tourist chaos that, most days, made the city's central precincts resemble a pitched battle in downtown Mogadishu; the army of keyboard Jedis and chest-thumping City boys that had, long ago, transformed London into a financial powerhouse; the all-night jamboree of nightwalkers in the city that never slept, mainly because it was hard to sleep when you were coked up to the eyeballs. Nine million souls ... Souls? Perhaps that was asking too much. But warm bodies, at least. Other cities asked for the tired and the poor. London actually *did* something with them, turning unpromising clay into a self-re-inventing empire of the bold and the beautiful. Or the damned. Probably the same thing, in the long run.

For coded into the city's genes was an instinct for survival, an ability to duck and weave and punch above its weight. Let other cities boast of art and music and vital longings; London had swagger. London was a fist clad in knuckledusters. If you survived London and lived to tell the tale, you became a part of the story, a little like the human after-shadows following a nuclear explosion. Or, if you wanted to be charitable, another romantic figure stitched into the urban tapestry of one of the world's great metropolises.

Q parked on the street in front of his home in Kennington, a stone's throw from the Oval Cricket Ground.

He felt his body exhale. Home. A three-storey Victorian townhouse, barely a twenty-minute walk from his former office. Some might have considered the place too large for the needs of a singleton with no children, but for Q it had felt just right, a coat you slip on and instantly know the tailor had you in mind all along. He was lucky to be able to afford it on a government salary, but the previous owner had been murdered by a lover in the upstairs bathroom in particularly grisly fashion, lowering the asking price.

He went through the house, made sure everything was as it should be. The *Death of Nelson* print above the fireplace, a scene to inject a shot of patriotism into the veins of any Englishman. His neatly organised kitchen, spotless, and surprisingly gadget-free. His carefully curated bookshelves. Medieval history. The Napoleonic Wars. Modern science. The classics: Dickens and Austen. But plenty of science fiction and fantasy, too. And the odd romance, the type he could get away with classifying, if pinioned, under the 'literary' banner. *The Horse Whisperer*. *The Bridges of Madison County*.

The intruder he had scared away would, no doubt, be back. But, for now, Q's castle was undisturbed.

He went to the basement door, punched a code into the keypad lock. A beep, and the door whirred back, and then he was moving downstairs. In the basement: a workbench and tools, some organised on shelves, others hanging from a metal pegboard. A space as clean and geometrically precise as an autopsy suite. Inset into the rear wall: a safe.

Q opened the safe, pulled out a titanium carry-on case. Stencilled on the outside of the case, the words: Q'S PICNIC HAMPER.

He checked the contents, then went up to the Caterham and placed the case in the boot. It was a tight squeeze and he was forced to move the car's mohair hood and weather gear to get the case wedged in.

Q thought about how long the house had been a sanctuary. No longer. Perhaps it had been a good thing that Pete's letter had summoned him to Wickstone. As awful as that was, at least the walls didn't close in every night at Sanctus Villa.

Life, post MI6. Q had been there so long he had all but become institutionalised. He had all the symptoms. A failure to adjust to the outside world. A desire to return.

His thoughts veered to his former office, his daily routine. About now he would be stopping for lunch, perhaps following a morning spent reviewing test results on the latest piece of field kit the lab had designed. Or a brainstorming session with the team. *No such thing as a bad idea, people. Except the crap ones.*

At the last such session before he had been forced out of MI6, a new recruit – a bespectacled Oxbridge *lateral thinker*, bless his squirrel-themed cashmere socks – had suggested a bicycle with a built-in laser cannon. Q had vetoed it on the grounds that he couldn't imagine a situation when a Double O might be on a

131

bicycle in the heat of battle. In Q's experience, Bond was unin-terested in any mode of transport that went at less than two hundred miles an hour and made him look anything other than a glamorous spy.

That was the odd thing about Bond. Other spies blended in. Indulged in spy-craft. Bond went in through the front door, a human battering ram. MI6 had stopped bothering to give him a cover, half the time. What was the point?

And yet the man got results.

There was something to be said for the direct approach.

29

CHECKING ON HIS HOME WASN'T the only reason Q had come to London.

He wanted to take a closer look at Pete Napier's stint working at University College London, before abruptly leaving to set up Napier Labs. Pete had spent seven years at UCL.

Every contact leaves a trace. Locard's exchange principle.

Seven years was a lot of contact.

UCL was a short Tube ride away in Bloomsbury. Post-COVID, the Underground system had become almost bearable. Less of a cattle crush. Instead of finding himself wedged into some City banker's armpit, Q had the luxury of a seat. And air-conditioning.

A man got on after three stops and began playing a stringed instrument. Q thought it might be a balalaika. The man's smell was a living thing. It sat down next to Q and put an arm around him. Began licking his ear. A woman in the seat opposite got up and ran for cover further down the carriage.

Q got off at Euston, then walked along Euston Road, joining the ranks of phone zombies flowing along both sides of the street. The mass of people gladdened his heart. Strange, the things you missed. He had always avoided crowds when he had lived here.

Bond had called him a misanthrope. It was true that he preferred his own company to that of others. His circle of friends had always been vanishingly small. But what was wrong with that? It wasn't as if he treated his colleagues as lepers, or shunned the occasional quiz evening at the pub. He simply valued his privacy. He worked in an environment where secrecy was the paramount currency. In other forums, oversharing might simply lead to a middle-aged meltdown on Facebook. But in the world of shadows Q inhabited, oversharing could compromise a mission and endanger lives.

And yet, others at MI6 balanced family, friendships and the demands of the job. Fair play to them. Q had never seen his own choices as a compromise.

He was simply who he was.

Q turned down Gower Street, then walked on to UCL's main campus, where a protest was going on in the quad. Several students were stretched out on the grey tarmac below UCL's Greek portico, drenched in what he presumed was fake blood. An earnest-looking young man sporting a shaggy beard bellowed through a loudhailer at a frightened-looking elderly couple. *'DON'T YOU CARE ABOUT CHILDREN DYING IN THE GLOBAL SOUTH?'*

Q remembered his own time at university, studying engineering. He had always been too timid to indulge in student radicalism. Though he had once bought a T-shirt with the slogan FITE DA POWA. He hadn't actually worn it because a) he hated the questionable grammar and b) he looked a bit of a tit in it.

Q navigated his way through the university to the UCL Quantum Science and Technology Institute.

The appointment he had made was still thirty minutes away. Q had always operated on the thirty-minute rule. Arriving early was the best way to avoid being late.

He was asked to sit in a small reception area, then led through to the office of Professor Mike Huang. Huang was on the phone and held up a finger as Q entered. The conversation went on for a few minutes, in what sounded to Q like angry Cantonese.

Huang set down his phone. 'Apologies. My mother is arranging a surprise birthday party for my father's eightieth. She expects me to drop everything and fly to Hong Kong tomorrow.'

Huang was casually dressed, in an open-collared shirt and jeans. His mouth and chin were smothered by a post-hipster beard, and his brown eyes were warm behind square-framed spectacles. He was squat and looked as if he worked out. He reminded Q of Robin Williams in *Good Will Hunting*, a sort of muscular therapist who bench-pressed three-hundred pounds and would happily punch a patient in the face if that's what it took.

Introductions were made. 'Thank you for agreeing to see me at short notice.'

'I was devastated to hear of Pete's death,' said Huang. 'An absolute tragedy.'

'How well did you know him?'

'I was his second-in-command when he established UCL's first quantum sciences research group. Our interests aligned. We both knew quantum computing was the future and wanted to be involved in making that future happen.'

'And yet you didn't follow him to Napier Labs?'

'He didn't ask.' Huang's expression revealed nothing.

'What did Pete do during his time at UCL?'

'*We* worked on the architecture for quantum computers. The hardware. There are many ways quantum computers can be put together. Using silicon-based technology, carbon nanotubes or superconducting-technology employing photons trapped in magnetic fields. The latter, in particular, requires cryogenic conditions – a fraction of a degree above absolute zero. That's always been the bottleneck in quantum computer advancement. The amount of space and energy you need to cool quantum computing hardware to near absolute zero. Pete and I helped refine those systems, made the hardware more practical. We achieved many world firsts here.'

'And then he left. Why?'

'Pete wanted to go his own way. There's no great conspiracy.'

Q knew that research showed that humans were terrible at detecting lies. For the same reason humans were so bad at detecting deep fakes. Yet, if crime fiction was to be believed, seasoned investigators could spot a liar from a million miles away. Gut instinct.

Pure bunk.

He remembered something Bond had told him about interrogation techniques. Not the bit about smashing the interrogatee on the bridge of the nose with an elbow. The other bit. About leaving silences.

Huang picked up a pencil. He looked as if he wanted to chew on it, then settled for sharpening it in a mechanical sharpener.

Finally, he spoke. 'OK. Fine. The man's dead now. What harm can it do? Pete fell out with UCL's ethics board.'

'How so?'

'It's essentially the same debate we're having about artificial intelligence. The potential dangers of quantum computing are enormous. Dangers from abuse, misuse or unintended consequences. Strong voices have been raised: slow down, let's put some ethical guardrails in place. Most universities have signed up to a call for increased government intervention and oversight. So that we don't make the same mistakes as we have with AI. Keep the genie on a leash.'

'But Pete didn't support such oversight?'

'He actively fought against it. As far as Pete was concerned the quantum computing frontier is the Wild West. Everything is up for grabs. If you hesitate, you die.'

'And setting up Napier Labs allowed him to circumvent ethical protocols?'

'Napier Labs is a private venture, funded by VC money. Technically, they're supposed to adhere to industry guidelines. But the secrecy they're working under is unprecedented. I mean, sure, we all operate a little in the shadows. We all want credit for getting to the peak first. But no one really knows what Napier Labs has been doing.'

'If you had to guess?'

'Aside from the obvious? That Pete was building the world's most powerful quantum computer?' Huang leaned back. 'Pete was chasing quantum supremacy.'

Q had read a little about this. It sounded like a Jason Bourne film. And was just as confusing. 'It would be helpful if you could expand.'

'Sure.' Huang knotted his fingers together and settled into what Q suspected was his lecturing pose. 'Currently no quantum computer can perform a meaningful task faster, cheaper or more efficiently than the very best classical supercomputer. At least not within a reasonable timeframe. This is because all quantum computing systems are subject to errors. Qubits – the fundamental bits of information employed by quantum computers – are highly susceptible to error – or noise, as we call it. Typically, today's quantum computers have error rates of around one in one hundred operations. What we need is to get that down to one error in one trillion operations. The holy grail of quantum computing is to build a self-correcting system that eliminates such noise.'

'And you think Napier Labs has succeeded in this?'

'I do. Or they're on the cusp of it. It will put them decades ahead of anyone else.'

'And what would Pete have done with this quantum supremacy?'

Huang grinned. 'Everything.' His smile faltered as Q continued to stare at him. 'Achieving quantum supremacy will unlock the true potential of quantum computing. All the things that have been posited that we *could* do with a quantum computer will suddenly become ... do-able.'

Do-able. Huang wasn't going to rank among history's great wordsmiths.

'Was there something specific that Pete wanted to apply this powerful new technology to?'

Huang hesitated. 'Yes. I believe so. But I wouldn't testify to it.'

Q waited.

Huang cracked his knuckles. 'Go talk to Jenny Grant. She heads up UCL's Centre for Future Crime.'

'Future crime?'

Huang shrugged. 'I know. Very *Minority Report*. You'll have to ask her. But I warn you. She can be . . . difficult.'

Q sat back. 'What kind of man was he?'

'Truthfully?'

'Yes.'

'Pete was an arsehole. And I say that as a former friend. Pete was an incredible scientist but he had no feel for people. Alienated almost everyone he worked with.'

Sounded familiar.

'Why *did* people continue to work with him?'

'Because he was making history. We are living through a momentous time. The AI revolution is comparable to the Industrial Revolution. The advent of quantum computing will supercharge the paradigm shift. Pete was one of the high priests of the new world order.'

It was a familiar refrain. Pete the wizard. Pete the oracle.

But being a genius was no protection from hatred or opprobrium.

Quite the opposite, in Q's experience.

Jenny Grant would not be available for a couple of hours.

Q headed into Bloomsbury for a late lunch. The streets were packed. Students and tourists. And psychotic office joggers with backpacks, steaming down the crowded pavements, cutting dirty looks at anyone who couldn't get out of the way fast enough.

He found a Thai place that looked presentable. He was seated at a small, square table in the corner, ordered a lamb pad thai and a beer. Why not? He wasn't on the clock anymore. He could drink a beer anytime he wanted to.

Rebel without a job.

Q could feel the case wind itself around him. The Pete that he had known was being raised from the dead. A flesh-and-blood figure. A man with weaknesses, chief among them unbridled ambition. An ability to upset those around him.

A man who made enemies.

Quantum supremacy. The words held a touch of glamour. Pete had clearly been on the verge of a breakthrough, one that would have had enormous repercussions. If Mike Huang was correct, achieving quantum supremacy would have allowed Pete's new quantum computer – already the most powerful in the world – to achieve unprecedented things.

Q was reminded of some of the exceptional criminals the Double Os had confronted over the years. Those who had financed powerful technological innovation so that it might be turned to destruction. The Double Os served as a secret force to hold such people to account. To stop them before they could wreak havoc.

But who did you send to stop *ordinary* men and women? Scientists? And even if you could, should you? Would Q go back in time and stop the first proto-human to harness fire? Fire – and its weaponization – had caused untold millions of deaths. But where would human society be without fire?

No.

You could never go back.

When he returned to the university, Q made his way to the Department of Security and Crime Science, where the Dawes Centre for Future Crime was housed. He remembered reading a paper that had come out of the centre a year ago. On autonomous vehicles and the potential for crime. Self-driving vehicles were, essentially, giant computers on wheels. And computers could be hacked.

Q had shown the paper to Bond, who had been banging on about the new Bentley prototype he had heard about, with a self-driving function. Bond had wanted Q to get hold of one and build a miniature intercontinental-ballistic-missile launcher into it. Q had told him that his latest budget had not been approved and, in any case, he wasn't certain that a ballistic missile inside a car that could think for itself was necessarily a good thing.

Bond had torn up the paper and stuffed it into Q's pocket.

Q believed in technology the way fish believed in water. Without technology, human beings would still be sitting around on the savannah clubbing each other over the head with bits of wood. Wondering if that bit of wildfire-barbecued antelope might be worth eating.

It was fine to be cautious with new technology. But Q couldn't understand those who actively opposed it. Those who banged on about the good old days. The truth was that the good old days were actually a bit shit. The life of an ordinary person in the Middle Ages had been awful. Technology was a great emancipator. And a force for social good.

And yet.

No one could deny that technology *could* lead to great harm. But the issue was not the tech. It was the people using the tech.

Q arrived at the department to find a party going on. Students were milling around in a ground-floor room with plates of food and little paper cups in hand. Cardboard hats and a sense of forced jollity.

Q was momentarily reminded of his own time at university. The freshers' luau. He had turned up in a three-piece suit when every other male attendee was dressed in a bomber jacket and aviator sunglasses. Q had rarely been out of Wickstone before. Everyone around him had seemed impossibly cool.

140

Jenny Grant turned out to be a large woman in a long, heavy dress with a grim expression, like a Victorian schoolmistress.

Q explained his mission. Grant seemed to debate something internally, then set down her plate of soggy sandwiches and beckoned him to follow.

They walked up three flights of steps and into a small office. Grant was wheezing by the second flight.

Grant took off her paper hat, crushed it viciously and dropped it into a bin. 'I suppose I should thank you for rescuing me.' She collapsed into a seat, bade Q sit. A MacBook was the only thing on her desk. The room, as a whole, was exceptionally tidy. Q approved. 'So,' she continued, 'you want to talk about Pete Napier?'

'Yes. Did you know him well?'

'Not really. We spoke several times about something he was working on.'

'And what would that be?'

Grant pulled a pack of cigarettes from her pocket. 'Do you mind? It's against the law, but I won't tell if you won't.'

Q did mind. But he suspected Jenny Grant wouldn't give a damn what he thought.

He waited while the woman lit up, took a puff, melted into her seat. 'God, I hate students.'

Q said nothing.

'Peter Napier. Mr Quantum Computing. A man on the cusp of changing the world, drowns in a river. How tragic.' She sounded anything but sympathetic. 'What do you want to know?'

'Did you work with him?'

She looked around for an ashtray, then opened a drawer and took out a plastic tray full of paperclips. She upended the tray, then flicked ash into it. 'Napier came to see me a few years ago. He was looking at the potential uses for the quantum tech he was developing. One of the things he cottoned on to was encryption. Or, rather, the fact that viable quantum computers will render all current encryption obsolete.'

Q's online research had revealed this possibility. To hear that Pete had actively queried this years ago sent a strange feeling up his spine.

'Encryption is how we safeguard data,' continued Jenny. '*All* data. Such as data we exchange when we communicate. Mobile phones. Voice over Internet. Social media. In fact, the very act of logging on to the Internet requires encryption. Think about it. Trillions of daily transactions, all relying on encryption. And this all works because the encryption methods we use today are based on mathematical problems that are all but impossible for even the most powerful supercomputers to crack. But a true quantum computer could break them in seconds. Micro-seconds. Imagine a world where all secured data and secure systems were instantly vulnerable to someone armed with a quantum computer.'

Q *could* imagine such a world. He had spent decades working in an institution that valued secrecy above all things. MI6's computers held secrets untold, locked behind layers of encryption, supposedly impervious to the efforts of the world's most ingenious hackers. Secrets that could bring down governments. It didn't bear thinking about.

'Did you end up exploring this with Peter?'

The woman prodded the mount of displaced paperclips on her desk with a finger. 'We talked about a possible joint project looking at the risks. But the next thing I heard he'd left UCL in a huff. That was the last I heard of him till Napier Labs was announced.'

'And you never contacted him? To pursue the project?'

'No. I had plenty on my plate and, frankly, my understanding was that true quantum computing was decades away. I'll be toes up in my grave by then. Turn the world to slag if you want. No skin off my nose.'

'You feel no responsibility for the next generation?'

'Sod the next generation. I don't have kids. Can't stand the brutes. Always up in arms about things they don't understand.'

'But you teach, don't you?' Q knew that he sounded plaintive.

'Only because I'm forced to. It's in the small print when they give you tenure. Academia is no longer the cosy sinecure it used to be. We're galley ships with bean counters lashing us along, cat o' nine tails in hand.'

30

'IKE I ALWAYS SAY, YOU can't go wrong with a fish finger sandwich.'

Kathy watched as Bob looked happily down into his lunchbox. Bob's lunches had become increasingly exotic of late. For a period, he had existed entirely on Gruel™, a liquid replacement meal developed in a lab. Bob claimed his bowel movements had never been more regular.

Kathy knew that Bob's lunches had once been made by his wife. Lorna had taken good care of him. But that was before ...

'How's Lorna?'

Bob stopped. Something passed behind his eyes. But his smile didn't waver. 'Good days and bad days. How was your date?'

'A bit like your sandwich. Pointless and a bit smelly.'

Bob grinned, lifted out the sandwich, took an enormous bite.

They were in the office, an open-plan floor at the stationhouse, going through the day's crime reports. A stabbing in a local park. A report of a possible cuckoo house. A man had flashed a pair of elderly women outside the local Waitrose. One of them had hit him below the belt with an umbrella. And so now he had filed a police complaint. Knowing the Crown Prosecution Service, they'd probably end up charging the eighty-two year old with aggravated assault.

Topsy-turvy world.

Kathy could see the slow erosion settling in. Wickstone was no longer a small village. In recent years, especially after the pandemic, there had been an influx of refugees coupled with those who could afford to get away from the city. Remote-working professionals who wanted clean air and the countryside on their doorstep. Selfies to send to their rat-race friends back in London. Perhaps that was the reason Pete had decided to site Napier Labs here.

But money attracted predators. And predators brought crime.

'Penny for your thoughts?' Bob was looking at her.

'I was thinking about Pete Napier.' Not quite true. She was thinking of Q. Which had led her to think of Pete. It bothered her that she hadn't heard from the man. Well, she certainly wasn't calling *him*, if that's what he was waiting for.

'He's got under your skin, hasn't he?'

Kathy frowned. 'I knew Pete at school.'

'I meant this new fella. Q. He's stirred the pond.'

Kathy picked up a stapler. 'He's convinced himself there was more to Pete's death than "misadventure".'

Bob put down his sandwich. 'OK. So let's give him the benefit of the doubt ... Why?'

'When we were fifteen, Pete told us he was going to change the world. What fifteen year old says that?'

'I wanted to be an astronaut,' Bob said. 'But my mum told me I was too fat. And stupid. She was a realist, my mum.'

'My point is that I just can't imagine Pete being careless enough to end up in that river. And there's no way he would kill himself. Too much of a narcissist.'

'We investigated it,' said Bob, mildly. 'Aren't you the one always saying cops should never second-guess themselves?'

Kathy said nothing.

'Do you remember why you wanted to be a cop?'

Kathy wanted to tell Bob that she had fallen in love with the idea when she was fourteen. A diet of cop shows. The thought of shoving a badge in a perp's face and telling him to spread 'em. Of piecing together a case singlehandedly and smugly revealing the killer's identity to an overbearing boss.

Policing hadn't quite turned out to be like that. There was a lot more paperwork than she had anticipated. And a lot of sitting around while nothing happened.

Bob reached into his lunchbox, took out a pot of yoghurt. Kathy saw that it was the kind with crunchy chocolate balls. She wished she had one. Several.

'Perhaps I'll pay Zak another visit,' said Bob. 'See if he's ready to tell us anything.'

'Do you really think he knows something about Pete's death?'

'No. I think he knows he's up to his eyeballs in it. He's clutching at straws. But there's no harm in finding out what he has to say.'

'If he'll talk to you.'

'Let me work on him. The old Bob magic.' A beat. 'In the meantime, why don't you have another chat with your pal? Q?'

Kathy snapped the stapler shut. A crumpled pin dropped out.

'He wasn't just a friend, back in school, was he?'

'No.' Kathy hesitated. Bob had always been more perceptive than he seemed. 'We dated. And then we got engaged. And then he left me.'

Bob whistled. 'And he's still breathing?'

Kathy looked away.

'Think you can be objective around him?'

'I don't need to be. He's a civilian.'

'Bit more than that. I googled him. Not much online. But there wouldn't be. He worked for MI6. The man's clearly no buffoon.' A pause. 'Why did he walk out on you? If you don't mind me asking. I mean, his loss, et cetera.'

'His mother died.'

'That's tragic. But hardly a reason to break off a perfectly good engagement.'

'She killed herself. An overdose.'

'Ah.'

'Q found the body.'

31

THE HOUSE HADN'T CHANGED.

Why would it? Houses didn't change. Not really. You could paint the exterior, add pebble dashing, a new front porch in uPVC and toughened glass. Posh things up a bit with a plaque bearing a fancy name. But ultimately, a home could no more change with age than a man's persona.

The lights were on.

Q knew that Mort was inside. He had gone to the library and they had told him Mort had gone home. He had thought long and hard about coming here. Perhaps he should have waited? Cornered his father at the library tomorrow.

He forced his feet to move. One step in front of another.

The bell seemed to go on for a long time. A melodious tune. Bach.

When Mort finally opened the door, his expression was one of shock. He reasserted control, then said, 'Come in.'

Q followed him along the corridor, weaving his way through a crowd of jostling memories. He remembered running up and down this corridor as a boy, a toy car in hand. He remembered sliding down the banisters, being shouted at by his mother.

The thought of her brought the memories to a standstill. They watched him solemnly, hands folded, as he made his way into the kitchen.

'Tea?' said Mort.

'Yes.' Q could think of nothing else to say.

He sat down awkwardly at the dining table.

The kitchen had been given a facelift. Gone were the Victorian tiles, his mother's Aga, the tacky bread gondola, the sepia-toned picture of ducks on the wall. The new kitchen had a space-age feel. A brilliant speckled white countertop made of some indestructible material. A microwave-cum-oven. An American-style double-fridge.

Q watched his father go through the routine of boiling water, setting out two teacups, adding teabags, creating the necessary space for them both to adjust to the moment.

As Mort reached up to open a cupboard, Q glimpsed a bright yellow mug. A deformed thing with wavy words painted on by a child's hand: WORLD'S GREATEST DAD.

Shock gripped him. How long had Mort held on to that? Why? The entire kitchen had been transformed, yet this single relic from Q's childhood had survived ... His feelings swarmed. Dark memories climbed out of the cellar.

Mort set down a bowl. 'Three sugars, right?'

Q nodded. His voice box had seized.

He regarded his father. Mort was still dressed in his suit. Some things hadn't changed. That same self-referential commitment to his own appearance. A preciseness that had impressed Q as a young man, so much so that he had adopted it in his own dress. Now it seemed forced. A battle against the inevitable.

His father was an old man.

The realisation was a hammer between the eyes.

Mort was old and Q had missed it. All those years, lost in grief, in anger. Blinding, white-hot anger. The thought cleaved him like a flaming sword. Time – and wisdom – had dampened the swirl of emotion. But you couldn't regain what had been lost.

Soon Mort would be gone. And then Q would truly be alone.

His heart thrashed around inside his chest. He didn't know how he should feel. His thoughts walked back along the corridor and tiptoed up the stairs. Into his mother's old bedroom. That last day. Her body slumped in bed.

Q clutched at his tea. The cup was too hot, seared his palm. The pain was welcome, returned him to the moment.

Finally, Mort spoke. 'I'm glad you came.'

Silence.

'I'm sorry about yesterday,' continued Mort. 'I was a little ... abrupt.'

'So was I.'

'I've never been good at this sort of thing. People.'

'Me neither.'

A movement beside his leg startled Q. He shot up, spilling his tea. 'There's something under the table.'

Mort leaned down and lifted a tortoise onto the tablecloth. 'Meet George.'

'You have a tortoise?'

'It seemed like a good idea at the time.'

George seemed impossibly ancient. He squinted myopically at Q, then began moving towards the edge of the table. Mort scooped him up before he could wander off into space. 'He's not the brightest.'

Mort cradled the animal.

Q was astounded. The idea of his father as a pet owner. A man who had banned animals in the house, had shut down Q's earliest pleas for a dog. Not that Q had been surprised. Mort had never been *that* kind of father. No dressing up as Santa on Christmas. No weekend kickabouts in the park. The Mort Q remembered had been a man of rules. So many rules.

'I have a dog,' said Q. 'His name is Bastard.'

Mort said nothing, reached for his tea.

Q took a deep breath. 'I need your help. I deciphered the note Pete sent me.' He reached into his pocket, set his translation down onto the table.

QUAERITE PRIMUM REGNUM DEI
SIC ITUR AD ASTRA
CAVEAT EMPTOR
HIC SUNT LEONES

'Latin,' said Mort.

'Yes.'

'And you couldn't work this out by yourself?'

There was a flash of the old Mort. 'I didn't study Latin.'

'No. You didn't.' Mort's gaze was direct. And then his eyes dropped to the paper. He set George on the floor, then reached into his waistcoat, took out a gold-plated Montegrappa.

Q watched the precise, looping hand dance across the paper. When he'd finished, Mort pushed the sheet back to him.

SEEK YE FIRST THE KINGDOM OF GOD
THERE YOU SHALL GO TO THE STARS
LET THE BUYER BEWARE
HERE BE LIONS

'What does it mean?' Mort's expression was unreadable.

'Pete was trying to tell me something. To direct me *towards* something. In the event of his death.'

'That's your interpretation.'

'Yes. But I think it's a logical one.'

Mort picked up his tea, then set it down again. 'Do you really want to pursue this?'

'I'm here, aren't I?'

151

'No matter where it takes you? You might find out things you don't want to know.'

'I'm used to it.'

Mort stood up, walked to the fridge, took out a packet of lettuce. Q watched as he emptied the pack into a bowl. George began moving eagerly towards the bowl. As eagerly as a geriatric tortoise could move.

'When Pete came back to Wickstone, did he – did he keep in touch with you?'

'He did.'

A beat. A slither of emotion around his heart. 'Did he ever talk to you about his work?'

'Only in the most oblique terms. Hardly my area of expertise.'

Q thought about discussing his trip to UCL, tracking down what Pete's lab might have been up to, but then changed his mind.

'Let's say you're right,' Mort went on. 'Do you think Pete's cipher was *literally* directing you to something?'

'Yes. Or someone.'

'Seek ye first the kingdom of God.' Mort's face became thoughtful. 'Pete lived and worked in Wickstone. Whatever he wanted to guide you to has to be here . . . The kingdom of God . . .'

'A church?'

'No. That would be too literal. Pete was too smart for that.' Mort's expression changed. 'What is the kingdom of God? Traditional ecumenical interpretation tells us that the "kingdom of God" is God's Christian rule over all creation. The fulfilment of his will on earth. But it can also be equated to the "kingdom of heaven" in Matthew. If we follow that logic through, we can reduce this to simply "heaven".'

'Is there a heaven in Wickstone?'

'No. But there is an Eden.'

*

152

After Q had left, Mort sat at the kitchen table and stared into his tea.

It had gone cold.

The boy's presence had left an imprint in the room, a swirl in the very air. Boy? No. His son was no longer a boy. A major in the army. Head of Q Branch.

Mort wasn't even sure what he should call him. By his name? That seemed too . . . intimate. After all that had happened between them. 'Q' would have to do for now. And Q had lived a whole life, a cloak-and-dagger existence that Mort could not begin to fathom.

Mort had always held a tight grip on his emotions. But now they were dragging him about by the coat-tails. Q's return had been unexpected. Mort didn't know if he should be helping him investigate Pete's death. He was deathly afraid that his own secrets would surface.

But Pete had brought Q back. Mort couldn't let the boy go. Not again.

George nudged his leg. Mort picked the tortoise up and set him on the table.

He hadn't told anyone why he had named the tortoise George. The gang at the library had expected him to give George a grand Roman name. Cicero. Augustus. Caligula.

But George was named after Lonesome George, a Galapagos tortoise who had been the very last of his species, what the naturalists called an 'endling'.

Mort felt an affinity with George. Other than Q, Mort had no living relatives. He and Bella had both been only children. Mort's mother had died a long time ago. His father had been a troubled soul. He had served in the Second World War, discharged following a skirmish in France. A sniper's bullet had taken out a testicle. What sort of war wound was that? You couldn't spin tales of courage out of such an injury. Nurses didn't fall for tortured souls whose claim to heroism was losing a testicle. An eye, yes. An arm, even. But a testicle?

His father had spent the rest of his life furiously embittered.

Mort had been determined to get away from that house, determined to put as much distance – physically and spiritually – between himself and his father.

Who knew better than a historian that history had a tendency to repeat itself?

For thirty years, Mort had lived in the mausoleum of his failed life.

He had lost a wife. He had lost his son.

He was alone. Utterly alone.

In a way, Mort too was the last of his kind.

32

THE NEXT MORNING, Q WIPED the steam from the bathroom mirror, picked up his razor.

He had spent a lifetime working with hi-tech gadgets but some things were best done the old-fashioned way. There was nothing like a hot shave with a good razor. Bond swore by it. As with so many things, Bond was right.

Routine. Human beings liked to pretend that they were spontaneous. Adventurous souls ever ready to leap out of aeroplanes or go off on romantic holidays with sexy Brazilian strangers. But research showed that most people preferred the predictability of an ordered life.

Q missed his routines. What was it Robert Duvall had said in *Apocalypse Now*? Something about enjoying the way explosives smelt in the morning. Well, Q loved the smell of his old life in the morning. And that smell was slowly fading.

He finished shaving, showered, dressed and went downstairs.

He made breakfast, then took it into the garden.

The garden was a metaphor for his life. Out of control, unruly, but with unexpected spots of colour. He smelled mint on the breeze. An early morning bee buzzed by his wicker-and-glass table.

Q relived the meeting with his father.

He was surprised that Mort had let him in the door. Even more surprised that Mort had chosen to help. The old man had mellowed.

Forgiveness. Could Q forgive? Forgiveness could be a deceitful bastard. He surely couldn't forget. Finding his mother overdosed in bed, a drool of foam snaking from her lips. His shouts turning to screams. The call to 999. Sitting there, head in hands, until the paramedics arrived.

He had had good reason to blame Mort, hadn't he? For years, Q had seen his father ignore his mother's obvious needs. She had been bipolar. Q knew that, now. But back then all he saw was a woman who switched from sunshine to storm, a lost soul in need of someone to help her find her way through the dark.

But Mort had chosen to run away. Into his career. Into himself.

And his wife, left alone, had turned to drink. And worse.

A vicious cycle.

Q remembered the funeral. His father hadn't cried. Q, then twenty, had torn into him. Had let him have it. Both barrels. After that, it was all a blur. He had packed his bags and returned to university. Finished his course and enrolled in the army, the Royal Engineers. He had worked on tanks and battlefield armour. By the time he was twenty-two he had been leading teams, a major at twenty-five.

And then MI6 had come calling.

All through those years, a part of Q had remained in that bedroom, holding his dead mother's hand, hating his father with every fibre of his being. Q had surrendered to grief, dragged grief around like the carcass of a dead animal. Fashioned a Greek tragedy of his own making.

But now he was back. Full circle. Back to investigate Pete's death, the son his father had wished he had had. Was that fair? What had fair got to do with anything, anyway?

Self-doubt sauntered out of the shadows, dressed in a long black coat, cigarette in hand, blowing smoke into his face … *Who did Q think he was, anyway?* He was an armourer. A man who

had spent decades employing science in the service of death ...
No. That wasn't right. Q Branch's efforts were dedicated to saving
lives, specifically the lives of MI6's field agents. Q was an *enabler*.
He helped the Double Os to achieve their goals. Need a special
thingy to hack into an unbreakable safe? Talk to Q. Modified
briefcase with concealed weaponry? No problem.

Miss Honeypenny trundled into the garden. 'Q, you have an
appointment at the Horse and Hound Veterinary Clinic at ten a.m.'

Q looked at his watch. 'Thank you, Honeypenny.'

'You're welcome, Q.'

On the way to the vet, Q tried to organise his thoughts.

At Q Branch he had always worked with a notebook and pen,
the notebook a Baron Fig Confidant, the kind with dotted grids
in pale grey. Many Q Branch gadgets had begun life on the
pages of a Baron Fig. Perhaps, hundreds of years from now,
historians would pore over his Leonardo-like doodlings,
murmuring at the genius of inventions that had failed to see the
light of day, cut down by the short-sightedness of civil servants
and the miserliness of government accountants.

Or perhaps not.

Q knew that he was out on a limb. The investigation was
spiralling out of control. Variables swirled around him like
maddened starlings. He was one man, on what amounted to
little more than a personal crusade.

And yet.

Pete's work had set off national security tripwires. His death
remained shrouded in mystery. Q's investigation had triggered
something: shadowy followers were dogging his steps. Who were
they? What were they afraid he would find?

The vet's name was Pru Argyle.

A vigorous presence in a pristine white lab coat with grey
hair and a wedge-shaped chin, Argyle took charge of the

situation with alacrity. 'A depressed dog. Commoner than you'd think. Let's have a look at you, boy.'

Q watched as Bastard was picked up and set down on a padded bench. Bastard seemed as interested in proceedings as a dead sloth.

Q's thoughts were still with Mort. And Mort's interpretation of Pete's riddle. Q had no idea why Pete would want to send him a riddle, but that was Pete. Always trying to show everyone how clever he was.

Only ... Something lay below the words in Pete's letter. A darker edge.

And then Pete had died.

He realised that the vet was speaking. 'Depression in dogs isn't so different from depression in people. They become withdrawn, inactive. They stop eating—'

'There's nothing wrong with his appetite.'

'*Or* they overeat. Like humans. The most common reason for this sort of thing is the loss of a beloved owner.'

'He *has* lost his owner. But I don't think he was beloved. In fact, I think he mistreated him.'

A frown. 'I know a lot of the dog owners in Wickstone. I don't think this animal has been here before.'

'I would be surprised if he had.'

'What did you say his name was?'

'Bastard.'

The vet raised an eyebrow. 'I suppose you think that's funny?'

'No. I— It was just something his previous owner called him ... It's not as if he knows what it means.'

'But *you* know what it means. Would you name your child that?'

Q opened his mouth, then closed it again.

Argyle turned away. 'I'd like to run a full battery of tests on him. Rule out any physical issues. Leave him with me.'

33

BOB PARKED OUTSIDE THE WICKSTONE Autoshop, then walked across the road.

Mechanics in blue overalls went about their business looking highly professional. He noted, approvingly, that there was at least one woman among the men.

Back in the day, Bob had fancied himself a bit of a grease monkey. Knew his way around an engine. The old sort. When cars were cars. Not these electric jobbies that were basically batteries on wheels.

He collared a young man with so much grease on his face he looked like a soldier in camouflage. 'Is Tony around?'

'In the office.'

Bob's meeting with Zak had been a bust. The boy had refused to divulge anything further. Had clammed up. The kid seemed nervous. It didn't take long for Bob to discover that Zak had been paid a visit by his employer.

Bob found Tony squinting at a computer screen in his office, a cup of coffee cooling at his elbow. Tony's pitted skull glinted in the overhead light. His crumpled face looked like it had done ten rounds with a forklift truck. Then again, it had looked like that as long as Bob had known him.

Word on the street was that Tony was now called Medium Tony. When Bob had first moved to Wickstone, Tony had styled himself Big Tony. Time had a way of cutting everyone down to size.

'Tone.'

'Bob.'

Tony leaned back in his seat. If he was surprised to see Bob, he didn't show it. 'What can I do for you?'

'A little bird tells me you paid young Zak a visit. At l'hôpital. That's French for hospital.'

'He's my employee. I went to see how he was doing.'

'And by employee you mean he's out stealing cars for you.'

'Zak is an apprentice at the Wickstone Autoshop. What he does in his own time is none of my business.'

'So you didn't send him out to boost Pete Napier's Bentley?'

'No idea what you're talking about. Nary a clue. Cup of coffee?'

'No. Thank you.'

Bob's eyes wandered around the cramped office. On the bulletin board behind Tony was a family photograph. Tony and his wife and their two kids. All wearing sombreros. Tony had still had hair when the photo had been taken. Great big curly mullet, by the looks of it. How the mighty fall.

Bob thought of his own boys. Good lads. Both in their thirties. One was working in Kazakhstan, teaching English to locals. Apparently, Kazakhstan was now oil rich. Not that his son was trousering any of that oil cash. Poor sod was barely making ends meet.

Kazakhstan.

Bob had had to look the place up on a map.

His other son had married a Bolivian shell artist and moved out to La Paz. Life was amazing. Who would have thought Bob would have a gay son? Bob was proud of the fact that he was proud of his son. Proud of both his sons. When Rory had come out, Bob had seen the terror in his son's eyes. In that instant, Bob had known what to do. He hadn't said a word. Simply grabbed his son and held on to him, felt the tension melt out of Rory's body.

That's what Lorna had taught Bob. That love, in its purest form, could cut through anything. Through hate, anger, prejudice. And there was nothing greater than love for your family. Family was everything.

Bob only wished that his sons would visit more often. But, then, neither of the boys were financially in a position to keep hopping back to the UK every five minutes. A good thing their old man was willing to put his hand in his pocket.

'These people you work for. They wouldn't happen to know anything about Pete Napier's death?'

'I don't work for anyone but myself, Bob.'

'Zak seems to think he knows something about it. That perhaps Pete didn't die of natural causes.'

'Misadventure isn't a natural cause, last I checked.'

'So you wouldn't know what Zak might be trying to tell us?'

'Kid's taken a knock to the head, Bob. Wouldn't trust anything the poor sod had to say, if I were you.'

Bob smiled. 'Lorna says I'm a people pleaser. Would you say I'm a people pleaser, Tone?'

'No harm in going about your job with a song in your heart, Bob. That's what I do.'

'Live and let live, is that it? The French have a word for that too. Lay-zay fair.'

'That's two words, Bob.'

'So it is. You dazzle me with your glory, old son.' Bob got to his feet. 'It's getting to be a war zone out there, Tone.'

'It's always been a war zone, Bob. Just a different kind of war now.'

Bob sat in his car and looked back across the road.

When he had first arrived in Wickstone, Tony's garage had been long established, handed down from father to son. But there had been no word that it was involved in unsavoury activities. It was only later that intel emerged to suggest that it was a chop shop. That's what an influx of wealth did.

Crime followed the money.

Bob wondered how much choice Tony had had in it all. In his experience, when the wrong elements made a man like Tony an offer of employment, it was the sort of offer a sensible man couldn't refuse. Not if he wanted to keep his brains where nature intended, instead of splattered across the nearest wall. If you wanted to get philosophical, you might even say Tony couldn't be held to account for his actions.

Then again.

Bob was certain Tony had just lied to him. Something tied Zak to Pete Napier's death. Maybe the boy wasn't full of it, after all.

Bob put the car in gear and pulled out into the road.

34

A S BUILDINGS WENT, IT WAS a statement to taste and subtlety.

As in: a complete lack of taste and a two-fingered salute to subtlety.

Q stood in front of the Seven Stars car dealership, housed on a retail estate on the edge of Wickstone-on-Water. The retail estate was named Eden Park.

Eden. Heaven.

Seek ye first the kingdom of heaven.

The dealership – like the retail park itself – was barely two years old. An imperious vision of glass and gold panelling. Bold lines. Bolder signage in a font size that was probably visible from outer space. A bright red sports car crouched on the roof, just in case the rows of sparkling cars out front and the eight-feet-high sandwich boards positioned every few metres failed to alert the casual onlooker as to the precise nature of the business.

The Seven Stars car emporium.

There you shall go to the stars.

This was what Mort had worked out the evening before.

The Seven Stars showroom on the Eden Park shopping estate.

A little local knowledge went a long way.

As for the last two lines of the riddle – *Let the buyer beware* and *Here be lions* – you didn't need to be a rocket scientist to work out what those meant.

It just so happened that Q *was* a rocket scientist. Of sorts. He had taken one module on aerospace engineering back at university. The course hadn't turned out to be as sexy as he had hoped. And the tutor had been a crashing bore, delivering his lectures with all the verve of a depressed gameshow host. But the work had proved useful later on when Q Branch had been tasked to tinker with vehicles for the Double Os. It was amazing the uses you could find for rocket-fuelled propulsion.

Let the buyer beware held a double meaning. A car dealership? Of course, the buyer should beware. But Pete had also been suggesting that there was something here to be wary *of*. And the final line confirmed it. *Here be lions.*

Why had Pete sent Q here?

No doubt, the answer would become self-evident.

He walked through the front doors into a climate-controlled paradise. Blinding white walls. Shiny floor tiles. Potted palm trees. Several luxury car models were displayed on stands, gleaming so violently Q wished he was wearing sunglasses.

He saw sales booths, immaculately dressed salespeople waiting for customers or talking to potential car buyers.

Q made his way to a counter. A beautiful young woman smiled at him. Her smile made him think of world peace.

'Could you tell me who runs this place?'

The woman's perfect brow crumpled. An unusual question. But she didn't let it faze her. Good for her. 'That would be Mr Gashi. Adem Gashi.'

'Is he here?'

'Yes. Do you have an appointment?'

'No. But I'm certain he will want to see me. Please tell him I'm an old friend of Peter Napier.'

164

The confused look vanished. She now had a mission. Her purpose in the grand scheme of things was validated. She picked up the phone and made a call.

Several minutes later, Q was directed through the sales deck to an office at the rear.

He entered to find a youngish man – early to mid-thirties – in a pastel pink suit and bright white shirt – no tie – standing in front of a desk the size of a snooker table. Middling height, with dark hair, gelled back, designer stubble and a single earing. Several gold chains graced a muscular neck. The shirt was open almost to the navel revealing an expanse of waxed chest. Beside him stood a woman – a little older – immaculately outfitted in a charcoal suit with faint pinstripes. The woman was striking, Q thought, dark-haired and dark-eyed. She held herself with a poise that he recognised as a sign of self-confidence and competence. She reminded him of Moneypenny.

The man held out a hand. 'Mr Boothroyd, was it? I'm Adem. Reception said you knew Pete Napier?'

'I did. We grew up together. I have some questions about his death. I wonder if you have a moment to chat?'

'Sure. Anything for a friend of Pete's. Though I have no idea what I can tell you. His death was a tragedy. We're still getting our heads around it.' Q caught a whiff of cologne. Something floral. He could sense the man's unease. The mere fact that Adem had entertained him, a stranger walking in off the street, asking questions about a dead man, spoke volumes.

Or perhaps he was just being solicitous.

'Adem.' The woman had spoken. 'Can we speak in private?'

'I'll take care of this, Debs. Why don't you get back to work?'

Q saw a sudden fury in the woman's eyes. Not that Adem noticed. He had already turned away, walked around the desk and dropped into an enormous leather captain's chair.

The woman looked as if she might argue. And then she nodded and left.

Q took a seat in front of the desk. 'Nice set-up you have here. I take it you're quite new?'

'We've been around a couple of years.'

'Strange place to site a luxury car showroom. A small town like Wickstone.'

'Wickstone is growing. A lot of professional couples are moving out here. Cash to burn. Austerity is over. People are enjoying life again.'

'Those who can afford it.'

He grinned. 'Life isn't fair. Some people drive Bentleys. Some people drive ... whatever it is they drive.'

'What do you drive?'

'A Lambo.'

Q knew that you could tell a lot about a man by the car he drove. For instance, you could tell if he was an idiot. A man driving around in a Lamborghini in Wickstone? Might as well put a big sign around your neck.

'How did you know Pete?'

'We have a contract with Napier Labs. We lease cars to their staff. Sell a few. Pete was one of our first customers. Got the business off to a flyer. Pete loved his cars.' He reached out to an intercom. 'Would you like something to drink? A snack? Honeyed peanuts? Very good for cholesterol.'

'No. Thank you.'

Adem pressed the button, ordered a soy milk latte with a sprinkling of hazelnut dust.

Q picked at a perfect crease in his trousers. 'You said you knew Pete?'

'We spent some time together. He grew up here. But you knew that. When I set up my operation, he offered to show me the sights. That took all of five minutes.' A burst of violent laughter. Once again Q had the sense the younger man was agitated and trying to hide it. Other questions surfaced. Wickstone *was* a small town but why would Pete have gone out of his way to be on friendly terms with a car dealer? One thing of which he was now certain: he had solved the riddle correctly. He was in the right place. But *why* had Pete sent him here?

'The Pete I grew up with would never have drowned. Would never have put himself in that position.'

'I can see why you would think that. The guy loved life. I mean, no one who drives a Bentley wants to kill themselves. Am I right?'

Q had read about the Bentley in the inventory list of Pete's home affixed to the back of the police report into his death. Q had more than a passing acquaintance with the Bentley range. Bond was a fan, more so after Q had gadget-loaded various models. Q found it irksome how Bond kept comparing the car to a woman. Q would like to see a woman who could unveil machine guns from her front headlights and blitz through a gang of international villains.

'What do *you* drive?' asked Adem.

'A Caterham.'

'Never heard of it. If you fancy trading up, I've got a great deal on a BMW X3. Careless Whisper pink. Great specs. Plenty of boot space.'

'No. Thank you.' Q hesitated. Play his hand or not?

'Mr Gashi—'

'Adem, please.'

'Before he died Pete sent me a note, directing me here in the event of his death. To this showroom. To you. Can you think why?'

The younger man seemed to freeze in his seat. The door opened and a woman came in with a cup. Adem took it and set it down on the desk. The woman left. The interruption had given him time to regroup. 'No idea. What sort of note?'

'Pete knew he was in danger. He pretty much predicted his own death.'

A tongue emerged, touched the man's bottom lip, then went back in. 'He never said anything to me.'

'When was the last time you saw him?'

'I don't know. Maybe a few days before he died. We went out for a drink.'

'Do you usually go out for drinks with your customers?'

'Wickstone is a small place. Not much to do. Pete and I got on. You might say we were friends.'

'And he gave no indication that he was upset?'

'Nope. I mean he was stressed about his work. But who isn't? Am I right?'

'Any personal issues on his mind?'

'Well, he wasn't too happy with his ex. And he didn't get to see his kid that often. Between you and me, his ex was a bit of a bunny-boiler. Turned his kid against him.'

'Pete said that?'

'Not in so many words. But you know the drill. Man meets woman. Woman turns out to be raging psycho. Man gets shafted.'

Despite Adem's discomfort – and unembarrassed misogyny – Q couldn't see any obvious reason why Pete had directed him to the man's showroom. What was he missing? *Here be lions.* 'Did Pete discuss his work with you? What he was doing at his lab?'

Adem blinked rapidly, then picked up a snow globe from the desk. Q could see a miniature giraffe inside the globe. 'I sell cars, Mr Boothroyd. I'm no scientist. All that computing stuff: way over my head.' He attempted a disarming grin, but his eyes remained on the snow globe. 'Are you working with the cops?'

Odd question. 'No. Why?'

Adem set down the object. 'Look, I get it. If I turned up dead, I'd want a mate to check it was all kosher. But in Pete's case I think we can safely say the man had his demons.'

Could we safely say that? Q didn't think so. 'I don't think Pete killed himself, if that's what you mean. I think he was murdered. And for some reason he sent me *here*.'

A frown. 'I'm not sure I like what you're implying.'

Q stood up. 'Thank you for your help.'

'That's it?'

'For now.'

Adem rose slowly to his feet. The smile was gone. Something about the set of the shoulders. Adem exuded strength. He clearly spent a lot of time in the gym. Beneath the linen jacket and the absurd shirt, his frame was muscular. Adem could easily have manhandled Pete into the river. The thought struggled to take off, like a flightless bird.

What motive could Adem possibly have to harm Pete?

Q saw that the man was quietly reassessing him.

'What is it you said you did?' said Adem.

'I didn't.'

Q stopped beside the Caterham, checked his phone.

No messages. He had been hoping Kathy might call.

The sun was high and the day handsome. Clouds made sheep-like shapes in a blue vault. The air shimmered. Around him cars drove into and out of the shopping estate. For an instant, his mind superimposed the Wickstone he had left thirty years ago onto this latter-day version. A growing town where a man could drive around in a Lamborghini and not feel like a complete moron.

'Caterham Seven. 620R. Supercharger, three hundred and ten bhp? I see you've opted for the large chassis.'

Q turned to see the woman that Adem had dismissed from his office standing behind him, unpeeling the wrapper on a pack of cigarettes.

'You know your cars.'

'You'd hope so.' She nodded at the showroom at her back. A couple were emerging, a sales rep with an arm parked around the shoulders of a dazed-looking older man in tweed. 'Did you get what you were looking for? From Adem.'

Q wasn't sure how to respond. 'I didn't catch your name.'

'Deborah. Debs to my friends.'

'And what do you do here?'

'I'm the general manager.'

'You work for Adem.'

Her jaw writhed. 'Yes.'

'Did you know Pete Napier?'

'Not personally. He was a customer. A very important customer. So, yes, in that sense, I knew him.'

'Did you ever meet him?'

'A few times.'

'Just before his death?'

'A couple of weeks before.'

'What did you meet about?'

'We were discussing Napier Labs' vehicle leasing contract. It was up for renewal. Standard client meeting.'

'Did Pete talk about his work? At Napier Labs.'

'In passing. But he couldn't go into details. It was all hush-hush.'

'Yes,' said Q. 'Did he seem ... agitated?'

She took out a cigarette, flamed it with a lighter. 'That's a loaded question. Are you saying you think Pete's death might not have been an accident? That he might have jumped in the river deliberately?'

'Is that what you think happened?'

'Well, he didn't walk in here wearing a T-shirt saying I NEED HELP ... He was a strange guy. Only really engaged when he was talking about science. Didn't read people well. Nerdy.'

Q frowned.

'Don't get me wrong. I like a nerd. The right kind of nerd. But Pete always seemed a little on edge. He didn't really get it. Watching him interact with regular human beings was like trying to watch a politician do the robot dance.'

'I'm sure he'd appreciate that character assessment.'

'Sorry. I thought you wanted an honest answer.'

Q hesitated, continued to hold her gaze. 'I think Pete was murdered.'

She blew smoke sideways out of her mouth, looked at him coolly. 'Sometimes we don't want to look at what's staring us in the face. Especially when those we love are involved.'

Had he loved Pete? Hard to say. But there had been something. An esprit de corps. Down there in the trenches of adolescent angst. Of all the people he had known, Pete had understood him best. But had Q ever really understood Pete?

That was the problem with genius. What was it F. Scott Fitzgerald had said? *Show me a hero and I'll write you a tragedy.*

Pete had been a hero. Of sorts. A hero of the new world order, where tech titans manipulated the future on a daily basis and held prince and pauper alike in the palms of their hands. If Pete had survived, Q had no doubt that Napier Labs would have made him a power player in the global technocracy. He would soon have been rubbing shoulders with the likes of Elon Musk and Mark Zuckerberg. What would Pete have done with that power?

More importantly, what would others have done to stop him achieving such power?

35

YOU TRIED TO SHUT OUT the thoughts. The feelings.
It was like trying to push the door closed on raging floodwaters.

Kathy's thoughts were with Q.

Last night she had had to physically stop herself from phoning him. From storming round and asking him what the hell he thought he was doing. Turning up here. Acting the amateur sleuth. Setting off uncomfortable memories, grenades going off inside her skull.

And had he apologised? For the way he had left things between them, thirty years ago? The wreckage he had left behind?

Had he bollocks.

The worst of it was that he now had her second-guessing herself.

Kathy had spent the morning reviewing the investigation into Pete Napier's death. Truth be told, it was still fresh in her memory. She had had doubts, to be sure, but not enough for her to make a crusade of it. But now, Q's analysis at the pub had made her twitchy. His belief that something had been missed.

Confirmation bias. That was the snake every detective was taught to watch out for, lying there in the long grass of your own ambition. With a verdict of misadventure laid down by the coroner, they had had little incentive to look for an alternative. Take the win. Notch another solved on the monthly stats board.

And Pete's colleagues at Napier Labs had been less than helpful. Bunch of arseholes, smarming around like God's gift to science.

Something rankled. Kathy just wished she knew what.

A shadow loomed over her. The new detective constable, Kieran Curtis, set a mug on the desk, then stepped back. 'The French press isn't working. I made it myself.'

She realised he was waiting for her to taste it, like a *MasterChef* contestant. For heaven's sake.

Three months ago, when the previous detective inspector had handed in his notice, Kathy had asked her superiors for a replacement. The rising crime rate in Wickstone-on-Water meant that the detective squad – namely, her and Bob, aided by a brace of uniformed foot soldiers – was struggling to keep pace. In response, she had been sent Kieran, a ginger-haired, newly minted detective *constable* who looked not much older than Kathy's own son.

But a detective, no matter how green, wasn't the sort of gift you could send back.

She picked up the coffee, gulped a mouthful. 'Mmm hmm.' Kathy gave him a thumbs up. What she wanted to say was that it tasted as if it had been filtered through a tramp's underwear. The young constable sagged with relief then went back to his desk.

The door opened and Bob walked in. Kathy watched him shrug off his jacket then collapse into his seat. Saddlebags of sweat radiated from under his armpits. 'Well, that could have gone better.'

'I take it Zak wasn't beguiled by the old Bob magic?'

'Beguiled. Nice word. I'll have to use it more in everyday convo.' Bob scratched his chin. 'Wasn't entirely a waste of time. Guess who came to see little Zak? Got past the lad on the door. Beguiled him, if you will.'

'Boris Johnson? Taylor Swift?'

'Tony. AKA Medium Tony. So guess who went to see Tony?'

'Roger Federer? The Pope?'

'Yours truly. Something definitely smells.'

'Yes, you could do with a change of shirt.'

Bob lifted his armpit, inhaled. 'Sorry . . . At any rate, I don't know what Zak knows but I'm sure he knows something. And that something he knows has something to do with Tony. Which means it has something to do with Tony's backers. Employers. Call them what you will.'

'The Albanians.'

'You said it, not me.' Bob looked across the room. 'I could murder a coffee, son.'

Detective Constable Curtis sprang up from his seat. 'Roger, sarge.'

Kathy watched him sprint off towards the kitchen. 'You know he's not here to make our coffee, don't you?'

'I suppose you made *that* yourself.'

She picked up her mug and passed it across the desk. 'Be my guest.'

Bob raised an eyebrow, reached out, lifted the coffee to his mouth. Kathy savoured the look on his face. 'The French press is on the fritz.'

'God. Don't tell me we're at the mercy of instant.'

Kathy's phone buzzed. She listened to the call, then stiffened. 'He's downstairs.'

'Who is?'

'Q.'

36

ADEM'S SMILE HAD VANISHED AS soon as the door
had closed.

Mirko's face hovered before him. Why hadn't he
listened to his uncle? Why had he let Boothroyd in the door?

He felt a sweat coming on.

As a rule, he didn't sweat. Mind over matter. It wasn't that difficult. Buddhist monks did it. And certain princes. Air-conditioning
helped, of course. In his office. His car. His home.

Home. The word was getting blurred somewhere inside his
head. For the past two years, Wickstone had been home. But
he was a Londoner born and bred. You could take the boy out
of London, but you couldn't make him feel truly at home in the
arse-end of nowhere. He'd put a brave face on it. It had been
an honour, after all. Being sent out here, given the responsibility
to break new ground. He had been asking for it long enough.

And everything had gone swimmingly. At first.

The dealership – his own idea – had done well, better than
he could have hoped. Not that that mattered. That wasn't why
he was here. The dealership was a front, a base of operations.
But Wickstone represented so much more. A stepping stone to
bigger and better things.

Such as Pete Napier.

That side of the operation had gone well, too. Until Pete had— Well, until Pete had died. Adem had almost lost it then. The investigation. The panic. The feeling that, sooner or later, someone would end up on his doorstep with an arrest warrant and a pair of handcuffs.

Growing up, Adem had always been insulated from the ongoing police interest in his family. Yes, he had cursed the cops like everyone else, spat whenever they were mentioned, but it had always been from a distance. A game.

When the coroner had made his ruling, Adem had breathed a huge sigh of relief. Pete's death was to be ruled an accident. End of. No more investigation. No more awkward questions.

And now here was this guy. Boothroyd. An old friend. Supposedly.

Adem thought about calling his uncle. But Mirko wouldn't be pleased that Adem had spoken with Boothroyd. Particularly when Mirko had specifically told him not to.

Ostensibly, the old man was semi-retired. Not exactly one foot in the grave but definitely tiptoeing around it. Grave adjacent. Mirko didn't want any waves around the Wickstone operation. If Mirko sensed Adem couldn't keep a lid on things, he would pass his concerns on to Papa John.

Adem didn't need Papa John turning up in Wickstone to handle matters. Papa John's method of handling matters usually involved kneecapping someone. Problem with the Amazon delivery guy? Kneecap him. Doctor's receptionist being a bit arsey? Kneecap her.

The man was a dinosaur. No subtlety.

Where did it say that just because you were a gangster, you had to act like one? It was the 2020s, for Christ's sake. Gangsters were reading poetry, sponsoring book festivals ... OK. So Adem didn't *personally* know any gangsters who did that, but there had to be some out there.

Adem had never thought of himself as a gangster. Yes, he had been born into a family of gangsters, but that didn't automatically make him one. He had studied business at college. Or at least, he had attended two weeks of college where he had notionally been enrolled on a business studies course. Adem thought of himself as an entrepreneur. A market maker. An ideas man.

But this new complication had rattled him. Who did this Boothroyd think he was, walking in and bracing Adem with his questions? Nice tie, though. Adem appreciated good dressing in a man.

A fresh wave of panic scalded his skin.

Adem had never been good at this. Dealing with guilt. Dealing with the consequences of his family's actions. It was the side of the family business he disliked the most. Adem's dream was the dream of Al Pacino in *The Godfather Part III*. Everyone said the film was crap, but that's because they didn't understand its message. Al Pacino's dream had been to go legit. Completely legit. Bring the family out of the shadows and into the light. Adem had been trying to get Mirko to watch the film for ages. But Mirko was too steeped in the old ways. If you couldn't shoot it or bribe it he didn't want to know.

Somehow his uncle had agreed to the Wickstone venture. A way of expanding the family's business horizons – in more ways than one. And, for a while, it had seemed it might work.

But now, with Pete Napier's death, it was all threatening to go sideways. And then downwards, like the *Titanic*.

Guilt gave his heart a friendly squeeze, closely followed by Panic, grabbing him by the proverbials and giving a good hard yank. Leering at him.

Adem wouldn't go to prison, not for this. He *couldn't*. Just imagine what those tattooed brutes would do to a guy like him. With his waxed pecs and moisturised skin? It didn't bear thinking about it. Which only made him think about it more.

No. He had to nip this in the bud.

He was suddenly conscious of the fact that his shirt was soaked through with sweat.

He wasn't cut out for this. Never had been.

Why were people so bad at facing the truth about themselves? Years of desperation rose inside him, years of knowing that he was living the wrong life. All those nights, listening to whispers in the dark. *You have nothing to prove to these people. They can't be your real family. You must have been adopted.* Doubt, working its way in like smoke.

Adem knew that he suffered – had always suffered – from that virulent disease few in his family had ever been afflicted by: a sense of right and wrong. He was a man nailed to the cross of his own inheritance. A greengrocer who didn't believe in vegetables. For as long as he could remember, he had wanted to walk out the door and never look back. Wake up a new man.

Fear had held him back. Fear of the unknown. Fear of consequences.

But now, a new terror was pushing him towards the cliff.

The terror of being found out. By Mirko. By Boothroyd. By the cops.

And yet ... there *was* a way out. Pete had shown him the exit from the maze. That last meeting. Just before he had died.

You can do this, Ade.

Ah, Pete.

In truth, Pete had only put into words the same solution Adem had considered for so very long; an idea never to be voiced, let alone acted upon. A permanent remedy to his predicament. A move that would get him out from under, once and for all.

Every day since Pete's death he had moved closer and closer to the point of no return.

It was time to step over the line.

For once in his life, he was going to put himself first.

Adem picked up the phone.

37

SITTING AROUND THE TABLE WITH Bob and Kathy, Q
was reminded of the finale from the classic western, *The
Good, the Bad, and the Ugly*. The three main characters
eyeballing one another, silently committed to a shootout to the
death . . . What did the Americans say? Never mix business with
pleasure. Not that this was strictly business. And it certainly
wasn't pleasure, judging by Kathy's less-than-enthusiastic response
to Q's summary of his recent activities.

'You did what?'

'I went through your investigation reports into Pete's death,'
Q repeated. 'I think the coroner was wrong. I think Pete was
murdered.'

Bob coughed into the silence. 'And how exactly did you get
hold of said reports?'

'I procured them.'

Bob looked at Kathy. Spots of red floated on Kathy's cheeks.

'The point is that Pete's death left behind unanswered questions.'

'Such as?'

'Do you know what Pete was doing at Napier Labs?'

'Building some sort of fancy computer,' said Bob. 'Bit over
my head.'

'A *very* fancy computer. One so powerful that it will change the world. Pete was working on capabilities that triggered a national security alert. *That* made him a target.'

'A target for who?'

Q hesitated. 'Dark forces. Bad actors.'

'Bad actors.' Kathy's voice was so cold it could have had liquid nitrogen asking for an overcoat.

'That's all I can say for now.'

'Well, blow me down,' said Bob. 'Poirot's only gone and solved it. Dark forces, you say? Why didn't we think of that?'

'There are other questions. Why did Pete take his clothes off at the jetty? If it was an accident, why undress?'

'You think he jumped in of his own accord?'

'No. Again, if he was going to kill himself, why undress? Why not just jump straight in?'

'People who kill themselves aren't usually thinking straight,' said Kathy. 'Besides. If he *was* murdered, why would his murderer have forced him to undress?'

'I don't know ... And what about Pete's drug taking? Where did he get the cocaine? How did he pay for it? There's nothing in his bank records.'

Kathy hesitated. This was something that had bothered her too. But she couldn't let Q have the win. 'We have a significant county lines operation here. Drugs aren't difficult to get hold of. And with the stresses Pete was under, it's no surprise he was snorting.'

'You didn't think it was worth finding out who supplied him?'

'What would that prove? You think he went out to Bishop's Point to buy drugs? That his dealer made Pete take off his clothes, then shoved him into the river? Why would he do that?'

'Criminals aren't exactly rational actors. Maybe they had a disagreement. Maybe they were stoned out of their heads.'

'He'd have to be pretty stoned to force Pete to take off his clothes.'

Q felt his wheels spinning. Kathy wasn't giving him an inch. He wondered how much of that was because of their past. 'I worked out the cipher in Pete's note. It led me to the Seven Stars car dealership, here in town. A guy called Adem Gashi runs it. He knew Pete. Leased – and sold – him cars.'

Bob straightened in his seat, glanced at Kathy. Q caught the look. 'You know him, don't you?'

Bob spoke first. 'I've been in the dealership a few times, getting the lay of the land. We believe Gashi has ties to the Albanian mob.'

'Bob.' Kathy's eyes were broadcasting the words *shut up*. In neon.

'He'll find out anyway,' said Bob. 'With his Secret Service magic wand.'

'Gashi claims he knows nothing about Pete's death. But Pete wouldn't have sent me to him if there wasn't some connection.'

'You're a civilian,' said Kathy. 'You can't go around accosting other civilians.'

Q had had enough. 'Look, I get it. No one likes to be told they did a shoddy job. But this isn't about you. It's about Pete.'

'Shoddy's a bit strong,' said Bob, mildly.

Q was spared from hearing what Kathy thought of his assessment of her work by her phone going off. She frowned at it, then answered as she got to her feet. 'Yes, sir.'

They watched her walk away.

'Saved by the bell,' said Bob. He raised an eyebrow. 'Brave call, that. Telling Kathy her work wasn't up to snuff. She tells me you were engaged, once upon a time. That you dumped her, practically at the altar. You must have bollocks the size of Bournemouth.'

'I meant no offence.'

'None taken. Speaking for myself.'

'Something isn't right. Pete brought me here. I'm not leaving until I've satisfied myself that I've done all I can.'

'Fair enough. A man has to stand by his convictions, or what's the point?' He scratched his jaw. 'Trouble is we haven't got anything in the way of leads. Other than—' He stopped.

'Other than?'

'Well, there's a local kid. Syrian immigrant. Zakaria Youssef. Zak. Stole Napier's Bentley. Crashed it into a church, if you can believe that. We've got him in the hospital. He initially claimed he knew something about Napier's death. Wouldn't tell us exactly what until he got a "deal". And then he went cold on the idea. Clammed up.'

'I'd like to talk to him.'

'What makes you think he'll talk to you?'

Q considered the problem. 'Does he have family here?'

'A mother. Sameera. Runs a local bakery.'

Bob was whistling as he nosed the BMW along the high street.

Q didn't know what the tune was. Arctic Monkeys, maybe. His colleagues at MI6 had always assumed he was a classical music connoisseur. Q could tell a sonata from an oratorio as well as the next man, but his musical tastes ran to strong lyrics and acoustic guitar solos. Years ago, he had bought a Yamaha fashioned from African mahogany. He had no idea if the African mahogany made a difference to the sound the guitar made, but it certainly couldn't resolve the problem of his eight-thumbed lack of talent.

'So. What exactly did you do at MI6?'

'I was the quartermaster.'

'Quartermaster. There's a word you don't hear much, nowadays. Like barnacle. Or rapscallion.'

Q said nothing.

'Must have been exciting. Mixing it up with secret agents and the like. What do you call them, again? Fancy word. Spooks?'

Had it been exciting? Q couldn't deny that. Being at the heart of MI6, the first to know the secret dangers of the world, a part to play in mitigating them. Even if no one but a select few would ever know.

But there were the other times too. When things went bad. Missions that blew up.

Q remembered attending the funerals of field agents. Closed doors and, more often than not, closed caskets. Coffins draped in the flag. Men and women he had worked with. Some dead because Q Branch's tech had failed them in the moment of truth.

Q carried that guilt around with him. There was no one else to give it to.

Bond had told him to shrug it off. Guilt was pointless, a drag. Q wasn't sure that Bond believed that. He had seen the man go through the wringer. Time and again. Bond took each loss personally. The cavalier façade kept him from drowning.

Bond's problem wasn't that he didn't care.

Bond's problem was that he cared too much.

'You really think Pete was the victim of foul play?' said Bob. 'I do.'

'Always wanted to say that out loud. Victim of foul play. Very Agatha Christie ... Sorry about that Poirot crack earlier.'

'Why are you helping me?'

'We want to know what Zak knows. Or what he thinks he knows. Personally, I think he's full of it. But just in case he isn't, maybe you can get him to open up.'

Q looked out of the window as they moved past his old school. Like everything else, it had changed. Ugly prefab buildings crowded the playground. He remembered the lonely classrooms, the cabbage-smelling canteen, the rugby fields out back. Cross country runs in the freezing cold, his squad of fellow losers bringing up the rear: Travis, with his constantly running nose; Glenn, who crab-ran, bent double as if hauling a fridge on his back. His friends. Not really his friends.

Strange thing, memory. They said it played tricks on you; but the truth was that life played tricks on the past. Distorted what you thought you knew, twisted history into strange shapes, made you reassess every decision, every act, in the light of self-revelation.

In his head, Q had *escaped* Wickstone.

But the truth was that he had run away.

38

THE TINKLE OF THE FRONT door chime alerted Sameera to an arriving customer.

She wiped her hands on her apron and walked out onto the shop floor.

Two men stood at the counter: Detective Sergeant Bob and a well-dressed stranger. A knot of fear settled inside her chest. *Be brave, Sameera.*

Behind the two men, she saw Mrs Bainbridge sitting at a table with a cup of tea and a slice of tamari kaak, a sandwich bread filled with grape molasses, tahini and mashed banana.

Mrs Bainbridge was a regular at the bakery. 'My father was in the war,' the stout old woman had told her. 'Used to say that he fought for an ideal. Fought against hate and prejudice.' Mrs Bainbridge had patted Sameera's hand. 'There are many instruments in God's orchestra and no symphony without each and every one.'

Mrs Bainbridge reminded Sameera of her late mother, bombed flat while visiting relatives in Darat Izza in north-west Syria. Mrs Bainbridge had told her about her own mother who, if Mrs Bainbridge was to be believed, had danced her way through the Blitz.

Humour. The British had a wonderful way of using humour to deflect horror.

'Sam,' said Bob, 'how goes it, love?'

'It goes fine, Detective Sergeant Bob.'

'Got someone here, wants to have a word.'

The man introduced himself. 'Pete Napier was a close friend. I'd like to talk to you about your son. What he may know about Pete's death.'

'Boothroyd,' echoed Sameera. 'Are you related to Mister Mortimer?'

'He's my father.'

Her eyes flicked over to Bob. 'Is he working for the police?'

'No. He's nothing to do with us.'

'Mrs Youssef. All I am asking is that you hear me out. I think I can help your son.'

Doubt buzzed in her ear. 'Very well. But I will speak only to you. I am sorry, Detective Sergeant Bob. But my son must come first.'

'Perfectly understandable. I'll stay here. Maybe check out some of this bread.'

Sameera turned and led Q through a tiny kitchen and into an even smaller room at the rear of the premises.

'Would you like some water?'

'No, thank you,' said Q.

The woman looked haggard. Dark hair pulled back beneath a headscarf, a touch of white that looked like flour. She wore a yellow apron with the legend: BAKING IS MY SUPERPOWER. There was a vulnerability to her that made Q hesitate. But beneath it he saw steel.

Sameera leaned against the wall and considered the man before her. A menu, partly covered in flour, was pinned to the corkboard behind him.

Damascus Delight. The name had been her own idea. A way of tethering her new home to her old . . . *Ah, Hassan! What would you think of your Sameera now? Alone in a land you spoke of so fondly, a land you promised to take me to so often but never found the time. And then time ran out. On us both.*

A lump swelled her throat. But tears were not the answer. She had to be strong. For Zak. For herself.

Sameera knew that she was losing her son.

Was she a bad mother? She had suspected that Zak wasn't fitting in. His troubles at school. His lack of friends. The fights. The attitude. She had seen that he was hurting. A boy who thought he was a man. Perhaps she should have refused to give her blessing when he told her that he wanted to leave school and join a local garage as an apprentice.

But Sameera had long ago passed the stage of what ifs. *What if* Hassan was here? *What if* Hassan hadn't gone with the men who had come to take him that day? *What if* she hadn't said the things she had said?

But fate rarely made compromises, and Death came unannounced.

And when you had lost almost everything, you became even more protective of the little you had left. If only she had managed to convince Zak to leave the garage, once she began to hear rumours of what really went on there! What Zak might really be doing there.

Each time she thought of it, it filled her with dread. The sort of dread she remembered from the dark days before they had left Syria. When she had felt trapped by her own knowledge of what was to come. A storm, like the great dust tempests that rode in from the desert, consuming everything in their path.

'Pete and I grew up together,' said Q. 'Here, in Wickstone. He wrote to me just before he died. He was afraid. I don't believe that his death was an accident. I'd like to talk to Zak. I don't care that he stole Pete's car. I don't care what else he has or hasn't done. And I don't think he had anything to do with whatever happened to Pete. But he's told the police that he knows something. I need to know what he knows.'

'Why didn't you go with Detective Sergeant Bob to the hospital? Why did you come here?'

'Because the only person who can convince Zak to speak to me is here.'

She gave a half-snort. 'Zak doesn't listen to me.'

'I don't think that's true.' A beat. 'Zak reminds me of myself at that age. I'm told that he loves maths. Loves tech. Has an affinity for it. It's no easy thing breaking into a modern car. Believe me, I know.'

She looked at him curiously. 'What *do* you do?'

'Did.' Q told her, saw her tense.

'We had secret police in Syria. They . . . They were not so secret. The things they did, everyone knew. They made sure we knew.'

'That's not the sort of work I did.'

Still she hesitated. The man's sincerity troubled her. Hassan had been a sincere man. A man who used words such as integrity and duty and meant them. In a place where such sentiments could get you killed.

'I have a friend,' said Q. 'Years ago, he was tasked to undertake a mission in Syria. The things he was told, about the regime, about what was happening out there, have stayed with him ever since. He brought back what he saw. He warned us of what was coming. We didn't listen.'

Tears stood in the corners of her eyes. 'I just want my son back.'

'I can't promise you that. But I *can* promise you that I'll speak up for him, when the time comes.'

'*If* he helps you.'

'If he helps me.'

Outside Zak's room, a new constable was on duty, a uniformed young policewoman who stood erect, twanging with the bearing of a North Korean presidential guard.

Bob signed Q in, then they walked into the room.

Zak was dozing on the bed, the TV on, remote control by his side. He awoke with a start. For an instant Q saw fear move across his features. The boy looked even younger than his years, notwithstanding the wispy chin fuzz he had clearly attempted to grow out.

As arcane Secret Service arts went, the turning of intelligence assets was right up there with black bag operations and the leaking of classified secrets via nubile interns.

Q had heard plenty of stories. The wooing of informers and double agents. Finding the right pick for the right lock. Slipping the knife in, once you had them on the hook. A morality mud bath, where all the actors flailed around, swiping blindly at each other, while barely able to hold their ground.

But that was the life. Those were the trade-offs.

It wasn't as if Q hadn't faced ethical dilemmas at Q Branch. Weaponry designed in his labs had been used to kill, discriminately, in the first instance, but, on occasion, the field of fire had spiralled outwards to bring an unintended full stop to the lives of innocents.

You lived with that. Or tried to.

But there were mornings Q had awoken with the screams of the newly dead ringing in his ears.

Sameera explained the situation to her son.

Zak focused on Q. 'I'm not telling you anything without some guarantees.'

Bob sighed. 'Son, I think it's time for a dose of reality. There isn't going to be any deal. Either you tell us what you know or we charge you for the stolen car. It's that simple. Breaks my heart to do it, but the law's the law.'

Zak stared at Bob, expression sullen. A million thoughts were fizzing through his head. About his situation, about Syria, about his father.

Zak missed his father. He missed Hassan's booming laugh, playing chess with him, the times they had gone out hunting in the desert. Once, his dad had accidentally shot a camel in the behind and they had had to leg it out of there with the beast on their tail.

Zak's heart twisted inside his chest. He looked at his mother. Frustration made him want to cry. Instead, he felt rage taking hold, a hand around his throat. 'This is *your* fault. Why did you come here? To this miserable country? If you had kept him in the house that day, he would still be alive. *You* killed him.'

Q looked at the Syrian woman. Her shoulders seem to sink inwards, her expression one of infinite sadness.

'I didn't kill your father, Zak.'

'I heard you fighting. I heard him leave the house. The day they took him away.'

Sameera's legs gave way. She sat down on a chair by the bed. 'I didn't kill your father. Your father is still alive.'

39

WHEN SHE THINKS OF DAMASCUS now, Sameera thinks of their home, a three-storey Ottoman-era villa near Abbassin Square, a fountain in the court-yard, the smell of cherry blossom and lemon in the summer, the cooing of birds in the dovecote.

Back then, before the war, before checkpoints and protests and mortar attacks, you could walk the winding alleys of the Old City to the bazaar, buy persimmons and oranges, walk back as the muezzin's call to prayer floated over the jostling streets. They said that Damascus was the oldest continuously populated city in the world. Sameera had always believed that, believed that there was something unique here, the city's soul, as old and as pure as the desert.

By the time suburban Damascus became a war zone, hardly anyone went out after dark.

Sameera had gone out into the streets when the protests had first begun. Not to protest, never that, but because there had been a heady sense of excitement in the air. In a life as staid as hers, a little excitement went a long way.

She had seen the young ones, no more than teenagers, up on platforms, making speeches through megaphones, wearing

T-shirts with the word FREEDOM emblazoned on them. What did that mean, anyway? Sameera had never not been free. Then again, she had never been entirely free, either.

Her father had been the regime's man. As had Hassan's father. As was Hassan.

One day, at such a gathering, she lost track of time. Stayed too long.

Out of the corner of her eye, she had seen the soldiers arrive. Unease had moved through her. She was glad she had left little Zak at home.

The soldiers' presence inflamed the crowd. The chants became louder.

Sameera began to back away. It was time to go home.

She must have been only yards from the sawboned old veteran at the rear of the crowd when he lifted the radio to his mouth.

Moments later, the first gunshot rang out. Followed by another. Then another.

A girl on the podium collapsed, her white T-shirt flowered with red.

A moment of suspended time ... and then chaos. Soldiers waded into the crowd, firing indiscriminately, attacking the children – and they *were* children, Sameera thought – with the butts of their weapons, with clubs, with knives.

Sameera saw a youth clubbed over the head. Once, twice, three times. His brain splattered onto the boot of his assailant.

She made it home but couldn't stop shaking.

The shaking continued, even when the maidservant, Mariam, came to soothe her with words that meant nothing, even when four-year-old Zak came to curl up in her arms, staring up at her with eyes that knew something was wrong, but not what.

By the time Hassan came home that night, she had readied herself. For years, she had played the role of dutiful wife, mother, never asking, never wanting to know. What use was there in knowing? What could she have done with that knowledge?

Sameera knew that her husband worked for the regime; that he held a senior position in the Mukhabarat – the secret police; that it afforded them a comfortable life, prestige, a future.

But her mind went again and again to the boy whose skull had cracked open in front of her, whose blood had stained that soldier's boot.

That night Hassan made the first of his many confessions.

He had ordered the soldiers into Abbassin Square. It was by his order that they had attacked the crowd.

In the year that followed, he told her of more horrors, ordered by the regime, ordered by him. Of nightmarish cruelties in soundproofed rooms, young Syrians tortured for intelligence, for sport, murdered, their bodies dumped in mass graves. Their crimes? Peaceful protest. Joining anti-government Facebook groups. Daring to ask for a better future.

Hassan told her that choice was a luxury they could not afford. They were tied to the regime. He could not disobey orders. He could not quit. Quitting would be a death sentence, for them all.

Had she believed him?

Yes. She had seen the pain in his eyes, the way he collapsed into bed each night, hollowed out by his own complicity. And yet this same man had admitted to crimes that had stolen her sleep, her ease. Stolen the life she had known.

And then, one day, the news of a boy. Thirteen. A boy taken by the security services, his body later returned, blackened with bruises, covered in cigarette burns, mutilated.

Sameera imagined Zak growing up to be such a boy, suffering such a fate.

They had fought. For weeks. Each day, Hassan returned to find a new Sameera waiting. A Sameera who would no longer accept. A Sameera who demanded action, a way out.

Would Hassan acquiesce? It didn't matter. She would keep chipping away, until he had no choice.

And then, on a warm Thursday evening, he had come home early, told her to pack suitcases. Handed her tickets. To England. She had stared at him, uncomprehending.

'The driver is waiting outside. I don't have much time.' He raised a hand, forestalling her protest. 'They'll be here soon. I have to go back. They *know*. The only way to get you both out is if I go back.'

Sameera had railed at him then. This was not what she had wanted.

Hassan had tried to make her understand. 'They won't kill me. They'll put me in a prison. Maybe, one day, when the war is over, I'll see the light of day again. The dawn of a new Syria. Until then, you have to be strong. For me, for Zak.'

As Sameera's voice died away, Q saw that Zak was struggling to hold back tears.

'You told me he'd been killed.'

'I needed you to accept our new life.'

'He might still be alive.' The boy's voice cracked. 'The war is over now. We can go back. Find him.'

Sameera said nothing, her face miserable. If she knew anything, had *ever* known anything, it was that if Hassan was, by some miracle, still alive, he would soon be arrested, tried and executed for his complicity in Assad's regime.

For a moment, Q thought the boy would erupt, let loose the dogs of anger howling inside him ... but then Zak seemed to deflate. He closed his eyes and lay back.

Sameera sat down beside her son, took his hand. 'We can never go back. Your father had one wish, his last wish. That we find safety. Here. Far from the regime. If you truly want to honour him, then be the man he wanted you to be. The man he wished *he* had been.'

Q spoke into the silence. 'I need your help, Zak. Pete Napier was my friend. I need to know what happened to him.'

The silence stretched.

'I don't know how Pete died,' said Zak, finally. 'But I saw him that night. I – I supplied him with cocaine. I mean, I was his courier. A delivery boy. That's all. He phoned me, told me to come out to Bishop's Point. When I got there, he was sitting on the jetty, naked.'

Bob frowned. 'Come again?'

'Pete's clothes were in the car. He was sitting there, visibly upset.'

'You didn't ask him *why* he was starkers?' said Bob. 'I mean, it was a warm night, but that seems like pretty eccentric behaviour, even for a boffin.'

Zak hesitated. 'I think someone else had been there. With Pete.'

'What made you think that, Zak?' said Q.

Zak cut a glance at his mother. 'I saw a condom. On the jetty. Used.' His face turned red.

Q directed himself to Bob. 'There was no mention of a condom in your reports.'

'That's because we didn't find one. Are you thinking what I'm thinking?'

'I have no idea what you're thinking.'

'I'm thinking Pete met someone out there for a little slap and tickle. That's why his clothes were neatly folded in his car. When he and his amore finished their little outdoor gymnastics routine, the other party left, and Pete ordered up a little post-coital Bolivian marching powder, courtesy of young Zak here.'

Q turned back to Zak. 'Did Pete say why he was upset?'

'He said he'd had a fight with someone he cared about. He said that person had threatened him. That he felt betrayed.'

'Did he say who?'

'No.'

'Got to be this woman he'd just had a roll in the hay with,' surmised Bob. 'Perhaps she's the one who shoved him in the river?' He glanced at Q. 'Assuming your murder theory holds water. Pardon the pun.'

'What pun?' Q frowned.

Bob opened his mouth, then closed it again. 'Never mind.'

'You're assuming it was a woman,' said Q.

'No evidence to suggest Pete was bisexual.'

'Pete was still alive when Zak got there. So it couldn't have been whoever it was he had just been with.'

'Nothing to say Condom Lady didn't come back after Zak left.'

Q turned to the boy. 'Were you Pete's regular courier?'

'Yes.'

'How did Pete pay for the drugs?'

'He didn't.'

'How's that?' said Bob.

'Pete never paid. He didn't have to.'

'Why not?' said Q.

'I don't know. I was told Pete could have as much coke as he wanted. As long as it didn't mess with his brain.'

'A conscientious drug dealer,' said Bob. 'Nice. Warms the cockles of my heart.'

Q considered the boy's words. He was certain Zak was telling the truth – though there was something about Zak's story that bothered him, something he couldn't put his finger on ... At least he now knew why Pete's finances had failed to indicate regular payments to cover his drug habit. And the mystery of why Pete had folded up his clothes and left them in the car was also solved. Pete had always been meticulous in that regard. Even in gym class, he would fold his clothes, place his watch on top, and leave them on the changing room bench. The other boys would watch this performance, then take the clothes and dump them in the toilet.

Funny how habits never changed.

'How did Pete get in touch with you?' he said. 'His phone records don't show any unaccounted-for calls.'

'He had a burner.'

'No burner phone was found at the scene.'

'Probably lost in the water,' said Bob. 'Along with the alleged condom. Or perhaps it was taken by our mystery woman.' He looked at Zak. 'Who supplied the drugs?'

'I can't tell you.'

'Can't or won't.'

'I can't put my mum in danger.'

Sameera jolted back to life, looked at Q. 'He has told you what you wished to know. You promised to help him.'

Q hesitated. He wanted more from the boy. He was certain there were still things Zak wasn't telling them. But a deal was a deal. It was in Q's interests to keep Sameera onside. 'Zak, your mother tells me you're incredibly bright. You'd have to be to hack into a Bentley 100 XT. I should know. When I was your age, I was taking apart TV sets and fridges and rebuilding them. Science was my lifeline. My escape. The decisions you make now will impact your whole life. I can't tell you what to do, but I can tell you that I've seen a lot of bad in this world. You're not a bad person. Not yet.'

Zak listened, mouth clamped shut.

Q turned to Sameera. 'I'll talk to Kathy. See what I can do.'

'Hang on,' said Bob. 'What makes you think she'll listen to you? I like the lad, but he's admitted to couriering drugs, and we've already got him bang to rights for the stolen car.'

'Haven't you ever needed a second chance, Bob?' Q's face turned stern. 'You've never seen true evil. I've seen men who would burn the world, just because they enjoy the sound of screaming. Zak's a child. It's not too late for him. If we let him slide into the abyss, that's on us.'

Back outside, Q waited while Bob thumped the soft drinks machine.

Eventually, it disgorged a Tango. 'Sure you don't want one?'

'I'm fine.'

'That was quite a speech in there.'

197

'I meant it.'

'Yeah, well, guess what I'm picturing? I'm picturing Kathy's face when you tell her you want to let the boy go. But what do I know? Maybe it's Hug-a-Hoodie month again. Anyway, we're none the wiser about Pete's death. Still no evidence of foul play.'

'But now we know Pete met with someone else that night. A lover. Who?'

Bob shrugged. 'So the man fooled around before he went tits up in the river. Doesn't mean he was murdered.'

'He was upset. He told Zak he'd been threatened.'

'Upset people often top themselves. Par for the course. I could murder a kebab. Interested?'

'I can't. I have to see my father.'

Bob glanced at his watch. 'Come to think of it, I should probably head home. Check on Lorna. My wife. She wasn't feeling too clever this morning.'

'Is she unwell?'

'Cancer. But we're fighting it. One day at a time, as they say. Not easy with the NHS limping along the way it is. Thank God for private healthcare.'

40

O N THE NIGHT BEFORE HE died, Caesar dined with Lepidus, his Master of Horse.

The two men got to discussing death. Lepidus enquired from Caesar what he considered the best form of death. To which Caesar replied: 'A sudden and unexpected one.'

Mort had often imagined Lepidus reacting to the news that, just twenty-fours later, Caesar had got his wish. Divination and prophecy had played a prominent role in the ancient world. Thousands of luckless animals had been sacrificed just so that their entrails could be examined for a glimmer of what the future might hold.

Mort wished he had a chicken to hand. A look at its entrails might give him some idea of what was to come.

The pipes in his office gurgled. A loud grunting noise: the sound of the toilet being flushed further down the corridor.

His emotions swirled around the room. Ghostly wraiths in pale robes.

Q's visit had unseated him. To see his son back in his childhood home. Impossible not to imagine Bella there in the shadows. Mort couldn't guess at what was truly driving the boy. But here he was, investigating Pete Napier's death, careening around town, kicking over rocks to reveal all manner of secrets.

How soon before Mort's own secret came slithering into the light? What would his son do then? How would Mort react?

At Oxford, the students – and no small number of his colleagues – had revelled in calling him the Mortician. Never to his face, of course. His starchy persona, his unwillingness to play the classroom buffoon, his utter lack of desire to *befriend* his students. Mort would rather have embraced a naked leper than sat down for an intimate one-on-one with the sort of entitled, mocha-bibbing neophyte that appeared to embody modern youth.

But that was the world now. A world Mort found increasingly difficult to navigate.

His phone rang. He picked it up, listened, then said: 'I'll be down in a minute.'

In the kitchen, Dave Potts looked up from *The Ladybird Book of Philosophy*. '"I think; therefore I am." Magic.'

The microwave pinged.

Mort watched Dave take out a bowl of something that resembled toxic sludge.

'Sure you don't want some? Plenty more where this came from.'

'I'm fine, thank you.'

'Your son's waiting out in reception.'

'Yes. I know.'

'You two made up, then?'

'My son is on a crusade. He thinks Peter Napier was murdered. That's why he's here.'

Dave whistled. 'There's a twist I didn't see coming. Anything to it?'

Mort said nothing. He had no idea why he had voiced his thoughts to Dave.

'Bumped into him once,' continued the younger man. 'Napier, I mean. Invited him to do a talk for us at the library. Told me to stick my invite where the sun don't shine. In so many words. Nasty piece of work.'

Mort suppressed the automatic flare of anger. Pete had rubbed people the wrong way. Mort knew that. But there had to be allowances for genius. 'Pete was a complicated man.'

'Sure. If complicated means he was an arse. Anyway, someone's crapped on the toilet floor again,' he added, conversationally.

Q walked in, trailed by Bastard. He looked at his father, opened his mouth, searching for a starting point. His mind went blank. And then: 'I'm in the mood for a kebab. Would you care to join me?'

Mort remembered the days when he had enthralled lecture halls full of the brightest minds in the country, revivifying for them the cut-throat politics of the Roman world. He remembered furiously debating matters of great academic import with the leading lights in the field, at the most august venues of learning in the world.

And now he was sitting in a kebab shop at a cheap plastic table while a balding man in jogging bottoms and a stained grey T-shirt took his order. The T-shirt rode up over the man's trapped-boulder stomach, revealing a mat of sweaty stomach fur.

Empire of Kebab. Established 2001. Which was news to Mort, because he was certain he had never seen the place before.

Or maybe he had and his mind had blanked it from his memory.

Mort looked at the menu. Stains made Mandelbrot patterns on the cheap card. The bottom edge of the card appeared to have dissolved. 'I'll have the grill platter.' It seemed the least dangerous option.

'Make that two,' said Q.

The waiter turned and screamed the order at an angry-looking bearded man sweating behind the counter. Mort wondered if it might have been easier for him to have simply screamed out his own order.

While they waited, Q recounted Zak's testimony.

Mort frowned. 'Zak Youssef? Sameera's son?'

'You know them?'

'Sam helps out at the library sometimes.'

Q nodded. 'You knew Pete. How bad was his drug problem?'

It took a moment for Mort to respond. Relief battled with a sudden overpowering desire to reveal his own dark truth. The boy would find out, sooner or later. Perhaps it would be better for him to hear it from Mort ... No. Not yet. 'If he had a problem, he kept it to himself. I don't think it interfered with his critical faculties. I saw less and less of him this past year. But each time I saw him he looked more strained. Perhaps he needed the cocaine just to keep going.'

Q raised an eyebrow. The Mort he had once known would have come down like a ton of bricks on the idea that work stress was an excuse for drug-taking. 'Do you know who the woman might have been? The one he met that night, at Bishop's Point?'

'After his marriage disintegrated, Pete soured on the idea of women. For a while. He was so busy at work, he barely found energy to make it home each night, let alone enter into a relationship. At least, that's what he told me.'

'Casual acquaintances?'

'Yes, of course. But that was another part of his life he stopped talking about. I have no idea who he was sleeping with.'

A beat. 'I know something isn't right. I can feel it.'

Mort looked down at Bastard, stretched out lifelessly under the table. 'What's wrong with your dog?'

'He's clinically depressed. And you just changed the subject.' Q leaned in. 'Pete's death wasn't an accident. And he didn't kill himself.'

'Why? Because he had sex just before he died? Because he snorted coke? Perhaps he was so high he forgot he couldn't swim? Or perhaps he needed the hit to get him over the line. No easy thing, taking your own life.' A hollow opened up inside Mort. His thoughts went to Bella, that awful day, his son's grief, a monster that had consumed the last vestiges of their fragile relationship ... 'I don't want to sound callous. Pete meant a great deal to me. I was shattered to hear of his death. But you can't save a soul who doesn't want to be saved. If your mother's death taught me anything, it was that.'

Q sat back. Could his father be right? Might all of Q's efforts simply amount to no more than a wild goose chase? Several geese, all flapping in different directions?

'Do you have any other leads?' asked Mort, carefully.

There was something odd in his father's tone. Q examined the old man's features, but Mort had found something infinitely intriguing in the tabletop laminate.

Bastard released a loud blast of wind under the table, breaking the tension.

Q responded to Mort's question with one of his own. 'Did Pete ever talk to you about his work?'

'Not really. It was outside my area of expertise. And much of it he couldn't divulge anyway. Intellectual property.'

'He was working on something that has the potential to jeopardise global security as we know it.' Q told Mort about the possibility that Pete had been developing an application of his new quantum computer that would compromise encrypted security protocols.

And Mort thought: How much like his mother he is! Bella, too, had been a woman of passionate crusades and heady opinions. An attentive mother, when her mood swings hadn't blown her out to sea. The sort of parent children adored: impractical, flighty, indulgent. Mort had never been that. Instead, he had been dutiful. But dutiful was not a memory children could warm their hands by. 'Seems to me,' Mort said, 'that if your murder theory is correct, then it's likely that someone who understood the dangers of his work *and* had the capability of orchestrating a killing would be the place to focus your attentions.'

His father's summation surprised him. Q had been moving towards the same conclusion. Mort, too, had clearly thought about this. Yet there were still shadows within shadows. Q still didn't understand why Pete had directed him to Adem Gashi.

And he needed to know who the woman was that Pete had spent his last hours with, out on that jetty.

But Mort was right.

Pete's work posed an existential threat to those whose sole reason for existence was security.

Security at a global level.

And that gave Q a starting point.

An hour later, back home, Q took out his phone.

The voice on the other end of the line seemed at once pleased and irritated by his call. 'You shouldn't be calling me on this line.'

'Is that music in the background? Where are you?'

'Official soirée. The former PM will be making a speech soon.'

'Which one? We've had quite a few in recent years. Do you mean the one that enjoys rugby-tackling toddlers or the one that destroyed the national economy and then wrote a book about how *we* were all deluded?'

'What do you want, *Major*?'

Major. Not Q. Moneypenny, ever the pragmatist. 'I need a favour. I want you to slot me into Q's diary. The new Q. I need to talk to him.'

Moneypenny barked out a laugh.

'It's important.'

'So is my pedicure, but I don't turn it into a national crisis.'

'"The woods are lovely, dark and deep, but I have promises to keep."'

'"And miles to go before I sleep." Bastard.' Moneypenny fell silent. 'Fine. But this is it. Even quoting Robert Frost won't get you any more favours.'

41

MIRKO WAS REMINISCING ABOUT THE good old days with his friend Vlodimir.

Vlodimir and Mirko had done business together, back near the beginning. Like most of Mirko's early ventures it wasn't the sort of business the taxman had needed to be troubled with. Mirko had been impressed with Vlodimir's efficiency and his small but well-oiled organisation. He had offered to buy Vlodimir out. Vlodimir had refused. Mirko, reluctantly, had decided he would have to kill Vlodimir.

But then Vlodimir had done something surprising. He had tried to kill Mirko instead. Which made no sense. It was like a mouse turning up at a lion's house with a rusty Kalashnikov and a couple of hand grenades.

Mirko had survived. His contemporaries had sat back and waited for a rain of hellfire to engulf Vlodimir's organisation. Mirko had thought about it. He quite liked the idea of raining hellfire on Vlodimir. No one could say Vlodimir didn't deserve it.

But something held Mirko back. He had already begun to learn that violence wasn't always the answer. Take children. Hitting children was something Mirko disapproved of. It rarely led anywhere but to long-term trauma for all concerned.

Mirko had gone to church, seeking guidance. Something about the expression on Jesus's face, up there on his cross, had planted an idea in his mind.

That evening he had left the house, taken a taxi, and turned up at Vlodimir's home. Unarmed and alone. Entirely at Vlodimir's mercy.

Mirko remembered that a birthday party had been going on. For Vlodimir's nonna. A ninety year old with an acid tongue and a recent hip replacement, who nevertheless insisted on dancing with the handsome newcomer.

If Vlodimir had been astonished at Mirko showing up on his doorstep, he hadn't shown it.

They finished the evening sitting in Vlodimir's garden, drinking expensive whisky and eating cheese.

By the time dawn came around, they had agreed on several things. That communism was dead; that John Lennon had been the best Beatle – despite that stupid stunt with the bed; and that neither Albania nor Ukraine would win the European football championships anytime soon. They had also agreed that war between their organisations would be pointless and destructive.

'I would hate to have to kill your entire family,' Mirko had said, taking the bottle from Vlodimir and refilling his glass.

Vlodimir had nodded, sagely. 'I would hate that too.'

'At the same time, I cannot let your attack on me pass without a response.'

'No. That wouldn't be right.'

'It is a quandary.'

'A genuine puzzle.'

In the end they had agreed that Vlodimir would pay compensation, and that his organisation, though remaining *completely independent*, would work exclusively for Mirko and at Mirko's express direction. And also that Vlodimir would cut off a finger, the way Japanese mafioso did when they had embarrassed themselves.

They had haggled for a while over which finger, how much to cut. Eventually, Vlodimir had gone with the little finger of his left hand, mainly because he was right-handed, but also because the tip of that finger had already been lost to a bullet and losing another centimetre didn't seem that big a deal.

They had sealed the pact with another whisky and then Mirko had handed him the cheese knife.

Now Vlodimir had diabetes and high cholesterol and bad kidneys and a rotten liver and claimed that life wasn't worth living anymore because all he could eat was rye bread and chickpeas. Not to mention the three litres of water he was forced to drink each day. For a man in a wheelchair that much liquid meant hardly thirty minutes went by without Vlodimir embarking on the complicated operation of going to the toilet.

'Adult diapers?' Mirko had suggested.

Both men had burst out laughing. The day that Mirko or Vlodimir succumbed to adult diapers was the day they would put a gun in their mouths.

Truly, Mirko thought, this was no country for old gangsters.

Papa John came in, stood there, hands folded, waiting patiently. Like the angel of death, Mirko thought.

He cut the call with Vlodimir.

'Boothroyd,' said Papa John. 'The man I told you about? He came into the Wickstone dealership. Spoke to Adem.'

Mirko's brow furrowed. 'Boothroyd?'

'The one who claims to be a friend of Napier's. The man who worked for the British Secret Service.'

Mirko turned in his chair and looked at his lieutenant. 'A spy?'

'A friend of spies,' said Papa John. 'I think this is a problem.'

'How big a problem?'

'I don't believe this man has just shown up out of the blue.'

'You think the security services sent him?'

Papa John said nothing. His expression said nothing. Even his new hair said nothing.

Mirko sighed. 'What should we do?'

'I have had him followed around Wickstone. I sent a man to his home in London. He went to Napier's house. He went to the lab, spoke with the American, Jed Ellis. He went to the dealership. I don't believe he will stop. I think we should neutralise him.'

Mirko sank further into his armchair. He hated euphemisms. If you meant, 'I want to hit this man over the head with a hammer, then chop him to bits, then disintegrate the bits in lime,' just say so. Don't say you want to *neutralise* him.

Mirko thought of the old Albanian saying: *He who shoots first, laughs last.*

But this wasn't Albania. And Mirko was no longer a trigger-happy young man. He understood the value of a life, the stain on the human soul of a life taken unjustly. What if this Boothroyd was telling the truth? That he was just a friend of Napier's? That would make him a civilian, a non-combatant. At least, until he became a direct threat to the organisation. And he was not that, not yet, no matter what Papa John said.

Besides, a man like that, trailing a past of shadows ... Who knew what monsters his death might unleash? 'No. You do nothing. For now.'

'And Adem?'

'What about him?

For the first time Papa John hesitated.

'Just say it.'

'Adem has never been reliable. You should never have sent him to Wickstone.'

'He's my sister's son.'

'I know.'

The clock on the wall ticked louder and louder.

'If Adem cracks, the whole house falls,' said Papa John.

Mirko closed his eyes. He wanted Papa John to go away.
But the man was right.
The Wickstone situation was precarious.
Napier's death had changed everything.
Something would have to be done.

42

MONEYPENNY HAD BEEN AS GOOD as her word.
It was the following day and Q had an eleven
o'clock with the new Q.

Q-lite. Mini-Q. *q*.

A month after Q had been jettisoned by MI6 he had realised
he was passing through something akin to the five stages
of grief.

Denial. Anger. Bargaining. Depression. And wanting to punch
someone in the face.

An unfamiliar nervousness grabbed him by the shoulders as
he negotiated entry into the building. He felt like a thief returning
to the scene of a crime.

They said buildings had personalities. The Great Pyramid of
Giza. The Basilica of St Peter. The Lubyanka in Moscow. Some
swaggered, some sang pianissimo. Some had stories to tell. The
MI6 building in London overlooked Vauxhall Bridge, a
neo-Mayan temple that, officially, was deemed the most secure
institution in Britain.

Q recognised only one of the security staff on duty. Mike
Little. In the way of these things, Mike was six foot eight and
the largest human being Q had ever met. And the unfriendliest.

Q was herded through the scanner, then roughly Mike-handled – at one point he wondered if the man might pull on a rubber glove. He hoped not. Mike's hand was the size of a dinner plate – and given a visitor badge to clip to his jacket, before being told to wait for an escort. An armed guard hovered close by.

It felt strange, watching others scurrying past, eyes cast down or at phones. Those that recognised him seemed to struggle to recall where they might have last met, an apologetic half-smile congealing on their lips, a tap of an imaginary watch, and then the brisk march onward.

So this was how it felt to be on the outside. Ignored. Barely acknowledged. Q felt the absence of his MI6 lanyard like a phantom limb. There had to be worse things in the world than a loss of privilege. He just couldn't think of any.

He recalled his last day in office. M had left no page unturned in the Book of Petty Bureaucratic Vengeance. Q had been forced to clear out his desk that very afternoon, pile his scant possessions into a cheap cardboard box – the foldable kind that sprang at you like a bear trap made by a vindictive Japanese origamist – and embark on a winding walk of shame through the building. He was accompanied by a guard at each elbow – overkill by a factor of two – through the vast open-plan area, where heads had bobbed up from behind workstation dividers to watch him pass – but not too far up, and certainly not for long enough to make eye contact. Could he blame them? If tramping around in the muck and mire of Service politics had taught him anything it was that it didn't do to pin your colours to the mast of a holed ship.

A small, grey-haired man in a dark suit and cheap shoes arrived. 'Mr Boothroyd? My name's Alan. I'll take you up to see Q.'

They followed a route Q had taken countless times. It seemed surreal that only months ago he, too, had been a master of the universe, walking these very corridors. And now he was being escorted around by a man in rubber-soled brogues.

There was no plaque on the door to Q's office. Protocol.

Alan knocked, opened the door, entered, ushered Q through, then pirouetted out again, closing the door behind him.

Q found himself facing his old desk, the same sturdy black-topped affair MI6's design contractor had installed over a decade earlier in the last facelift. But that was the only point of familiarity. Everything else about the room had changed. He was standing on a garish rug imprinted with a motif that reminded him of pavement vomit. A plastic palm lurked in one corner, beside a new floor lamp in the shape of a flamingo. Q's bookshelf had been replaced with a wall sculpture, a 3D shape he suspected had been fashioned by an artist on the edge of insanity. One wall – the wall formerly exhibiting a map of the world, marked with Q Branch tech deployments – was now taken up entirely by framed photographs.

Q was ambushed by a sudden memory. Bond charging into his office, having once again wet the budgetary bed, demanding the impossible. Q patiently explaining that you couldn't squeeze blood from a stone. Bond replying that you could if you shot it in the head.

The biggest change was sitting behind the desk.

Q knew who the *new* Q was, of course. Following his ousting, he had feverishly tracked the Internet for word of his replacement. But seeing the man in the flesh, sitting in his old chair, did strange things to his insides.

Kris Ramakrishnan was in his early forties, wearing a checked shirt that was probably a crime in several countries and a badly knotted cartoon tie. A *personality* tie. His shaggy hair was held back by an Alice band, giving him the look of a professional footballer. Not that Q was aware of any footballers who were twenty kilos overweight. A designer stubble, pockmarked with patches of clear skin, made it look as if Ramakrishnan had come off worse in a fight with an electric shaver.

But the man's smile was genuine.

Q watched him advance around the desk on suede moccasins, hand outstretched. Q's own hand fluttered at his side unable to make up its mind. Kris grabbed it, pumped it enthusiastically. 'The man! The myth! Please, sit, sit.' They took their seats. 'When Moneypenny told me you wanted to meet, I was mystified. What could the living legend want to talk to *me* about?'

Q blinked. 'Living legend?'

'I can't go five minutes here without someone telling me how the old Q was the absolute dog's bollocks. Pardon my Latin ... Tea? Coffee?'

Q watched him violently attack the intercom.

His eyes wandered to the wall covered in photos. He knew that Ramakrishnan, a Brit, had studied in the States, then worked in Silicon Valley running his own very successful cybersecurity company. So successful that he had been invited to serve as a security consultant to the US government. The photos were largely of Ramakrishnan with B-list celebrities and politicians. Perhaps this was the modern way. The newest incarnation of the Secret Service. You no longer found people who understood the need to remain in the shadows. You picked self-aggrandising entrepreneurs in clown clothes—

'So. What can I do for you?'

'Are you familiar with Pete Napier? Napier Labs?'

'The quantum computing guy? Died recently? Yeah. Sure. I've heard of him.'

'Pete was my friend. We grew up together. The coroner ruled his death an accident. I think he was murdered and that it might have something to do with his work.'

Kris leaned back, put his hands behind his head, revealing a pinprick hole in the left underarm of his shirt. 'Tell me more.'

Q explained his theory, then: 'I'm trying to figure out who has an active interest in how Pete's work might undermine encryption protocols. Specifically, bad actors.'

A thoughtful look. 'Not exactly my area of expertise, but I'm guessing *that* sort of breakthrough would really put the Rottweiler among the babies. I have a friend at GCHQ who could help. I could give her a call?'

GCHQ. The intelligence organisation responsible for gathering and deciphering encrypted communications. During the Second World War, GCHQ – then based at Bletchley Park – had cracked the Enigma codes. 'Wouldn't that be against protocol? I mean, I don't work here anymore.'

'You're hardly an outsider. And if there *is* anything to what you say, then Q Branch really should be across it.'

Q watched as the man video-dialled from his laptop. A pale face appeared on a giant monitor on the wall.

'Sheila. Got a friend here. Interested in the quantum computing apocalypse.'

Sheila was a narrow pair of shoulders above which hovered a head of frazzled blonde hair, bespectacled brown eyes and a pert nose. 'You still owe me a bottle of Glenfiddich from the last time I did you a favour.' The accent was northern, Cumbrian. Sheila focused on Q. 'What do you want to know, Mr . . . ? You look familiar.'

'This is Boothroyd. The Q before me.'

'Ah. Yes. Well, how can I help?'

Q explained the situation. Sheila frowned. 'The Chinese and Russians have been chasing quantum supremacy for a long time. If it's true that Napier Labs have already got there then it will be a matter of intense foreign interest.'

'You think these "foreign interests" might have killed Pete to prevent him getting to quantum supremacy before them?'

'I don't know if anyone killed your friend. But, yes, if it *is* true that he was murdered then there's always that possibility. If Napier Labs has truly achieved what you think they have, then they will soon be capable of breaking existing encryption protocols. It would be a global catastrophe if such a capability got into the wrong hands. Think about it. All sensitive data, applications and transactions will instantly become vulnerable.' Sheila hesitated, expression troubled. 'I probably shouldn't tell you this ... I assume you're still bound by the Official Secrets Act?'

'I am.'

'We've modelled a Doomsday scenario based on encryption becoming obsolete. It's not ... good. So, yes, I can imagine that foreign bad actors might wish to steal the tech or stop us from developing it. And if that means drawing a line under men like your friend, then ...'

'When you say foreign bad actors ... Do you mean agents in Wickstone?'

'I don't know. But a few years ago, two suspected Russian military intelligence officers attempted to murder Russian double-agent Sergei Skripal, then living in Salisbury. Intel chatter tells us that the Russians – among others – are closely monitoring the sort of work Napier Labs are doing.'

Q remembered the Skripal case. The Russians had used a Novichok nerve agent hidden inside a perfume bottle. It was the sort of thing Q Branch might have developed. 'Explain to me why Napier Labs' work is so dangerous.'

'Encryption employs mathematical problems, such as factoring. Encryption is *only* secure because factoring large numbers is very, very hard. If I ask you for the factors of six, it's simple. Three and two. Six and one. But what if asked you to calculate the factors for six billion, three hundred and forty-eight million, five hundred and six thousand, two hundred and twelve?' Sheila pursed her lips. 'Normal computers, even the most powerful, can't solve such a problem, not in a reasonable timeframe. Quantum algorithms will be able to do it easily. But to run such algorithms you need a quantum computer more powerful than anything anyone in the world currently has access to.'

'Except Napier Labs.'

'Yes. If we believe the hype. As I said, it's exceedingly difficult to get any information out of Napier Labs. Their people sign confidentiality contracts. They won't talk because they know they'll be sued into the Stone Age.'

Q recalled how cagey even a former employee such as Helen Banner had been.

'Would killing Pete actually prevent this encryption-hacking scenario?' asked Kris. 'Wouldn't others at Napier simply take the ball and run with it?'

'Possibly,' said Sheila. 'But Pete was the driving force at Napier Labs. At the least, his death will delay things. Remember the atom bomb? It was the fear that the Germans would get there *ahead* of the Allies that drove the Manhattan Project. If the Germans could have killed Oppenheimer, I'm sure they would have. Take out the head, send the body into shock.'

Q considered her words. Could Pete have been the victim of an international conspiracy? It seemed incredible. A foreign agent turning up in Wickstone, intent on taking Pete out of the picture. He couldn't imagine a Chinese or Russian assassin in his hometown.

His thoughts tilted. Why did he think the assassin had to be a *foreigner*? Wouldn't it be easier simply to get someone local, someone close to Pete to do the deed? His thoughts went to the mystery woman Pete had had a sexual encounter with on the night of his death ... How much money would be enough to convince someone to cross the line? To commit murder?

A knock at the door. Alan entered. 'M would like to see you, Mr Boothroyd.'

Q frowned. 'I don't have a meeting scheduled with M.'

'You do now.'

43

J ED ELLIS WAS STARVING.

He looked at the clock. Still an hour until lunch. Not that he couldn't just order something now. But he was putting on weight. Stress eating. Like Elvis.

He lingered on the clock. Early in his career, Jed had worked on a quantum clock. The clock was designed to deviate one second every three billion years. Not bad for a team of junior researchers. But that was the quantum world. A Wild West of opportunity. For those with the guts to take it.

Jed had never believed in that old saw about scientists doing it for humankind. What had humankind ever done for him? Most humans were idiots. There was a reason why sports stars who could barely spell their own names earned millions while men like Jed were paid peanuts ... Why shouldn't scientists enjoy the trappings of success? Why shouldn't they be feted? Scratch any great scientist from history and you'd find an ego that would make a rutting stag feel inadequate.

Jed thought of the long road that had brought him to Napier Labs. The years of gruelling slog, the slow climb up the academic ladder. Bidding for ever-dwindling research funds, administrative forms resembling finely-tuned instruments of torture.

Government ministers ready to gobble the congratulations for scientific breakthroughs but unwilling to pony up. Not just morons, but cheap morons.

Jed had had enough.

Jed had drawn a line in the sand.

When the tailgate drops, the bullshit stops. As his late grandmother had liked to say.

A knock on the door. 'Come in.'

Astrid Simmons walked in, sat down opposite him, set a folder onto the desk. 'The latest test results.'

'And?'

'We're still not there.'

Jed picked up a stress ball, squeezed it a couple of times. Then he threw it at the wall.

'Feel better now?'

'No.'

'There's nothing we can do. It will take as long as it takes.'

Jed glared morosely at his colleague. 'We're going to have to face it, sooner or later. We're not going to be able to do this without Pete. Or Helen.'

'Pete's dead. And Helen . . .'

Jed was silent. His thoughts lingered on Pete. On the consequences of actions. Pete was a casualty of war; Helen: collateral damage. 'I'm going to have to tell . . . *them*.'

Astrid pushed her glasses up her nose. 'And how will they take it?'

'How do you think?'

She leaned forward. 'Entropy always increases. And Einstein had dandruff.'

Jed smiled, leaned across and placed his hand on Astrid's. 'What would I do without you?'

'Collapse into a black hole.'

Jed took a breath. 'The guy who came to see us. Boothroyd. Claimed he was a friend of Pete's . . . He's been asking questions. Awkward questions.'

'Is it a problem?'

'It could be.'

Astrid hesitated. 'I showed him BETSY. He told me you'd authorised it.'

Jed gave a mouth shrug. 'I don't care that he knows what our quantum computer looks like. I care that he's digging into how Pete died. Into what Pete had got himself into, the lab into.' He ran his hands over his face. He hadn't shaved. 'It didn't have to be this way. God, what I wouldn't give to turn back the clock.'

Astrid stood up. 'The arrow of time only moves in one direction. And Pete ... Pete got exactly what was coming to him. Come on, let's get something to eat.'

Jed stood up. He marvelled at the look on the young woman's face. Determination. Implacable resolve. Joan of Arc in a lab coat. Just looking at her gave him strength. 'That's not quite true. About the arrow of time. Did I tell you about the quantum time loop experiment I worked on for NASA?'

Astrid walked around the table, hooked her arm through his. 'No. But it sounds fascinating.'

44

'**M**ONEYPENNY.'
            'Major.'
            'You haven't changed,' he said.
'I'd be surprised if I had. It's only been a few months.'

Q smiled. He had no idea what he was saying. Moneypenny's presence – the smell of her perfume, her immaculate sense of dress, her perfect diction – always caught him off-guard. It had been a decade since he and Moneypenny had danced the dirty dance. But the memories were still humid. And tender.

Sometimes, in the pit of night, Q would wonder at the road not taken. What had held them back? The answer: MI6. The rules that wrapped around them all like iron hoops. Internal liaisons were forbidden, a potential security risk. And since neither of them had wanted to leave the Service, they had taken the difficult decision to end the affair and move on.

At least, he assumed it had been as difficult a decision for Moneypenny as it had been for him. Tears had been notable by their absence. Moneypenny wasn't the sort of woman who cried over lost love ... Love. Had it been that? Q had never quite been sure. As close as he had come since Kathy, perhaps.

He knew that Moneypenny had been seeing someone else recently, someone outside the Service. He hadn't had the courage to ask.

'How have you been?' asked Moneypenny.

Q felt the urge to lie, to tell her he had been having the time of his life. Every day a carnival. 'It's been a hard landing.'

'I can only imagine.' Moneypenny sat down. At times it seemed to Q that she had been behind that desk forever, an office Sphinx who would remain at her post even should the walls come crashing down around her. Fiddlers on the *Titanic*? They hadn't a thing on good old Moneypenny.

'M wants to see me.'

'Yes.'

'Any idea why?'

But Moneypenny only smiled her enigmatic smile.

Fifteen uncomfortable minutes later, Q was ushered into M's office.

A woman sat behind the desk, dressed in a navy power suit. Small, with a round face and brilliant black hair, chopped into a pageboy cut. Cheeks as shiny as a ventriloquist's dummy. A smear of chilling red lipstick. Pale blue eyes.

'Boothroyd.'

'I'd prefer Major.'

The temperature fell to Arctic depths. 'Do sit down.'

Q took a seat.

'I won't ask you what you're doing here. I've already spoken to Ramakrishnan. Care to explain yourself?'

'I had an enquiry and I thought he might help.'

'I see.' M picked up a pen and worked it in her fingers. Her hands were the first thing Q had noticed about her. Muscular hands. Strangler's hands. 'I hadn't realised that MI6 had become a drop-in clinic. Perhaps we should open ourselves up to the general public? All your Classified Secret needs in one place.'

Q said nothing.

'You do realise that you don't work here anymore?'

Q said some more nothing.

M's eyes glowed like lasers. 'As I understand it you believe there is some sort of international conspiracy afoot in your hometown. You believe that – in spite of a thorough police investigation into his death – your childhood friend, Peter Napier, did not commit suicide, but was the victim of assassins. You believe that his lab is about to initiate a cyber apocalypse.' A thin smile twisted her lips. 'Has it occurred to you that this might all be symptomatic of a desire, on your part, to remain at the heart of things? That, having left a role that you occupied for so very, *very* long, you are now manufacturing ways to stay involved?'

'I didn't leave. You pushed me out.'

Her features froze. Q thought the pen might snap in her hands. He had a sudden image of the old M, sitting in that same seat, a toad in his hole. The old M had been a man of quiet action. See problem, shoot problem. As tough as they came. But M's leathery heart had given out a year ago, in a Greggs of all places. He had fallen face first into a shelf of assorted doughnuts. An ignominious end to a great career.

'Change is the only constant,' said M. 'Every organisation needs new blood. You no longer fit. Sometimes the hole changes shape. Some may believe the peg can adapt but, in my experience, it's an exercise in futility. It's the difference between a purpose-built rocket and retrofitting a piece of junk to fly to Mars.'

A piece of junk. Nice.

'Napier Labs is on the cusp of something that could change the world order,' said Q. 'A new arms race.'

'We are well aware of Napier Labs.'

'We?'

'The intelligence services. Believe it or not, we're not fools.'

222

Q's eyes widened in sudden realisation. 'The inquest into Pete's death . . . *You* put the national security tag on it. *You* ordered the coroner's report to be kept private. Which means you knew what Pete was doing. Why didn't you tell me?'

'Tell *you?*' That single word, delivered with the condescending majesty of a blue-blooded daughter of empire, chopping his legs out from under him and setting the bloody stumps back in his lap. M raised her chin. 'Because some things were, are, and will always be above your pay grade, *Major*. And it was never a matter for Q Branch. But others have been keeping tabs. Peter Napier was a person of interest.'

'You knew that his team was working on algorithms that will make encryption redundant.' A statement, not a question.

'We knew of the possibility. But our assessments suggest that this is an unlikely eventuality. In the near term, at any rate.'

'If you knew of the danger, you could have saved him.'

'Everyone is expendable. In the long run. I'd have thought you would have realised that by now. Napier's death, while tragic, may well serve the greater good.'

Q's lips felt dry. A terrible thought had just struck him. 'Did MI6 have something to do with Pete's killing? To prevent him from achieving his goal?'

M's snake-like smile vanished. 'MI6 had no involvement in Peter Napier's death. Any suggestion by you to that effect, in any public forum, will be met with the strongest response. And if that isn't clear enough for you: if you do anything to drag us into your conspiracy fantasy, I will personally have you hung, drawn and quartered. Do I make myself clear?'

Q stared at her. Anger throbbed at his temples. He remembered their last meeting again, on the day he had been made redundant, the way M had crumpled him up like a ball of paper on which extraneous jottings had been rendered, jettisoned him towards the wastebin. Those jottings: his life's work. 'All this because I humiliated you at an oversight committee.'

A scarlet flare raced across her cheeks. 'You arrogant shi—'
She stopped herself. Her jaw worked silently. 'You will stop your
investigation into Napier's death. *Now.*'

Q stood. 'There's nothing you can do to me anymore. *Ma'am.*'

She leaned back. 'In that, you are very much mistaken.'

45

THE ANGER SAT WITH HIM all the way back to Wickstone, waving at passers-by from the passenger seat. Cupping a hand over its mouth and pointing back at the lunatic behind the wheel. *Crazy guy alert*.

M's attitude shouldn't have surprised him. The woman had made no secret of her desire to oust Q from the moment she had arrived in post ... Who was she anyway? A civil servant with no substantive security background that Q could dig up. And he had tried. M's principal claim to fame appeared to be that she had once served as the ambassador to Nauru, a Pacific Island nation holding the title for world's fattest country. Practically everyone on Nauru was clinically obese.

He wondered briefly what it would take to kill the woman. A stake through the heart – assuming you could find it – followed by incineration. And then, just to be sure, you'd want to scatter the ashes to the four winds. Preferably hurricanes.

The thought made him feel better.

He focused on the investigation. M's threat had rattled him, but a good scientist didn't give up just because of the danger of the lab exploding around him. *Especially* not the former head of Q Branch. Explosions in the lab were practically mandatory.

It seemed obvious to him now that Pete's work might have attracted bad actors – foreign and domestic. He mentally added his former employers to the list of suspects. But how did this fit with the letter Pete had sent him, directing him to Adem Gashi? What did Gashi – and his possible links to the Albanian mafia – have to do with any of it?

Only one way to find out.

Evening had closed in by the time he arrived at the Seven Stars dealership.

In the dark, the showroom glowed brightly, a constellation of Disneyland-style artificial stars lighting up the roof, gleaming the bodywork of the red coupe parked up there.

He entered and walked to the counter. Minutes later, the woman he had met the last time he had visited – Deborah – came out to greet him, designer heels clicking across the showroom floor.

'Mr Boothroyd. You're back. How can I help?'

'I'd like to speak with Adem.'

'I'm afraid he's not here.'

'Where can I find him?'

A bright smile. 'I'm not at liberty to give you that information.'

'Then I need his phone number.'

'Need?' She tilted her head. 'Forgive me, but you seem agitated. Is everything all right?'

Q stared at her. Words failed him. He could feel the anger rising again.

Lies and obfuscation. Frustrated at every turn. No wonder Bond so often circumvented the rules or made them up as he went along.

Q knew that he was out on a limb. But that was what you did, wasn't it? When the stakes were high enough to matter. You did what you did because you were the guardian, the watcher on the wall, the clockwork soldier who marched on even when the small gods of politics and misrule pulled out your batteries and threw you on the slag heap. You did what you did because some things couldn't – *must never* – be allowed to stand.

Taking away a lanyard made no difference. That's what M failed to understand – and perhaps Q had only truly understood it at this very moment.

'That's fine. I'll find him myself.'

46

THE DJ WAS GUSHING ABOUT retro pop.

Adem loved retro pop. Bouffant quiffs like Wham! in the eighties and sexy leather trousers? *Count me in.* Under normal circumstances. But now, the music only provided an anxious backbeat to the muddy orchestra of his thoughts.

Adem was nervous. He had made the call. Had well and truly crossed the Rubicon.

To be fair, he had never quite understood that whole thing about the Rubicon. I mean, it was just a river. You could turn your horse around and just ride back across it. But it was a good saying. Caesar was the don when it came to sayings. All that render unto Caesar's business. And, of course: *I came, I saw, I conquered.* Classic!

Of course, you had to walk the walk to come up with stuff like that. *I came, I saw, I shat myself* hardly had the same ring.

Adem wasn't frightened. Telling himself that every five minutes probably made it true. Probably. What was there to be frightened of, anyway? He had taken the only logical course of action. And it wasn't as if it had been a snap decision. He had been building up to this for a long time. Years. That inner voice, forever whispering in his ear.

And then Pete, just before his death: *You can do this, Ade.*

Now, having made the decision, a weight had been lifted from Adem's shoulders. Clouds had parted. He was cantering to the sunlit uplands, whinnying his way towards a new life.

He tried not to think of the consequences. The aftermath.

He tried not to think about Mirko. And Papa John.

He couldn't afford to think like that. There was too much at stake. His life, for one.

If he had any regrets it was about Deborah. Debs would be disappointed in him. But it was time for her to learn that, contrary to her apparent belief, he *was* capable of doing the right thing. Just not right for her. Or for Mirko.

A breath of fear touched Adem's mind as he thought of the message he had received, shortly after he had made his call. The message asking him to meet up. Strange place to ask for a meeting. Up on Jane's Hill.

Then again, an isolated setting was probably for the best, given the nature of the discussion.

Fear was not an option. It was time to put on his big boy pants.

Adem turned up the music. The speakers thumped out 'When the Going Gets Tough, the Tough Get Going'.

Now *this* was more like it.

47

THE WINE GLASS BEFORE HIM was almost empty. A house red.

Q seethed. His chest felt tight, alive, a wriggling sack of barely suppressed emotions.

'Mind if I join you?'

He looked up to see Kathy. His thoughts scattered like panicked sheep. 'What are you doing here?'

'It's a pub. I'm off duty. It's been a long day. You work it out.' She slipped off her jacket and sat down. 'I'll have an IPA. And a packet of crisps. Black pepper. Make that two.'

Q stood and made his way to the bar. His legs felt altogether too steady. Then again, drinking himself into a stupor had never been his thing. Nor Pete's.

Q returned with the beer. And the crisps.

Kathy tore open a packet, shovelled a double handful into her mouth, then chased the crisps down with a large gulp of beer. Q sipped on his wine, wondering what she might do for an encore.

'Sorry,' mumbled Kathy. 'Missed lunch.'

'How did you know I was here?'

'I didn't. I was driving past, saw your Marvel superhero car outside.'

They drank in silence for a minute. The pub was quiet, filling up slowly.

'So,' said Q.

'So,' said Kathy.

A big lump of awkwardness writhed on the table between them.

'Bob tells me you spoke with Zak Youssef,' said Kathy. 'He tells me the boy says Pete was busy schtupping someone just before he died. A mystery woman.'

'Schtupping. Is that a police term?'

'Bob says Zak delivered coke to Pete that night. That he's confessed to drug dealing.'

'He's not a bad kid.'

'And how would you know this? Your years of experience working with troubled teens?'

Q refrained from commenting that working with the Double Os was probably a lot like dealing with hormonal teenagers. Particularly Bond. 'I just ... sense it. The boy needs a break.'

'Of course he does. Tell you what, why don't I call up the home secretary and ask her to set free every con in the land? Tell her they all need a break.'

'We're getting off point.'

'What is the point, Q? Do tell.'

'The point is that we now know there is a lot more to Pete's death than your initial investigation threw up. We know he met with a woman that night. Who is she? Why were they meeting out at Bishop's Point? And there's more. I went to MI6 today. I spoke to people who understand Pete's work. They believe that there may be hostile agents in this country, perhaps even in Wickstone, intent on stopping Napier Labs. Parties that had a reason to harm Pete.'

'Stopping Napier Labs from doing what?'

Q hesitated. In for a penny, in for a pound, Official Secrets Act be damned.

He told Kathy about the impending encryption Armageddon.

Kathy sat back and folded her arms. 'Have you any idea what you sound like? Russian assassins prowling around Wickstcne bumping off scientists hellbent on creating some sort of Doomsday weapon?'

'I didn't say it was Russians. And Napier Labs isn't working on a Doomsday weapon. They're not working on a weapon at all. It's the law of unintended consequences.'

'I won't claim to understand exactly what Napier Labs are doing but I'm pretty sure they're not about to unleash some sort of cyber apocalypse. As for your mystery woman ... Has it occurred to you that Zak might be lying? The boy's a criminal. He works for criminals. And even if Pete did get his leg over just before he died, so what? There's no evidence of foul play. None.'

'Pete directed me to Adem Gashi for a reason. Bob told me that Gashi is suspected of ties to the Albanian mafia.'

'*Suspected*. We don't know for certain.'

'I tried to track Gashi down tonight—' Q stopped. 'I think we should get him in and question him.'

'We? Who is we?'

'Fine. I'll question him myself.'

'No. You won't. You have no authority here.'

'You can't stop me from speaking to a private citizen, Kathy.'

Kathy's eyes blazed. She picked up the second packet of crisps and tore it open so violently crisps went flying in all directions. A young couple at a nearby table looked over, then went back to their drinks. A rowdy crew bustled into the pub, made a beeline for the bar.

'We should talk,' said Q.

'We are talking.'

'I think we need to clear the air.' Q paused. 'Kathy ... I had to leave. After Mum died, I— my heart imploded.'

'Imploded. Fancy that.'

'I can't explain it. I needed to get away, cut all ties with this place. I wouldn't have hurt you for the world.'

'Don't give yourself the credit. A week after you buggered off I was out on a date with Larry Hopkins.'

Q paused. 'Larry? *Larry?* The guy who was always ... *overexcited* in gym class?'

'That was one time. Jesus.'

Q stood up. 'Go ahead.'

'What?'

'Take a swing at me. Get it out of your system.'

Kathy stared at him. And then a smile twitched her lips. 'Sit down, you silly sod ... No. Don't sit down. Go and get me another packet of crisps.'

When Q came back, he said, 'Tell me about yourself. How's your family?'

'Dad died last year. After he retired from the bank, he had an epiphany. Decided he was going to become a druid. Wore a robe and made craft animals out of wicker. Sold them at fairs. After his death, Mum moved to Australia to live with my brother. Apparently, she's seeing a man named Scooter. My seventy-five-year-old mother is getting more action than I am. What do you think of that?'

Q gazed into the dregs of his wine. 'Bob told me you married a cop.'

'Jeremy. We're divorced.'

'Were you married long?'

'We had a good run. And then the wheels fell off. He asked for the divorce.'

Q said nothing.

'This is where you gallantly tell me he was a fool.'

'Was he?'

'No. Cops make for awful life partners. I knew it was over when he started clipping his toenails at the breakfast table.'

'Kids?'

'The one. Eleanor. Twelve. Lives with her dad.'

'Isn't that—?'

'Unusual. No. Not when the child asks for it.'

Q sensed the minefield ahead, decided to back away. If life at MI6 had taught him anything, it was that, in certain situations, fleeing the field of battle was the better part of valour.

'What about you?' said Kathy. 'Married?'

'No.'

'Ever?'

'No.'

'Girlfriend?'

Q sensed another potential landmine up ahead. Kathy's enquiry was deliberately pointed. What could he tell her? That his last meaningful relationship was four years in the past? That it had consisted of three dates, the last ending in a disastrous restaurant meal, a pastiche of misunderstood signals, attempts at humour that missed their mark and some embarrassment over the bill. Not to mention the chipped teeth. And the black eye. Turned out his date, a mild-mannered museum cataloguer by day, had recently taken up cage-fighting.

'I date. Been a little busy lately.'

'Doing what?'

Being made redundant, actually.

'I'm taking some time out. Reflecting on the next stage of my career.'

'And so now you're back in Wickstone, auditioning for the *Columbo* remake.'

Q said nothing.

'Why were you booted out of MI6?'

'I wasn't—' He stopped. What was the point? He explained the situation, M's antipathy towards him.

'This M sounds like a woman who knows what she wants.'

'She's the type who'd waterboard her own mother.'

'Have you considered the possibility that you simply don't like the fact that she's a capable woman who was given authority over you?'

'She's not qualified for the job.'

'Next you'll be telling me she slept her way up the pole.'

'No one sleeps their way up the MI6 pole. It's studded with razor blades.'

Another silence passed.

'Why did you really come back here? And don't give me that crap about Pete.'

Q hesitated. 'You're wrong. Pete's death hit me harder than I could have imagined. I suppose I thought of him as my last link to Wickstone. To my father. To you. And, yes, after MI6, I needed ... something. A purpose. Pete's letter gave me that purpose.'

She stared at him, then stood up. 'Come on.'

'Where?'

'You'll see.'

Q trailed Kathy's BMW in his Caterham.

Five minutes out from the edge of town they turned onto a country road, following it out to Bishop's Point. The thought came unbidden: *This was the road Pete took on the night he died. The road that had led him to his death.*

A short while later, Q peered through his windscreen as Kathy parked on a grass apron at the foot of the Bishop's Point jetty, then slid in beside her. A screen of elm trees with their backs to the wind reached up into the darkness.

Q got out and followed Kathy onto the wooden pier. The jetty had been long neglected, the boards cracked and gasping for a coat of all-weather lacquer. A full moon glimmered the slats, milky light rippling over dark water gently slapping against the posts.

Surrounded by forest, the jetty was a secluded spot, once a favourite of lovers and fishermen. As Q approached the furthest edge, his steps faltered. This is where Pete had died. His last moments on earth had fallen through the hourglass on a night like this, only weeks earlier.

He stood beside Kathy and looked out across the sluggish river. On the far side, the bank dropped several feet to the waterline, choked with weeds. When Q had been young, otters had played here. It was the sort of river Ratty and Mole had messed about on, in their little rowboat. A wholly English river from a time that now seemed lost.

A dull ache beat inside Q's chest. Memories swarmed around him, thick as flies. Pete's grin, when he knew he had plotted his way to checkmate in a game of chess. Pete's irrepressible braggadocio. Pete's irresistible momentum. Had Q been jealous of his best friend? Of course he had. But it had been a benign envy, one that had inspired Q to scale his own heights.

He tried to assemble the facts in his head.

Pete had been under immense pressure at work. His research had become the target of bad actors, perhaps foreign agents, perhaps agents closer to home. MI6.

On the night of his death, Pete had met with a woman, here, just hours before he died. They had had sex, and then the woman had left. Next, Pete had called Zak Youssef and asked the boy to deliver cocaine to him. Zak had found Pete sitting naked on the jetty. What had been going through Pete's head? What storms had raged through that beautiful mind?

After Zak had come and gone, Pete had ended up in the water, a man who couldn't swim. Earlier that day, Pete had written a letter to be sent to Q in the event of his death, summoning him back to Wickstone and obliquely directing him to Adem Gashi, a man involved in organised crime.

Something was missing.

236

After Zak had left the jetty that fateful night, Q was certain something else had gone on here, something that had led to Pete ending up in the river. Pete *hadn't* killed himself. And his death was no accident.

Which meant that someone else had been here *after* Zak. Someone who knew Pete well enough to know that he couldn't swim. Someone who had come here to end Pete's life.

Might it have something to do with Adem Gashi? The man knew *something*. Q was sure of it . . . What would Bond do? That was easy. Bond would beat the shit out of Gashi. And then he'd ask Gashi the questions he needed answers to.

Q heard his name being called. His real name. It seemed to come out of the night sky, a disembodied voice. And then he realised that the voice was coming from behind him.

Kathy had stepped backwards, away from the edge of the jetty. 'Let it go. Let it go or the past will eat you alive.'

Q stepped closer. 'I know you don't believe me, Kathy. But I'm certain Pete didn't kill himself.'

'I'm a cop. I need facts, evidence.'

Q stared at her. Her face. Her eyes. Her lips. Time dissolved; memories tumbled through the dark. He felt an unbearable feeling of loss. For Pete, for himself, for his lost youth. For everything that might have been.

A fierce longing gripped him; adrenalin flooded his heart.

He hadn't come back to Wickstone for *this*. At least, not directly. But there had always been the possibility that he would run into Kathy.

Q moved forward until they were practically touching. His eyes held Kathy's. How well he knew this face. Which, itself, was a lie. He knew – had *known* – the girl. And yet it scarcely seemed to matter that she had aged. Wasn't that the heart's greatest trick? That, at the twitch of an invisible dial, loved ones could be returned to any age you desired? In the fantasy chamber of the mind, you could breathe life into the past and make it whole again.

Q's gaze rested on Kathy's mouth. The way moonlight puddled on her lower lip. He leaned down—

Kathy's phone rang.

She stepped backwards, drew a long breath. Then she turned away and answered the call.

When she turned back, Q saw that her demeanour had changed.

She looked at him with a strange mixture of bewilderment and ... was that fear in her eyes?

'I have to go. There's been an ... incident.'

He looked at her stupidly. 'You're off the clock.'

'This is— A body has been found. I'm needed at the scene.'

'Whose body?'

But Kathy simply shook her head and began walking back to her car.

Q moved quickly.

He jogged to the Caterham, went to the boot and took out his 'picnic hamper', the titanium case that he had retrieved in London, carrying his equipment. A few Q Branch essentials that he had accumulated over the years. In the spy game, you never knew when such kit might come in handy.

From within, he removed a small drone – barely the size of a sparrow – from its moulded housing and activated it using his smartphone. The drone, a mechanical miracle encased in shiny black metal, hummed to life.

Moments later, it shot off after Kathy's departing BMW.

Q followed the vehicle on his smartphone, a bird's-eye view of Kathy speeding back towards Wickstone, then along several roads skirting the edge of town, until she turned onto a winding dirt track that, he knew from memory, led up to the summit of Jane's Hill.

Q remembered climbing the minor hill with Pete, the sun as bright as a ten-pence piece, seeds blowing from the hedgerows, kestrels breaststroking the thermals high above. They had stopped halfway up the hillside at the crinkle-crankle wall. The technical term for the wall's unusual serpentine shape was *sinusoidal*. Pete had told him that.

Q saw Kathy approach the summit, where several other vehicles had gathered.

Flashing lights. Crime scene techs in boiler suits.

He saw the BMW stop, Kathy get out. DS Bob Lazarus walked over to her, said something, then turned and led her away.

A momentary twinge of guilt. Spying on Kathy? What would she say if she found out? But this was the spook's dilemma. How did – *could* – you unlearn a lifetime's instincts? Those instincts were like keeping a gun in the house. No matter what you told yourself, when the moment came, you used them.

Q realised that someone was sitting on the old Second World War memorial bench. The man, dressed in a shiny suit, seemed to be asleep, hands folded neatly on his lap, head lolling on chest.

He couldn't bring the drone any lower; couldn't risk detection. The drone was built for stealth, but it wasn't entirely invisible. Instead, he focused its powerful videocam onto the bench.

He watched as Bob Lazarus, with great care, lifted the man's head with a gloved hand.

Q knew that face.

Shock reverberated through him.

The man on the bench was Adem Gashi.

48

THE NEXT MORNING BROUGHT WITH it rain.

Q awoke early, a night of troubled sleep, slipped on a bathrobe, shoved his feet into slippers, then went downstairs.

Coffee. Strong and black. That was the ticket. Clear the head, calm the bull rampaging through his inner china shop.

If he had learned anything in the Service it was that death was the one variable you could rarely account for. He remembered a meeting in Q's office, M, Bond, another Double O – 004 – and a man from German intelligence. A Berlin op that had been blown, several wounded field agents – British and German – whose lives remained in the balance. 004 – a Scotswoman who was, arguably, the best sniper in the Service – had been on point. An unexpected variable had entered the theatre of action late in the day. 004 had reacted. Civilians had perished. Bond had cleaned up the mess, but not before some of it had stuck to him.

In the aftermath, it was almost impossible to pinpoint the exact moment that Death had walked into the fray, banging a tambourine.

Could Adem Gashi's murder have been prevented? And how did it link to Pete's death? That there *was* a link, Q had no doubt. Pete had very deliberately sent him Gashi's way. Q's impression of the young man had been that he had been hiding something. And then there was the fact that Gashi was linked to organised crime ... The thought occurred to Q that perhaps his visit might have been the catalyst behind the man's death. Had someone decided to permanently prevent him from speaking with Q? If so, why?

Q knew that he needed more information. About Gashi. About the people he had really worked for. And about how they might have been tied up with Pete Napier—

The doorbell.

Q set down his coffee, walked through the hall and swung back the front door.

Kathy stood there, a few yards back. Outlined in a halo of white light.

A star went nova inside Q's chest. The previous evening, that moment on the jetty, returned in a crashing rapture. He had spent much of the night wondering if Kathy – in between dealing with a dead body – had felt a similar swelling of past emotions.

And then his eyes were dragged to Bob Lazarus, clambering out of the black BMW.

Why was Bob here? Q focused on Kathy. Something was missing. A smile. Kathy's expression was grim.

'Kathy? What's going on?'

'Where were you last night?' said Kathy, as Bob drew along-side. 'Between seven and eight p.m.?'

Q blinked at her. Was she serious? His gaze slid over to Bob's sombre face. 'What's this all about?'

'Adem Gashi,' said Bob. 'Local car dealer. Found dead last night. Up on Jane's Hill. Murdered. Little bird tells us you went to see him recently. And then, last night, you made another trip to his dealership. Just before he died. Kathy says you were hell-bent on tracking him down.'

The halo around Kathy winked out.

'We'd like you to come down to the station,' said Bob. 'Answer a few questions. If you don't mind.'

'Am I under arrest?' His voice sounded faint to his own ears.

'No,' said Kathy.

'Not yet,' said Bob.

'Right.' Q's vision went white. 'Give me a moment to get dressed.'

'Now don't try to run,' said Bob. 'It may not look like it, but I've got a fair bit left in the old afterburners. And frankly I've just had my breakfast and I'd rather not throw it all up.'

The interview room was smaller than the ones at MI6.

Q looked at Kathy, sitting rigidly beside her junior officer. Colour rose to her cheeks, but she said nothing.

White noise filled his thoughts. This is what came of letting people in. One day you're sharing lingering looks, rekindling lost love from the ashes of the past; the next they're dragging you to a police station to interrogate you about a murder.

In the Service, betrayal was hardwired into the field of play. That it still had the power to shock – spies changing sides, politicians peddling influence, bureaucrats pushing invisible levers that materially altered the dynamics of geopolitical influence – was a testament to the human reluctance to confront the seductive power of treachery.

How many times had he seen this scene play out? On TV, in his favourite cop shows. The cramped interview room. The cynical senior officer with the I-need-a-cigarette eyes. The tubby sidekick. The sleazy lawyer ... There was no lawyer. And the only one in need of a cigarette was Q. Not that he smoked. But now was probably a good time to start.

'I had nothing to do with Adem Gashi's murder.'

'Never said you did,' said Bob. 'We simply wanted to ask you a few questions.'

'I only met the man once. A couple of days ago.'

'In pursuit of your enquiries into Peter Napier's death?'

'Yes.'

'And what did you and Mr Gashi speak about?'

'Adem told me Napier Labs was a customer of his car dealership. He told me he and Pete had become friends, that they met a few days before his death. He told me Pete was under great strain.'

'But you were unsatisfied with these answers,' Bob continued. 'You were determined to go and talk to him again. Hold his feet to the fire, as it were.'

'Bastard.'

Bob coloured. 'I've heard it all, mate. Insults won't change what's happening here.'

'My dog. His name is Bastard. He's not well. He's home alone.'

'This won't take much longer,' said Kathy.

'Well, that depends,' said Bob.

'On what?' said Q.

'On how truthfully you answer our questions. You knew that Adem had connections to organised crime. Perhaps you concocted a theory that Adem might have had something to do with Pete Napier's death. Perhaps you tracked him down last night. A confrontation ensues. One thing leads to another.'

'How was he killed?'

Bob hesitated, glanced at Kathy. The DCI nodded. 'He was stabbed. Multiple times.'

'Stabbing is an inefficient way of killing someone. You have to get up close. Plenty of potential for blood spatter, DNA transfer. No guarantee of putting down your opponent, unless you know what you're doing.'

'But you do know, don't you?' said Bob, softly.

Q said nothing. Armourer. No matter how far he went, he would always end up here. He was a man who had spent his life designing weapons of death. At one time he had been one of the world's foremost experts on small arms. Handguns had been his speciality. The work had evolved over time, but he still knew his way around most forms of weaponry.

Bob spoke again. 'We know that you went to the Seven Stars dealership last night at around 7.20 p.m. An hour later, DCI Kathy Burnham approached you at the Knight Shift Inn. We know that Adem Gashi died roughly in that interval. Where were you between leaving the Seven Stars dealership and arriving at the pub?'

Q looked directly at Kathy. A light flashed in her eyes. A tremble in her cheeks. Still she said nothing. 'I don't know. I— I drove around for a while.'

'Why?'

'I was upset.'

'With Mr Gashi?'

'No. I—' But he had no wish to share with Bob his feelings about M.

Bob nodded, as if Q had actually replied. 'Here's the thing. You say you had nothing to do with Mr Gashi's death. But a witness at the Seven Stars showroom tells us that you were in an agitated state. Your car was later caught on camera on the edge of town, not far from the road that leads up to Jane's Hill, the site of Mr Gashi's killing. How do you explain that?'

Q felt his stomach drop. He said nothing, then: 'Do I need a lawyer?'

'I don't know. Do you?'

A knock on the door. The door swung back and two men walked in. A short, paunchy white man in a dark suit, swinging a battered leather satchel. And Mort.

The man swung his briefcase onto the interview desk, rested a hand on it. He looked down on Bob and Kathy. 'I'm Donald Finkelstein. Mr Boothroyd's solicitor. My client will be saying nothing further at this time.'

Bob spoke to Q. 'Who says wishes don't come true?'

49

'WHERE ARE WE GOING?'

'To talk,' said Mort. 'A talk we should have had a long time ago.'

Q glanced at his father. Mort's eyes were on the road. The Volvo XC40 nosed along the high street. An earlier passing shower glistened the tarmac.

Fifteen minutes later, they arrived at the graveyard.

Mort got out. Q waited. He had no desire to get out of the car. He knew where they were headed. His legs had suddenly doubled in weight. He saw that his father was waiting patiently for him. Immaculately dressed, as always. That cold blue gaze. That impenetrable expression. Q felt himself rushing towards a singularity, a moment in space–time where the rules of physics broke down.

He opened the door and got out of the car, trudged behind his father as Mort led them through the graveyard.

They reached the grave, then stood, side by side, looking down at Annabelle Boothroyd's headstone.

Silence. The sound of a car leaving the car park. A dog barking.

Mort knew that it was time. Whatever Q had got himself into, chasing the mystery of Pete's death, it had gone far enough.

No more secrets. No matter the consequences. 'Your mother sparkled,' said Mort. 'That's the best way I can describe her. We were madly in love. But there was something wrong with her. I knew it, of course. From the beginning. But I ignored it. I wanted her to be perfect. I *needed* her to be perfect. Anything less and it was an indictment on me. Mortimer Boothroyd doesn't make mistakes. And so I ran from it. I ran from her. I should have helped. I should have listened.'

'But you didn't.'

'You can't understand. Unless you've loved someone and then seen them turn into something altogether unrecognisable. It twists you inside out. It's terrifying. I was afraid. I wanted to control the situation. I failed.'

Q felt the earth lurch under him. Mort, the man made of granite. The monolith.

In that instant, Q saw a boy and his father, standing on opposite sides of a wall, unable to hear each other except as voices echoing in the dark. But then a door opens. Did they have the courage to walk through?

'It wasn't just her that needed you. *I* needed you too.'

'I know. I'm sorry.'

And Q thought: The dead don't really die. Death simply makes them more powerful, more present, kept alive by the monstrous reanimator that was memory.

His mother was a light dancing in the air.

For the first time in an age, Q thought he saw her smile.

And then Mort turned to him. 'I killed her. I killed Bella.'

50

MIRKO ALWAYS KNEW WHEN PAPA John had bad news for him.

The big man would come in with a glass of Mirko's favourite whisky. Mirko's doctors had cut back his alcohol intake; the Glenfiddich only came out on special occasions. A birthday. A wedding. A toast to the departed. And when Papa John came bearing bad tidings.

Mirko knew it wasn't because the messenger was afraid of being shot. Mirko was long past the point of being a physical threat to anyone.

It was because Papa John cared.

Papa John was as close to a son as Mirko had. Mirko adored Adem, but Adem was his flesh and blood. He had no choice but to love the boy. But Papa John ... A long time ago, Mirko had paid a man to dig into Papa John's past. What he had found had profoundly disturbed him. Fostered and then returned. Time and again. Papa John had never had a home, a family. Mirko had paid another man to unseal sealed records. He had read pages of notes detailing a litany of horror that had raised the fury of angels inside him.

There were monsters in this world. Mirko might have done things that others considered morally dubious, but he was no monster. The men who had preyed on Papa John were unfathomable to Mirko. What made them that way? Were they, too, part of God's design? If you believed in God's omnipotence, then you had to believe that, didn't you?

Mirko had tracked down Papa John's birth parents. The mother lay six feet below ground in a cemetery back in Albania. But the father was still alive. He had completed a lengthy prison sentence and was living in the north of England. Was he still tormented by his predilections? Mirko didn't doubt it. Men didn't change.

Mirko had never told Papa John. The past was something Papa John kept locked tightly within himself. Like a pin in a grenade. And so Mirko had left the man's name and address in an envelope, to be given to Papa John after Mirko's death.

Perhaps Mirko should have had the man killed. Perhaps the man had harmed other defenceless little innocents since his release? Would that weigh against Mirko when he stood before St Peter? He hoped not.

Papa John sat down. Mirko felt a bloom of fear. Papa John rarely sat in Mirko's presence. And he was refusing to meet Mirko's eye. A bad sign.

'Adem is dead. He was murdered last night. In Wickstone.'

Mirko's lungs collapsed. The armchair's jaws closed around him.

Mirko was a child again, on the day that news of his grandfather's death had come home. He remembered the women wailing, the men's stoicism, talk of revenge and retribution. Mirko had walked in the shadow of Death his whole life and now Death had sauntered into Mirko's home, parked His boots on Mirko's desk, and looked Mirko squarely in the eye: *Sooner or later we all pay for the choices we make.*

Papa John watched his boss. He knew Mirko wouldn't ask. Not yet.

It didn't really matter *who* had killed Adem, not in this moment. The time for that would come later.

'Deborah?' said Mirko. It sounded like the gasp of a dying man.

'She's fine. She's making enquiries.'

Papa John wished he could put his arms around the old man. But that could never be. He stood. 'I'll make the necessary arrangements.'

Mirko closed his eyes, hand clutched around the whisky. A tear leaked out from under the lid of one eye.

Papa John turned and left the room, unable to bear the sight of the old man weeping.

He thought it might break his heart.

51

Q BLINKED IN A SUDDEN BURST of sunlight.
His father's words clanged against the side of his head ... *I killed Bella* ... A monstrous vision of Mort forcing pills into his wife's mouth hovered in the air ... A darkness reared up inside Q, threatening to overwhelm him. His mouth opened, but his voice had gone AWOL.

'I had an affair with Pete's mother,' said Mort. 'That's why his father left. That's why I took such an interest in Pete. I felt responsible.'

Q felt himself floating away. A sense of unreality engulfed him. The moment expanded ... He found his voice. 'Mum knew?'

'She found out. Just before she died. I think— I think that's what sent her over the edge.'

A sparrow sang into the sudden silence.

Q's legs gave way. He sat down on the grass. The grass was wet. Moisture soaked through his trousers.

A moment passed, then Mort sat down beside his son.

Q realised he could hear the sound of his own breathing, a rasp in the still air. Everything around him seemed outlined in brilliance, painful to the gaze.

A young couple at a nearby grave looked at them, concern on their faces.

Nothing to see here, thought Q. Other than the elephant on fire and the three-lane pile-up that was his life.

Was this what they meant by the long dark night of the soul? A crisis in faith and spirit. It had all come crashing down at once. He had lost his job, and with it the carefully ordered life that he had built. A barricade against the floodwaters of the past. Why had he really come back to Wickstone? Kathy's question had been a valid one. The truth was that Pete's death was simply the catalyst for a return that had been a long time coming.

Truth. Life was a constant battle for the truth. But the fight for truth was an asymmetric one. Because no one really wanted the truth. Not about themselves.

Q looked at his father. What did he see? A broken man held upright by the fragile scaffold of his own vanity. How had Mort made it through all these years? Q understood now why his father had never remarried. Carrying all that guilt around, displacing it into a career and a set of principles that precluded honesty. For how could Mort be honest about the one mistake that had cost him everything?

Q had a choice. Walk away and never come back. Forget Pete. Forget Kathy. Forget his father.

Or he could stay, and together he and his father could face down their demons.

'My arse is soggy,' said Q.

'Mine too,' said Mort.

52

'**M**OCHA COOKIE CRUMBLE FRAPPUCCINO. JUST the way you like it.'

Bob handed the coffee to Kathy, then sat down. They were back at their desks.

'Penny for your thoughts?' said Bob.

Kathy said nothing.

'I know this can't be easy for you, what with him being your ex. Truth be told, I can't see him for this. A career scientist stabs a guy he barely knows? Nah. Gashi was dirty. That dealership of his is a front. More than likely, this is gang related.'

When she had been young Kathy had known everything. Or thought she had. About love, about the world, about the way people worked.

She remembered the first time she had kissed a boy. Not Q. It hadn't been horrible, but it hadn't been pleasant either. But the first time she had kissed Q, it had felt right. In spite of his braces, in spite of the way he had closed his eyes and puckered his mouth five minutes ahead of time. A valve had opened inside her; she had never really been able to shut it again.

Last night, thirty years had vanished into the sky. There were no feelings as strong as those you experienced as a teenager, no love that lingered in the dells and hollows of the heart as potent as first love.

Kathy knew that Q hadn't murdered Adem Gashi. Even if they brought her a bloody knife with Q's DNA and fingerprints on it, she wouldn't believe it. People changed, but not that much ... *Why hadn't she stood up for him?* Did being a cop, doing things by the book, matter more than Q? She heard herself speaking. 'Do you remember when Charles and Di were married, they gave away spoons to all the schoolkids?'

'I was a little too old, love.'

'I kept that spoon for years, even after Q left, even after Jeremy and I separated. I thought if I can hold onto this one thing, this one little symbol of love, then maybe love can still be real.'

'Charles and Di divorced. He was never in love with her.'

'That's the point. The spoon was a reminder of all the times love goes wrong. Because love only works when you're with the person you're meant to be with.'

Bob sighed. 'I've been with Lorna for nigh on forty years. The prospect of losing her terrifies me. I can't imagine a day when she's not there, when we don't talk, when I can't look up and rest my eyes on her. It's uncanny. Her face has changed, but each time I look at her I see the girl I first fell in love with. I think— I think, when she's gone, my heart might just fly away. Go south for the winter. I'm afraid it might never come back.'

Kathy put down her coffee. 'I'm sorry. I'm being a selfish bitch, aren't I?'

'You're being human,' said Bob.

53

THE CHURCH WAS EMPTY.

They sat in a pew at the front.

Q had no idea where to begin. Why couldn't he and Mort have had a normal relationship? Other fathers and sons assembled garden furniture, talked sports, went for a beer every Friday. Q knew a man at MI6 who had recently gone on a trip with his dad to Venice simply to retrace locations from the film *Don't Look Now*. That's what father–son bonding was supposed to look like. Not sitting in an empty church with wet backsides and the ghost of a dead woman squeezed between them.

'Thank you for coming to the police station.'

'You sent me a text. What was I supposed to do?'

A beat. 'Aren't you going to ask me if I did it? Killed Adem Gashi?'

'Did you?'

'No.'

Q knew that he was in shock. He had to be. He had been questioned in connection with a murder. He understood that he couldn't be a serious suspect, not for long. Whatever the police thought they had would collapse under any real scrutiny. But Kathy's betrayal had stung. He knew why she hadn't spoken up,

254

of course. What could she have said? *We've hauled you in on the off chance that you might be involved in a local stabbing, and, by the way, please don't mention the fact that we almost fell into each other's arms last night.*

Technically speaking, she *couldn't* vouch for him. Kathy had no idea where he had been between turning up at the Seven Stars dealership and arriving at the pub. So, in that sense, she was only doing her job. And yet . . . It hurt that she hadn't spoken up. It hurt that she had turned up on his doorstep to brace him in her official capacity, instead of just calling him.

And then, to round off his morning, his father had told him he had had an affair with Q's best friend's mother, an affair that had nudged Q's own mother over the edge into the abyss. 'Why did you keep it from me? About Mum?'

'What would I have said?' Mort looked up at Jesus on his cross. 'When Pete died, the police questioned me. Someone had told them how close Pete and I were. I could have told the truth then. About the affair. But I didn't.'

'Did Pete know?'

'Yes. I told him.'

'When?'

'On the day he died.'

Q froze. Time seemed to slow. A dull knocking sounded in his ears. 'Why then, after all these years?'

'Because Pete's mother had just died. She moved out of Wickstone years ago. Met someone. A fisheries worker in the Highlands. He wrote to me, at her request, after her funeral. She died still wanting forgiveness, for Bella's death. She felt responsible.'

Q remembered Pete's mother, Briony, a pale presence, always in the background. Pete's father, Alan, had been an overloud man, fond of making speeches about the English football team. Q had barely known them.

'I told Pete because I couldn't keep it in any longer. I wanted to tell you too. Write to you. But Pete asked me not to.'

And now Q understood the final line in Pete's note. *Mort won't be pleased. But that's neither here nor there, is it?* He'd written that note on the day he had died. Presumably after Mort had told him about the affair. Yet, Pete had still retained enough self-control to write the letter and leave it somewhere for it to be sent to Q in the event of his death ... Could the revelation of his mother's infidelity have pushed Pete into that river? Had Q got it wrong, after all? But then why would Pete leave that letter behind? It occurred to Q that this might all be an elaborate game, Pete's attempt to get back at Mort. By making Q chase his own tail around. By forcing him back to Wickstone and a confrontation with his father.

No. That simply didn't make sense.

He took a deep breath. 'And you didn't tell the police this?'

'No. I lied. I told them I hadn't seen Pete on the day he died.'

'Is that why he went out to Bishop's Point? Because of what you'd told him, about his mother? About you and her?'

'I've been asking myself that same question.'

Q could see that his father was hurting. He examined his own feelings. He was shocked and disappointed. Of course he was. But time softened most things. Finding out thirty years after the fact that his father had cheated on his mother ... The admission quickly lost its potency.

He considered again how Pete might have taken the news. Granted, they had drifted apart, but Q couldn't imagine Pete being so devastated by the news of his mother's infidelity that he would have ended his life because of it. He and Pete had been alike in many ways. Driven. Ambitious. Coldly analytical. Each had suffered emotional upheavals in life. Each had similar mechanisms for dealing with it. Throwing themselves into their work. Running away. But suicide? No. Q didn't think so.

A shout came from the entrance to the church as someone popped their head in the door, bellowed for 'Philip', then backed out again.

'So, what now?' said Mort.

Q thought about it. 'Schrödinger's Cat.'

Mort swung his head around. 'I'm sorry?'

'Schrödinger's Cat. A thought experiment devised by physicist Erwin Schrödinger. A cat is put in a box together with a beaker of poison, a radioactive source and a Geiger counter. If the Geiger counter detects a single atom decaying from the radioactive source, the beaker cracks and the poison escapes. The cat dies. So, in theory, until someone looks in the box, the cat might be dead *or* alive. It's the way quantum superposition is usually explained to the laity.'

Mort looked unimpressed. 'I hate cats.'

'My point is that I'm here and not here. A part of me still exists in the life I created in London. But another part of me is now back in the life I left behind in Wickstone. It doesn't really matter *why* I came back. I'm glad that I did. I'm glad that I've had the chance to reconnect with you, with Kathy. If any good can come of Pete's death, then I'll take it. But now I'm invested. I don't think Pete killed himself. I think he was murdered.'

'And you have evidence for this?'

'Not precisely. But I'm building up a picture. And the picture is crooked.'

Mort looked at his son. Mort could still see the boy in the man. He remembered Q's first steps, his first faltering words, the boy he had read stories of ancient Rome to in place of Roald Dahl. Love was a force powerful enough to move planets. To displace time.

But there were limits even to love.

Mort couldn't tell Q that there had been moments when he had wanted Bella dead. Wanted the unhappiness to end. Hers and his. He couldn't tell Q that he had hated himself, had wanted so very badly to reach out to his son and make things right.

Fides rupta. Broken bond. Fate had broken bonds in a way that had seemed impossible to repair. But now, here was Fate again, smiling down on Mort. Everyone deserved a second chance, didn't they? Even a man who had betrayed his family.

'I'm hungry,' said Mort. 'Would you care for another kebab?'

If Kebab Guy recognised them, he was doing a good job of not showing it.

Mort noticed that the constellation of stains on the front of his T-shirt had changed. Perhaps it was another shirt. Perhaps he had a set of them, a different one for every day of the week. Perhaps he considered it a crime to wash them, the way some artists refused to clean paint-splattered garments.

As they waited for their order, Q set out what he knew. 'Pete's lab is developing the world's most powerful quantum computer. One of the applications of that technology will be to enable all current encryption methods to be overridden. That scenario is frightening to a great many powerful people. In a sense, it's a weapon. Many would kill to prevent such a weapon coming online. Or kill to obtain it.'

'And you think one of these parties had Pete killed?'

'It's a possibility. Which means that perhaps someone at Napier Labs knows precisely who might have wanted Pete dead.' Q paused. His thoughts went to Jed Ellis, Napier Labs' Chief Operating Officer. When Q had spoken to him Ellis had been evasive. He had mentioned the strain Pete had been under; had been keen to push the suicide narrative. But if Pete *had* been threatened – about the technology Napier Labs was developing – it would put a new light on things. On Pete's behaviour. On the circumstances of his death. *Could* someone from the lab be involved?

'And then there's Adem Gashi,' Q continued. 'Pete took the trouble to direct me to his car dealership. Why? Adem told me he and Pete were friends, that Napier Labs was a valued customer. The police say Adem was linked to organised crime. We know Pete had cocaine in his system. It's not a big leap to think Pete was buying drugs from Adem – or Adem's associates. But I can't see why any of them would want to kill him.'

Mort picked up a bottle of extra hot chilli sauce, examined it, shuddered, then set it down again. 'These scenarios sound outlandish. Given that the easiest explanation is still that Pete either drowned himself or that his death was an accident.'

'Adem was murdered. Surely you don't think that's a coincidence?' Q tapped a finger on the tabletop. 'We know that Zak Youssef met with Pete out at Bishop's Point on the night he died. Zak believes that, prior to his arrival, Pete was with a woman, and that there's a strong possibility that Pete had sex with her. Pete was clearly alive when this mystery woman left, but it's not beyond the bounds of possibility that she returned later that night, after Zak had come and gone.'

'And you think this woman is Pete's killer?'

'It's possible.'

'But you have no idea who she is?'

'No.'

'Forgive me, Sherlock, but you don't seem to know very much.'

The clatter of the lunchtime crowd rose around them. His father was right, of course. What did he really have? Speculation. A web of barely glued together facts, as thin as gossamer.

And yet.

Q cast his mind back over the past days. Everything he had learned, everyone he had spoken to. He knew, from his years at Q Branch, that, more often than not, a solution presented itself only when you allowed the mind to slip its leash, to roam free and reflect.

His thoughts kept returning to the mystery woman. Might *she* be the bad actor at play here? A woman who had seduced Pete, and then killed him? In the pay of those who wanted Pete's work stopped? At all costs.

Pete had been working flat out. He would hardly have had time to go looking for female companionship. Which meant that he would have cast his net closer to home. And home, for Pete, in the months before his death, had been his lab.

And, suddenly, Q was back in Helen Banner's house.

Q had asked Helen if she knew anyone who might have wanted to harm Pete. Helen had deflected, had instead told Q to talk to Astrid Simmons, the young scientist who had shown Q around Napier Labs. Helen had also told her that Astrid had taken over her work at the lab. Something in Helen's tone had struck Q as odd at the time. A tightness in her throat. What had Helen said? ... *'Astrid. Pete had a lot of faith in her.'*

It wasn't *what* she had said, but the way she had said it.

Q made an intuitive leap.

It was time for another talk with Astrid Simmons.

54

'I REALLY SHOULDN'T BE DOING THIS.'

Why did people say things like that? When it was clear they had every intention of doing precisely the thing they thought they shouldn't be doing?

Deborah smiled at the man sitting behind the desk. His name was Gavin. Gavin was the forensic pathologist assigned to Wickstone. A man approaching retirement, with mouths to feed, including a wife with expensive tastes. Deborah had done her homework.

She reached into her handbag, took out a thick envelope, and set it down on the desk. 'The family is grateful for your help.'

Gavin blinked in the bright white lighting. A tongue flicked out to touch his bottom lip. Gavin reminded Deborah of a lizard. The kind that sat around all day waiting for flies to buzz into its mouth. A hand snaked out and pulled the envelope into a drawer. *Gulp.*

Gavin turned to his computer and fiddled with his mouse. A printer whirred to life. He stood, walked to the machine, returned with papers. 'The autopsy report. There isn't much there. Mr Gashi was stabbed through the heart. Multiple wounds, by a large, bladed weapon – a kitchen knife or one of those street knives young gang members carry around these days. His right ventricle was pierced. Death would have been quick.'

'The knife hasn't been found?'

'Not yet.'

'Was there anything indicating who might have done this?'

'There were no defensive injuries on Mr Gashi. Which implies that he knew his assailant. Or was unafraid of him.'

Deborah said nothing. Adem had known few people in Wickstone. Whoever he had met up at Jane's Hill would be someone Adem either trusted or who had somehow compelled Adem to meet him, in secrecy. That narrowed the suspect list.

'I spoke with the crime scene coordinator,' continued Gavin. 'No forensic artefacts were found at the scene.' He hesitated. 'But it's early days.'

Deborah stood. 'Thank you for your help.'

'Would you like to see the body?'

'I've already seen it. I identified it for the police.'

Gavin said nothing. His nervousness was a fog gradually filling out the room.

Deborah felt an unnatural calm. Adem's death had come as a shock. But there was work to be done. Mirko was relying on her. Wickstone was too important to allow a single death to interrupt the family's plans.

Perhaps it was time to visit Jed Ellis again. Was Napier Labs still on track? It was hard to be sure. Deborah hoped so.

For everyone's sake.

55

TAKE THE BULL BY THE horns.

Q had never understood the sentiment. On the list of top ten most stupid things to do, taking a rampaging bull by the horns seemed a clear winner. The expression had originated in the Wild West where bored cowboys wrestled steers for fun. This probably explained why so few cowboys had grown up to be cowmen.

Nevertheless.

Astrid Simmons had not struck Q as the type to take kindly to intrusive questions about her personal life. He doubted that she would respond well to an interrogation into her relationship with Pete Napier. Q debated with himself whether he might enlist Kathy's help but quickly dismissed the idea.

The idea of facing Kathy any time in the near future gave him heartburn.

Which meant that he would have to do this on his own.

Where did Astrid Simmons live? How could he find out?

Q worked the problem. A thought struck him. Perhaps he was overengineering this. There *was* a simple solution here.

He took his car keys out of his pocket and headed for the door.

*

Q drove out to Napier Labs.

At the gate, he tried his luck with the guard. 'I'd like to speak to Astrid Simmons.'

The guard stared at him. 'Sorry. Miss Simmons won't be able to speak to you today.'

'But she's on the premises?'

'That's neither here nor there, is it?'

'Do you know what time she usually leaves?'

'Sir. If you wouldn't mind exiting the premises.'

'I'm not actually on the premises.'

The guard frowned. This was clearly higher-level thinking in the world of security guarding. Sitting around in a booth all day left plenty of time for esoteric thought. Einstein had formulated his theory of relativity whilst working as a lowly clerk in a patents office. Perhaps the guard had been busy delving into the mathematical secrets of the cosmos during his booth tenure. Q doubted it.

He turned and headed back to the road.

Q sat in the Caterham for a couple of minutes, watching the guard through the windscreen. He saw the man pick up his intercom. Q lifted a small device from the passenger seat, set it on the dash, and pointed it at the booth. The device was connected by wires to equipment on the seat. Q slipped on a pair of headphones.

The Spectra laser microphone had a range of four hundred metres and could eavesdrop through walls.

The guard's voice crackled through, loud and clear. '*Miss Simmons? That guy was back. Boothroyd. You asked me to let you know if he showed up again.*'

Interesting. Q slipped off the headphones, started the car, executed a perfect three-point turn, drove a few hundred metres around a bend in the road, then turned into a small layby. Parking the Caterham, he returned the eavesdropping kit to his 'picnic hamper' and removed something else from it, placed it in a satchel, then made his way back towards Napier Labs on foot, through the woods leading up to the facility. When he was approximately a hundred metres away, he settled himself behind a tree and took out a Pulsar Axion thermal imaging monocular from the satchel. Setting it up on a collapsible stand, he pointed it at the main gate and peered through the lens.

From his vantage point, he could see the gate and the guard booth beside it. He would be able to monitor every car that came out of the compound, with a direct view through each windscreen. If night fell, the monocular's thermal imaging capability would come into its own.

All he had to do was wait.

Q was familiar with the mythology of the Hollywood stakeout.

Sweaty men parked in cars littered with fast food cartons and coffee cups, peering in at glamorous suspects obligingly undressing in uncurtained windows. Witty banter hinting at an undercurrent of tension or, in the right circumstances, romance. And then the moment when everything kicked into gear, feet pounding on pavement, doors battered down, guns going off.

What he hadn't realised was just how boring the actual act of surveillance was.

An hour passed. The woods were quiet. Animal noises faded into the background. No cars rattled along the road towards Napier Labs. No cars left the compound.

Q wished he had a stool. His knees were already aching. How did the professionals do it? Bond had been on plenty of surveillance ops. Though Bond's idea of surveillance often appeared to be to just walk in the front door and announce himself. Then order a martini. It was a wonder the man didn't wear a hat embroidered with the words 'I AM A SPY'.

Thinking of Bond jolted a memory. Days earlier, Bond had asked him to call, to discuss something. Instead, Q had enlisted him in his own investigation. The thought bothered him. The fact was that, even after all these years, Q had no idea whether Bond considered him a friend, not in the truest sense of the word. It wasn't as if they spent much time together socially. MI6 didn't do karaoke nights.

Q still remembered the first time he and Bond had met, early on in Bond's tenure at the Double O section. Q had advised him on his choice of handgun. True to form, Bond had thought he had known better. But, in the end, he had grudgingly bowed to Q's expertise. Perhaps that was the difference between them. Q had all the theory in the world but Bond had actually *seen* the world. Been there, done that.

Now, for the first time in his life, Q was out in the field. It was exhilarating. And more than a little terrifying.

He briefly tried to imagine Bond at a karaoke mike. What song would 007 pick?

Q took out his phone, logged on, dialled.

No reply.

Bond was probably deep into a mission. Probably jumping over crocodiles or seducing some femme fatale with a prominently scarred and sociopathic boyfriend.

The hours passed. Q lowered himself to the cool earth, set his back against the tree. A beetle crawled across his hand. A movement in the shadows turned out to be a deer. He watched it for a while before it turned and trotted away.

The sun wheeled across the sky and began its downward trajectory into oblivion.

More time passed.

Q had all but given up when cars began leaving the compound. He rose slowly to his feet, set his eye to the monocular.

An hour later, he saw Astrid Simmons leave, hunched over the wheel in the driver's seat of a canary yellow Mini Cooper with a black roof. She paused to say something to the guard.

Q jogged back to the Caterham, started the engine and pulled onto the road.

He revved the engine until the Mini Cooper's tail-lights came into view.

Keeping a discreet distance behind, he followed Astrid back into Wickstone.

56

Q CHECKED HIS WATCH.

He was parked outside The Olive Taverna, Wickstone's only Greek restaurant. Astrid had gone inside some ten minutes earlier.

Another stakeout. Q briefly toyed with the idea of marching in and simply sitting down at her table. It's what Bond would have done. And Astrid would probably have melted at the sight of him, told him everything he wanted to know.

But Q wasn't Bond. He didn't have Bond's occult powers with the opposite sex.

He settled into his seat. He would wait her out. And then, follow her home. Doorstep her, as the journos said. Yes. That was the way to go—

A knocking on his window jolted him out of his thoughts. Q looked around. Astrid was staring down at him.

Q blinked rapidly. He hadn't seen her come out of the front door. Which could only mean— He slid down the window.

'If you're going to follow someone perhaps you shouldn't do it in a fluorescent green sports car?' Astrid folded her arms. 'What do you want?'

'I – I'm sorry. I wanted to ask you some more questions about Pete. I had no idea how to get hold of you.'

Her gaze continued to evaluate him. And then: 'Come on. You can buy me dinner.'

The restaurant was busy for a weekday evening.

Q and Astrid ordered. The woman had quite the appetite, Q couldn't help but notice. And she wasn't shy about ordering an expensive bottle of wine. Not with Q picking up the tab.

'Are you going to ask me a question or just sit there staring at my chest?'

'I wasn't—'

'I'm joking. You seem a little uptight. What can I do for you, Mr Stalker?'

'I wasn't stalk—'

'Relax.' Astrid checked her phone, then set it down.

Q licked his lips. 'I think Pete Napier was murdered. In fact, I'm sure of it. On the night he died he met with a woman, a woman he had— had a sexual encounter with. Out at Bishop's Point.' Q stopped.

Astrid stared at him. The wine arrived. The waiter poured for them, then stepped smartly away. Astrid picked up her glass. 'Are you asking me if I slept with Pete or whether I murdered him?'

Q picked up his own glass. 'Did you?'

Astrid seemed to consider this. 'Yes. And no ... Yes, I slept with Pete, though not on that night. And no, I didn't kill him.' A noise at a nearby table turned her head. They waited as a happy birthday recital was inflicted on an unsuspecting octogenarian, a cake brought out with great ceremony, waiters leading the applause. The old man at the centre of the fuss looked mortified.

Astrid turned back to Q. 'Pete and I had a thing. When I first joined Napier Labs. It was no big deal. We were both single and it didn't last long. We kept it under the radar. I didn't want to be known as the woman who slept with the boss.'

'But you did,' said Q. 'Sleep with the boss.'

'That's the patriarchy talking,' said Astrid. 'I graduated top of my class at Stanford. I am one of the world's leading quantum computing software coders. Everything I do, I do because I can, because it suits me. Pete Napier pursued *me*. I made my own decision. I slept with Pete because I wanted to.'

'I'm sorry, I didn't mean—'

'Yes. You did.' An uncomfortable silence ensued, before Astrid continued. 'As I said, it didn't last long. I got bored of Pete. We agreed to move on.'

'Did it affect your working relationship?'

'No. We were adults.'

'And you weren't with him that night? The night he died?'

'Categorically not.'

'Can anyone vouch for that?'

Q thought she would go on the attack, but instead she simply flashed a thin-lipped smile. 'Fine. I'll humour you. No, no one can vouch for me. I spent the night alone. At my home. And, no, I didn't get up, wander into the woods, shag Pete and then murder him. Not that I didn't want to.'

'I don't understand.'

'Pete was a hard taskmaster. He was driving everyone crazy. At the lab. I think he was having a breakdown. I think that's why he killed himself.'

'Pete didn't kill himself.' Q tapped the rim of his glass. 'Do you know who else Pete might have been sleeping with? Who this mystery woman might have been?'

Astrid shrugged. 'Pete liked sex. He was too busy for a relationship. He took what he could get, when he could get it. There were plenty of others for him at Napier Labs, a few around town. He wasn't conventionally handsome, but he had a monomaniacal charm. And money. Pete didn't mind splashing the cash. On the things he enjoyed in life. Cars. Women.'

Q studied her face. Was she lying? 'Why did you have the guard look out for me? What is it that you and Jed Ellis don't want me to find out?'

Their food arrived. Astrid's eyes remained on Q. When the waiter left, she said: 'Do you know what Combat Sambo is?'

'No.'

'It's a Russian martial art. I took it up several years ago. I could knock your nose back into your brain.'

'I would rather you didn't.'

'Then how about you stop insulting me and tell me what this is really all about?'

'I've already—'

'What do you know that I don't?'

Q hesitated. And then he plunged. 'Is Napier Labs using its new quantum computing capability to develop software capable of breaking current encryption protocols? Are you leading that effort?'

Astrid picked up her wine. 'I can't speak about my work.'

'NDAs?'

Astrid nodded. 'Plus it wouldn't be ethical.'

'But it's true, isn't it? And that work placed Pete in danger. Is that why he was murdered? Do you know who killed him?'

Her eyes hardened. 'I think it's time for you to leave.'

'I—'

'Leave. Before I start screaming.'

Perhaps he was coming at this all wrong.

Q sat in the Caterham, thinking through the encounter with Astrid. It was obvious to him that there were things the woman wasn't telling him. But were those secrets relevant to Pete's death? Was Astrid the woman who had been with Pete that night, despite her denials? Like Jed Ellis, there had been something evasive in her manner.

As he sat there, running through the permutations in his mind, Q was hit by a sideways jolt of comprehension. He realised that there might be another way to crack the problem, a thought that had been lurking at the back of his mind without quite making itself known ... It wasn't so much who Pete had been with that night, but *how*. How had this mystery woman gone out there to meet with Pete? The traffic camera on the road up to Bishop's Point had only captured one vehicle that evening: Pete's car. The footage clearly showed him alone in his vehicle. No other vehicles – or pedestrians – had passed that way during the relevant timeframe.

Could someone have walked there through the woods, avoiding the road?

Highly unlikely. The woods would have been dark, the trail hard going. And a long way. It would make no sense.

And then it hit him. A flare going off inside his skull. How had he missed it?

There was *another* person who had gone out to Bishop's Point that evening.

Another person who hadn't appeared on the traffic cameras.

57

THE HOUSE BEFORE Q WAS stuccoed, semi-detached, and looked a little embarrassed to be under scrutiny. A large and faded flag, the cross of St George, draped from an upper window.

Every town had a street like this. A postcode that estate agents preferred not to talk about. When they sold property here, they used terms such as *exotic* and *quaint* to describe the locale. Q remembered a friend from school who had lived here. Milo. Whose dad was rumoured to have spent time in prison. Not much fun for Milo. At home or in the playground.

Q ignored the front door and instead walked down a side alley to a secondary door. He rang the bell, then stepped back. The light was fading. Dusk was on its way.

The door opened to reveal Sameera Youssef. 'Mr Boothroyd.' Her surprise was evident.

'I hope it's not an inconvenient time? I was hoping to speak with Zak.'

A hesitation. But then she nodded and gestured him inside.

The room was cramped, with the impression of barely imposed order on a natural state of chaos. Unfamiliar smells drifted from an adjoining kitchen.

Sameera watched Q nervously.

'I went to the hospital,' said Q. 'They told me Zak had been discharged.'

'Yes. The doctors said he could come home. Detective Sergeant Bob has questioned him officially. About the stolen car. He will have to appear at magistrates' court. If he pleads guilty, Detective Sergeant Bob thinks Zak has a good chance of being given a suspended sentence.'

'It could be worse,' said Q.

'Yes. Thank you for helping him.' A brittle smile transformed her features.

'Zak gave the police information about Peter Napier's death. He helped himself.'

She was silent a moment. 'He is not a bad boy.'

A mother's eternal lament. 'I need to ask him a few more questions about the night Pete died.'

A look of worry crossed her features.

'It's quite important.'

Still she hesitated.

'I don't think Zak had anything to do with Pete's death,' Q said. 'But I do need to talk to him.'

She relented, turned, and led him to a door leading off the living room. A metal sign screwed to the door read: KNOCK BEFORE ENTERING. AS A SMACK IN THE TEETH OFTEN OFFENDS.

Q knocked. A voice called out. Q grabbed the handle and entered.

Sameera began following him in but was distracted by the sound of her phone ringing from the kitchen. She hesitated, then turned back, leaving him to it.

Zak was sitting up in bed, focused on a TV screen and operating a controller in his lap. Q could see that he was playing a video game, decimating hordes of animated creatures streaming across the screen.

'Hello, Zak.'

The boy looked up. Confusion crossed his brow. 'What are you doing here?'

Q looked at the screen. 'Is that *Zombie Rampage on Planet Blood*?'

'You're a gamer?'

'No. But I've come across the gaming community in the course of my work. The metaverse is an important field of research at Q Branch.'

'I've managed to reach Level 6, the torture chamber of Zargon IV. But I can't seem to get past Lena, the Man-Eating Warrior Queen.'

'Zak, I need to ask you something important. How did you get out to Bishop's Point that night? To deliver Pete his cocaine?'

The boy frowned. 'I cycled.'

'Through the woods?'

'Yes. There's a camera on the main road. I try to avoid cameras.'

Q nodded. 'I think that's also how Pete's killer got there that night. It was too far and too dark to walk out to Bishop's Point. And no individual – or vehicle – went past the traffic camera except Pete. A bicycle through the woods is the only realistic way that anyone could have got to Pete. Without being seen, that is.'

Zak set down his game controller.

'The question is,' Q continued, 'how can I find out who that bike belonged to? There must be hundreds of bikes in Wickstone.' Q knew that might be an understatement. With the open lanes of the countryside on the town's doorstep, plenty of newly minted Wickstonians had probably taken up biking. There were probably hordes of lycra-swaddled middle-aged men with pasty legs and pot bellies huffing and puffing along local arteries, blocking up traffic.

'Bike club,' said Zak.

It was Q's turn to frown. 'What?'

'There's a bike club in Wickstone. A lot of people cycle together or compete against each other for the number of miles they cycle in a week.'

'How do you know this?'

Zak scraped his tongue over his teeth. 'I have a friend who … has a strong interest in bike ownership in Wickstone. Bikes are high-ticket items these days. Worth hundreds, sometimes thousands of pounds. Many have inbuilt GPS trackers. A lot of them are registered to ride-tracking apps.'

'Ah,' said Q. 'I take it your friend's interest in high-end bikes is similar to your own interest in high-end cars?'

Zak said nothing.

'I don't suppose you could call your friend and ask him a couple of questions?'

'I don't think he'd like that.'

'I'm not the police, Zak. I don't care what your friend does. I just want to track down the person who might have cycled out to Bishop's Point that night. You mentioned ride-tracking apps? If the person I'm looking for was a member of a local bike club, then perhaps their journey might be logged on such an app?' Q suppressed his rising excitement. He could sense that he was on to something.

Zak looked conflicted, then said. 'We don't need to call my friend. I wrote the rootkit malware that he used to hack Bike-A-Long, the most popular ride-tracking app in Wickstone.'

'You used a RAT?' A remote access trojan. The boy seemed surprised that Q knew the term.

'Yeah. I control it via a botnet swarm.'

Q imagined that most civilians would understand one word in three of this strange shibboleth. He was reminded of meetings with the top white hat hackers at Q Branch, smart young things who talked so rapidly it sounded like machine-gun fire.

Q waited as the boy fired up his laptop, ran the code and hacked into the Bike-A-Long app. A sense of unease drifted over Q. What they were doing was, technically, illegal. Did the end justify the means? MI6 had certainly operated with that principle. The Double Os were licensed to kill for a reason. Sometimes the only way to get the job done was to operate outside of the lines.

'What was the date you were looking for? And the time?'

Q told him.

Zak ran a search, then sat back. 'Here you go.'

Q could see a cycle journey on the laptop's screen, superimposed on a map of Wickstone. A red line snaked from the centre of town out to Bishop's Point. The time stamp indicated that the journey had been made shortly before Pete had died.

'You're lucky,' said Zak. 'Our rider didn't set up a privacy filter. Their journey is recorded end to end.'

'Can you find the originating address? Where the journey began?'

Zak attacked the keyboard. The address popped up in a bubble on the screen. It took a second for the information to register . . . Q was stunned. The address was one he recognised, had been to recently.

Zak hit another key. 'By the way. There's a second journey, same as the first. Not long afterwards.'

Q looked at the screen. The boy was right. Just over an hour after the first, a second pair of lines showed another journey from – and back to – the same location. The same rider had made two trips out to see Pete that night. Which made perfect sense.

'Does that help?'

Q looked up. 'Thank you. That's very useful.'

'Tell the cops I helped out,' said Zak. 'Maybe the magistrate will go easy on me.'

'I probably won't tell them about hacking into the ride-tracking app. And what your friend uses it for.'

Zak frowned. 'Maybe you're right.'

Q took out his phone, checked the time. 'Did Pete ever talk to you about his work? Did he ever mention any . . . danger that he might have been in because of it?'

The boy allowed a silence, before speaking. 'He'd talk about the lab, sometimes. About the lab's work, about the impact it might have on the world. Good. And bad. I'm not sure he thought I understood everything he was talking about. But I wasn't stupid. I like maths. Pete knew that. He told me I could work for him one day. *If* I went back to school.' A cynical snort. 'He was talking shit. He would never have hired a boy who once delivered him drugs.' A beat. 'He did say something, on the day he died, out on the jetty. I think he was quoting some film. "I am become death, destroyer of worlds." Or something like that. He seemed . . . sad.'

The door opened and Sameera walked in. 'Is everything all right?'

Q glanced at her, standing there, anxiety draped heavily over her shoulders. A woman haunted by the past, by her husband's uncertain fate. Battling an equally uncertain future, in a country that wasn't sure that it wanted her, and a son who wasn't sure that he needed her.

And the boy? He seemed smaller, sitting there with his game controller, a cast around his ankle, trapped in this tiny room, the guillotine of the future hanging over his bed. Q remembered what it was like to have few friends, to be uncertain of one's place in the world. He remembered something a colleague had once said to him: *Inside every bad kid is a good kid trying to get out.*

'How are you getting on here?' Q asked.

'This place is tiny,' said Zak. 'Back in Syria we lived in a mansion.'

'I take it someone else is living in the flat upstairs?'

'Mr Saunders,' said Sameera. 'He's very nice.'

'He's a racist old fart,' said Zak.

'No,' said Sameera. 'He is not.'

'He's got that flag in his window.'

'That does not make him a racist.'

'Has he insulted you?' said Q.

Zak looked sullen. 'No.'

'Has he made you feel unwelcome?'

A hesitation. 'No.'

'He brought us dinner,' said Sameera. 'He made it himself.'

'It was pork,' said Zak.

'He didn't know,' said Sameera. 'He's a kind man.'

Q found words in his mouth. 'You've had a rough time of it, Zak. You didn't ask to be here. But here is where you are. Britain isn't your enemy. Britain isn't trying to steal your identity. Britain has given you a home. A safe harbour. Ask yourself: have you earned the right to criticise us? Nations are like people. Imperfect. But the greatness of Great Britain lies in the fact that each time we fail, we learn, and we go back into the fray with a desire to be better, to be a force for good in this world. That's the Britain I believe in, the Britain I've spent my life defending. It's the same with people. Give them a chance and they might surprise you.'

Zak looked uncomfortable.

'Perhaps it's time for you to examine your own prejudices?' said Q.

'I *can't* be racist,' Zak muttered. 'I'm brown.'

58

Q KNOCKED ON THE DOOR, THEN stepped back.
The thudding of his heart counted out the seconds.
The door swung back.

Helen Banner stood in the doorway squinting into the sun. Dressed in gymwear, a sheen of sweat on her arms and face. Hair pulled back into a workmanlike ponytail.

'Mr Boothroyd.' If she seemed taken aback to see him, she hid it well.

'I have information about Pete's death. Do you have time for a few more questions?'

She checked her watch, opened her mouth, then seemed to change her mind. 'I'm not sure why I checked my watch. It's not as if I have anywhere to go. Come in.' She turned and walked inside. Q followed. She threw words over her shoulder. 'I've always lived in big cities. When Pete told me he'd set up shop in his hometown, out in the countryside, I imagined a seething hotbed of rural angst. It hasn't quite been that.'

They walked into a large drawing room. Helen picked up a towel and wiped down her arms and the back of her neck. 'Sorry, I've been Pelotoning.'

'You Peloton?'

'A lifelong cyclist. Semi-professional, for a while. I prefer to get out into the roads. But sometimes it's nice to get online with a pro. Something to drink?'

'No. Thank you.'

He watched her pick up a bottle of water and tilt it back. 'So, what's this all about? Are you still convinced Pete didn't kill himself?'

Q had no experience of this. He had charged in here without the requisite authority or having thought through the consequences. It wasn't every day that you accused a woman of murder in her own home. What if things turned ugly? Q's military training was decades behind him. There may have been a time when he could have incapacitated an opponent with his bare hands, but he hadn't needed that particular skillset for a while. And Helen Banner looked like she could take care of herself.

Was there someone else in the house? Her son? With his tousled Young Hugh Grant hair and rugby player thighs? Q couldn't imagine the young man standing by while Q performed some sort of citizen's arrest on his mother.

'Why are you here, Mr Boothroyd?'

Q took out his phone, fiddled with it, then held it out to the woman.

'What am I looking at?'

'It's an image, taken from GPS tracking data. The red line follows a bicycle that was ridden out to Bishop's Point on the evening of Pete's death. The bicycle originated – and returned – to this address. The bike is registered to you.'

Helen's mouth fell open. No sound emerged. And then her legs gave way. She flopped onto the sofa. An oxblood chesterfield. You didn't see sofas like that anymore, thought Q. Everyone wanted neon-coloured sofas you could sink in to, the kind that looked good in adverts, couples in colourful socks, pretending to watch TV, snuggled in each other's arms.

Q spoke into the silence. 'Were you and Pete having an affair?'

She seemed to revive. 'Have the police seen this?'

'Not yet.'

'But they will?'

'Yes.'

Another brief silence. 'I fell in love. It wasn't planned. I'd never been attracted to Pete. As I mentioned before, we worked together, briefly, in France. A long time ago. Nothing. No spark. But something happened here in Wickstone. Working together on this project. Watching him up close. I suppose I had never really understood just how incredible he was. To be that close to someone who might change the course of human history. You can't imagine how intoxicating that is.' A blink. 'Henri, my husband, found out. It ruined our marriage. That's why he's away, in France. A trial separation. I don't think he's coming back.'

'I presume the affair was why you were asked to leave Napier Labs?'

'No. I left because Pete and I fundamentally disagreed over the work we were doing. I know it sounds crazy. We were lovers, but in the lab Pete was a different animal.'

'What did you disagree about?'

'I can't—'

'Was he asking you to develop algorithms that would undermine global encryption protocols?'

She stiffened. 'Who have you been talking to?'

Q leaned forward. 'Why did you go out to him that night?'

She was shaking her head. '*He* called *me*. On a burner phone. I know how it sounds, but we kept them so we didn't have to use our actual phones. Our colleagues were getting suspicious. It just made things easier.'

'You went out there on your bike? Through the woods?'

'Yes. I knew there was a camera on the road out to Bishop's Point.'

'What happened when you got there?'

282

'We had sex. We talked. Pete was upset about something. Something personal he'd discovered about his mother. He wouldn't say exactly what. And then there was the lab. Worries about the project, about his stakeholders. People he had to answer to.'

'What people?'

'I don't know. That was his and Jed Ellis's domain. I expect he meant his VCs. Venture capitalists. Have you ever dealt with VCs? They can be quite brutal. Like the Terminator, if the Terminator had a business degree. I suspect they were threatening to pull the plug.'

'Why? Wasn't Pete on the cusp of turning Napier Labs into a highly lucrative enterprise?'

She hesitated. 'Some of his results might have been exaggerated.'

Q masked his shock. 'Pete was making up results?'

'Not making up. Just . . . He was under pressure to deliver to timescales that were ridiculous. Our funders needed to see progress. As did new funders – we needed more money, all the time. So Pete massaged some of the projections.'

Q's mind whirled. 'If that had come out, it would have destroyed Pete's reputation. And the reputation of everyone at Napier Labs.'

'Possibly.'

'Is that why you killed him?'

A twitch of the cheek. 'I didn't kill Pete. I loved him. Or thought I did.'

'But he didn't love you back.'

A beat. 'No.'

'Is *that* why you killed him?'

'He was very much alive when I left him that evening.'

'I agree,' said Q. 'After you left, Pete called his drug courier and ordered a delivery. But here's the thing. The courier says Pete was upset. That the person he had been with had threatened him, had betrayed him. What did you say to Pete?'

'I simply told him that if we didn't stop working on the encryption-busting algorithms I would go public with everything I knew. About the work, about the massaged results. I would break my NDA, no matter what it cost me.'

'You were angry with him. Furious.' Q fiddled with his phone again and held it up. 'Half an hour after Pete's drug courier left, your bicycle made another journey out to Bishop's Point. You went back. Maybe you wanted to have another crack at Pete. But when he refused to listen, something snapped. You pushed him into the river. Knowing he couldn't swim. You watched him die and then you cleaned up the evidence. And then you went home.'

Helen's face froze. She seemed to stop breathing. When she spoke again, her voice was faraway. A clarity had come into her features.

Resignation, thought Q.

'Yes,' said Helen. 'I killed Peter Napier.'

59

THERE HAD BEEN A MOMENT, back in the late Noughties, when the world, as it did now and again, had seemed to hover on the brink of catastrophe. Unrest in the Caucasus. The Middle East embroiled in war. Superpowers rattling sabres across a map of the globe.

Q and Bond had been in M's office, discussing an infiltration op into Pakistan. A Pashtun warlord had made forays into the enriched uranium marketplace. Bond, posing as a British arms dealer, had agreed a meet in Karachi. Bond wanted to use the opportunity to permanently end the warlord's sudden uranium craving. MI6 preferred to ask the man a few questions first, if Bond wouldn't mind.

Q had been tasked to fit Bond out with a lead-lined case of fake uranium, just real enough to pass the basic chemical and radiological tests that a tribal warlord might have at his disposal. Bond had argued that he be allowed to rock up with the real thing. Unfortunately for 007, no one else thought that handing him a suitcase full of enriched uranium would be a good idea.

Partway through the conversation, Bond had looked up. 'M? Are you OK?'

M had been silent a while, a lugubrious expression slackening his bullfrog features. 'My wife, Jane, you've met her, haven't you, Bond? This morning, at breakfast, she tells me she wants a divorce. That she's in love with an ornithologist from Clapham. Been going on a year, it seems. What do you make of that, 007?'

Bond had straightened, exchanged glances with Q.

'You know, in this business, you can account for anything,' M continued. 'Greed, malice, sheer bloody-mindedness. But the one thing you can never plan for is the monstrous nature of love.'

It was two days after Helen Banner's arrest, and Q was sitting opposite Bob Lazarus at the Wickstone police station.

No sign of Kathy. Just as well.

'You'll appreciate I can't talk about an ongoing investigation.' Bob blew the froth off his coffee. '*Off* the record, I can tell you that you've done well there. Nice bit of sleuthing. How did you get Banner to confess? Used the old MI6 interrogation handbook, eh?'

'I confronted her with the evidence,' said Q. 'She confessed.'

'Often the way. No such thing as a criminal mastermind. Most offenders are as thick as two short planks. Not the case here, obviously, but you'd be surprised how quickly they fall to pieces when faced with proof of their evildoing.'

'Has she said anything else?'

'She repeated her confession in a police interview room after we arrested her. Voluntarily gave us access to her bike app data. Though we managed to get a warrant for the data anyway, expedited at warp speed off the back of her confession. Kathy likes to be thorough. Belt and braces. By the way, how exactly did *you* get hold of said data?' An inquisitively raised eyebrow, to which Q said nothing. 'Doesn't matter, I suppose. Banner hasn't changed her story. She killed Pete. No further details yet. She's hired herself a lawyer, bail hearing imminent. But your little GPS trick has her bang to rights. Let's see you wriggle out of that one, Little Miss Quantum Scientist.'

Q looked around the station. A young officer sitting at a nearby desk was desperately pretending that he wasn't trying to listen in.

In the two days since Helen Banner had confessed to Q, something strange had happened. Once the initial euphoria had worn off – he had solved the puzzle! He, Q, had found Pete's killer! – doubt had crept in. Through the back door and up the darkened steps into the attic.

Something was wrong. Q was certain Helen Banner had killed Pete, but something about the *why* of it remained unclear. A crime of passion? Possibly. Then again ... Pete's murder had been followed by a second killing: Adem Gashi. A man who had known Pete, a man Q had spoken to *about* Pete. What were the chances that his killing was unrelated to Pete's death? Had Helen Banner been behind both? If so, why? Did it have something to do with Pete's work at Napier Labs? And the revelation that perhaps Pete had not been entirely truthful about the lab's progress? ... Who would that have impacted? What would they have done about it?

Q's thoughts returned to his earlier conjectures about bad actors being involved in Pete's death, agents of chaos interested in stopping or procuring the lab's work, specifically the algorithms that would allow global encryption protocols to be circumvented.

'You look troubled,' said Bob.

'Something doesn't feel right.' Q remembered the feeling when an op went to plan. Objectives met. Threats neutralised. Everyone back home safely. He didn't have that feeling now. Loose ends. In detective fiction, there were always loose ends, keeping the detective up at night. More often than not, they led to a vital new discovery that turned an investigation on its head.

Bob appeared to have read his thoughts. 'Princess and the pea.'

'Sorry?'

'That old yarn about the princess and the pea. How she couldn't sleep on account of a pea under the mattress.' A reflective pause. 'To be clear, you're the princess in this scenario.'

'Yes,' muttered Q. 'Something like that.'

'Now, me, I sleep the sleep of the dead. Bought myself a top-of-the-range mattress. Titanium alloy springs. "Gravity-defying comfort". Lorna needed it, on account of the cancer. Who knew sleep could be so expensive?'

'How *is* your wife?'

'Dying. Slowly. But she's a trooper. Lorna's always had a good sense of tumour.'

Q said nothing.

'Sorry. Cancer jokes. Always a bit hit and miss. Lorna loves them.'

'How long?'

'As long as I can make it last.'

Q was about to say *I'm sorry* but stopped himself. Bob didn't need apologies. He didn't need people to be understanding. He was a man in love with his wife. A man who would soon lose the person he needed most in the world. Q could not imagine the strength it took for Bob – and Lorna – to face each day.

He marshalled his thoughts. 'Adem Gashi.'

Bob put down his coffee. 'What about him?'

'Any leads?'

'Another open investigation. Afraid my lips are sealed.'

'Kathy isn't here.'

'If Kathy *were* here she'd have you escorted off the premises. By way of the window.'

Q suspected Bob was right. His one meeting with Kathy after Helen Banner's arrest had been short, terse and unpleasant. Then again, what had he expected? He had, effectively, overturned Kathy's initial investigation into Pete's death. Made her look, at best, incompetent, at worst, a fool.

Bob smiled. 'Frankly, we have nothing. No forensic evidence at the scene. No witnesses. No murder weapon. No motive – other than the fact that we suspect – frankly, *know* – that Gashi was involved in organised crime.'

'I'm no longer a suspect, then?' Q's tone could have stripped paint.

'That's policing for you. We go where the leads take us, without fear or favour. No hard feelings.'

Q's phone rang. It was the vet, Pru Argyle, with Bastard's test results. 'Yes, of course. I'll bring him right over.'

'There's nothing physically wrong with him.'

The vet's back was turned, fiddling with a water cooler.

'Then what's the problem?'

'Trauma. Abuse. That would be my guess.'

Q looked at Bastard. Bastard looked at the floor.

'What do I do about it?'

'Frankly, I'd start by doing the basics. Treat him well. Praise and reward. Unconditional love.'

Unconditional love? Was there such a thing? Q had yet to see it, even among humans. 'Isn't there some medication we can try?'

Argyle's look became grave. 'I do *not* prescribe Prozac for dogs.'

60

'SOMEBODY WILL COME IN.'

'That's what makes it exciting.'

Jed Ellis hesitated, but it was clear that Astrid had only one thing on her mind. They were in the server room, banks of tall black server racks, lights winking like fireflies across polished surfaces.

Jed had read that there were over one hundred million servers in the world, in data centres and server rooms just like this, guzzling energy, generating heat and emitting greenhouse gases as if it was going out of style.

Jed didn't give a damn about all that. Climate change? Let the plebs worry about forest fires and floods. Let the politicians bang on about carbon reduction targets. Sanctimonious twats. With enough money you could stick a thumb in the eye of climate change. As for the next generation . . . What had they ever done for Jed? Let every generation fend for itself. That was Jed's motto.

'Sex among the servers,' murmured Astrid, leaning into him, reaching for his mouth with her own. 'Eat your heart out, Mills & Boon.'

Jed allowed her to kiss him and then pushed her gently away. 'No.'

'It'll take your mind off things.'

'Things? You mean the avalanche of crap headed our way? You mean the end of life as we know it?'

'You can fix this. *We* can fix this.'

'Not without Pete. Not without Helen.'

Astrid stiffened, stepped backwards.

Jed sighed. 'I didn't mean—'

'It doesn't matter.' She folded her arms. 'Stop feeling sorry for yourself. You want to get out of this, do something about it. You're every bit as smart as Pete. In your own way.'

'And what should I do, exactly?'

Astrid wasn't the type to pout. Jed knew she was annoyed because she pushed her spectacles up her nose. Christ, how had he got himself into this? He still remembered the day Pete had come calling. *Together, we'll change the world . . .* Pete, the quantum messiah.

What Pete *hadn't* told him was the hustling he had had to do to get his project off the ground. And to keep it there. The people he had got into bed with.

Chickens, thought Jed. He had never liked the little bastards. Sooner or later, they always came home to roost.

'Well, Helen's not exactly going to be able to help, is she?' said Astrid. 'We need to deliver what we've promised. Better late than never.'

Jed said nothing. Helen's confession, days earlier, had rocked Napier Labs. Jed was still reeling. A confession! What was wrong with the woman? Helen would go down for Pete's killing. What a waste.

What Astrid was saying made sense. In theory. There were only two small problems. The people who mattered didn't like the idea of *late*. It wasn't a word they were used to hearing. And there was also the issue of *never*. Because Jed Ellis was now fairly certain that, barring a miracle, they would *never* deliver what Pete had promised.

291

And then there was the small matter of Adem Gashi's killing. A death that only added to the bubbling cannibal's pot Jed found himself in.

'Adem?' Astrid looked at him quizzically. He must have spoken out loud.

Jed wished he hadn't told Astrid about Adem. In truth, he wished he hadn't told her any of it. But it was hard to keep secrets when you were naked in bed with someone. That's how state secrets got out. Some femme fatale seduces a government minister; next thing you know classified military documents are plastered all over the Internet next to cute family pictures of dogs on skateboards.

Did the dogs agree to be skateboarded? A question that had always bothered Jed.

Jed felt like Indiana Jones racing through an underground cavern full of booby traps. He could see the treasure waiting at the end, but the likelihood was that he would end up guillotined by a scythe or hit in the eye with a poison dart.

Why was life so hard? All he had ever wanted was a few million dollars and a house in the mountains. And to live well into his eighties.

Choices. You lived and died by them.

Jed had made his choice. He had taken his thirty pieces of silver.

And now he had to live with the consequences.

61

K ATHY HAD SLEPT BADLY THE whole week.
On the whole, insomnia didn't bother her. More hours
to get things done.

Occasionally, it left her wanting to shout at people, but that
wasn't necessarily a bad thing.

Her life was spinning out of control, a car twirling on ice.
Q's return, the murders of Pete Napier and Adem Gashi.
Q crashing around Wickstone like a doomed prime minister
on the campaign trail.

To be fair, he *had* proved them all wrong – Helen Banner
had confessed to Pete's killing and that wasn't to be sniffed at.
Once she had got over her anger – and setting professional
embarrassment to one aside – Kathy could appreciate the end
result. Justice had to prevail otherwise what was the point? Cops
had a bad rap, as it was. If you weren't being called a fascist
lackey by some tree-hugger stretched out on the M25, you were
being told by spineless politicians that you were lazy, incompetent
and predatory.

A pot bubbled on the hob.

The doorbell rang. Kathy frowned, glanced up at the clock.

Ten thirty.

She walked down the hallway, swung open the door.

'Hi,' said Q.

The kitchen stretched to a set of patio doors looking onto a small garden. Bar stools encircled a central island. A pot of something cooking on the hob wafted strange odours his way.

'Goulash,' said Kathy. 'Have you eaten?'

'No,' said Q.

Kathy turned back to the hob. She was dressed in shorts and a plain T-shirt, hair pinned back. Sandals. Q watched her a minute, then sat down on one of the stools.

Kathy stirred the pot with a red-handled ladle. 'If you're waiting for me to apologise, we could be here a while.'

'What could you possibly have to apologise for? Other than accusing me of murder, hauling me to the station and grilling me like a villain in an episode of *Vera*.'

'I didn't accuse you of anything. You were a legitimate person of interest.'

'Person of interest,' echoed Q. How often had he heard those words? Being labelled a 'person of interest' by MI6 usually meant that your life expectancy dropped to that of a mayfly's.

Kathy set down the ladle and looked at him. 'I'm a cop. It's my job.'

'You think I killed Adem?'

'Of course not. But I haven't seen you in three decades. And then you waltz back in and suddenly people are dropping dead left, right and centre.'

'One person. One person dropped dead. Adem. Pete was dead *before* I got here. He's the reason I came back.'

She stared at him. 'Of course he was. I mean, what other reason could you possibly have for coming back to Wickstone?'

'I didn't mean—'

She spun back to the hob. 'Forget it. My point is Adem is probably dead *because* of you. Your informal investigation clearly stepped on someone's toes.'

'So you *do* think there's a link between Pete's death and Adem's? We agree on something.'

'This is Wickstone, not South Central LA. Two murders, of two men who knew each other, in such a short space of time? Yes, I think they're connected.' She grabbed a bowl, ladled goulash into it and pushed the bowl in front of Q. Caught in the headlights, he hesitated; and then a spoon willed itself into his hand.

The goulash tasted of dead mouse marinated in raw sewage. He resisted the impulse to retch.

'Well?' Kathy looked at him anxiously.

Q swallowed. 'Delicious.'

'You've turned green.' She went to the fridge, returned with a bottle, poured him a white wine. Q drained the glass.

'Jeremy always said I had the instincts of a prison cook.' She went to the fridge again, took out a Charlie Bigham ready meal, microwaved it, then served it on china plates. Paella with chicken, king prawns and chorizo.

They ate in silence. Q was suddenly conscious of Kathy's bare legs, her neck, her ... closeness ...

'Q,' said Kathy. 'International man of mystery.'

'Hardly. I've lived half my life in a lab.'

'Bob told me you came to the station today. That you think Banner isn't telling us everything.'

Q set down his fork. 'There has to be more to Pete's death than an affair gone wrong.'

'Has to be or you want there to be?'

'Meaning what?'

'Have you ever thought that this isn't about Pete. That it's about you?'

M had said the same thing, more or less, days earlier. 'Reductive,' said Q. 'And I'm quite aware of my own motivations. They have nothing to do with me leaving MI6 or needing some sort of quixotic purpose to bring meaning to my existence.'

'Normal people don't use the word "quixotic" in ordinary conversation. You do know that?' She sipped on her wine.

Q picked up his own glass. 'I've spent my life working out solutions to complex problems. I think I have good instincts. Something about this doesn't add up. And then there's Adem's murder.'

'Adem Gashi came from a prominent Albanian crime family. We believe he was involved in an organised crime operation, here in Wickstone. County lines drugs. Setting up in Wickstone as a beachhead to the local region.' A beat. 'Adem's family are well known to the authorities. They have a reputation for extreme violence. You're a civilian, not a cop. I can't imagine they'd be thrilled about you digging into his death.'

Something in her tone ... Q reached out and touched the back of her hand. Kathy pulled away. 'Don't.'

'Kathy—'

'We can't. *I* can't.'

'The other night, I sensed something ...'

'Let's be honest with ourselves. I'm trailing the wreckage of a bad marriage and you're a gay bachelor. Or whatever they call your sort nowadays. How long will you stay in Wickstone before your feet start to itch? A month? A year?'

Q said nothing.

'That's what I thought.' She pulled her arms around herself. 'I'm sorry, Q. I can't invest in you. Not again.'

62

Q SAT AT HIS KITCHEN TABLE with a mug of coffee and his laptop.

Bastard lay at his feet, a rug with paws.

Bastard's demeanour looked much like how Q felt. Of course, Kathy's summation of the situation made sense. It was silly to think he could waltz back into her life, that they could pick up where they had left off. Where *he* had left off.

Thirty years. They were different beings. Crabs. All hard shells and claws.

And yet.

Who was it had said you only get one true love in any given lifetime? Kathy was Q's one true love. If he'd doubted it before, he didn't now.

He pushed Kathy to the back of his mind. Which was as easy as shoving a hippo into a wardrobe. Nevertheless ... He still had an investigation to conclude. Kathy's warnings about Adem Gashi's family were well meant, but Q couldn't abandon his quest to find out the why behind Pete's death, and how it linked to Gashi's murder. He owed Pete that much. He owed himself.

Loose threads.

A call to a former Metropolitan Police commander, a woman Q had worked with on the government's Future Policing initiative – essentially *Robocop*, but without the bionic weaponry and indiscriminate violence – resulted in a second call to a senior contact at the National Crime Agency. An hour later Q had a wealth of information about Adem Gashi and his ties to the Albanian mafia.

Adem hailed from a prominent crime family, led by a Mirko Demaçi, a man on several wanted lists. The NCA's own list. Interpol. The FBI.

Mirko was in his seventies, rumoured to be in semi-retirement. His gang's operations covered the gamut of criminal activity: drugs, human trafficking, gun-running. A 2019 *Guardian* article detailed how Mirko's outfit had taken control of the UK drug trade by cutting out the middlemen and going direct to South America. The gang had flooded Europe with vast quantities of cheap cocaine, disposing of anyone disinclined to appreciate their entrepreneurial attitude. Cocaine prices had never been lower, creating more demand; a virtuous circle that had made everyone in the supply chain vastly wealthy. As one commentator had remarked: 'If they were on *Dragon's Den*, everyone would be giving them money.'

Q sat back and thought through his next move. Adem Gashi had been a spider at the centre of a crime web, here in Wickstone. A web that had caught many flies, some of whom had ended up working for the spider. Adem's business had been drugs. And drugs needed to get from A to B, from supplier to consumer.

Q picked up his phone and dialled Zak Youssef.

'Hi.' The boy sounded nervous.

'Zak, I need to ask you a question and I'd like an honest answer. The drugs that you supplied Pete with – did they come from Adem Gashi? I don't mean personally from him, I mean his outfit.'

A silence, and then: 'Yes.'

'Was he the one who asked you to steal Pete's Bentley?'

'I didn't deal with Adem.'

'Who did you deal with?'

Another hesitation.

'Zak, this is important. This isn't about you, you have my word. Adem was murdered. I think his murder is tied to Pete's death in some way. I'm trying to figure it out.'

Q could practically hear Zak's thoughts ticking over in the silence.

'My instructions always came via the Wickstone Autoshop. You need to talk to Tony.' Zak explained the chop shop's workings, the fact that the Albanians had taken over when they had arrived in Wickstone. 'There's something else. I hacked into Tony's records. I think he's been skimming. I don't think the Albanians know.'

The doorbell chimed. 'Thank you, Zak,' said Q, and cut the call.

As he walked to the front door, he realised that the boy's fate had become important to him. Why, he could not have put into so many words. Perhaps the same reason he had always felt the fate of the Double Os so acutely: they were the closest thing to a family he had known.

Q remembered the first time one of Q Branch's modified cars had come back riddled with bullets. As had the field agent inside it. It had hit him then that what they did in the lab had consequences out in the real world. Lives were at stake. Not just the lives of the agents, but those who depended on the success of their missions. A single faulty chip could jeopardise millions. The fate of nations.

MI6's field agents were human. All the training and equipment in the world couldn't minimise risks to zero. One day, even Bond would die, as indestructible as he was. One day, he would react a second too late, or his gun would jam at the wrong time, or he would simply be in the wrong place when a bomb went off. No last-second heroics. No *deus ex machina* to save the day.

And no one but a select few would know how much he had done, how many times he had risked his life. For them, for the world. In the Service, he was a legend. The ultimate death-or-glory merchant. A man whose very name was a magic spell. But when Bond walked down the street, no one recognised him. No one came forward to grasp him by the hand and thank him. No one was waiting at home when he came back from a botched mission to tell him it would be fine. That tomorrow would be better.

A lonely grave awaited Commander James Bond.

At the door, Mort was brandishing a bottle of wine.

Minutes later, they were installed at the kitchen table, glasses in hand.

The silence stretched. Q had come to terms with the fact that his father had had an affair all those years ago, that that affair had probably sent his mother over the edge, to her death. But that didn't make it easy to sit and drink with him. Perhaps in time.

'I thought congratulations might be in order,' said Mort. 'I hear you found Pete's killer.'

'Perhaps.'

Mort's confusion was evident. 'You're not certain? Helen Banner confessed, didn't she? It was on the news.'

'She did. But I think there's more to it. The note that Pete sent me, the note that brought me back to Wickstone, directed me to Adem Gashi. Adem was murdered. There has to be a link to Pete's death.'

Mort loosened his bow tie. 'Let the police do their jobs.'

'Because they did such a great job before?'

Mort raised an eyebrow. 'I hope you didn't say that to Kathy?'

Q picked up his wine. 'Have you heard of the Wickstone Autoshop?'

'Oldest garage in town,' said Mort. 'I don't use it myself, but I hear good things. Don't you remember? You did grow up here.'

'You never let me drive your car. And I couldn't afford one of my own.' Q paused. Mort sniffed but said nothing. 'It's a chop shop. A front for the Albanian mafia.' Q explained Adem's connection to the garage. Zak's too. He laid out his plan to talk to the garage's owner, Tony.

Mort set down his glass. 'No.'

'No?'

'You've done all you can do. Putting yourself in danger is foolhardy. And you're not a fool.'

'It's a conversation with a mechanic.'

'A mechanic with ties to a mafia outfit. I would rather not have to identify your bullet-ridden remains.'

'You're catastrophising.'

'Am I? Wasn't Adem Gashi stabbed to death? Is that catastrophising?'

'*Alea iacta est*,' said Q.

Mort's eyes became dark. 'The die is cast,' he murmured. He stood up. 'You never listened to good sense back then. Some things don't change.'

After his father had left, Q sat and drank some more.

He looked at Bastard who had barely blinked through the whole exchange. Must be easy being a dog. Dogs never had to have difficult conversations with their fathers. Dogs never sat around drinking morose glasses of wine, dwelling on past mistakes.

Was Mort right? Was Q being rash?

Perhaps it *was* silly to walk into the lion's den. Back at MI6, ops sometimes collapsed. Bad intel. Bad judgement. Bad execution. Bond had told Q many a hair-raising story. The times he had almost died. Not that the man seemed to mind. Some people were only alive on the razor's edge.

But here was the thing.

This wasn't Bond's op. This wasn't MI6's op.

This was his op.

And Q was damned if he was going to back away.

63

'**N**ICE PIECE OF KIT.'

Medium Tony nodded at Q's Caterham. He had just walked out of the garage to see the car slice to a halt on the opposite kerb, a well-dressed man get out, a dog in tow, and head purposefully across the road.

'Bit out of my range of expertise,' Tony continued. 'I'd take it to a specialist.' He mangled a cloth in his hands, then slipped it into his overalls.

'I was told you might help. By a mutual friend. Zak.'

Tony's gaze was cool. 'You're the guy asking questions all over town.'

'And not getting many answers,' said Q. 'I think Adem Gashi's murder is linked to Pete Napier's death. Pete was my friend. My understanding is that you worked for Adem.'

'Zak told you that?'

Q said nothing. Need to know. The mantra of the services.

'I need something to drink.' Tony set off along the road, Q falling into step beside him.

'Can I offer you some advice? Go back to London. Forget Adem. Draw a line under this.'

'You knew Pete, didn't you? He grew up in Wickstone. He brought his cars to you. The cars he purchased from Adem's dealership.'

Tony stepped into a mini-supermart. Q followed him around as he picked up enough packets of crisps, chocolate bars and cans of soft drink to start his own obesity epidemic. 'Fancy anything?'

'No. Thank you.'

Back outside, Q said, 'I need to know more about Adem. His family.'

'I'd strongly advise you to stay away from Adem's family.'

'An organised criminal gang run by a Mirko Demaçi. That family? What was Adem's interest in Pete?'

'Adem ran a car dealership. Napier Labs was a customer.'

'There has to be more to it than that. Drugs? What else?'

Tony stopped and faced Q. 'Way I hear it you were hauled in by the cops on suspicion of *involvement* in Adem's killing.'

'I had nothing to do with it.'

'His family isn't the type to split hairs. If I were you I'd forget the whole thing. Go back to whatever it is you were doing before you decided to get mixed up in this.'

'I can't do that. I genuinely believe Adem had something to do with Pete's death.'

'Helen Banner confessed to killing Napier.'

'I'm not saying she didn't kill him. I'm saying the motive might be a bit more complicated than she's led the authorities to believe.' Q hesitated. 'I want to talk to Mirko.'

A very large man with a very small dog walked by. Tony watched the tiny dog snarling its way along the pavement, then turn and bark at his visitor's dog. The bulldog slipped behind his master's legs, looking whipped. Several things went through his head at once. And then he said: 'Fine. My understanding is the police have released Adem's body. The funeral is two days from now. In London.' He gave Q the details.

'Thank you.'

'When I was young, my father told me there are two kinds of people in this world. Those who crack the whip and those who enjoy finding out what it looks like inside the lion's mouth. I'd wish you well, but what's the point?'

Q grimaced and headed back to his car.

As the Caterham slid away, Tony took out his phone and dialled Papa John. 'You wanted to know who might have killed Adem?' He summarised Q's visit. 'For what it's worth, I think the guy's harmless. But I've sent him your way. Find out for yourself.'

Tony hung up, then rested the phone against his lips. Had he done the right thing? Of course not. He had deliberately flung a piece of red meat at Mirko's chief Rottweiler. Bought himself some time. A dirty business. But so was life. Tony had a family to think of. He didn't need Papa John coming to Wickstone looking for Adem's killer. Looking at Tony's operation. Looking through Tony's books.

Tony had always thought of himself as an honest man. Stealing from thieves wasn't dishonesty. Not when you thought about it. But the thing about men like Papa John . . . They were old school. Scorched earth. Take no prisoners.

Tony didn't like throwing Q to the wolves. Didn't like himself for doing it.

But the man had asked for it. Literally.

Be careful what you wish for.

64

TWO DAYS LATER, Q WAS back in London, standing outside a church in Clapham.

The men on the door looked like bouncers. They looked like their days probably involved delivering bad news, with extreme prejudice.

Q knew all about extreme prejudice. The Double Os were often tasked to prosecute missions with extreme prejudice. Q had never had a problem with that. The world was full of madmen with bad haircuts. Sometimes the only way to stop them was to take them off the board. That's what made agents such as Bond indispensable. There weren't many capable of understanding such a sentiment and then acting upon it.

'Good afternoon, gentlemen. I'm here to pay my respects to Adem.'

'You knew Adem?'

'Yes. We met in Wickstone.'

The man who had spoken looked at his partner. They both wore sunglasses, the insolent kind favoured by FBI agents and minor celebrities at tennis matches. Both looked as if they spent considerable time in the gym, in tiny tank tops, lifting very heavy weights, urging each other on with ear-shattering grunts.

'Are you police?'

'No,' said Q.

The man gestured Q inside with his wrecking-ball chin.

Q walked into the church. Many of the mourners were already seated. Others were lined up beside an open casket, displayed at the altar.

Q walked to the casket, looked inside. Adem lay in repose, in a black suit and tie, hands crossed at the waist. A cross attached to a bead bracelet could be seen wrapped around his wrist. The handsome young man looked at peace. Vulnerable in a way he probably couldn't have shown when he was alive. What a waste.

A commotion turned Q around. A small party had entered the church. At their head was an elderly man with a cane in hand. A dark suit hung off him. The sunglasses looked too big for his wizened face.

All eyes turned to Mirko Demaçi as he made his way to Adem's casket. Those around Q melted away. A large, thickset man sporting interesting hair and a five o'clock shadow appeared in front of Q. 'Mr Demaçi would like some time alone with his nephew.'

'Yes. Of course.'

Q walked back along the aisle and took a seat next to an elderly dowager in a black dress. The woman looked at him, then pointedly stood up and drifted several aisles further back. A young girl – perhaps eleven, maybe twelve; he could never tell – turned to Q. 'I don't recognise you.'

'I don't recognise you either,' said Q.

'Were you Adem's friend?'

'Yes.'

A pause. 'Adem was very nice.' Another pause. 'He liked boys, not girls. We're not supposed to talk about that, but everyone knows.'

Q turned back to Mirko. The man looked genuinely distressed. His cheeks glistened. Q saw him take off his sunglasses, lean down into the coffin and plant a kiss on his nephew's shoulder. Mirko whispered something into Adem's ear, then straightened. His minders turned him around, steered him to the front pew.

A robed priest emerged from the sacristy and ascended a lectern. The youngish man looked incredibly nervous, thought Q. Wouldn't want to mess this one up. Not in front of a roomful of armed, emotionally charged and, quite probably, unstable men.

Q recalled a mission in Columbia, 0013 in covert attendance at a funeral, an injudicious comment by a family member, all hell breaking loose. Automatic weapons had suddenly appeared. They had ended up burying eight instead of one. Including the priest. And poor old 0013.

Q remembered the young man scoffing at the notion of an unlucky number. 'In this business, you make your own luck,' he had told Q, firing off a few rounds with the modified Heckler and Koch machine pistol Q had handed him. 'You wouldn't know. You've spent your life hiding in a lab.'

MI6 had since retired the number.

Adem's funeral service went off without incident. Several eulogies painted him as a bright young thing, full of ideas, a Richard Branson in the making, a fan of rap music, bling and colourful clothes. Finally, Mirko Demaçi made his way to the lectern. He peered out at the audience. Q thought the man looked spent. Done with life and all its demands. Perhaps *haunted* was a better word. Mirko looked haunted. Too many ghosts. 'Adem was my nephew.' Mirko's voice was hoarse. 'But I loved him like a son. Whoever did this ... will pay.'

Q watched as Mirko was helped off the platform by the brutish man with the odd hair. Clearly a key lieutenant.

The priest resumed the lectern, wrapped up the service, then detailed the next step in proceedings. The burial.

Forty-five minutes later, Adem was safely in the ground and cars were overtaking each other in their haste to get away.

As Q looked for an opening to approach Mirko, the two bouncers from the door appeared before him as if pushed up out of the floor. 'Mr Demaçi would like to speak with you.'

Q nodded. 'I would appreciate the chance to express my condolences to him too.'

'Not here. At his home.' They gave Q the address.

Q watched as Mirko was shuffled out of the church by his minders.

Mirko Demaçi lived in an affluent suburb in the eastern part of the city, where the homes were of the type that graced architectural magazines or featured in reality shows about rich housewives with Oompa Loompa tans and eccentrically shaved dogs.

Mirko's mansion was surrounded by a reinforced steel fence, with guards at the gate. A man walkie-talkied in Q's arrival and he was let inside. He drove up to a carriage driveway with space for a small fleet, parked beside an impotence-inducing Range Rover. Q had worked on smaller tanks.

More black-suited men greeted him. He was frisked and then led through an enormous reception to a kitchen. Glass concertinaed doors looked out onto a wide lawn. Several young girls were playing in the garden, including the girl who had spoken to Q at the funeral.

A few minutes later, Q was pushed into a study where Mirko Demaçi sat in an armchair, still in his funeral suit.

Mirko's lieutenant emerged from the shadows, waved Q into a seat. 'My name is John. My friends call me Papa John. You have something you wish to say to Mr Demaçi?'

Q cleared his throat. Suddenly, sitting here in this lightless room, with men who had probably killed or ordered the killing of uncounted souls, he felt vulnerable. Back at Q Branch, he had dealt with murderous megalomaniacs – but only at a remove. Only through Bond and the other Double Os. He had never been this close to an actual killer. Unless you counted the Double Os themselves.

He bought time by feigning interest in the room. His gaze fell on a sideboard, a series of family photographs in triptych wooden frames. One picture showed Mirko with a young Adem and a slightly older girl. Q was momentarily arrested by the picture.

Something about the photograph, the girl … And then Mirko's scratchy voice broke into his thoughts. 'Did you kill Adem?'

'No.'

The old man went flaccid, seemed to melt into his armchair.

Papa John spoke into the silence. 'The police arrested you in connection with Adem's death. You went looking for him on the night that he was killed. You told a local detective that you wanted to speak with him, question him. Why did you want to speak with Adem?'

Q's brow furrowed. Something about Papa John's words had pinged an alert. But he couldn't put his finger on exactly what it was that had set off his radar. 'I think Adem had something to do with Pete Napier's death. Pete was my friend. I simply want the truth.'

'Helen Banner killed Napier. It's in the news.'

'But *why* did she? That's the question. I think it has something to do with Adem. And what he was doing in Wickstone.'

Papa John folded his arms. 'Please. Tell us your theory.'

'Adem was sent to Wickstone to further your operations. He set up a car dealership to establish a legitimate front, possibly to launder the proceeds of illegal drug distribution. Pete became a valued customer. Of Adem's cars *and* your drugs. The staff that Napier Labs brought to Wickstone worked in a high-pressure environment. They were well compensated. Exactly the kind of people your organisation preys on. Adem used Pete to build up a base of well-heeled drug customers. Recreational cocaine users. How am I doing so far?'

'You still haven't told us what this has to do with Adem's death.'

'I don't know why Adem was killed. Or who killed him. But I think Pete was killed to silence him. Or stop him.'

'Stop him doing what?'

'At first, I thought it might be to stop Pete going to the police about Adem's drug-running. But I don't think Pete would have done that. He needed the cocaine. And he wouldn't have endangered his own reputation or that of his lab.' A beat. 'I think it's to do with the work Pete was spearheading at Napier Labs. The quantum computer and its applications. Was Adem somehow involved?'

Papa John's eyes were flat. 'We're not in the science business.'

'No. But Pete needed money. He'd burned through his initial venture capital funding. He was struggling to raise more. And so he began exaggerating his success. Massaging his results. Hoping that someone would come to his rescue. Perhaps he found someone. A partner with cash to burn. A partner looking for a legitimate investment for illegitimate funds ... I think he found Adem. Adem was already in bed with Pete through the cars and the drugs. Perhaps Pete convinced Adem or Adem convinced Pete. Perhaps they convinced each other. It doesn't really matter. In the end, Adem came back to the family. He convinced you to make Pete an offer he couldn't refuse.

'And then, later, when you discovered that Pete was lying, that your investment might end up in the crapper, you turned on him. Pete had to be punished. Maybe Helen Banner was persuaded into becoming your instrument. A willing assassin who knew Pete and could get close to him. A woman with her own grudge against him.'

Q's words hung in the room. Papa John was stony-faced. 'Presumably you have some proof for these colourful theories?'

Q said nothing. Proof. A valid question. Much of his conjecture was little more than that. Darts aimed into the darkness. But he sensed that he had come close to the board. Or, at the least, hit a punter in the eye.

Papa John stepped closer. He seemed to grow taller, bigger. 'Let's say you're right. Let's say we went into business with Peter Napier. As silent partners. Does it make sense that we would wish to see dead the one man who might turn Napier Labs' fortunes around? What purpose would killing Napier serve? And how would we convince Helen Banner to carry out his murder?'

'I don't know.'

310

'It seems to me you don't know very much at all.'

'It's only a matter of time before I put it together. I'm a very persistent man.'

Papa John straightened. Q sensed the sudden change in atmosphere. There was a genuine sense of violence in the air, an electrical discharge as pungent as the whiff of ozone.

'Let him go.' Mirko spoke without turning his head.

'I think we should—'

'I said, let him go.'

Papa John seemed to twist on the spot. Q could sense the man's desire to ignore his boss. But this was not the time or place for the tail to wag the dog.

'I'll escort you out.'

Q stood, then turned to Mirko. 'What did you whisper into Adem's ear? At the church?'

'Besa,' said the old man in his papery voice.

Papa John led Q back to his car.

Q looked back up at the house. 'What does *besa* mean?'

'It means to keep one's promise.'

As Q drove away, Papa John slipped his mobile phone from his pocket. Over the years, he had learned to act on instinct. In recent times, as Mirko had gradually faded from view, Papa John had had to rely more and more on his own judgement.

This man Q would not stop. Papa John had recognised that in him right away. He had met men like this before. Beholden to their own sense of moral righteousness. A peculiar brand of vanity.

Often fatal, in Papa John's world.

He made a call.

65

THEY CAUGHT HIM ON THE outskirts of Wickstone. Two large black SUVs forced the Caterham to a halt. Men with automatic weapons approached, gestured him out, pulled a hood over his head and bundled him into the back of one of the vehicles. Twenty minutes later, he was sitting on a metal seat in a space that smelled faintly of urine and old paint. And a smell just below that, a faint signature of something that set his teeth on edge: blood.

The thumping drumbeat of his own heart, his breathing a loud rasp against the cloth of his hood. His hands were bound. Cable tie. He tested the tie but knew that it was pointless. Panic flooded through him, borne on whitewater rapids of adrenalin. He had heard enough stories about rooms like this, situations like this. From Bond, from others.

Torture rooms. Rendition cells. The scene wasn't difficult to imagine, hood or no hood. Instruments laid out on trestle tables. Grey-faced men with the stomachs of butchers. Questions. Over and over, punctuated by the grammar of pain. And, beneath it all, the understanding that, no matter what was said, what was exchanged, the end was already written.

Q realised that his watch was still on his wrist. Did he need to know the time? What did it matter? . . . No. There was another reason his thoughts had landed on the watch. Something to do with Bond. The watch was a Bremont Broadsword Bronze. Another souvenir from MI6. Bremont served as official watch suppliers to the British Armed Forces. Q Branch had modified several models for the Double Os ... A match flared in the murk ... *Of course!* ... The fingers of his right hand locked around the watch. He felt his way around the edge of the dial, pressed buttons.

A door swinging open, hinges squeaking like mice trapped in a box. Q heard footsteps clack across a stone floor. Two men. Maybe three.

They came to a halt before him. The sounds of fumbling, a cigarette being lit.

Bond had told Q war stories about being interrogated. Tortured. Nothing to it, apparently. But Bond had been *trained* to resist. How much torture could Q withstand? A spot of waterboarding? Probably. He liked swimming. Sleep deprivation? Bring it on. He was an insomniac anyway. Britney Spears played day and night into his eardrums? He'd crack like an egg.

'Do you smoke?'

'No.'

Q thought he recognised the voice. He had only heard the man utter a few sentences, but he thought it was Papa John.

'I'm going to ask you some questions. If you answer me with lies, you will be hurt. There will be a lot of pain. Do you understand?'

Q's throat went dry. His head nodded of its own accord.

'Why did you come to the funeral?'

'I want the truth. About Pete.'

'The truth can be dangerous.'

'So I'm discovering.' A beat. 'I was right, wasn't I? Pete took money from you. You have a stake in Napier Labs.'

'We don't have a *stake* in Napier Labs. We own it. All of it. We bought out Peter's original investors. Offered them a golden exit. They were happy to accept. Word had already got back to them that the work wasn't going as smoothly as Peter had told them it would. Delays. The possibility of not achieving his goal at all.'

'But *you* believed him?'

'We were willing to take a chance.'

'Why?' Q could smell the cigarette smoke filtering through his hood. 'It couldn't have been just because you needed a front for laundering drug money. Not with what it would have cost to buy out Pete's original investors ... You wanted the encryption-busting tech. Why?'

Papa John said nothing, leaving Q to follow the winding path of his own conjecture. 'Because you have buyers lined up. Buyers willing to pay a fortune for it. Buyers who want to use the tech to subvert security protocols, protocols protecting the most secure organisations in the world. Military bases. Intelligence outfits. Government institutions. The only buyers who would pay enough to make this worthwhile for you would be state actors. Governments. I'm guessing the Russians. The Chinese. Iran.'

Seconds ticked away. Q could feel sweat soaking the hood.

'I checked you out, Mr Boothroyd. You are an intriguing man. In another time and place, you might have been useful to us. Our business is changing. We have enough thugs, enough men steeped in the old ways. But the modern world is a new environment and we must adapt. There are new ways of making money. There are some within our organisation who understand this. Adem understood this too. His only problem was his incompetence.' A pause. 'I must know what you know. I must know if you have held anything back.'

Q heard words barked in a language he could not follow. Moments later, he was pulled up, dragged backwards, his arms lifted over his head. He felt the cable tie slide over a hook. He was on tiptoe, practically hanging, shoulders straining at the sockets.

'Wait a min—'

The first punch hammered into his midriff, knocked the breath from him. Pain crumpled him forward, but the hook kept him upright. His body swung through a short arc; and then a second blow landed. And another. And another.

Front. Back. Front. Back.

Q felt nausea ride up through his gullet. His head sang. He bit his lip, tasted blood.

His mind went away. He was aware that questions were being fired at him. He stumbled out answers, but they made no sense to him. Not that it mattered. None of this mattered. This wasn't real. He was a man of science. Men of science weren't hung up on hooks and pummelled like slabs of beef. Men of science sat in quiet rooms, smoking pipes, thinking their way around corners.

A good thing they hadn't gone for his face. Couldn't afford to lose his looks. Not with Kathy potentially back in the frame. Not that their last meeting had been encouraging. Wonder what she would make of him now? And Mort. No doubt his father would trot out some anecdote about the hardiness of ancient Romans. Didn't build men like that these days. Namby-pambys who couldn't take a little friendly beating. And poor little Bastard. Who would look after Q's depressed dog? Somehow Bastard's fate seemed more important than anything else.

His thoughts became thicker. What was he doing here, anyway? Why had he come back to Wickstone? Peter. Something to do with Peter. Was Pete out there now, beyond the squeaky door? Squeaky. Funny old word. Perhaps he and Pete could play a game of chess, the way they had when the world was young. Perhaps Q's mother might bake them a cake. She had loved baking. Fiend for it. Where was *she* now? Somewhere over the rainbow. Why had he said that?

The world went dark.

66

Q FLOATED IN THE RIVER WATCHING Pete sitting on the jetty, bare feet tracing circles in the water. A cascade of stars above, the Milky Way glittering with the brilliance of dreams.

'It's funny,' said Pete, 'you think you know the rules. And then the rules turn to smoke.'

'Did you know about their affair?' said Q. 'Before Mort told you? My mother. Your father.'

'Molecules. Atoms. Quarks. None of it is real. Not in a way we can touch and feel.'

'We were friends. You could have asked for my help.'

A sad smile. 'But who would have helped *you*, old friend?'

Q awoke into darkness.

A moment to clamber out of chaos, and then his senses returned.

He lay face down on what felt like a thin mattress, the hood still over his head, hands now bound behind him. He couldn't hear anyone else in the room. A tiny squeak might have been a mouse. Or a rat. He hoped it was a rat. Rats he could deal with. Nature's ultimate survivors.

His body woke up, coughed politely in his ear, then turned the mood music to full blast. Pain thrummed around Q's torso. The acrid taste of blood in his mouth.

He allowed a minute to pass, then slipped his brain into gear, scrambled painfully to his feet, took stock.

He was alone, but for how long? How long before they came back for another round of beat-the-prisoner? His thoughts were muddy but he was fairly certain he hadn't told them anything useful. Not that he had much to tell, beyond conjecture. He suspected that Papa John was simply a very thorough man. Q could appreciate that. Perhaps he would have appreciated it more if the man hadn't used him as a human piñata. But credit where credit was due.

What would happen when Papa John had satisfied his curiosity? Was it a good sign that they hadn't removed his hood? Q couldn't hang around to find out.

He fumbled behind him at his watch, fingers pressing buttons. A whirring sound.

Q winced as the three-quarter-inch sawblade nicked the inside of his wrist. He concentrated and manoeuvred the blade until it had cut through the cable tie. Hands now free, he pulled off his hood, then retracted the blade back into the watch.

The room was small. Bare concrete walls, a mattress in one corner, a metal bucket, a foldable chair and a solid hook screwed into the ceiling. No windows and just the one door. The only light source a dim-wattage fluorescent tube.

Q walked to the door, bent to examine the lock. A cheap tumbler lock. Q Branch had a million gadgets capable of picking a lock like this. But Q wasn't at Q Branch. He was here, on his own.

Q fumbled in his pockets. They had taken his wallet, his phone and his keys. But all the other odd junk remained. A pack of tissues. A Werther's toffee. A safety pin. And his Montblanc.

Never go anywhere without a Montblanc. Particularly when the Montblanc in question was a model developed at Q Branch. Like the watch, it was more than it seemed.

He twisted the cap off the pen, pressed a small button just above the nib, then pointed the nib at the lock. A second button squirted a jet of nitric acid into the lock. Q stepped back, waiting for the acid to do its work, destroying the pins within the lock. A minute later, having applied force to the ruined lock, the door was open.

Q hesitated, took a deep breath, then walked out of the room.

Into a deserted corridor, dimly lit, patchily creamwashed walls.

He moved quietly past several doors, then stopped at a corner, glanced into the adjoining corridor. Light spilled from an open doorway.

Q edged to the doorway, looked in.

An incongruous sight faced him. A farmhouse kitchen, with an old-fashioned fireplace and a wooden dining table. On the table lay a walkie talkie. Of its owner, there was no sign. Beside the walkie talkie, Q saw his wallet, keys and phone. He scooped them into his pockets, then walked to the fireplace, plucked a poker from a galvanised bucket. The makeshift weapon felt reassuringly solid in his hand.

He began walking towards a door at the back of the room. Five steps, and then the sound of a toilet flushing. Another, smaller side door opened. A man walked out. A large man. Q recognised him from the church. One of the two bouncers at Adem's funeral. The man was still tucking in his shirt. Had he even washed his hands? Q couldn't stand men who didn't wash their hands after using the toilet.

The man's jaw fell open. And then Q moved forward, swinging the poker. A meaty thud and the man went down. Q dropped into a squat, pulled the man's pistol from its holster. A Desert Eagle Mark XIX, chambering .50 Action Express rounds.

Gas-operated, semi-automatic. A big, clumsy gun that looked powerful but lacked velocity. A gun for show-offs and idiots.

Q jogged to the kitchen's rear door, stepped out into the night.

He was in a field, the smells of the country around him. Several outbuildings wore a deserted look. No sign of the Caterham. Perhaps it was parked at the front of the farmhouse? He began to walk towards the side of the building when a voice split the air. 'Stop!'

He turned to see a second goon framed in the kitchen doorway. The man was reaching for his weapon. Q reacted instinctively. He raised the Desert Eagle and fired. A bullet whacked into the plaster beside the door, a good metre from the thug. Q had fired a lot of pistols over the years, back at the test range. He was one of the world's top experts in small arms. But he had never fired live rounds at another person before. And he was no marksman.

Q turned and ran, spilling over a nearby fence. Suddenly, he was clumping through a muddy field. The smell of manure stung his nostrils. Gunshots cracked the air. He reached behind him, fired again. The heavy gun's blowback spun him off balance and he ploughed into the earth. Grass tickled his nostrils. And the smell of gunpowder. He scrambled to his feet, headed towards a copse of trees.

Just before he reached them, he tripped, fell into a ditch. The gun slipped from his grasp. He scrabbled blindly around for it but couldn't locate it in the dark.

Bullets thwacked the top of the ditch. Q ducked down.

A voice barrelled through the warm air. 'You could have killed me, you stupid bastard!'

Pot, kettle, thought Q.

His thoughts raced. He needed a weapon. *Any* weapon ... His right hand closed around a heavy stone.

Q peeked up over the edge of the ditch, saw a large silhouette hurtling towards him in the dark.

Q threw the stone.

Not even close. The man kept coming. Then, thirty metres away, he tripped, fell face forward, the gun twisting in his grip. A loud retort. Q saw the man's head jerk back; and then he lay still.

Q could feel sweat congealing on his forehead. Maybe God did have a sense of humour after all.

Another noise. Q spun around to see a leather-clad shape in a biker's helmet pointing a gun at him from the edge of the ditch. The gun had a silencer attached. The figure must have slipped up on him from the copse at his back. A gloved hand raised the helmet's visor.

It was the Deliveroo rider-from-hell.

Q's thoughts went into freefall. He blinked, rapidly. 'Who are you?'

'Does it matter?'

A beat. 'Yes. It matters. If you're going to kill me, it matters quite a bit. I'd like to know.'

She seemed to debate this, lowered her weapon. 'I work for certain interests. Interests that have a stake in the work at Napier Labs. I was sent to Wickstone to monitor things. Unobtrusively.'

'Riding around in leather pretending to be a Deliveroo rider is unobtrusive?'

A grimace. 'It's a cover.'

'You don't work for the Albanians,' said Q. An assertion, not a question. 'You work for whoever is paying the Albanians a fortune for Pete's tech. Is it the Chinese? The Russians? Someone else?'

'Time's up,' she said, and raised her arm. And Q thought: *I'm going to die here. In this muddy ditch, in a deserted farm, under a Van Gogh sky.* An obituary would probably mention little of his time at MI6. And he was survived by no one. *When I'm gone, it will be as if I had never been.*

A bullet rang out. Q heard a bird whir out of the branches of a tree.

And then the woman fell over, slipped down into the ditch.

Q looked around. A shadow detached itself from the trees, gradually resolved into the shape of a man. Tall, broad-shouldered. Holding a gun.

Even through the veil of shock, the shape, the man, looked familiar.

'Hello, Q,' said Commander James Bond. 'Enjoying retirement yet?'

67

'WOULD YOU SHOOT BABY HITLER in the face?'
Bond looked at Q. 'Because, when all's said and
done, that's what it boils down to. That's the job.'
Q walked to a cabinet, plucked out a bottle of Scotch, splashed
several fingers into two crystal tumblers. Bond accepted the
whisky, leaned back into the sofa's cushioned embrace. Q took
the armchair opposite, raised the glass to his lips, closed his eyes.

They had made it back to Sanctus Villa an hour earlier. Q
had showered, changed – into straight-legged tracksuit bottoms
and a T-shirt – and returned downstairs to find Bond hard at
work in the kitchen, cooking and carrying on a conversation
with Miss Honeypenny. The robot was giggling in a way Q
thought sounded dangerously close to coquettish. The man had
actually managed to charm a *machine*.

As they sat to eat – Bond's speciality: scrambled eggs on toast
– Q filled the commander in on everything that had happened
since Q had set foot in Wickstone. When he had finished Bond
waved a fork at him. 'Never thought you had it in you. An actual
gunfight.'

'This isn't funny.'

'Dicing with death never is. How's the undercarriage?'

'I don't think anything's broken.'

'Try toothpaste on the bruises. Works wonders.'

Bastard wandered in. 'Hello, boy,' said Bond. The dog perked up, lolloped over to Bond, leaped onto the sofa, set his head on Bond's lap, and looked up at him with adoring eyes. Q gaped at the animal in disbelief.

Bond rattled the ice in his glass. 'So . . . what next?'

'We should call the police.'

'Pointless. By the time they get to the farm the site will be clean. No bodies, no torture room, no signs of conflict. These people aren't amateurs.'

'MI6 then.'

'Will M listen to you? Will she care? By your own admission, Napier Labs have failed. Or at least they aren't going to create the tech you're talking about anytime soon. Encryption protocols are safe. For now. And if a handful of gangsters or state-level bad actors are left out of pocket . . . who cares? Perhaps they'll turn on each other. Result.'

Q knew that Bond was right. But it stung nonetheless. He had been through all of this, almost *died*, and . . . it didn't matter. Not in the grand scheme.

He saw that Bond was scrutinising him. 007's eyes suddenly pulled back into shadow. 'Do you know why it took me so long to respond to your SOS?' A nod at Q's watch. Q felt the weight of it on his wrist. He had programmed its inbuilt radio transmitter with a simple Mayday signal – to be sent direct to Bond's phone – a long time ago, had never imagined he would need it. Why Bond and no one else? A question that didn't really need answering. 'I was on a cargo plane back from South Sudan,' Bond continued. 'A female suicide bomber with a baby strapped to her back detonated an IED at a political bigwig's birthday party in Juba. A man I'd been sent to retire. Fifteen dead. Mainly children. The bigwig survived. For a little longer . . . How do you process something like that? How do you get that out of your head? And the worst thing? We have to work with the ones behind the bombing. They're currently on our BFF list.'

'BFF?'

'Best Friends Forever. You're showing your age, Q.'

Q had no answers. Bond was smarter and subtler than many gave him credit for.

Q had watched Commander Bond evolve over the years. The best field agent MI6 had ever produced. A killing machine, a man who had done things for King and Country that few would ever know or understand even if they did. In place of a life Bond had spy-craft. Working undercover – and the psychological trauma that wrought; living off the constant rush of adrenalin; beholden to his own, sometimes warped, code of honour.

But Q knew there was more to the man. It wasn't all fistfights on top of speeding trains or sex in silken-sheeted hotel suites. Behind that devil-may-care façade lay an astute mind, and a sense of loyalty that had led him into danger more times than even Q knew about.

Bond was hurting. Q knew it, had known it for some time. All those accumulated horrors. Sooner or later, they took their toll. But Bond couldn't show weakness. He was James Bond, the last soldier at the edge of the wasteland. When 007 fell, they would all fall. Bond knew that and so he kept going, long after lesser men would have surrendered. To the pain and the terror and the wickedness.

The old M had known how to handle Bond, when to give Bond his head, when to rap him over the knuckles. When to listen. But the new M? Q suspected she saw Bond as a relic, a man-eating tiger that might one day devour her. She would chew Bond up first, a piece of human gum, stick him on the underside of her desk and forget about him.

'You left me a message,' said Q. 'A while ago. To get in touch. What did you want to talk to me about?'

Bond's brow furrowed. His mouth opened. For the briefest moment, Q thought that perhaps, for once, Bond would drop the act and reveal something essential, allow him into that secret chamber where his innermost thoughts and feelings resided. And then Bond smiled. 'It doesn't matter.'

The doorbell rang. Q stood up, pitched himself towards the hallway. Every movement sent pain stabbing around his midriff. Had Papa John's brutes broken a rib? Should he go to the hospital? They would probably insist on a police report. And that Q could not do.

It was Mort. Q stared at him. 'Now is not a good time.'

'It is for me,' said Mort, and pushed past him.

In the living room, Q introduced his father to James Bond. 'James is an old friend.'

'Charmed,' said Mort, looking anything but.

'Likewise,' said Bond. 'Scotch?'

'Thank you.'

'So,' said Mort, after Bond had handed him a glass and he had settled into a chair, to train his hawkish gaze back on Q. 'You seem to be in some pain. I take it you didn't listen to my advice? Someone give you a pasting? Was it Medium Tony? Or the thugs he works for?'

The man missed nothing. 'I'm perfectly fine.'

'He really isn't,' said Bond, cheerfully. 'If I hadn't turned up tonight, he'd be lying dead in a ditch with a bullet in his skull.'

Q stared daggers at Bond. What sort of friend told tales to your dad?

Bond shrugged. 'He has a right to know.'

Mort pinched his trousers into place, then: 'Well?' The tone regressed Q to when he had been eight years old and found himself in trouble at home. Was there any point resisting?

He told his father everything.

Mort's expression flattened. 'So this is your new life? Playing musical chairs with Death?'

'Dad—'

'Are you having a mid-life crisis? Because that's the only rational explanation for your behaviour.'

'No. I'm pursuing an investigation. I hadn't expected it to take such a ... rough turn.'

Mort looked unhappy. A silence wandered into the room, checked the temperature, then slunk out again.

'Let's work the problem,' said Bond. 'What do you know?'

Q was glad of something else to focus on. 'I know that Helen Banner, an ex-colleague of Peter Napier's, has confessed to killing him. On the face of it because of an affair they were having. But I think there's more to it than that. We know that Adem Gashi was killed by parties yet to be identified. We know that he befriended Pete, that he worked for a crime syndicate that has made inroads into Wickstone and that secretly financed Napier Labs, with the intention of securing the tech Pete promised them would incapacitate global encryption protocols. Tech that *they*, in turn, had promised to international bad actors in return for what we can safely presume is a fortune. We know that Pete lied to them, that he massaged the results. The tech is worthless. For now.'

'A motive for murder,' said Bond.

'Yes. But why use Helen Banner to carry out that murder?'

'Plausible deniability. Banner and Napier had an affair. It went wrong. He fired her. If she's caught, that's a lot of motive.'

'Why would she do it?'

Bond shrugged. 'Maybe they offered her a fortune. Maybe they threatened her. The woman was angry. Wouldn't have taken much to push her over the edge.'

'And Adem? Why kill him? *Who* killed him?'

'Perhaps that lovely Deliveroo rider of yours. Perhaps it was retaliation by your "bad actors" for being conned by Adem's Albanian mobsters.'

The theory made sense. But there were certain things niggling away at Q. Something he had seen in Mirko Demaçi's office. A photograph. Something he had heard, a throwaway remark by Papa John that had burrowed into his brain like a tick.

He realised that Bond was watching him intently. 'If you're going to get through this, you need to chill out.'

'Said the pathologist to the corpse.'

'What?'

'Sorry. It was a joke I heard once.'

Bond stared at him, then burst into wild laughter. Q wasn't sure if Bond was laughing at him or if he had just got the joke.

Bond reached into his kitbag, took out a gun, checked the clip, then held it out to Q. 'Take this.'

'No,' said Q.

'They might come for you again.'

'I know more about guns than you've probably forgotten,' said Q. 'But I don't ever want to fire one again. Not at another human being.'

Bond looked at him. 'You think I don't get tired of shooting people in the face? The endless carnage? The meaningless sex?'

'Frankly, no.'

Bond seemed about to protest, then gave a shrug. 'Fine.' He tucked the gun away.

'What is it you said you did again?' said Mort.

'I'm a ... mechanic.'

'Ah. Euphemisms. The last refuge of the illiterate.'

Bond looked at Q. 'I can see where you get your winning personality.'

Mort checked his watch. 'I have to go. George needs his evening feed.'

Q led his father down the hall. At the door, Mort turned back and said: 'Are you sure you should be hanging around with that man? He seems like a bad influence.'

'I'm a little old to be told who I can be friends with, Dad.'

Mort's mouth pursed. 'Fine. Just try not to get yourself killed. It would ... upset me.'

Q knew that was the best he was going to get. He watched his father get into his Volvo and drive away. When he returned to the living room, he saw that Bond had fallen asleep on the sofa. Q went upstairs, found a thin quilt and fluttered it over the man. Gently, he prised the tumbler from Bond's hand and slipped off his shoes.

He stood a moment looking down at him.

James Bond. 007. Part-man, part-myth.

Q couldn't imagine Bond's life. For so long, they had run along parallel tracks – neither had married, neither had children. None that Q knew of, anyway. But Q wasn't Bond. Bond had a licence to kill and the willingness and skills to exercise that licence. Q had spent his life in a lab. Bond had lost assets, lost people he loved. Sometimes because of his own actions.

They were the same, but not the same. Opposite sides of a coin, perhaps?

Bond murmured something unintelligible in his sleep. His eyelids twitched. And Q thought: there's a gentleness to the man in sleep that's never visible when awake.

Pay attention, James. How often had he said those words to Commander Bond?

Q knew that, somewhere inside him, he loved this man. For everything that Bond stood for, everything he was prepared to do. For all that he inspired in those around him. He loved Bond because Bond said: *Nothing is going to hurt you, not while I have strength to fight.* At the end of time, when the stars shook and the heavens fell, Bond would be there, standing at the gates of hell, facing off against the Devil.

But who rescued the rescuer? Who went in to save the soldier when the soldier had had enough? Bond would never ask for help. Bond knew six ways to choke out a man with his bare hands, but he couldn't tell another man that he needed him.

Think of yourself as dead. You have lived your life. Now, take what's left and live it properly.

Marcus Aurelius. *Meditations.*

The problem was, Bond had never read Marcus Aurelius.

Truly, thought Q, there was no place in heaven or hell for a spy who had lived too long.

68

Q AWOKE TO FIND BOND GONE.
The commander had folded the quilt into a square and left it on the sofa. Atop it lay a folded piece of paper. On the front were the words: YOUR EYES ONLY. CLASSIFICATION: BAD SHIT.

Inside, in Bond's surprisingly neat hand:

Do you feel alive?
Don't stop.
And watch your back.
James.

What, no Xs? Q crumpled the note and threw it in the bin. Five seconds later, he excavated it again, uncrumpled it, folded it neatly and stuck it inside his wallet. A talisman.

Q made breakfast, took it out into the garden. He sat in early morning sunshine, a captive storm at the centre of tranquillity. His body vibrated with pain. He had almost died last night. The thought filled him with wonder. And something else. Death – *near* death – should come with a disclaimer. The experience was almost religious. It changed a man, converted him.

Q was angry. Angry with himself, with his carelessness. He had blundered about, stepping into minefields with gay abandon, believing himself untouchable.

Hubris. Born of a life lived under the protection of the bullet-proof umbrella that was MI6.

But now he was out in the cold. Bond couldn't rescue him each time he got into trouble. And, as they had both discovered last night, Q was no field agent.

Bastard slunk into the garden, looking even more morose than usual. He was followed out by Honeypenny. 'Will Commander Bond be coming back, Q?' Her tone sounded wistful.

'Oh, for God's sake,' said Q. 'He's just a man!'

Q focused on the case. He powered up his laptop, checked the news sites. Nothing about the events at the farmhouse. And nothing more about Helen Banner's arrest or Adem Gashi's death. The media was all but silent on the killing fields of Wickstone.

Q's thoughts lingered on Banner.

Why did Helen Banner *really* kill Pete Napier? Q didn't think a woman as intelligent, as competent, as seemingly sane as Banner could have snapped in that way. Then again. He recalled the case of the jilted American female astronaut who had driven across the States to try to kill the man she had been having an affair with. She had worn adult diapers so she wouldn't have to stop for bathroom breaks. A woman that had passed every psychological test NASA had devised.

And now another, sharper question shimmered into view.

Why did Helen Banner *confess* to Napier's murder? Q remembered the sudden turn in their conversation, how Banner had simply blurted out the truth. What had made her do that? Something Q had said? All he had done was go over the GPS evidence of her two journeys to the crime scene. One journey to meet with Pete, to have sex with him on the jetty. The second to go back and kill him. A woman scorned. A woman hurting ...
Or was there more to it than tha—?

A star went nova inside his brain. Q sat perfectly still, mind blazing ... The thought he had been chasing swam away. And then swam back, tantalisingly within reach ... And then he had it.

Excitement rippled through him. He knew he was on to something. An answer, perhaps, to the questions that still plagued him about Pete's death. Disparate facts snapping into place. But there was only one way to be certain.

He needed to confront Helen Banner.

But, before he did so, he had another murder to solve.

Adem Gashi.

And now the photograph he had seen in Mirko's office, the thing he had heard, returned. He bent the sunlight of his focus onto the thought. Something Papa John had said had bothered Q. Now, in the silence of the garden, with no distractions, he finally had a chance to examine the feeling properly.

It took a few minutes, but then it popped into his head, a conclusion fully formed.

Q thought he knew who had killed Adem and why.

But to get to that endpoint, he needed to fill in missing links in the chain.

He initiated a video call with Zak. It took an age for the boy to pick up, and when he did he looked bleary-eyed, as if awoken from a crypt. Q guessed that, like most teenagers, Zak was allergic to early mornings.

Q said: 'I think I know who murdered Adem. I need your help.'

Zak looked hesitant.

'You told me that Adem was the senior representative of the Albanian operation in Wickstone. But he wasn't the only one, was he?'

For a long time Zak said nothing. 'No. There was someone else. My ... benefactor.'

'I think I know who that is. I just need you to confirm it.' Q said the name.

Zak's reaction told him everything he needed to know.

69

E NDGAME. IN THE INTELLIGENCE COMMUNITY, the term referred to a very specific phase of an op, a dance macabre where one or more parties literally danced with Death. Q had been here many times, in the situation room at MI6, with M, and others, waiting, breath baited, as the final moves of a mission that might have taken months to set up played themselves out.

And now here he was, playing out his very own endgame.

No MI6. No M. No Bond.

Just Q.

The only difference Q could see in the Seven Stars dealership since the last time he had been here was that the company flag was fluttering at half-mast. He presumed this was in tribute to the death of its founder and chief car enthusiast, Adem Gashi.

The showroom was open. Business was business and cars still had to be sold, whether anyone wanted them or not.

Q walked inside and spoke to the receptionist.

Minutes later, he was sitting in the back office, Deborah seated across the desk, evaluating him with an inscrutable expression.

'The chair suits you,' said Q, eventually. 'Particularly given that you've always been in the driver's seat. Pun intended.'

Deborah cocked her head. 'I'm sorry?'

'*You* are in charge. Of your family's operation out here in Wickstone. And I don't mean selling cars.'

She looked at him as if seeing him for the first time. 'Who told you? Someone at Adem's funeral? I know you were there.'

'There was a photograph of you and Adem at Mirko's home. There was a stronger family resemblance when you were younger. But I can see him in you now. Adem was your brother. I had it confirmed by one of your off-the-books "employees" here in Wickstone.'

A silence spun itself out. Then Deborah spoke. 'Yes. Adem was my brother. We were very close.'

'I did some desk research. You went to Cambridge. A degree in business and technology. Adem, on the other hand, flunked out of college. My guess is *you* were the one pushing bright ideas about how to reshape the family enterprise. County lines. Investing in Napier Labs. And then the powers-that-be – namely, your uncle Mirko – decided Adem would head up the Wickstone operation. Adem was younger than you. You were older, smarter. How did that make you feel?'

The woman's mouth drew into a grimace. 'What makes you think I want to have this conversation with you?'

'I was almost killed yesterday. I think you owe me.'

She picked up a phone, spoke quickly. Seconds later, a young man entered.

'Do you mind?' said Deborah, gesturing.

Q stood, allowed himself to be searched. A wand was passed over his body. His phone, watch and tie-pin were taken.

'You'll get them back when we're finished.' She shooed the young man out, then sat back a moment holding Q with her eyes. 'Adem was gay,' she said, finally. 'Suffice to say he didn't find it easy, not in our line of work. Not in our family. He tried to fit in, desperate to prove himself. The trouble was he was never very bright. When I told him about my ideas – expanding via county lines, then funnelling that cash into legitimate tech companies – he leaped on the idea. Took it to Mirko as his own. I stood by and said nothing.'

'Why?'

'Because he needed it. Because I loved him. Because we live in a society where an incompetent man is still preferred to a competent woman, more often than not.' A sad smile. 'He was sheepish about it afterwards. Told me he had asked for me to be his second-in-command here in Wickstone. I accepted – only so that I could keep an eye on him. I guess I failed.'

Q could sense the depth of emotion the woman was struggling to hold back. 'Why weren't you at Adem's funeral?'

She looked away. 'I – I couldn't.'

'You know I had nothing to do with his death, don't you? Despite what Papa John might have told you.'

She looked back, met his eyes. Then: 'I believe you.'

Q breathed out. Now came the tricky part. 'Did Adem have anything to do with Pete's killing?'

Her eyes flared. 'No. Adem would never have hurt Pete.'

'How can you be so sure?'

Her smile turned grim. 'Because Adem *loved* Pete.' She paused to allow this to sink in. 'My brother fell in love with Peter Napier. It wasn't reciprocated, of course. I had to sit back and watch him pine for a man who simply wasn't interested. But Pete and Adem did become close. And Adem listened to Pete.

'My brother's heart was never in the family business. He was never ruthless enough, committed enough. And the deeper Pete got in, the longer he was in bed with us, the more *he* regretted it. Until, at some point, he decided enough was enough. Pete managed to convince Adem that walking away from his family,

335

his obligations, was the right thing to do. That his family was involved with people who would use Pete's tech to commit untold harm, on a global scale.

'Adem was conflicted. He spoke to me about it. About going to the authorities with Pete. Coming clean about everything. He wanted me to join them. I told him not to be ridiculous. I told him to stay the course, to trust his family. To remember who he was.'

'But Adem didn't listen, did he? He was going to *betray* his family. That can't have gone down well with Mirko.'

'Mirko didn't know about it. I begged Adem not to do anything rash. I thought I could work on him, find a way to stop him, to change his mind.'

'Because you knew it would be a death sentence if Adem went to the authorities. Are you *sure* Mirko didn't know?'

'Mirko loved Adem like a son. He would never have ordered Adem's—' She stopped.

Q saw the steel in her features. He realised he had underestimated the woman, misjudged her when they had first met. He changed tack. 'Why was I taken yesterday? Why the interrogation?'

'That was Papa John. What happened to you was unsanctioned. And unfortunate.'

'Unfortunate? I pissed blood this morning. I almost *died*.' Q breathed out, throttled his fury. That wasn't why he was here. 'I think I know who killed Adem. And why.'

She pressed back into her seat. 'I'm listening.'

'I need my phone.'

'Why?'

'To call the police.'

Kathy and Bob arrived in thirty minutes.

Seats had been arranged for them in Deborah's office.

Kathy's eyes found Q. 'You said this was urgent. What's this about?'

'Adem Gashi. I think I know who murdered him.'

Bob broke in. 'Hang on. Is this a confession?'

'No.'

'If you have vital info about an ongoing murder investigation then we need to get you down to the station, do this formally. We're not half-arsing it.'

'Let him speak,' said Deborah.

Kathy looked between the woman and Q. Something was going on here that she didn't understand.

Q put his voice into neutral. 'Yesterday I was in the home of Mirko Demaçi, Adem's uncle and patron. A man named Papa John – Mirko's right-hand man – was there too. He said something that struck me as odd, though I couldn't put my finger on it at the time. His exact words were: "The police arrested you in connection with Adem's death. You went looking for him on the night that he was killed. You told a local detective that you wanted to speak to him, question him."'

Bob broke into the sudden silence. 'So? So what?'

'Here's the thing,' said Q, directing his gaze at Kathy. 'How did Papa John know what I had said to Kathy that night?'

Bob frowned. 'What are you saying? That Kathy was involved? That *she* told Papa John what you'd said?'

'No, Bob. I'm saying that Kathy told *you*. And then you told Papa John.'

The air seemed to leave the room. Kathy and Deborah both turned to stare at Bob.

'My guess is that you've been secretly working for Papa John for a while now,' Q continued. 'Ever since the Wickstone operation got off the ground. You needed the money. Perhaps it started off simply to help pay for private medical treatment for your wife. But once you were in, you couldn't get out. I suspect you were told to report only to Papa John, to keep your ear to the ground, and a watchful eye on Adem – and Deborah. You were Papa John's spy.' A beat. 'But then Pete died and everything went sideways. Adem was in a highly volatile state. He was upset that the man he loved, Pete Napier, was dead. He suspected his family's hand in Pete's death. He wanted out of the family business. And so he decided to go to the authorities. I can't say for sure why he took that final step when he did. Perhaps it was when I came knocking on his door? Perhaps he thought the game was up.

'And so he went to you, thinking you would be the best person to talk to about his plan to testify against his family ... Why you? Again, I'm guessing here, but I think you went out of your way to cultivate some sort of contact with Adem, while he was in Wickstone. You told me earlier that you had visited his car dealership on several occasions. "Getting the lay of the land." Perhaps you presented yourself as the friendly face of law enforcement. Whatever the reason, Adem approached you and told you he wanted to come clean, about everything. About the Wickstone operation, Napier Labs, what he thought he knew about Pete's death. Adem probably laid out the deal he expected in return. Leniency. Witness protection. But that's not what he got.

'You did what Papa John had paid you to do. You called him. And Papa John ordered *you* to deal with the problem. To deal with Adem. It was finally time to earn the money he had been paying you. Papa John knew that Mirko would never sanction the killing of his own nephew. So he did what he thought was right. To protect the organisation. To protect the family. He ordered you to kill Adem.'

Bob's face was a stone mask. A deathly silence descended on the room.

Q continued: 'You called Adem up to Jane's Hill. You probably told him it was to discuss his exit from the gang, a cloak-and-dagger meeting far from prying eyes. Whatever you told him, it worked. Adem trusted you – that's why there were no defensive wounds on the body. You called him up there and you killed him.'

338

'Adem wouldn't have trusted just anyone,' said Deborah. 'It had to be someone he knew. It had to be someone he believed would help him.' Her eyes were hollow.

Bob's lips were dry. 'This sounds like the plot of every bad gangster film I've ever seen.'

'Follow the money,' said Q. 'I worked for the intelligence services for a very long time. Believe me when I tell you that no matter how secure you think the money trail is . . . it isn't. It won't take long to confirm your involvement with Mirko's outfit.'

Kathy looked as if she had stopped breathing. 'Bob?'

Bob's mouth opened, but nothing came out. The awful perfection of Q's logic had clogged up his chest, made breathing difficult.

The truth was that Bob had been waiting a long time for the trapdoor to open. Make a deal with the Devil and sooner or later the Devil comes to collect.

Bob saw himself as a good man drawn into darkness. He had rolled the dice. And for a while it had all seemed to work out. Watching Lorna being treated by the very best doctors that money could buy, no waiting lists, no worrying about the cost of tests and medication. Helping his boys out. After all, what was the point of a man if he couldn't look after his family?

But Bob's luck had finally run out. The truth was that killing Adem had not been on the agenda, not when he had made his pact with Papa John. All Papa John had asked of Bob was a little local information direct from a local cop. A helping hand for the gang's new Wickstone drug operation. What harm was there in that? In Bob's experience if people wanted to buy drugs, they would find a way, Bob or no Bob. And so Bob had made the deal and pocketed the cash.

But killing a man? No. Bob hadn't signed up for that.

Not that Papa John had given him a choice.

Either you kill Adem or I pay your wife a visit.

No choice at all really. Didn't matter that Lorna was dying and that Adem was a young man with everything to live for. You looked after your own. Law of the jungle.

But killing Adem had changed something. Bob hadn't been the same since that day. Which is why it was almost a relief that Q had rumbled him. A relief that he didn't have to walk around with a head full of guilt anymore. A relief that he didn't have to face Lorna each day with a lying heart.

When Bob spoke, his voice was firmer, steadier. 'You can't know what it's like. To see the person you love most in the world wasting away before your eyes. I did what I had to. That's all.'

Later, Q would have time to relive the moment. The way Bob had crumpled, the confession. Kathy arresting him, the Japanese-tea-ceremony formality in her conduct, the stunned coldness in her voice. The silent anger in Deborah's features, the restraint that had told Q that this was far from over. He suspected that prison wasn't going to be safe enough for Bob Lazarus. The other side of Mars wouldn't be safe enough.

What made men do the things they did? Bob had justified to himself getting into bed with the likes of Papa John. He had told himself it was for his wife, his family. But Q suspected that it was more Bob's need to demonstrate – to himself – that he was doing all that he could, as a husband, as a father.

But all the money in the world couldn't buy back a life.

70

THE DAY WASN'T DONE.

Q drove from the showroom to Napier Labs.

The guard at the gate greeted him with a sneer. 'You're persona non grata.' He relished the expression. Probably been practising it in front of a mirror, hoping that Q would be foolish enough to come back. And now that he had: *bam!*

'Tell Jed Ellis I'm here. He'll want to see me.'

'Doubt it. Mr Ellis doesn't see anyone anymore. And certainly not you.'

'Tell him I've met with his investors. His *real* investors. Believe me, he'll want to see me.'

The guard deflated. He looked ready to argue but then turned and phoned it in.

Ten minutes later, Q was sitting in Jed Ellis's office, the American behind his desk, Astrid Simmons leaning against the wall.

Haggard. The word swam around Q's thoughts as he looked at the man. Jed's eyes were bloodshot, expression hunted. Fast food cartons littered his desk. A row of empty beer bottles were lined up against the wall as if waiting to be shot. His lab coat was crumpled, a splash of what looked like dried ketchup – or blood – on the lapel. Jed had clearly been drinking and not bothering to hide it. He looked like he hadn't shaved – or washed – in a while. There was a sour odour in the room and not just from the lack of hygiene.

Fear. Q had sensed it before, in Double Os about to venture into dangerous terrain. Ops where the possibility of death was more than likely. Some dealt with it by channelling nonchalance; others with a grim seriousness. And some hid from it, inside a whisky glass. Or worse.

'You're persistent,' said Jed. 'I'll give you that.'

'Here's what I know,' said Q. 'Pete Napier got into bed with the Albanian mob. Napier Labs ran out of money and they bailed him out. Perhaps Pete thought it was legitimate funding, perhaps he knew from the very beginning. At some point he knew for certain. But that wasn't the problem. The problem was that Pete hadn't been honest. And when his investors realised that Pete wasn't going to come up with the goods – specifically the encryption-busting algorithms that had got them interested in Napier Labs' quantum computer operation in the first place – things turned nasty.'

Jed picked up a beer bottle, took a slug. 'Pete had a dream. He sold that dream to all of us. Build the world's most powerful quantum computer. Use it to do good. It never even occurred to him that his machine might be used for less than benevolent purposes. Oh, he *knew* about the potential downsides, of course. But he thought he could control it. Control who had access to the machine, who did what with it. He was a narcissist. Comes with the territory, I guess. He couldn't admit he might be wrong. And so he over-egged the pudding. To get the funding he needed.'

'You mean he lied.'

'Overpromise and underdeliver. That was Pete's mantra. But when our results began to stutter, our tests began to fail, it became obvious we weren't going to deliver anything. No quantum computer – at least not the massive leap forward that

Pete had advertised – and no groundbreaking apps. Pete tried to hush it up, keep the markets from knowing the full extent of what was going on. But word began to leak. The stock market listing kept being pushed back. The money ran out.'

'And that's when the Albanians came in.'

'What would you have done? I don't blame Pete. We were all heavily invested by then. In the work. In our stock options. If the work stops, the lab shuts down. If the lab shuts down, everything turns to shit. This whole thing' – he waved the beer bottle around – 'becomes a giant fire sale. And so Pete took the Albanians' money. He didn't know who they were, not then. They sent a lawyer, a Brit, shiny suit and a cut-glass accent out of *Downton Abbey*. Said he was representing a conglomerate of overseas investment firms. Sign on the dotted line and we'll give you all the money in the world. And so Pete signed and didn't ask questions. Don't look a gift horse in the ass, right?'

'When did he realise who he had partnered with?'

'Not long after. Our new friends paid us a visit. To clarify certain expectations. They'd neglected to tell us that they'd come into this deal with a single agenda. They didn't care about all the incredible things our quantum computer might enable. Medical advances, a revolution in science and technology. They wanted only one thing: the ability to crack existing encryption protocols. A killer app. To sell to the highest bidder.'

'And this is where Helen Banner came in?'

'Helen was our best programmer. Pete convinced her to work on the algorithms. But as she got closer and closer, she eventually realised exactly what her work might be used for and by who. She got cold feet. Frankly, she only went as far as she did because she and Pete began an affair.

'But, in the end, she refused to continue. And so Pete fired her. Astrid took over the work. She tried to finish what Helen had started. But she ... failed.'

Q saw the woman twitch. Astrid's eyes blinked angrily behind her spectacles. 'I cannot finish the work,' she said. 'Not when the quantum computer itself doesn't work. The two go hand in hand. Algorithms are meaningless unless they can be implemented by the hardware. And if the hardware fails ...'

'You have no qualms about finishing Helen's work?' said Q. 'Handing it over to ... bad actors?'

Astrid's tone was neutral. 'We are scientists. It is not our job to police the world.'

'Funny,' said Q. 'I'm a scientist too. And I've spent my whole life trying to do exactly that.'

An uncomfortable silence fell on them. 'Why exactly are you here?' said Jed.

'I'm trying to figure out who killed Pete.'

'This again?' The American glowered. 'Helen Banner killed Pete. She's admitted it, for Christ's sake.'

'I don't believe that. In fact, I'm pretty certain Banner is innocent.'

'Fine. Then here's another scenario for you. Pete got to a point where he couldn't see a way out of the mess. Our investors – our Albanian friends – wanted their pound of flesh. And they weren't subtle about it. Pete was under incredible stress. He was doing coke like it was going out of style. He took the easy way out.'

'I don't think you really believe that.'

'Look. I don't think the Albanians would have helped Pete into that river. They threatened him, but they knew they needed Pete. If there was any chance of recovering their investment it lay with him. I'm not sure they feel the same about me.' His eyes became hollow. 'I haven't left the lab for weeks. I live in this office. They threatened *me*. Deliver what Pete promised or else. They showed me pictures. People who had disappointed them.' He shuddered.

Q saw Astrid place a hand on Jed's shoulder. 'It'll be all right.'

Jed reached back and laced his fingers through the young woman's. Q sensed their fear, riding on the back of despair.

'Pete was a genius,' Jed said. 'But he was also a fraud. And he made a fraud out of me. Out of us all.'

'There's another possibility,' said Astrid. 'Perhaps Pete killed himself to *stop* the work? Or at least delay it. He didn't want the tech ending up in the hands of terrorists any more than the rest of us. He didn't want to be responsible for a digital world war. Perhaps he wasn't such a narcissist after all.'

Q got to his feet. 'I think there's a little truth in everything you've said. Pete *was* a genius. But he got himself into a hole he couldn't get out of. He made a mistake, an error of judgement. And then he had second thoughts. About finishing the work. About enabling our enemies. At least, that's what I choose to believe.' A pause. 'But Pete didn't kill himself. He may have thought about it, may even have gone out to that jetty thinking he would do it. In the end, I just don't see it.'

'So you genuinely believe that Pete was murdered?' Astrid sounded unconvinced.

'I do. And I think I know who by.' Q leaned over the desk, picked up a notepad. He took a pen from his pocket and scribbled a name and a number onto the pad, pushed the pad back across the desk.

'Moneypenny,' mouthed Jed, reading aloud.

'Call her. Tell her Q gave you her number. And then tell her everything. The truth and nothing but. She'll know what to do.'

'And she'll help ... us?'

'She will.'

'How can we trust her?'

'Because *I* do.'

71

A ND NOW IT WAS ALMOST done.
What he had to do next he hated. Was this how
Bond felt? In the final moments of a mission? The target
in his sights, a life in the balance, the twitch of a trigger finger
all that stood between his quarry and the ultimate abyss. And,
in those final seconds before the flaming sword was swung, did
doubt ever creep in? Did Bond ever think about the life he had
chosen, the decisions he was forced to make?

One day, Q would ask Bond about Nikolai Sakharov, Q's
murdered friend, his one-time Russian equivalent. And Bond
would smile that enigmatic smile of his and say: *Isn't it just like
you, Q, to have a Russian for a friend?* But Q would have his
answer. As was only proper between two men who had seen the
world for what it was: a place of darkness and light, where the
pendulum swung back and forth between these endpoints,
between the darkness of war and the illusory grey light of peace.
Two warriors of Albion, knights of the Round Table. Arthur and
his Merlin. Gunsmith and the wielder of the gun. They would
share a last drink, and then, and only then, with their deathbed
confessions, would there be no more secrets between them.

*

'No one sees the gorilla.'

'What?'

'The Chabris-Simons test,' said Q. 'An experiment designed to test selective attention. Two teams, one in black shirts, one in white, throw a basketball around. The viewer is asked to count the number of passes between the white-shirted team. Halfway through, a man in a gorilla suit walks between the players. Almost half of viewers never notice the gorilla. Their concentration is focused elsewhere; the gorilla doesn't even register.'

Helen Banner pressed her lips together. 'I'm sorry. I don't understand why you're here.'

Q had driven from Napier Labs to Banner's home. He knew that Banner had been released on conditional bail – she would wear an electronic monitoring tag and be subject to a curfew until her sentencing hearing. Q knew that bail in a murder case was unusual, but the fact that Helen Banner had pled guilty to the murder of Peter Napier and had no prior criminal record had clearly swayed the judge.

On the way, he had lined up his thoughts. He felt in control. He could see the final moves like a set of runway lights. The only thing left to do was land the plane.

'May I borrow your watch?

Helen's confusion deepened. 'I don't—'

'I'd like to show you something. It will clarify everything.'

Helen blinked and then took off her watch and handed it to Q. Q slipped his iPad mini from his pocket, then connected the watch to it via a short cable. His fingers flew across the iPad as he ran the app he had downloaded onto it earlier. Within moments, he had hacked into the Apple Watch and was hunting down the data he needed. Finally, he turned back to Helen. 'Apple Watch's GPS data is incredibly accurate. It tracks where you've been. On the night of Pete's murder you went out to the jetty.'

'You've already established that. Via the GPS tracking data from my bike.'

'Yes. That data showed that you went out to the jetty twice. I assumed it was because you went out there first to meet with Pete and then later went back to kill him. But here's the problem.' Q leaned in. 'Your watch data only shows you going out there the once.'

Helen's face seemed to freeze. Time slowed.

'You didn't kill Pete,' said Q, softly. 'You didn't go back a second time. But someone else did. Someone who had access to your bike. Someone with the means, motive and opportunity to murder Pete. That's what it always boils down to, doesn't it?'

Q became aware of a presence at his shoulder. He turned, saw that Helen's son, Ricky, was standing in the doorway. The boy's eyes were glassy. A swampy quiet enfolded the room.

Q got to his feet, faced Ricky. 'You killed Pete because he had an affair with your mother. You blamed him for the collapse of your parents' marriage. For your father leaving.'

'Don't say a word.' Helen's voice stabbed into the room.

Ricky stared mutely between them. And then he began to speak, words spilling from him like water over a cliff. 'I didn't mean to kill him. I just went out there to talk to him. My mother came back from seeing him that night. I confronted her. She told me where she'd been. She told me she loved Pete and there was no chance she would get back with my dad. And then she went up to her room, to shower.

'I was so angry, I couldn't think straight. I took her bike and went out to Bishop's Point. Pete was just sitting there, naked, on the jetty. He stood up as I approached. I guess he thought I would say something, and then maybe he'd explain why he'd wrecked my parents' marriage. But neither of us said a thing.

'And then he reached out for me, as if – as if he wanted to put his arms around me. To comfort me. I reacted. I pushed him away. He fell back, into the water. He started thrashing around, couldn't make the jetty. I could see he was in trouble. I stood at the edge, tensing myself to dive in after him . . . and then I didn't. I watched him drown.' His words came from a long way away.

'Oh, Ricky.' Helen's anguish swelled around Q. He wasn't sure what he had expected when he had come here, but he realised now that he wasn't prepared for this. His triumph at having solved Pete's murder had turned to ash. Because for Pete's ghost to find rest would mean throwing a young man's life onto the bonfire.

Would you shoot baby Hitler in the face?

Is that what justice meant? Q knew there could be no negotiation with the truth, with what was right. Surely, if his time in MI6 had taught him anything it was that?

Semper occultus. MI6's motto. Always secret.

But some things couldn't remain a secret.

If Q did nothing, Helen Banner would take the blame for her son's actions. Q had no doubt that Helen *did* blame herself. Her affair had led directly to Ricky being on that jetty that night. Perhaps he should allow a mother to sacrifice herself for her son?

What would Bond do?

Q felt the weight of responsibility drive down his shoulders. His thoughts crackled with static, a grey blizzard of indecision ... And then the fog cleared.

It didn't matter what Bond would do.

It only mattered what Q would do.

'I'm sorry,' said Q. 'Pete was my friend and you killed him. You went out to the jetty via the woods instead of the main road. Why? Because you didn't want to be caught on camera. Because you went there with the intention of harming Pete. Maybe you didn't intend to kill him but you wanted to warn him off. You made a bad decision and it cost a man his life.'

72

WHO DID STORIES BELONG TO?

In prehistoric times stories were the preserve of the storyteller. Gathered around a fire, tribal orators would recount the taking down of a great mammoth, the passing of an elder. Later, the Greeks refined storytelling into a mythic enterprise, a tradition that continued until the modern era when it was supplanted by the desire for immediacy, for instant narratives.

In one hundred and forty characters or fewer.

Bond was a man with stories. And the scars that went with them.

But Q had stories of his own. Granted, Q's stories didn't involve exotic women or throwing people out of aeroplanes, but they were important nonetheless. His stories – like the stories of the majority of ordinary people – were simple stories. A job well done. A nice meal. A good book. The portrait that was life.

But stories could take on a life of their own. Could fly out of control and crash into the side of a mountain.

Helen Banner's life was such a story.

Q's mother's life was such a story. And his father's.

And to a certain extent, his own.

*

Flowers on a grave.

This is what normal people did.

When all was said and done, in between the fantastical, one-in-a-million dream scenarios and childhood wishing-for-what-could-never-be, wasn't normalcy, the soothing lullabies of an ordinary life, what most people yearned for?

A life in the shadows wasn't all it was cracked up to be. There was something to be said for boring.

Q placed the roses – three red, three white – onto his mother's grave, then rose to his feet. Bastard settled onto his paws beside him.

So there it was. An ending. Perhaps more than one. That was the problem with stories. Sometimes they didn't know when to end. Sometimes fictions cemented themselves into place around you and you ended up clanking around in an armour of lies. Or half-truths.

Q thought of the shadow world in which he'd passed so many years. Where justice itself was a notion sanctified by blood. *Who was he to talk of right and wrong?*

The sound of boots crunching on gravel. He turned, watched a moment, then turned back.

When the newcomer reached him, he said nothing, merely crossed his hands before him and looked down at Annabelle Boothroyd's grave.

A lark sang in the silence.

'So what happens to Bob Lazarus now?' Mort said, eventually.

'He'll plead guilty to murder. He'll go away for a long time.'

Mort shifted on his feet. 'And young Zak?'

'Zak cooperated with the authorities. Provided valuable assistance on both investigations.'

'But you can't guarantee anything?'

'I don't have any influence over the case. Zak committed a crime. Ultimately, his punishment is for the justice system to decide.'

A brief silence. 'How will Napier Labs fare?'

Q slid his hands into the pockets of his jacket. There was a nip in the air, unseasonal. Or perhaps not. Seasons seemed to have gone the way of the necktie. Out of tune with the prevailing ideology but always threatening to make a comeback. 'They'll have to come clean. I believe Jed Ellis is preparing a public announcement. To the effect that they've wildly exaggerated their claims of progress on their quantum computer. The lab will be investigated. There may be prosecutions.'

'And their backers? The Albanians? I suppose they walk away clean?'

'The source of Napier Labs' funding will be traced back to offshore companies. I suspect that's where the trail will run cold.' He allowed a pause. 'Ultimately, Pete took money from people he shouldn't have. And then he lied to them. They might have wanted to kill him, but they didn't. They needed him. But our Albanian friends have others to answer to. Clients, who, if my past experience is anything to go by, are not the kind to sit on their hands when someone takes them for a ride.'

'Are we talking poison-tipped umbrellas?'

'Something like that.'

They turned as one as a family walked noisily into the plot, a woman admonishing a young child slathering at an ice cream.

'One cannot help but feel some sympathy for Helen Banner,' said Mort. 'A mother, put in that position. Perhaps it's not so hard to understand why she tried to take the blame for Pete's killing.'

'She acted in haste,' said Q. 'There was no actual way to prove that Pete had been pushed into the water. I suspect if she had brazened it out, if she hadn't confessed, if her son hadn't admitted to Pete's killing when I confronted him, they might have got away with it. I think it was the moment when I told her about the second journey back to the jetty, recorded on her bike's GPS, that she realised it had to be Ricky. And she reacted out of maternal instinct.'

His phone rang. Kathy. 'Excuse me,' said Q, turning aside, and then: 'Kathy.'

A deliberate pause, before she spoke. 'This is going to sound absurd, but I have a job offer for you. Your work on the Napier and Gashi cases has caught the attention of my superiors. There's a cold case they'd like you to take a look at. It involves a murdered man and a golden compass. Our civilian consultant rates are competitive. Or so I'm told.'

'You don't sound too pleased.'

'Do you blame me?'

'You're upset. Because this is a situation you can't control.'

'Hah! You think *I'm* the control freak? This from the man who wouldn't accept any of the evidence from our investigation into Pete's death.'

'I was right.'

He imagined her mouth flapping open. A gust of wind hammered in his ears.

'I need time to process the idea. Of working with you. But before that, *you* need to decide if you intend to stick around.'

'I—' Q began, but Kathy had already cut the call.

He wandered back to his mother's grave.

'Trouble in paradise?'

'The word eavesdropping is said to have come from wooden figures Henry VIII had built into the eaves of the Hampton Court Palace ceiling, to prevent gossip and potential dissent among his courtiers. Eavesdropping is actually illegal in many jurisdictions.'

Mort gave a small snort, then reached inside his jacket. 'I thought you might like this.'

Q took the photograph. To his surprise, it was a picture of Mort and Q. Q was about three years old, sitting not on his mother's lap, but his father's. Mort was grinning from ear to ear; Q was caught mid-laugh looking up at his father with delight. There was no sign of his mother.

Q stared at the picture for a long time.

How strange life was. A series of shutter clicks, burned on to the back of the eye. The past was another country. One where the language was alien, the food gave you diarrhoea and men in sweaty T-shirts waited to mug you around every corner.

'Your mother was behind the camera. In case you were wondering.'

Q's lips moved of their own accord. '*Mors vincia omnia.*'

'Death conquers all,' whispered Mort. 'Your Latin isn't as bad as you make out.' Seconds ticked away. 'In Inuit culture, when an elder decides their time has come, they walk out onto the ice, lie down under the stars and wait for the night to take them.'

'That's your answer, is it?' Q could feel anger in his throat, sitting there like a dog that had caught the postman's scent . . . Did he have a right to be angry? Q didn't know how to feel. So much of his time back in Wickstone had been dedicated to investigating Pete's death that he had barely had time to process his own emotions. Coming to terms with his mother's death. Reuniting with Kathy. Salvaging his relationship with his father.

How would Bond have handled it? An orphan who walked around with the devil in his pocket? Had anyone ever asked James Bond what *he* wanted? Q doubted it. How did that shape a man's decision-making? When others assumed you were resilient enough to handle anything and everything?

Q looked at his father, really looked at him.

Had anyone ever asked Mort what *he* needed?

'It's OK to regret, Dad. It's OK to admit that you were wron—'

He stopped.

Mort raised an eyebrow.

'It doesn't matter,' said Q. They turned back to contemplate the grave.

Q felt Pete's shade hovering at his shoulder. His mind looped back to the beginning, to Pete's letter. Was this how Pete had imagined things panning out? Pete dead and Q lured back to

Wickstone, to embark on a personal crusade to uncover the truth. But truth was a slippery thing. Truth carried with it no guarantee of moral rightness.

When all was said and done, he had followed his own conscience. That had to be enough.

Finally, he said: 'Shall we rejoin the world of the living?'

'Let's do that ... son.'

As they turned back towards the car park, Mort said: 'Tell me, didn't anyone use your real name at MI6?'

'No.'

'It was your mother's doing. I wanted to call you something sensible. Tiberius. Cassius.' The ghost of a smile. 'Q... I suppose I'd prefer to be called something else too, if my real name was—' Bastard began to bark, drowning out the sound of Mort's voice. As father and son walked briskly away, the dog began to follow, then stopped, looked briefly back at the church, before turning and merging with the shadows at their heels.

And inside a large, formless grey building, as forbidding as any ogre's keep in a fairy tale, a man in a dark suit stands by as a seated man in a white shirt and grey tie reads a report.

When he finishes, he picks up a packet of cigarettes and lights one.

He smokes for a while, seemingly staring into thin air.

The standing man breaks the silence. 'How should we respond? What I mean is, how would you like me to handle things with our Albanian ... partners?'

Smoke makes shifting patterns in the air. 'Kill them. Kill them all.'

Author's Note

THIS BOOK CAME ABOUT BY ambush. In the summer of 2023 I was invited, by Corinne Turner and Simon Ward, the head honchos at Ian Fleming Publications Limited (IFPL), the publishing arm of the Ian Fleming estate, to a meeting. I thought we were simply saying hello – me being the Chair of the UK Crime Writers' Association at the time and IFPL being sponsors of our Ian Fleming Steel Dagger Award – but halfway through our meeting – at their cosy offices in central London – I was asked a simple question: *Would I be interested in writing a mystery series featuring Q?* Fair to say that I was momentarily stunned. It's not every day you get invited to take on one of the most iconic characters in fiction.

My connection to James Bond goes all the way back to first watching Roger Moore in *Live and Let Die* as a teenager. My father was a huge fan of Moore – as Bond. My mother, not so much. She would insist on me averting my eyes whenever Mr Bond became amorous – which was a lot – fearful that 007 might corrupt my malleable teenage brain.

Brain rot or not, I have never lost my love of Bond. Like any Bond fan I have, of course, watched every single film, and read the books, including several of the continuation novels by authors following in Ian Fleming's footsteps. In every incarnation, there is something new to enjoy.

Why does James Bond continue to resonate? For me, it is because Bond is more than just a spy/unstoppable killing machine. He is a symbol. Of values that stand for a Britain many of us believe in. A Britain that stands up to evil, that puts itself on the line for what is morally right. Just as Bond does. And, by extension, Q does.

Writing Q has been one of the greatest honours of my life. The challenge was fourfold. Firstly, who exactly *is* Q? Very little of him is mentioned in the books. The public perception of Q comes almost entirely from his role in the Bond films, particularly Desmond Llewelyn and, latterly, Ben Whishaw. So my first challenge was to create a Q distinct from these two portrayals, but familiar enough for fans not to feel entirely at sea. The second task was to give Q a meaningful backstory and a cast of characters from his past who might stay with him through several novels. I had particular fun with his father Mortimer Boothroyd. I love Roman history, so making Mort a Roman historian seemed a no-brainer. Making him a crotchety old bastard was also a no-brainer. My third challenge was a plausible plot. Something that allowed Q to flex his Q muscles. Truly effective quantum computers are a lot longer away than I have depicted in the book but they are, nevertheless, very real and will be game-changing when they finally arrive. (And yes *Quantum of Menace* was my own title – one of only two that I have ever been allowed to keep.) The last and perhaps key task was *tone*. Throughout my earlier novels I have employed a dry brand of humour. (Do check out my Malabar House series set in 1950s India, of which *The Times* said: 'Think Mick Herron in Bombay!'). Wit and satire help keep the darkness at arm's length. And there *is* darkness at the heart of *Quantum of Menace*. We live in an increasingly fraught world. War, economic strife, political misdeeds. Navigating this quagmire of angst isn't easy, but, by adopting that famous British resolve and attempting to make light of the dark, we may persevere.

One final thing to say: just how personal this journey has been for me.

I still remember writing the scene between Bond and Q towards the end of the novel. Halfway through I had to stop and sit back, momentarily overcome. That I, having grown up watching and adoring these iconic and beloved characters, now found myself entrusted to bring them to life in a new outing seemed both outlandish and intimate in a way I cannot describe. I know my late dad would have got a great thrill out of this. If you take nothing else away, take this: I am immensely grateful to have had this opportunity, and even more grateful to each and every one of you for giving me the gift of your time in reading the book.

As far as I'm concerned, you're all Double Os. With the odd Q.

Acknowledgements

THEY SAY IT TAKES A village to raise a child. This book has involved an entire town. So bear with me while I thank what might seem like half the world's population. To begin with: Corinne Turner and Simon Ward for bringing the project to me, and the members of the Ian Fleming board for supporting them in so doing, and for working with me at every stage as we fleshed out the details. And to Julia Bradley for her sterling efforts on the marketing side and Frederika Park on the audiobook. One could not hope for better support.

To Kelly Smith, the publisher at Bonnier who took a chance on this project, and has provided such valuable insight with her editor hat on, making this a vastly better book. And to the rest of the Bonnier team who, like a gang of banditos shooting up the town, have had such enormous fun with this project. I am incredibly grateful for the brilliant publicity and marketing campaign they have put together. And so I shall name them all: Blake Brooks, Head of Marketing; Lucy Richardson, Publicity Director; Beth Whitelaw, Senior Press Officer; Holly Milnes, Marketing Executive.

And a nod too to cover designer Will Speed for an absolutely brilliant design, the audiobook team: Chelsea Graham and Laura Makela, and audiobook narrator, Alexander Armstrong, as well as those sales agents whose mission it was to get this book into your hands: Vincent Kelleher, Stuart Finglass, Stacey Hamilton and Evie Kettlewell.

To my agent, Euan Thorneycroft, at A. M. Heath, and the agents for this project, Ciara Finan and Jonny Geller, at Curtis Brown, thank you for your sterling work steering us through the contractual side of things.

To my late parents, who worked their socks off so that I could fulfil my dreams.

To my family: my wife, my brothers and sisters, nephews and nieces, and wider family, who never cease to amaze me with their wonderful achievements.

To my author friends across and beyond the crime and thriller community, especially those who came in with early reviews (you know who you are), and my daily WhatsApp therapy group Ayisha Malik, Imran Mahmood, Alex Khan, A. A. Dhand, and Abir Mukherjee.

To Alex Read and the gang at the Caterham factory who gave us a wonderful tour of the premises and allowed us to pretend to be racers.

To the community of readers, critics, reviewers, bloggers, book-groupers, booksellers, and word-of-mouth enthusiasts who have helped get me to this stage in my career. (And a special word for my many friends in Newcastle: I hope you didn't mind the little fun I had at your expense!)

To my friends and colleagues at University College London, especially at the Department of Security and Crime Science and the Dawes Centre for Future Crime. I am continually inspired by the amazing work they do each and every day to make the world a safer place.

To the Bond fans and enthusiasts who have *got* this project and really put their fandom behind it.

And, finally, to Ian Fleming, whose spirit endures. I don't know what he would have made of this book but I suspect he would have had a belly laugh or two at some of the zingers, and, I like to think, might have misted up a little at the scene between Bond and Q. I hope I have captured the essence of his creations.

Turn the page for an exclusive look at the next Q Mystery

THE MAN WITH THE GOLDEN COMPASS

Coming soon

Prologue

CHANGE.

As the owner of a vineyard, Harry Simms understood the imperatives of change. Spring was underway, and the great British countryside was feverishly awakening from its winter slumber. Soil temperatures were up. Sap was rising. And not only in Harry's vines.

Vines were self-fruitful. They pollinated without the assistance of bees or wind.

Harry, too, had always been self-fruitful. Sounded rude, but Harry knew what he meant. He had tried working for others, but it tended to end badly, usually with someone face down in a ditch.

But that was the past. Life was all about change, after all. Until it wasn't.

Harry pulled his Range Rover Sport into the deserted car park, switched off the radio and got out. Trees leaned in on all sides. The nature reserve's visitor centre was a ghostly shape in the darkness. Strange hoots and slithers. Christ, what a stupid place to meet.

Still, no chance of being disturbed. Probably for the best.

He checked his gold Rolex. He was early. An old habit. The watch caught the pale moonlight in a pleasing way. His wife had complained at the expense, but a man had to keep up appearances. You couldn't run a boutique vineyard dressed like a tramp.

On that note. He took out his phone, punched up the mirror, checked his appearance. He looked good, all things considered. Though a facelift wouldn't go amiss. Perhaps he could write it off as a business expense? Not that Rosie minded. Why would she? Bit of a cliché – buxom country barmaid falling for wealthy city gent – but Harry wasn't complaining.

As for Harry's wife. What she didn't know wouldn't hurt her. And there was a lot Samantha still didn't know. Despite recent ... revelations.

He had overdressed for the meeting. An old trick. His former boss had once told him: a good suit makes you bulletproof. The man had been shot dead a week later, proving that no one could be right all the time.

He heard the car before it arrived, watched it turn into the car park, beams lancing into the dark.

The woman that emerged was immaculately dressed, projecting urbane, with a side order of prim. Jet-black hair. Probably dyed, he thought. Or a wig. Designer glasses.

Too old for Harry's taste, of course, but he appreciated the effort.

Her shoes – thick boots, he saw, very unsexy – crunched across the loose soil. 'Thank you for meeting me.'

'You didn't really give me a choice.'

'Unavoidable, I'm afraid. Given the importance of the matter at hand.'

'Important to you. I don't respond well to threats.'

'Yet here you are.' The woman stepped closer. 'We want to know where it is, Mr Simms.'

'"It"?'

'Don't be coy.'

Harry considered a denial. But what was the point? What could this old bag do to him anyway. 'Look. If I did once have it, I don't now. I only came here out of courtesy, to put the matter to bed—'

'You came here because if you hadn't I would have ended up at your home.'

Harry had had enough. 'I'm done. I don't have what you want. Don't contact me again.' He turned on his heel, headed back to the Range Rover.

'I wouldn't go anywhere, Mr Simms.' He heard the soft click of a handgun's safety being taken off. He'd heard the sound many times in his life, never in pleasant circumstances.

The woman looked at him with eyes as cold as marble. 'Get in the car.' She indicated her own vehicle.

Harry stared at her, then burst out laughing. 'You can't be serious.'

The gun's retort was deafening in the silence. The bullet thwacked into the dirt beside Harry's foot. He heard something running away in the woods.

'Jesus Christ! Have you lost your mind?'

She gestured with the gun. 'Now, please.'

Harry cursed himself. How had he let a *woman* get the jump on him?

Seemingly resigning himself to the situation, he trudged towards the car. And then, at the last instant, he pretended to stumble ... and leapt at her. They grappled, fell to the floor ... The gun went off.

A few seconds of ringing silence, and then the woman heaved Harry's body off of her own and scrambled to her feet. She looked down at the prone man, a dark stain spreading across his shirt. 'Damn.'

Moments later, she was back in her car, and pulling into the darkened country lane.

1

'KING GEORGE V. DYING WORDS.'

Q looked up. 'What?'

'Four across.' His father, Mort, set down the folded newspaper. 'Three words. King George V's dying words.'

'Wasn't he the Queen's grandfather? King Charles's great-granddad?'

'The very same.'

'Right. Well, I have no idea what his dying words were.'

'God damn you.'

Q raised an eyebrow. 'That's a bit harsh, isn't it?'

'No. His dying words were "God damn you". Aimed at his doctor. Who euthanised him with a lethal injection of morphine. Wanted him ushered out before midnight so that the announcement could appear in the morning edition of *The Times*.'

They were sitting in Empire of Kebab, a restaurant in the centre of Wickstone-on-Water. Restaurant was probably overegging it. The hole-in-the-wall joint dealt mainly in takeaways, of the type where one didn't question exactly what went into the kebab. Q had introduced his father to the place several weeks ago and had regretted it ever since. Mort, a gourmand most of his life, had made the restaurant his second home. Q's seventy-eight-year-old former history professor father was now on first-name terms with the staff.

Talking of which. Mustafa loomed over the table. Q noted that the man had ditched his filthy T-shirt in favour of a full-sleeved white shirt with a tie. And cufflinks.

He suspected Mort's influence.

They ordered. Q waited for Mustafa to bellow the order to the grizzled cook behind the counter, but, instead, he wrote it painstakingly down on a chit, then walked the chit over to a spike and pinned it there.

'Is this your doing?' said Q.

'One tries.'

'Does one? And has one heard of cholesterol? Or food poisoning?'

'Don't be such a prig.' Mort picked up a can of Coke, opened it theatrically and poured it into an almost clean glass. 'So, have you decided to take the job?'

'I'm not sure.'

'Because of the case? Or because of Kathy?'

Q hesitated. His father was a perceptive man. Thirty years of estrangement hadn't changed that.

He regarded Mortimer Boothroyd, one-time don at Oxford University's Faculty of History, long retired, but a long way from his dotage. Immaculately dressed in a dark, three-piece suit, cold blue eyes staring from lean features graced by a short, greying beard and set beneath a bald dome. That slightly supercilious sneer that Q had always associated with his father. Mort had never suffered fools. Or even fairly bright people.

The fact that the pair of them were sitting here, at the same table, still filled Q with wonder. Thirty years earlier, following the suicide of his mother, Annabelle – Bella – Q had left town, vowing never to speak to Mort again. Rightly or wrongly, he had blamed his father for his mother's death. It had taken the death of Q's childhood friend – and his own unexpected ouster from MI6's Q Branch – the division of Britain's Secret Service dedicated to producing field weaponry for the Double Os – to return him to Wickstone.

The rapprochement with his father had been far from a simple affair. Q wasn't entirely certain that hostilities had ceased.

'Did you know Lawrence Noble?' he asked, focusing on the matter at hand.

'He came into the library once. Prickly character.' Q knew that Mort ran a historical society at Wickstone Library. If his father considered Lawrence Noble 'prickly' it probably meant that Noble had had the temperament of Caligula. Which would fit with some of the reading Q had done around the case.

Following his recent reinvestigation of the mysterious death of his friend, quantum computer scientist Peter Napier, Q had been offered a role as a civilian investigator with the local police force, specifically to look into the slaying of one Lawrence Noble, fifty-seven-year-old tech entrepreneur – a man who had made his fortune in the world of online computer gaming – turned antique trader. Noble had moved to Wickstone some years previously, buying a stately home on the edge of town and living there pretty much as a recluse until his gruesome murder almost a year earlier. Despite a thorough investigation, the case remained unsolved.

The problem wasn't the case. The problem was who was doing the asking.

'You never were very good with girls,' said Mort. 'Do you remember Fiona Cartwright? You mooned after her all summer. Never got up the nerve to ask her out. And then that fat boy with the goggly eyes swept her off her feet.'

'They went on one date. To the chippie. He made her pay for her own chips. She squirted West Indian pepper sauce in his eyes.'

'Point being: you're not a teenager anymore. Stop acting like one.'

'It's complicated.'

'Is it?' Mort tucked a napkin into his collar as Mustafa set down their order. The big man stood back and looked nervously at Q's father as Mort inspected the plate. No food critic at a Michelin-starred restaurant could have engendered greater terror.

Mort nodded. 'Looks good, Mustafa. My compliments to the chef.'

The man wilted with relief.

Q checked his watch. 'I have to go. My interview is at two. Wish me luck.'

'Luck is for the ill prepared and the incompetent. I raised you to be neither.'

Q scraped back his chair, stood up. 'Gee. Thanks, Dad.'

'You're welcome.'

Listen to the MURDER JUNCTION podcast

British crime writers Vaseem Khan and Abir Mukherjee bring to life history's most intriguing murders, both true crime and fictional, in the company of the world's best known crime writers. They make murder ... fun. Listen in on iTunes, Spotify, Spreaker or your favourite podcast app.

Join Vaseem's Newsletter

You can also keep up to date with Vaseem's work by joining his newsletter. It goes out approximately six times a year and includes:

*Extracts from Vaseem's next book
*Exclusive short stories
*Competitions – win signed copies of books
*News of forthcoming events and signings

You can join the newsletter in just a few seconds at Vaseem's website:

WWW. VASEEMKHAN.COM

IAN FLEMING PUBLICATIONS

Ian Lancaster Fleming was born in London on 28 May 1908 and was educated at Eton College before spending a formative period studying languages in Europe. His first job was with Reuters news agency, followed by a brief spell as a stockbroker. On the outbreak of the Second World War he was appointed assistant to the Director of Naval Intelligence, Admiral Godfrey, where he played a key part in British and Allied espionage operations.

After the war he joined Kemsley Newspapers as Foreign Manager of *The Sunday Times*, running a network of correspondents who were intimately involved in the Cold War. His first novel, *Casino Royale*, was published in 1953 and introduced James Bond, Special Agent 007, to the world. The first print run sold out within a month. Following this initial success, he published a Bond title every year until his death. His own travels, interests and wartime experience gave authority to everything he wrote. Raymond Chandler hailed him as 'the most forceful and driving writer of thrillers in England.' The fifth title, *From Russia With Love*, was particularly well received and sales soared when President Kennedy named it as one of his favourite books. The Bond novels have sold more than 100 million copies and inspired a hugely successful film franchise which began in 1962 with the release of *Dr No*, starring Sean Connery as 007.

The Bond books were written in Jamaica, a country Fleming fell in love with during the war and where he built a house, 'Goldeneye'. He married Ann Rothermere in 1952. His story about a magical car, written in 1961 for their only child, Caspar, went on to become the well-loved novel and film, *Chitty Chitty Bang Bang*.

Fleming died of heart failure on 12 August 1964.

www.ianfleming.com

X TheIanFleming

O Ianflemings007

f IanFlemingBooks

(007)

By Ian Fleming

Fiction

Casino Royale
Live and Let Die
Moonraker
Diamonds are Forever
From Russia with Love
Dr No
Goldfinger
For Your Eyes Only
Thunderball
The Spy Who Loved Me
On Her Majesty's Secret Service
You Only Live Twice
The Man with the Golden Gun
Octopussy and The Living Daylights

Chitty Chitty Bang Bang

Non-fiction

The Diamond Smugglers
Thrilling Cities